ANYA KELNER

Faith

Rise of the Red Claws (Book 4)

Copyright © 2025 by Anya Kelner

All rights reserved. No part of this publication may be reproduced, stored or transmitted in any form or by any means, electronic, mechanical, photocopying, recording, scanning, or otherwise without written permission from the publisher. It is illegal to copy this book, post it to a website, or distribute it by any other means without permission.

This novel is entirely a work of fiction. The names, characters and incidents portrayed in it are the work of the author's imagination. Any resemblance to actual persons, living or dead, events or localities is entirely coincidental.

First edition

This book was professionally typeset on Reedsy.
Find out more at reedsy.com

Contents

Rise of the Red Claws series   vii

I   Seeds of darkness

Chapter 1	3
Chapter 2	7
Chapter 3	12
Chapter 4	16
Chapter 5	20
Chapter 6	25
Chapter 7	29
Chapter 8	31
Chapter 9	36
Chapter 10	39
Chapter 11	42
Chapter 12	47
Chapter 13	51
Chapter 14	55
Chapter 15	58
Chapter 16	62
Chapter 17	66
Chapter 18	70
Chapter 19	74
Chapter 20	79
Chapter 21	86

II One of tainted blood

Chapter 22	93
Chapter 23	98
Chapter 24	103
Chapter 25	107
Chapter 26	110
Chapter 27	116
Chapter 28	122
Chapter 29	124
Chapter 30	129
Chapter 31	131
Chapter 32	135
Chapter 33	138
Chapter 34	142
Chapter 35	145
Chapter 36	148
Chapter 37	151
Chapter 38	154
Chapter 39	161
Chapter 40	165
Chapter 41	169
Chapter 42	174
Chapter 43	178
Chapter 44	180
Chapter 45	183
Chapter 46	187
Chapter 47	190
Chapter 48	194
Chapter 49	198
Chapter 50	204

Chapter 51	209
Chapter 52	213
Chapter 53	217
Chapter 54	221
Chapter 55	226
Chapter 56	231
Chapter 57	233
Chapter 58	239
Chapter 59	242
Chapter 60	246
Chapter 61	251
Chapter 62	256
Chapter 63	260
Chapter 64	264
Chapter 65	269
Chapter 66	274
Chapter 67	279
Chapter 68	281

III   Eminence of abominations

Chapter 69	287
Chapter 70	291
Chapter 71	295
Chapter 72	297
Chapter 73	299
Chapter 74	301
Chapter 75	304
Chapter 76	307
Chapter 77	311
Chapter 78	314

Chapter 79	318
Chapter 80	321
Chapter 81	324
Chapter 82	329
Chapter 83	332
Chapter 84	336
Chapter 85	340
Chapter 86	343
Chapter 87	346
Chapter 88	349
Chapter 89	353
Chapter 90	369
Chapter 91	372
Chapter 92	375
Chapter 93	378
Chapter 94	381
Chapter 95	383
Chapter 96	386
Chapter 97	389
Chapter 98	393
Chapter 99	397
Chapter 100	401
Epilogue	404
Dear reader	406

Rise of the Red Claws series

Part 1: Awake
Part 2: Hunt
Part 3: Legacy
Part 4: Faith

I

Seeds of darkness

Chapter 1

Faith watched her bare foot sink into the wet sand, feeling each individual grain shift beneath her skin. Even this simple sensation reminded her of what she was — human nerves heightened by vampiric senses, allowing her to experience the world in ways that belonged to neither realm completely.

She was a vampire born, rather than turned, unique among mortals and immortals alike. She was aging in human years, having gone from a helpless babe feeding at her mother's neck, suckling on life-giving blood, to standing here as a grown woman two decades later.

Faith felt alone and adrift on the isolated beach at the northern tip of Scotland. The remote location and dark skies amplified her sense of isolation. Like so many other frigid, lonely days, her thoughts roiled and swirled like currents on troubled water.

She raised her head and looked out.

The North Sea stretched endlessly before her, steel-gray waves crashing against Scarfskerry's rocky shore. Salt spray carried on the biting wind, each individual droplet clear in her enhanced vision. The late September sun was settling into its winter routine, already dropping toward the horizon, though it was barely past four in the afternoon. Soon the light would fade entirely, but that hadn't bothered Faith for a long time. Darkness was as much her element as daylight.

These solitary walks along Scarfskerry's shore marked the boundaries of her world — the furthest she dared venture from home alone. Beyond that lay only the carefully choreographed trips to the nearby town of Thurso for supplies, her parents always flanking her like protective shadows, steering her clear of crowds.

Even being here on the beach felt dangerous sometimes, exposed beneath the vast sky with nothing but sea and sand around her. But at least here she could pretend to be normal, if only for a while, without her parents' watchful eyes tracking her every move.

Her keen eyesight caught something in the corner of her vision. She turned to inspect it more closely — a discarded glove half-buried in the sand, probably dropped by one of the few tourists who ventured this far north.

Faith usually avoided touching abandoned items — her 'gift' was unpredictable — but in her distracted and somber mood, she bent and picked up the glove. It symbolized life, humanity and other souls. It somehow made her feel less alone in the barren landscape.

The wool was still warm. Her fingers had barely brushed the inside of the fabric when a wave of vertigo hit her. She quickly dropped to her knees, then sat hard on the cold wet sand to prevent herself from toppling over. She felt the wetness of the sand slowly soaking into the seat of her jeans, nipping at her skin.

Then the vision slammed into her without warning.

**

Sarah stood in the cramped London flat, her hand shaking as she pulled off the glove.

"You can't just expect me to leave everything behind, James! My whole life is here — my job at the gallery, my sister, my friends. And now you want us to move to the absolute middle of nowhere because

CHAPTER 1

of some fishing business you inherited from an uncle you barely knew?"

"It's not just a business, Sarah," James pleaded, his once youthful face drawn with anxiety. "It's an opportunity. A chance to get away from London. Isn't that what we wanted after Alfie was born? Uncle Malcolm's fleet might be small, but it's profitable. We could have a real life there."

"A real life? In Scarfskerry?" Sarah's laugh was bitter. "I meant moving to the suburbs, or the countryside perhaps, at a stretch. There's nothing in Scarfskerry but cold, wind and sea. Is that what you want for Alfie? For him to grow up in some backward fishing village instead of going to a proper school?"

Their eight-month-old son slept in the next room, oblivious to the argument that would change his life.

Sarah looked down at the expensive sheepskin and wool gloves clutched in her hands, remembering how James had gifted them to her last Christmas, back when things were still good between them. Back before postpartum struggles and sleepless nights with a restless baby had chipped away at her sanity and driven a wedge between her and her husband.

"I can't do this," she whispered, throwing the gloves onto a nearby coffee table. "I won't do this. If you want to run away to Scotland, go ahead. But Alfie and I are staying here." She was resolute.

But Faith could see further — this was both her gift and her curse. She had a father who could peer into the past and a mother who could glimpse the future. Faith was a union of the two, both darkness and light.

She could see that Sarah would eventually give in and make the move north. So far north from the cosmopolitan comforts of London.

She could also see the tragedy years later.

The sea turned violent. Rain fell like needles. The boat's hull splintered against rocks in a storm that seemed to materialize from nowhere. James was trapped in the wheelhouse as icy water rushed in. His final desperate gasp, his last thought of Sarah and little Alfie before darkness took him, leaving Sarah a widow in the very place she had never wanted to be...

Chapter 2

Faith dropped the glove. She was immediately thrust back onto the beach. Back to the here and now.

She recoiled from the glove, her breath caught in her throat. She scrambled backward through the wet sand. Her heart hammered in her chest — another reminder of her otherworldly nature. Pure vampires didn't have heartbeats. Pure vampires didn't get dizzy from visions of the past and future. Pure vampires didn't have to carry the weight of knowing how people would die.

The vision of James's death struck her particularly hard. She knew his fishing boat — the 'Sarah Jane', named in a gesture of appreciation for the wife who'd reluctantly followed him to what seemed like the edge of the world. Faith occasionally saw the boat with her extra-sharp vision as she trudged the gray beaches on her lonely walks.

That same boat would be found battered and capsized off the coast, James's body never recovered. And here was the gifted glove in front of her, a small piece of their story lost and discarded on the beach, like James's dream of a fresh start for his family.

"Stop it," she whispered to herself, digging her toes deep into the sand. The coarse grains helped ground her in the present moment. "Stop it … just stop it."

She wrapped her slender arms around her knees and pulled them toward her, hugging herself. She hung her head and heaved ragged breaths.

She thought she was getting better at controlling when the visions came. Four years had passed since the incident with Mr MacPherson at the village shop in Thurso, when a simple transaction turned into a vision of horror.

He had been placing coins in her hand when his finger brushed her palm. The world swam in her vision, then she witnessed the massive heart attack that would take him days later. She saw him clutching his chest as he collapsed behind the counter. She wanted to warn him, but who would believe a sixteen-year-old girl's premonition? Now she carried his death with James's — the futures she had seen but was powerless to change.

The damp sand had soaked through her jeans, and the chill wind of northern Scotland made her legs feel like ice. She slowly got to her feet and dusted off the wet sand that clung in clumps to her clothes.

Something else caught her eye as she stood.

This time in the water.

A boat appeared on the horizon, cutting through the choppy waters.

Thankfully, it wasn't the Sarah Jane. There were no characteristic ornate letters on the side of the vessel. Faith wasn't sure she could handle seeing the Sarah Jane after the tragic vision she had just experienced.

Faith tracked the boat's progress with eyes that could count the individual barnacles on its hull even at this distance. Two men worked on deck, their movements sluggish in thick green waterproof gear. Their heartbeats carried across the water to her preternaturally sensitive ears — strong, steady rhythms that made her throat contract and her body thrum with a primal thirst.

Faith swallowed hard and took a step back from the shoreline. Her parents had taught her to hunt animals, never humans, but the craving never fully went away. It was an innate part of what she was

CHAPTER 2

— another 'gift' from her vampire side, along with the strength, speed and enhanced senses.

At twenty, she was now the same age as her mother. They looked like sisters rather than mother and daughter. Time had stood still for Nell Cartwright — she would remain twenty for all eternity. But neither woman could discern the path that fate had in store for Faith Laura Deverell. Would she continue to age? Would there come a day when she looked like her own mother's mother? Faith was unique in history. Her story was yet to be written.

She picked up a smooth stone and ran her fingers over its surface, trying to suppress her spiraling thoughts.

The boat was closer now, approaching the small wooden dock that served this part of Scarfskerry. Something about its movement caught Faith's attention. It cut through the water too smoothly, as if gliding on glass instead of the choppy surface. Her sharp vision picked out details that sent warning signals shooting through her nerves — no wake behind the boat, no spray around the bow.

The sun dipped lower, painting the clouds in shades of crimson that reminded Faith of blood on water. She took unconscious steps backward as the boat neared the dock. All her senses screamed danger, a symphony of vampire instinct and human fear creating a uniquely hybrid response.

A figure emerged on deck — female, dressed in dark clothes and wearing a hood that rippled in the wind. She moved with inhuman grace, each gesture liquid and smooth. Faith recognized what she was even before she caught the pale gleam of the woman's skin as the hood shifted back in the wind — or noticed the complete absence of a heartbeat.

Faith's body instinctively shifted into a defensive stance — a movement drilled into her muscle memory through endless sparring matches with her father in the wild terrain around their home. Yet even with all her training in self-defense and honing her abilities, Faith felt woefully unprepared for whatever was approaching.

The stranger's sudden appearance shattered the fragile illusion of safety Faith had built around herself in this remote corner of Scotland. Her sanctuary, her hiding place from the world, had been breached. The realization made her feel small and vulnerable in a way that even her supernatural abilities couldn't counter.

She turned to leave, but the woman was suddenly standing between her and the path back to the house. Faith hadn't seen her move — vampire speed, too fast even for her extraordinary senses to track.

Up close, the woman was beautiful in the way all vampires were, with features that seemed carved from marble. Her skin was porcelain smooth, completely flawless. She had defined cheekbones, an angled chin and a narrow nose, giving her an almost feline appearance. Her eyes were pools of black. Her dark hair whipped around her face in the wind, but her eyes remained fixed on Faith with unsettling intensity. There was something familiar about them that made Faith's skin crawl. She gave off a scent of sandalwood and spice — earthy, heady, old.

"Let me see what you are, child," the woman said in a silky yet cold voice, reaching for Faith's face with long, elegant fingers. Her voice carried traces of an accent Faith couldn't place — something that spoke of centuries rather than decades.

Faith grabbed the woman's wrist before she could make contact. While the stranger was quick, Faith was no slouch either. Her hand motion was a blur.

The moment their skin touched, she heard a scream — and then the world around her fractured into chaos.

***

CHAPTER 2

Blood cascaded down old stone walls in crimson waterfalls, hot and thick, filling the air with an overwhelming copper stench. Ritual circles carved into the stone floor erupted with dark flames, their arcane symbols writhing like living things.

The chanting began as whispers but quickly grew, voices merging into a wall of sound that pierced Faith's skull. "Rasie sufletul morților și aduc viață nouă." Each syllable vibrated with unnatural power, threatening to shatter her mind from within.

Images flashed through her consciousness: a woman kneeling, her tattered shawl failing to contain cascading dark hair. Tears carved paths down her sharp-featured face — high cheekbones, prominent nose. Her anguish felt ancient, sacred, terrible.

The vision twisted, reality bending like smoke in the wind. A stone box cracked open, and from within rose a figure that made Faith's blood run cold. His features mirrored the woman before her, but twisted into something darker — sharp angles and burning eyes that spoke of calculated cruelty. Blood dripped from elongated fangs as his lips curved into a smile, one hand reaching toward Faith.

Around the edges of her vision, bodies lay crumpled like discarded dolls, their flesh gray and withered. Empty vessels drained of life, tossed aside without ceremony or care.

The ritual circles pulsed with increasing intensity, their energy seeming to devour what little light remained. The chanting built to a fever pitch, becoming a physical force that threatened to tear reality apart: "RASIE SUFLETUL MORȚILOR ȘI ADUC VIAȚĂ NOUĂ!" The words crashed through Faith's consciousness like thunder, each repetition more devastating than the last — louder and louder and louder…

Chapter 3

Faith wrenched her hand free with a scream that was half-human, half-vampire snarl.

The woman vanished as suddenly as she had appeared, leaving Faith alone on the beach with her heart racing and her hands trembling. The clouds had darkened and the sun hung lower in the sky. How much time had passed?

A burning sensation drew her gaze to her palm.

An ornate letter 'R' was branded into her skin, its edges already fading as her healing ability kicked in. The mark pulsed with dark energy, reminding her of the ritual circles in her vision. Faith watched as the brand completely disappeared, but the questions it raised burned brighter than the mark itself.

Who was the woman? Who was the cruel man in her vision? Answers whispered in her mind, carried on the bitter wind from the sea.

She recalled her parents' stories, which felt like fables, removed from her mundane existence, almost like supernatural fiction.

She glanced toward the dock, but the boat had vanished as completely as its mysterious passenger. Only the churning waves remained, dark and foreboding under the fading sky. Like James's future grave, she thought, then immediately wished she hadn't. Faith wrapped her arms around herself, though the biting Scottish wind had never bothered her too much. This chill came from within.

Memories flooded back — fragments of conversations she had overheard over the years, whispered discussions between her parents. Her sensitive hearing had caught words like "prophecy," "chosen," and "danger". But whenever she asked directly, they were reluctant to provide details.

One name stood out, spoken in fearful, almost revered tones through the years: Zachariah Redclaw. All she really knew was that he had once led a fearsome vampire army, had held her mother captive, and had died in the war of the night creatures twenty years ago.

Faith quickened her pace along the shoreline, her bare feet barely touching the sand. The sun was almost gone now, painting the beach in deepening shadows. Most humans would be hurrying home, driven by ancient instincts that warned against darkness. But Faith felt her other nature awakening as night approached — the part of her that belonged to the shadows, the same part that let her see deaths before they happened.

She paused to pick up her boots, left by a cluster of rocks. A flicker of movement drew her attention — someone watching from the cliffs above? But when she looked up, there were only gnarled trees bending in the wind. Still, she didn't linger. The encounter with the vampire had shaken her more than she wanted to admit.

The path home wound through thick gorse bushes, their yellow flowers still visible in the gathering dark. Faith could have run at vampire speed and covered the distance in seconds, but she forced herself to walk at a human pace. It was one of her father's rules — never draw attention, never reveal what you are, never take unnecessary risks.

They'd lived in Scarfskerry for twenty years without the villagers suspecting anything about the reclusive American family in the old stone house. Of course, they were seen as slightly eccentric for choosing an isolated existence over a more conventional life closer to civilization. But there were no mutterings of the supernatural. Yet.

However, isolation had its price.

Faith's step faltered as she thought about the acceptance letter from the University of Edinburgh, now hidden beneath her mattress like some shameful secret. Even the act of applying had felt like a betrayal — not just of her parents' careful protection, but of everything they'd built here in their safe isolation. Her heart ached with impossible dreams of lecture halls and library stacks, of friendships and normal experiences that could never be hers.

Yet the very thought of being surrounded by so many people made her breath catch in her throat. One accidental touch, one moment of lost control, and her secret might be exposed. Worse, she might witness someone else's death, like Mr MacPherson's, like James's, and again be powerless to prevent it. What if the person was a friend?

No, it was all impossible. A dead end. She shouldn't have even bothered. Her destiny was to live in the shadows, where it was safe.

A twig snapped in the darkness beside the path.

Faith spun toward the sound, her senses stretching out into the night.

Nothing.

But the hair on the back of her neck stood up, and she could have sworn she caught a whiff on the wind — the same earthy scent as the woman with those cunning dark eyes.

She broke into a run then, no longer caring about maintaining human appearances. The trees blurred past as she pushed her speed to its limits.

Faith raced toward home — not just the physical building, but the cocoon of safety it represented. The stone walls had been her fortress against the outside world for twenty years. Each step closer made her feel like a frightened child fleeing from shadows, but she didn't

CHAPTER 3

care.

She reached home in mere moments.

The old stone house appeared just ahead, warm light from the fire spilling from its windows. She could hear her father's guitar through the walls, smell the wood smoke from the hearth, and sense her mother's presence inside. Home. Safety. Love. Protection.

Faith passed their battered old Volvo parked in front, its dark paint dulled by years of salt spray from the sea. Living this far north meant that having reliable transportation was essential, even if they rarely ventured beyond Thurso for supplies.

As Faith reached for the door handle, she looked down at her palm where the strange brand had been — or where she thought it had been. The skin was smooth now, completely healed, but she could still feel the phantom burn of that ornate 'R'.

Beneath that sensation, a deeper fear was taking root: the fear that her isolated but safe life was about to change forever. She kept returning to the vision of the man with the blood-stained smile.

The final rays of sunlight vanished behind the horizon as Faith stepped inside, closing the door on the gathering darkness. Yet, she couldn't shake the feeling that something from the night had followed her in — something that had been waiting two decades to find her.

Chapter 4

Faith gently closed the door behind her and leaned against the rough wood, pausing to catch her breath. Her acute hearing picked up the distant crash of waves against Scarfskerry's rocky shore, accompanied by the cries of seabirds flying inland ahead of an approaching storm. Yet, these familiar sounds felt wrong — twisted and distorted, as if the world had suddenly tilted on its axis.

She scanned the room and saw her father in his usual spot by the hearth, his acoustic guitar balanced on his knee as his fingers danced across the strings, picking out an intricate melody she recognized from countless evenings before.

Her mother sat curled up in the worn leather armchair beside him, a book open in her lap, her dark hair falling forward to conceal her face as she became engrossed in the story.

The domestic scene made Faith pause. How many evenings had she watched them like this? A family engaged in the mundane aspects of life during their self-imposed exile. These quiet moments were her sanctuary — just the three of them wrapped in their own private world, safe from whatever lurked beyond their stone walls.

She breathed in the familiar scents of woodsmoke and freshly picked lavender, trying to calm her racing heart.

"Someone was at the beach," she said, finally finding her voice. "A vampire. She…"

CHAPTER 4

Faith faltered as both her parents turned sharply to look at her. Christopher's fingers stilled on the guitar strings, and the sudden silence felt deafening. Nell snapped her book shut with a crack that made Faith flinch.

"… she moved so fast," Faith continued, her voice trembling now. "Faster than I could track. And when she touched me… I saw… I saw…"

Her hands shook as she hugged herself, the memory making her wish she had never ventured down to the beach. She should have stayed within sight of the house.

She held out her palm, where the 'R' brand had once been, even though her healing ability had erased all trace of it. Still, the phantom burn lingered like a flame against her skin.

Christopher quickly set his guitar aside, the polished wood gleaming in the firelight. He crossed to her with an urgent yet fluid grace, his movements reflecting an extra measure of control, as if he were restraining his own predatory nature. He was apprehensive — that much she could tell. He took her hand, cool fingers examining the unmarked skin with careful precision.

"What exactly did you see when she touched you?"

His voice was low and measured, but Faith sensed the underlying tension.

"Blood. So much blood." The words felt thick in her throat. "Running down stone walls. And there were these circles carved into the floor, burning. There was also chanting in a language I didn't understand… it hurt my ears."

She watched her parents exchange a loaded look. Her keen senses registered the slight dilation of their pupils and the almost imperceptible stiffening of their postures.

"And I saw a face," she added. "The one from Mom's drawings."

Faith had connected the dots.

Nell went still, the book sliding from her lap to thud against the stone floor.

"Which drawings?" she whispered, her eyes wide.

"The ones you hide in the locked drawer beneath your easel."

Faith noticed her mother's fingers clench, her knuckles turning even whiter.

"The man with the sharp face and dark eyes that burn like coals. You draw him when you think no one's watching, as if you're trying to exorcise him from your mind."

The crackling fire filled the heavy silence, while outside, the wind whistled through the gaps in the old stonework.

Finally, Nell spoke, her voice barely above a whisper.

"Zachariah Redclaw."

"The one who held you captive?" Faith asked, though she didn't really need an answer.

Over the years, Faith had pieced together fragments of the story from whispered conversations between her parents, usually when they thought she was deep in her restorative trance. She recalled her mother's nightmare mutterings and the deep pain that occasionally haunted Nell's eyes when she thought no one was watching.

"Yes," her mother replied simply.

Nell rose from her chair and moved to the fire, seeming to seek warmth, though Faith knew pure vampires felt neither heat nor cold. It must have been a reflex from her previous mortal life — a search for comfort in the dancing orange flames.

"There are things we haven't told you, Faith. Things we hoped would never be a part of your life," her mother said, turning to her.

"I'm not a child anymore!" Faith's voice came out harsher than she intended, echoing off the stone walls. "I deserve to know the truth — everything. What really happened back then?"

Christopher moved to the window, his attention now divided

between their conversation and the outside. Faith recognized the slight tilt of his head; he was using his sensitive hearing to scan their surroundings. Her own supernatural senses picked up on his rising tension.

"Zachariah had a brother," Nell said, her fingers tracing patterns on the rough stone of the fireplace. "Damian Redclaw. He died twenty years ago during a battle in Alaska. But there was also a sister — Mary. Amara discovered her in the census records from over a century ago."

That name again — Amara. Faith had heard it mentioned a handful of times over the years. It sounded exotic to her sheltered ears, yet she had no idea who it referred to.

"No one knew where Mary was," Nell continued. "She was absent during the entire Red Claws saga. But Zachariah must have been in contact with her. Family and blood meant everything to him. He was a man obsessed with purity. I was sure Mary was a chess piece purposely left off the board, kept in reserve in case the worst befell the bloodline."

Suddenly, the woman's face from the beach loomed large in Faith's mind — her defined features and dark eyes burning with maniacal intensity.

Christopher's body tensed, muscles coiling like a predator ready to strike. Faith strained to hear what had alerted him. Then she caught it.

Footsteps rustled through the wild grass outside, multiple sets moving with an eerie uniformity. Her father's superior senses could undoubtedly determine exactly how many were out there, but Faith knew enough: they were surrounded. The boat carrying Mary must have been the vanguard, with reinforcements following close behind.

Now they were trapped.

Chapter 5

A familiar woman's voice sliced through the air, causing Faith's skin to prickle.

"Send out the hybrid child and no harm shall befall you. My business is solely with the Eminence of Abominations."

The what? Faith's eyebrows shot up.

"What did she just call me?" she asked, looking between her mother and father. They remained silent. "Abomination, am I?" She took a moment to calm herself. "What does she want with me?"

Faith's gaze swept around their home — the worn furniture, the shelves brimming with books, the marks on the walls that tracked her growth over the years. The thought of leaving this sanctuary made her feel physically sick. Here, she knew who and what she was. Here, she was simply Faith.

"Your blood." Nell's voice was taut with bitter memory. "The same thing Zachariah wanted from me. The same thing that poisonous family always seeks from us. The power that flows in our veins."

Nell reached out, her trembling fingers brushing against Faith's cheek.

"Blood connects all," she said cryptically. "Blood is the liberator. Blood is the destroyer. Blood is the answer."

Nell seemed distant, lost in thought. It frightened Faith. That weight of memory. The lingering trauma of captivity. You could escape in body but never truly in mind. After all these years, Faith had come to understand that much about her mother.

Nell snapped back to the present, her eyes sharpening with resolve. Righteous fury crept across her features.

"But I swore they'd never do to you what they did to me," she declared fiercely. "Not to my girl."

Christopher positioned himself by the door, every muscle coiled for action. His normally bright blue eyes had darkened to midnight — a sign Faith had learnt meant his predatory instincts were rising.

"The car. On my signal," he hissed. "Use your speed. Both of you."

"One life for two," Mary's voice echoed, now closer, as if the very stones of the house had absorbed her words. "The trade I offer is just. You took two of my kin, yet I ask only for the girl."

Faith glanced at her parents — her father standing fiercely protective, her mother's face set with determination and anger.

Thunder rumbled in the distance as the storm unleashed its fury. Through the window, Faith glimpsed dark robes shifting in the twilight. The fire popped and crackled, each noise causing her to flinch as her heightened senses tracked every movement and sound outside.

"Remember your training," Christopher said, more softly. "Everything we taught you…"

"… was for this," Faith finished, her heart racing.

Years of training to control her strength, harness her senses, move with stealth and speed, and fight like a vampire while thinking like a human had prepared her for this moment. It hadn't just been about surviving in a hostile environment or confronting feral wildcats and rutting red deer — it had been preparation for this moment. Now that the moment had come, she felt hopelessly out of her depth.

A new sound sliced through the encroaching darkness: low chanting in a strange language that echoed her vision.

"*Rasie sufletul morților și aduc viață nouă ... Rasie sufletul morților și aduc viață nouă ... Rasie sufletul morților și aduc viață nouă ...*" The words scraped against her skull, causing her teeth to ache. She noticed her mother's face grow even paler.

"That's the same chanting from my vision," Faith whispered, struggling against rising panic. "What does it mean?"

Before either parent could answer, Mary's voice pierced through the ominous murmurs.

"We can do this without bloodshed, or we can paint these stones crimson. Either way, I will have what's due to me. The circle awaits."

Ritual circles — just like in her vision. Faith's mind raced.

Christopher's voice was like steel.

"You won't fucking touch her, bitch," he shouted.

Mary's laugh chilled the air like winter frost.

"Really, caretaker? You, the neophyte and the cursed child, against all of us? Count them — how many do you sense out there? How many can you fight while protecting the Eminence of Abominations?"

That damning title again.

Faith saw her father's jaw tighten. Whatever number he sensed with his superior abilities couldn't be good.

She recalled the woman's impossible speed at the beach. How many more like her lurked in the shadows? Were they all that powerful?

"Mom?" Faith's voice sounded small, like the child she was so desperate to prove she wasn't. "What do we do?"

Nell moved closer, her expression resolute despite the fear radiating from her.

"We run. We fight. We survive."

She placed her hands firmly on Faith's shoulders.

The chanting outside grew louder, seeming to echo from all directions. Faith felt a palpable tension in the air — a pressure, a darkness that screamed warnings to her senses.

CHAPTER 5

Rain began to fall, drumming against the stone walls as lightning split the sky. Through the sheets of water streaming down the windows, Faith glimpsed the figures in dark robes. They moved with an unnatural synchronization, forming a tight circle around the house.

"Raslie sufletul morților și aduc viață nouă ... Raslie sufletul morților și aduc viață nouă ..." The chant continued endlessly.

"Time's up," Mary called over a crash of thunder. "None of us can escape our destiny."

Faith pressed herself against the familiar rough stone wall, wishing she could sink into it and disappear. She had spent her entire life within these protective boundaries, learning every crack and crevice. The thought of being forced into the unknown world beyond filled her with panic.

The weight of the moment bore down on her.

Throughout her life, she had been different — not fully vampire, nor fully human — caught between two worlds. Now she understood why her parents had hidden her away, why they had chosen this remote corner of Scotland.

Yet, as Mary's words about her blood echoed in her mind, she couldn't help but wonder: was there something within her that even her parents feared? A darkness in her tainted blood just waiting to be unleashed?

The chanting grew louder, reaching a fever pitch, as lightning once again illuminated the dark figures surrounding their home. Faith could hear footsteps approaching, multiple bodies pressing against the outer walls.

She glanced at her parents, seeing their determination and readiness to fight. To protect her. To die for her.

But another question flashed in her mind, perhaps more terrifying than the gathering vampires outside: what if running wasn't the answer?

She recalled her visions of death — James and Mr MacPherson. What if Mary Redclaw was right? What if there was no escape from what she truly was?

Chapter 6

The front window shattered, sending Faith's heightened senses into overdrive. Time seemed to splinter alongside the glass, each shard catching the firelight like falling stars as she tracked their chaotic dance through the air.

Moments later, the smells overwhelmed her — rain-soaked air rushed in, mingling with the metallic tang of blood as the first dark figure crashed through, his hands slashed by the broken glass.

Thunder rumbled overhead as the vampire landed in a predatory crouch, wet boots crunching on the scattered shards. Dark blood pooled from the cuts where the window had sliced him, but he didn't seem to notice; his focus was entirely on Faith, lips pulling back to reveal teeth too sharp to be human.

Two more figures surged through the ruined window behind him, the wind and rain howling in like harbingers of doom.

"Take her alive," the first vampire commanded, his voice resonating unnaturally. He bared his fangs in what might have been a smile. "But that doesn't mean unharmed," he added.

The other vampires spread out, their movements measured. They were herding her, aiming to capture rather than kill. Somehow, that was even more terrifying.

Faith stumbled backward, nearly tripping over her own feet. Her heightened senses betrayed her; every detail seared into her mind with horrifying clarity — the blood staining their hands, the precision of their movements, the hungry intensity in their eyes.

She pressed herself against the far wall of what had once been her sanctuary, desperately searching for an escape as the vampires fanned out to cut off any retreat.

In that moment, despite her supernatural strength and speed, she felt like the frightened child she'd tried so hard to prove she wasn't.

Outside, the chanting pulsed in the air: *"Rasie sufletul morților și aduc viață nouă..."* The words crawled under her skin. Every shadow harbored a threat. Every movement demanded a response.

Amid the chaos, she glimpsed her parents in action. Christopher moved with lethal precision, his hands empty yet deadly. One of the vampires lunged at him wielding a curved blade that gleamed wetly in the firelight. Her father seized the attacker's wrist and twisted, the snap of breaking bone echoing in the storm. Leaning in, he tore out the assailant's throat with his teeth, dark blood spraying onto the stone walls, desecrating their once-peaceful home.

Nell fought with cold grace, each movement economical and brutal. The second vampire through the window produced an ornate silver sword — a fatal mistake. In one fluid motion, Nell caught his sword arm, twisted until bone snapped, and wrenched the blade from his spasming fingers.

The blade sang through the air as Nell sliced through the oncoming vampires with chilling efficiency. This wasn't the woman who curled up by the fire with poetry and Harmony Constance fantasy novels; this was a different person entirely — a predator fiercely protecting her child.

A rush of displaced air warned Faith just in time. She ducked and stumbled to the side as a blade whistled past the spot where her ear had been. Her attacker moved with impossible speed, the gleaming metal already reversing for another strike. Faith barely managed to deflect it with her forearm, the sharp edge slicing a deep gash that intensified her focus amidst the chaos.

As the attacker's hood fell back, Faith glimpsed a face that might have once been motherly, now sharpened by vampirism into something predatory. High, angular cheekbones cast deep shadows beneath eyes blazing with an unnatural amber fire. Her alabaster skin, nearly translucent, revealed delicate blue veins beneath. A thin scar traced from her left temple to the corner of her mouth, twisting what might have been a serene expression into a permanent half-sneer. But it was her expression — a chilling mask of conviction — that truly unsettled Faith, reflecting a willingness to sacrifice everything for a higher purpose.

"Your blood will restore us all," she hissed, launching into another lightning-fast combination of strikes.

Faith was forced to retreat to the far side of the room, her reflexes barely keeping her ahead of the blade. She was being driven into a corner, further away from her parents. The vampire's attacks came with supernatural speed and precision.

"Faith!" Christopher's voice broke through the din.

She caught the glint of metal as he kicked a fallen vampire's sword toward her. Instinctively, she snatched it from the air. Its weight felt foreign in her hands.

The attacker lunged again.

Faith's hands trembled on the unfamiliar hilt as she attempted to parry, but the sword felt awkward and unwieldy. The blade wobbled, far too heavy towards the tip.

The vampire's next strike nearly tore the weapon from her grip, the impact sending painful vibrations up her arms, forcing a cry from her lips.

Faith lurched backward, terror rising in her throat as she fought to maintain her balance. Her enhanced reflexes were her only lifeline, and they barely held her together.

Each desperate parry came a moment too late; each panic-fueled block was too weak. The vampire's blade slipped through her defenses repeatedly, leaving small cuts on her arms and shoulders as she aimed to incapacitate rather than kill.

Sweat mingled with rain on her face as Faith struggled against rising panic. She frantically tried to mimic her opponent's stance, searching for a way to hold the sword that didn't feel completely wrong. She had the raw speed and strength to survive, but none of the skill or finesse needed to truly fight back.

A wild swing left her overextended, and the vampire seized the moment, stepping inside her guard with alarming speed. Faith recognized her mistake as she saw the blow aimed at her eyes.

Only her quick reflexes saved her; she twisted away at the last possible moment. The sword sliced through her collar instead of her face, tearing fabric but sparing her flesh. She staggered, nearly losing her footing on the slick stone floor.

"Focus!" Christopher shouted over the crash of thunder.

Faith stumbled again, awkwardly holding her sword in front of her like a shield. Her foot caught on an uneven part of the floor, and she began to fall.

The vampire pressed her advantage and lunged forward. But in her eagerness, she slipped on the rain-slicked floor, her own feet sliding out from under her.

As Faith fell, she instinctively thrust her sword arm out to break her fall. By sheer chance, the blade caught the vampire at neck level as she fell forward.

Faith's strength, combined with the vampire's momentum, drove the steel through flesh and bone with shocking ease. The sound was like a wet branch snapping beneath the howl of the storm.

For a brief moment, time seemed to stand still.

Chapter 7

Faith could see individual raindrops suspended around them, every detail of the vampire's face shifting from surprise to disbelief. Hot black blood sprayed across Faith's face in a crimson arc as the head separated from the body.

The vampire's head tumbled backward, its mouth frozen in shock, before both it and the body began to disintegrate. Faith landed hard on her backside, staring in horror at the scene before her. Her hands shook violently on the sword hilt as she tried to process how her clumsy fall had resulted in her first kill. Pure, dumb luck — nothing more.

She watched in horrified fascination as the flesh of her attacker turned to ash, spreading from the point of severance outward like paper burning at the edges. Within moments, all that remained was a pile of ash mixing with the rain pooling on the stone floor.

Faith tasted blood; she had been spattered with enough of it to feel it on her lips. The musty scent of ash and copper flooded her senses. Her sword arm trembled, the blade slick with the quickly dissolving dark vampire blood.

She had just ended a life, taken something that could never be restored. The realization hit her like a physical blow, making her stomach lurch. Training was one thing. This was real. This was final.

Faith caught her father's gaze across the room.

In that fleeting moment, she sensed a mixture of relief and sadness — the expression of a father who had dedicated years to preparing his child for this moment while secretly hoping it would never arrive. In that brief connection, Faith realized something profound: every training session, every harsh lesson, every admonishment, every time he pushed her beyond her limits, it hadn't been about survival or punishment. It had been about love.

But the moment shattered as another vampire leapt between them.

Faith sprang to her feet and turned to face the attack. The sword still felt heavy and unwieldy in her hands, yet she managed to block the strike just in time.

A pained grunt rang out amidst the turmoil — a sound Faith had never heard her father make before. She turned toward him, her keen vision capturing every harrowing detail of the scene with stark clarity.

Christopher had thrown himself between an oncoming blade and Nell's exposed back. The weapon had sliced through him from hip to sternum, the wound so deep that Faith glimpsed white bone beneath the torn flesh.

Dark arterial blood pulsed from the wound, rapidly soaking through his shirt. The rich, metallic scent hit Faith's heightened senses like a gut punch. This wasn't just any blood; it was her father's blood, the very life force that flowed in her.

Chapter 8

Christopher staggered against the wall, one hand pressed to the gaping wound while the other still clutched his sword, though the blade now trembled in his grip. His face, typically composed and confident, had turned ashen. Faith had spent her entire life viewing him as invincible — her protector, her teacher, an immortal vampire of immense power. Now, however, he looked vulnerable, almost mortal.

The sight sent an icy chill coursing through her veins. This was wrong — fundamentally, terrifyingly wrong. Her father couldn't bleed. He couldn't feel pain. He couldn't die. The foundation of her world seemed to crack as she watched him struggle to remain upright, his lifeblood seeping between his fingers.

"Dad!" The word tore from her throat, raw and primal. Every fiber of her being wanted to rush to him, to help, to fix this impossible reality unfolding before her eyes.

"Stay focused!" Christopher snarled through gritted teeth. He pushed off the wall and rejoined the fight despite his injury, but Faith could see he was moving slowly.

The battle devolved into a whirlwind of steel, blood and storm-driven rain. Faith lost count of how many vampires surged into their former sanctuary.

Her mother's sword became slick with blood. Each time she cut one down, two more took its place.

Faith's senses were overwhelmed by the metallic smell of blood, the rumble of thunder, the sounds of chanting, bright flashes of lightning and the crush of bodies in the confined space.

She found herself back-to-back with Nell, both breathing heavily as vampires circled them. Lightning flashed outside, illuminating the chaotic scene — dark robes, pale faces and raised blades surrounded them.

"We have to reach the car," Nell urged. "Your father's losing too much blood."

Faith nodded, tightening her grip on her sword.

They fought their way toward the back door, protecting Christopher's flanks as he struggled to keep up. Nell did most of the fighting while Faith guided her father.

The storm raged outside, thunder drowning out the clash of steel. Rain poured in through broken windows, turning the stone floor treacherous with a mix of blood, water and ash that had become a gray sludge.

Just as they neared the back door, Mary materialized from the shadows. In one moment, the path was clear; in the next, she stood before them, wielding a sword that seemed to absorb the little light left in the room.

"Impressive display," Mary said, eyeing Nell. "I see the blood of the Omni-Father truly runs through your veins. But do you really think you can run forever?"

Another flash of lightning highlighted Mary's striking looks. In that instant, Faith recognized the family resemblance to the face from her mother's drawings — the same ebony eyes, the same fervent zeal.

"Your mother's blood is powerful," Mary continued, now directing her attention to Faith. "But you..." Her smile revealed too many perfect white teeth. "You are something else entirely. The fusion of

CHAPTER 8

bloodlines. The key."

The remaining vampires drew back, forming a circle around them. The chanting outside grew louder, making Faith's head spin. The air felt thick with energy, pressing against her body.

"I don't want any part of this," Faith said, hoping mere words could end the madness. Her voice sounded weak even to her own ears.

Mary laughed, the sound like shattering glass.

"*Want* has nothing to do with it," replied Mary, coldly. "This is birthright."

With the speed of lightning, she moved, her sword a blur of motion. Faith barely raised her blade in time. The impact sent shockwaves up her arms — Mary was impossibly strong. Their blades locked together, their faces inches apart. Mary's eyes seemed to pierce into Faith's soul.

"Can you feel it?" she whispered. "The power. The rage. It's calling to you."

The worst part was that Faith could feel it. With each beat of her heart, she sensed a fire growing within her. Dark and heady. It energized her, but demanded blood in return. She thought of the life she had already taken. Her moment of distraction came at a cost.

Mary's blade slipped past her guard, carving a deep gash across Faith's chest. Pain shot through her, immediate and intense. Stumbling backward, Faith watched in disgust as Mary raised the sword to her lips. She dragged her tongue slowly along the flat of the blade, her eyes rolling back as Faith's blood touched her tongue. A sound escaped her throat — something between a moan and a growl.

Mary's body convulsed violently, her spine arching at an unnatural angle. The sword clattered to the stone floor as her fingers spasmed and curled into claws. Dark veins spread like spider webs beneath her pale skin, pulsing with each beat of Faith's blood flowing through her system. When Mary opened her eyes again, they were entirely black, resembling deep wells of ink that seemed to absorb the firelight.

"Oh yes," she breathed, her voice distorted and multi-toned, as if multiple voices were speaking through her simultaneously. A thin line of Faith's blood trickled from the corner of her mouth, steaming in the cold air. "Your blood... it sings with power. The perfect union. Pure. Primal." Her jaw stretched unnaturally wide as she spoke, revealing rows of teeth that appeared to multiply and sharpen before Faith's eyes.

Mary's body twitched and shuddered, her bones cracking audibly as Faith's blood surged through her veins. Her fingers elongated, nails turning into black talons. The transformation was horrifically mesmerizing.

"Get away from her!" Christopher hurled himself at Mary despite his injuries, but she dismissed him with contemptuous ease. He slammed against the wall and sank down.

"Dad!" Faith rushed toward him, but Mary blocked her path, moving with a fluidity that defied the laws of nature, as if her body had become liquid. Her black eyes fixed on Faith with predatory intent.

"Enough games," Mary's distorted voice rasped. "The circle awaits, and your dear father is becoming a distraction."

Mary picked up her sword and turned toward Christopher. The air crackled with dark energy.

Her father struggled to rise, one hand pushing against the wall while the other clutched his still-bleeding wound. His once-graceful movements resembled a wounded animal's desperate flail.

Mary raised her sword slowly, savoring the moment. The blade caught the firelight, casting crimson reflections across her face. Her eyes blazed with an almost religious fervor as she glared down at Christopher. Faith could see the muscles in Mary's arm tensing, preparing for the killing blow.

CHAPTER 8

"Dad..." The word slipped from Faith's lips in a broken whisper.

Christopher met her gaze. In that frozen moment, Faith didn't see the fighter who had protected her but simply her father — the man who had read her stories, held her after nightmares and loved her unconditionally despite her cursed heritage. Now, he could barely lift his hand.

Nell was too far away, still battling two vampires.

Faith's sword felt like lead in her trembling hands. Her combat skills had abandoned her. Her strength had failed her. Mary was too powerful. Yet there was something else — something that had been within her all along.

Chapter 9

Faith let her sword fall from her fingers. The blade clattered against the stone floor, the sound echoing like a bell tolling in the charged air. Every head turned toward the noise, including Mary's.

Faith lunged forward, her hands outstretched.

Mary's eyes widened in surprise as Faith's palms pressed firmly against her temples. The contact felt raw, skin to skin, as Faith flung open the mental doors she usually kept locked tight.

Instead of glimpsing the future or the past, she unleashed everything — the deaths she had witnessed in her visions, every moment of pain and loss, the final, agonized breaths. Despair, anger, isolation, grief, loneliness, broken dreams and forlorn hopes flooded into Mary's mind in an unrelenting torrent, crashing through their connection like a tidal wave.

Mary's scream began low and guttural, escalating to a piercing shriek that shattered the remaining windows. She clawed at her head, desperately trying to break free. But Faith held on, her fingers digging into Mary's flesh as she poured out the terrible burden of her gift, of her life.

The surrounding vampires fell back, their perfect synchronization disrupted by their leader's anguished cries. Faith's vision began to blur at the edges as she pushed harder.

"Now!" Nell's voice cut through the chaos like a sharp blade. "Out!

CHAPTER 9

Run!"

Faith felt her father's arms wrap around her waist, propelling her toward the back door. He was healing, regaining strength. She broke the connection with Mary, who crumpled to her knees.

They dashed through sheets of rain toward the car. Faith's heightened hearing caught Mary's rage-filled screams shifting to commands: "Stop them! Don't let them escape!"

They flung open the car doors and piled inside. Christopher twisted the key that was already in the ignition. The engine coughed once, twice. Faith's heart nearly stopped.

"Come on, come on!" Christopher urged as dark shapes emerged from the storm behind them.

Finally, the engine roared to life.

Christopher slammed his foot down, tires spinning on wet gravel as the car fishtailed with vampires closing in from all sides. One vampire grabbed the trunk handle, his face a mask of feral hunger. Another leapt onto the hood, amber eyes blazing as she raised a blade.

Christopher shot the car into reverse, then forward again. The sudden motion dislodged their attackers, sending the vampire on the hood flying off. The tires found traction and they shot forward into the darkness.

But in the rearview mirror, Faith saw a terrifying sight: Mary had recovered, her face twisted with fury as she stretched out her hand. The air itself seemed to ripple with dark energy, causing the car to shudder violently.

"Hold on!" Christopher yelled, wrestling with the steering wheel as they skidded on the rain-slick road. The engine screamed in protest.

Through the rear window, Faith watched in shock as more vampires emerged from the storm, moving with inhuman speed in perfect formation behind them. At their head was Mary, her pace matching the car's despite its acceleration. Blood trickled from her nose and mouth, but her eyes burned with obsessive determination.

"She's gaining on us!" Faith cried as Mary closed the gap.

Christopher slammed the accelerator to the floor.

The old car shuddered as it was pushed beyond its limits. They took a corner nearly on two wheels, almost sliding off the road entirely. Faith was thrown against the door.

When she looked back again, their pursuers had finally fallen behind, swallowed by the storm and darkness. But Mary's final scream still pierced through the howling wind.

Huddled in the backseat, Faith's mind reeled from everything that had just happened. The car's headlights pierced the downpour as they sped away from the only home she had ever known. Her chest still burned from Mary's cut, though the wound was already healing. She could still taste blood on her lips, a reminder that, after tonight, she was not merely a death-seer, but also a death-dealer.

"Where are we going?" she asked, her voice low.

"Somewhere safe," Nell replied from the front seat, avoiding Faith's gaze in the rearview mirror as she pressed a cloth against Christopher's side to staunch the bleeding.

Faith gazed out the window at the storm-ravaged landscape flying past her. Mary's words echoed in her mind: "Can you feel it? It's calling to you."

She watched lightning dance across the sky as she fled from everything she had ever known.

Chapter 10

The car jolted over another pothole on the dark coastal road, sending waves of pain through Faith's battered body. Although her wounds were healing — one small mercy of her nature — every muscle screamed in protest against the night's violence.

She pressed her forehead against the cold glass of the window, watching as lightning split the sky. The Scottish countryside rushed past in stark flashes of illumination: gnarled trees bent by coastal winds, stretches of wild heather and ancient stone walls dividing the landscape into a patchwork of shadow and storm.

In the front seat, her mother continued to press the cloth against Christopher's side. The once-white fabric was already stained black with blood, and the scent filled the enclosed space of the car — a copper tang that made Faith's throat constrict.

The instinctive hunger disgusted her; this was her father's blood, spilled in their protection. Yet her body reacted as it would to any feeding opportunity, serving as another reminder that she wasn't human, no matter how much she sometimes wished to be.

"The bleeding's slowing," Nell said, her voice tight as her hands trembled while applying pressure. "But you're taking too long to heal."

"The blade that cut me …" Christopher replied through gritted teeth, "… it was hexed."

His knuckles were corpse white on the steering wheel as he fought to keep the car steady on the rain-slicked road. "Dark magic," he continued. "I can feel it fighting my natural healing."

Faith's breath caught. She had never seen her father truly injured before, and the sight of him struggling tore at her heart.

"Let me drive," insisted Nell.

"No," Christopher replied. "I'll be okay. My senses are sharper. We can't afford to lose time."

"How much further?" Nell asked, glancing nervously at the rearview mirror.

Faith knew she was checking for pursuers, though the storm made it impossible to see far behind them.

"Another four hours to Aberdeen," Christopher informed, wincing as the car hit another bump in the road. "Then we need to find St Machar's."

"The cathedral?" Faith asked, her interest piqued.

Growing up alone in rural Scotland, she had spent countless hours reading about the country's rich history, finding comfort and escape in tales of historic battles, crumbling monuments and feudal politics.

"Why there?" she enquired.

"St Machar's is one of Scotland's oldest vampire sanctuaries," Nell explained, her eyes still fixed on the rearview mirror. "During the Scottish Reformation, when the country broke away from the Catholic Church, the cathedral was abandoned."

"And that's when the ancient vampires seized their opportunity," Christopher continued. The discussion seemed to provide a welcome distraction from his suffering. "They embedded a talisman in the cathedral's foundations — supposedly a crystallized tear from Mary Magdalene."

"Is that really true?" Faith asked, intrigued by the merging of Christian and vampiric lore.

CHAPTER 10

"The tear's origin is mostly legend," Christopher replied softly. "But the talisman's power is real. It creates an impenetrable barrier around the cathedral's crypt. Anyone approaching with malign intent cannot cross the threshold." He paused, his voice taking on an almost reverent tone. "That sanctuary has sheltered our kind for centuries, protecting vampires from those who would destroy us in the name of their God."

Faith closed her eyes, trying to process everything. Her head throbbed from the sensory overload — the storm, the scent of blood, the lingering echoes of combat and the bloody history of her country.

Behind her eyelids, she kept replaying the moments of her first kill: the spray of blood as her sword found its mark, the shock on her victim's face as flesh turned to ash. Her hands trembled in her lap. It didn't go unnoticed.

"You need to go into trance," Nell said, turning to Faith. The worry in her mother's eyes made Faith's chest ache. "Your body needs time to heal, not to mention your spirit," her mother added.

Faith shook her head. "I need to stay with you. Alert. What if they're following us? What if Mary …"

"I won't let anything happen to you," Nell assured her, reaching back to squeeze Faith's knee. "Please, sweetheart. Rest."

The gentle concern in her mother's voice broke something inside Faith. She nodded reluctantly and let her eyes drift closed, allowing her consciousness to sink into the restorative dormancy that was neither sleep nor vampiric death.

Her last thought before the trance took her was of Mary's words: "The circle awaits."

Chapter 11

When Faith opened her eyes, the car was still. Through the rain-streaked windshield, she glimpsed the looming granite walls of St Machar's Cathedral silhouetted against the pre-dawn sky.

Twin towers rose into the darkness like ancient sentinels, while elaborate stained glass windows captured the scant light that remained amid the storm. The medieval stone walls seemed to pulse with a subtle energy, causing her heightened senses to tingle — akin to the moment just before lightning strikes.

The streets of Aberdeen were mercifully empty at this early hour, yet Faith still felt exposed as they hurried toward a small side door nearly concealed by a buttress. Her heart raced in her chest; she had never been in a city before.

The urban environment overwhelmed her with its intensity — the echo of their footsteps bouncing off the building walls, the hum of distant traffic and the lingering scents of countless people who had passed this way. After a lifetime of isolation in the wilds of northern Scotland, being here felt wrong. Dangerous. Her instincts screamed at her to flee back to the safety of their remote home. If only.

She thought again of her acceptance letter from the University of Edinburgh. Applying had been a fool's errand; that city would have swallowed her whole.

Rain plastered her hair to her face as Christopher raised his palm

CHAPTER 11

and gently pressed it against the old wood of the small door. She heard a locking mechanism shifting, and then the door swung open, revealing a darkness beyond. Her eyes adjusted with supernatural speed.

"Old Magick still lives in the new world," Christopher said, casting Faith a small wink.

Faith followed her parents down the worn stone steps into the cathedral's crypt, leaving the storm behind. The air grew cooler and still, heavy with centuries of silence. Ornate stone columns rose into the shadows overhead, while carved figures peered down from alcoves with sightless eyes. The space felt both threatening and welcoming, as if it recognized them as kindred spirits to those it had sheltered for hundreds of years.

Christopher scanned the floor before picking something up from the corner of the room. It was an antique-looking flintlock lighter made of dulled steel, with a carved wooden handle that resembled something from a steampunk encyclopedia. He began lighting the wall-mounted lanterns, casting dancing shadows through the forest of columns.

"The talisman's power has been fortified by every vampire who has sought sanctuary here," Christopher said softly. "They all gave something of themselves for the greater good while they were here. We will, too. The walls are imbued with that energy. We're safe here."

Faith ran her fingers along the rough stone wall, marveling at the subtle current she could feel radiating from it. It felt like a warm hum of protective energy — a comforting sensation after the chaos of the night.

Faith watched her father suddenly struggle to remain upright against a stone column. His usual composure was gone, replaced by jarring, unnatural movements that made her heart ache. Christopher had always been her rock — teaching her to fight, showing her how to control her enhanced senses and protecting her from a world that would never understand what she was. Now he could barely stand.

"Let me help," she whispered, moving closer.

"I'm fine." The words came through gritted teeth. Always the protector, he never wanted to show weakness.

But this time, she ignored his protest, ducking under his arm to support his weight just as he had once supported her first stumbling steps. His skin felt cold — too cold, even for one of their kind.

"You taught me to never let pride get in the way of survival," Faith said softly, echoing his own lessons back to him. "Remember?"

A weak chuckle escaped him.

"Using my own words against me?" His attempt at humor couldn't hide the pain in his voice. "When did you get so wise?"

"I had a good teacher."

She helped him slide down to sit against a wall, trying not to wince at the dark blood still seeping from his side. The hexed wound refused to heal completely, spreading angry black lines through nearby veins like poison.

Christopher caught her examining the injury and reached up to cup her cheek — just as he had done to comfort her after childhood nightmares. His hand trembled slightly.

"I'm sorry," he whispered.

"For what?"

"For not being strong enough tonight. For not protecting you better." His voice cracked. "A father should be able to keep his daughter safe."

Faith grasped his hand, squeezing it fiercely. "You've spent my whole life protecting me. I couldn't ask for more. But I still need my dad."

He wrapped an arm around her and, for a moment, she was transported back to countless nights spent like this — him teaching

CHAPTER 11

her guitar, explaining vampire history or simply holding her when the weight of loneliness and being different became too much.

Faith felt him tense as another wave of pain hit. She held him tighter, willing her own strength into him. They sat in silence for a while, the roles of protector and protected quietly shifting between them, if only for a brief moment.

Nell sank onto a stone bench nearby, her face drawn in the flickering lantern light. Now that they had stopped running, the terror of the night seemed to catch up with her all at once, and her shoulders began to shake with silent sobs.

"Mom?" Faith moved to sit beside her. She had rarely seen her mother cry.

"I'm sorry," Nell whispered, her voice breaking. "I'm so sorry, Faith. I thought we could keep you safe. I thought if we stayed hidden, if we were careful enough…" She pressed her fist against her mouth, trying to hold back tears.

"None of this is your fault," Christopher said firmly, moving to kneel in front of them despite his wounds. "We knew this day might come."

"But why?" Faith asked. "What makes my blood so special that she would hunt us down? That she would kill to get to me?"

Her parents exchanged a look that made Faith's stomach clench. There was more they hadn't revealed, secrets buried beneath the surface of their quiet life.

"You should try to rest," Nell suggested.

"Not until you tell me why this is happening." Faith straightened against the cold stone wall. "Why Mary called me… what she called me."

A distant rumble of thunder punctuated her words. The storm seemed to be following them, as if nature itself was unsettled by what was happening.

Nell exchanged a glance with Christopher, who nodded slightly. The wound on his side had stopped bleeding, but angry black lines still spread through the nearby flesh.

"It starts with two brothers," Nell began, her voice soft in the vast space.

Chapter 12

"Vlad and Radu Tepes," explained Nell.

Faith recognized these names from her mother's stories, but something in Nell's tone sent a chill down her spine. One of the lanterns sputtered, casting shadows that danced across the carved figures watching from their alcoves.

"Vlad became known as The Impaler," Nell continued. "A ruler so cruel that his name became synonymous with darkness." She traced patterns on the stone bench, avoiding Faith's gaze. "Radu was different — noble, just. Where his brother brought death, Radu tried to preserve life."

A cold draft whispered through the crypt. Faith noticed her father tense at each small sound, his protective instincts still alert despite their sanctuary.

"What does this have to do with me?" Faith asked, though apprehension was already tightening her stomach.

Christopher shifted, wincing as the movement tugged at his wound.

"Those brothers began two distinct bloodlines," he explained. "Two opposing forces, you could say."

The implications began to dawn on Faith just as something scraped in the murkiness beyond their circle of lamplight. All three of them froze, listening intently.

Just rats, Faith reassured herself, but her heightened senses remained on guard.

"Your father carries Radu's blood," Nell said, once the sound faded. "The light, the nobility, the strength to resist darkness."

Faith turned to look at Christopher. Even injured, he exuded an innate nobility — in his bearing and in how he had thrown himself between that blade and Faith without hesitation.

A lantern flickered out, the glass cracking softly in the silence. Faith's night vision kicked in, bringing her parents' grave expressions into sharp focus.

"And you?" she whispered to her mother, already knowing the answer but needing to hear it.

"Vlad's blood runs in my veins." Nell's fingers curled into fists. "The force Zachariah used. The power he tortured me to access."

"So I'm both," Faith asked, her voice barely above a whisper. "Light and dark. Noble and cruel. Is that why Mary wants me?"

"You're the first one," Christopher stated. "In all our history, to be born of these bloodlines. You're…"

"An abomination?" Faith's voice cracked on the word.

"No." Nell knelt before her daughter, taking Faith's cold hands in hers. "You're unique. You're precious. You frighten them because they don't understand you."

The stone walls seemed to close in, the weight of centuries pressing down upon them. Faith felt the talisman's energy pulsing around them like a heartbeat, providing protection against those who would try to take her, use her, or break her like they had her mother.

"Your blood holds power," Christopher said softly. "But that power doesn't define you. You're not merely a prophecy or a bloodline."

"Then what am I?" Faith asked, feeling more lost than ever.

"You're our daughter," Nell said fiercely. "You're the love of our lives… our miracle baby."

Another rat scuttled across the stone floor, causing Faith to jump.

CHAPTER 12

Her amplified hearing picked up its tiny heartbeat, the drip of water somewhere in the darkness and the distant rumble of thunder above. The cathedral felt alive around them, as if the very walls were eavesdropping on their secrets.

Nell had grown very still, her gaze fixed on something far away. Faith recognized that look — her mother was lost in memories she tried desperately to bury. The dripping water grew louder, echoing like the steady fall of drops in a prison cell: tap, tap, tap.

"Mom?" Faith whispered.

Nell's fingers traced unconscious patterns on her wrists, where manacle scars would have been had vampire healing not erased them. Her breathing quickened, a mortal reflex resurfacing.

"He would count," Nell said softly, her voice distant. "One drop at a time. He said it helped him savor each moment, each scream. Such precision in his cruelty."

Faith watched her mother's face transform, shadows creeping into her usually warm features. Even after all these years, Zachariah's influence still loomed over her.

"He liked to talk while he…" Nell's voice broke. She hugged herself tightly, as if trying to comfort a previous version of herself. "Such a cultured voice, discussing art and music while he…" She shuddered, the name catching in her throat like broken glass: "Zachariah."

The sound sent visible tremors through Nell's body, like ripples in water.

Faith instinctively reached out to comfort her mother, but the moment their skin touched, a vision slammed into her like a freight train.

***

Darkness. Complete and absolute.

Then hands everywhere — clawing, grasping, tearing. Fingernails like knives ripping into flesh.

Her mother's emaciated body burned with agony, every nerve ending screaming. This constant, unrelenting torture had defined her existence ever since she left the safety of a place called Vhik'h-Tal-Eskemon.

Rough hands seized her hair, dragging her across uneven concrete like a broken doll. The pain surpassed anything that could be expressed through screams. Yelling only invited more torment — extra sets of fangs piercing her flesh, fresh cuts carved into her abdomen, mocking laughter echoing as they fed on her terror as much as on her blood.

In the dank underground prison, time lost all meaning. Days bled into nights in an endless cycle of torment and brief, fitful unconsciousness that provided no real rest.

Through the hatch in the ceiling, his face would appear — Zachariah, with greedy eyes that devoured her suffering. His sneering voice sliced through the darkness: "Look how far you've fallen, special one."

The proud, defiant woman who once fought back had vanished, stripped away piece by piece until only raw survival remained. The only thing that kept her sane was fleeting flashes of Christopher's face, reminding her why she had walked willingly into this hell — to keep him safe. To protect them all...

Chapter 13

Faith ripped her hand away from her mother's skin, bile rising in her throat.

The depth of trauma, savagery and humiliation she had just witnessed made her entire body shudder. Now she truly understood why merely mentioning Zachariah's name could drain the last remnants of color from her mother's face. The haunted look that sometimes crossed Nell's expression, the way she flinched at unexpected touches — all of it became clear. It was why Nell was so desperate to keep Faith hidden from the world.

"Mom..." Faith whispered, her voice breaking.

But no words could encompass what she had just experienced, no comfort could erase the memories etched in blood and pain.

"I saw it," Faith said, her voice raw. "Mom, I'm so sorry. I didn't mean to..."

Nell pulled her into a fierce embrace.

"You have nothing to be sorry for. I just want to protect you from ever experiencing anything like that. I couldn't bear it if they hurt you the way they hurt me."

"Which is why we need help," Christopher interjected, a note of resolve in his tone. "The American Council has resources, allies. They can help us fight back. I need to call Kavisha to set the wheels in..."

"NO!" Nell's voice cracked like a whip, echoing around the chamber.

"I won't have Faith drawn into their politics, into their wars. Look what happened last time. They couldn't protect me then, and they can't protect Faith now."

A long silence followed.

Faith watched her father examine his wound again, his face tightening in pain. She pretended not to notice the tremor in his hand or the way her mother kept glancing anxiously at the stairs leading up to the street. They were trying to conceal their fear, but their bodies revealed the truth. Even in this sanctuary, they were counting exits, measuring distances and preparing for the worst.

"We can't stay here," Christopher began.

"Then we need to find somewhere even more remote," Faith replied, her voice shaking as horrific images from her mother's memories flooded her mind — the endless torture, the sheer helplessness, the degradation. Her stomach lurched. "Further north, maybe. One of the outer islands — the Orkneys, Shetlands or even Iceland. Somewhere they'll never think to look."

The thought of facing Mary again made her hands shake uncontrollably. She could still taste copper on her tongue, still see the spray of blood as her wild, desperate swing had somehow found the vampire's neck. One lucky kill didn't make her a warrior; it only highlighted how close she'd come to being captured.

It could have easily been her strapped down in a dark basement, enduring the same torment as her mother. The vision of Nell's torture was still so vivid that she could feel the phantom pain of fangs tearing into flesh and hear the echoes of mocking laughter.

"Faith..." Christopher began gently, reaching for her with his injured arm — a reminder of how even her immortal, powerful father could bleed.

"No!" she interrupted, backing away along the bench until her back hit one of the stone columns. Her voice echoed off the ancient walls.

CHAPTER 13

"I'm not ready for this. You saw me tonight; I can barely fight. I stumbled around like a child playing with her father's things. I only survived because someone else slipped." Her breath came in ragged gasps. "If we go to America, if we get involved…" She couldn't even begin to fathom the magnitude of that country.

The shadows cast by the lanterns began to stretch and twist unnaturally, reaching toward them like grasping fingers before snapping back to their original forms. Faith couldn't tell if it was a trick of the light or something sinister testing the sanctuary's barriers.

She hugged herself tightly, her fingers digging into her arms as another wave of her mother's memories washed over her — the feeling of being nothing more than a blood bank, a thing to be used and discarded.

"I'll just get us all killed. Or worse…" She couldn't finish the thought, couldn't voice her deepest fear — that she would end up in some dark pit like her mother had, stripped of everything but pain and terror.

The tears she had been holding back finally spilled over. Her strength faltered, and she slid off the bench to sit on the cold stone floor. Years of training meant nothing. She was still just a scared girl pretending to be something she wasn't, and now she knew exactly what happened to those who were weak.

Nell knelt beside her daughter, pulling her into a fierce embrace.

"It's okay to be scared," she whispered, stroking Faith's hair as she had done when Faith was little. Her touch was gentle, a stark contrast to the cruel hands from the vision.

Faith buried her face in her mother's shoulder, inhaling her familiar scent, feeling like a small child again. "How did you survive it?" she whispered. "How did you stay sane through all that pain?"

"By remembering why I was there," Nell replied softly. "By holding on to love."

"I don't want to fight," Faith choked out. "I don't want to be special or powerful or whatever Mary thinks I am. I don't want to end up..." She shuddered, unable to finish. "I just want to go home. I want everything to go back to how it was."

But home was gone now, reduced to blood-stained stones and shattered glass. Their quiet life of books, music and long walks had been destroyed in a single night of carnage. Somewhere in the storm-wracked darkness, Mary was hunting them, gathering her forces, preparing to do God knows what to get what she wanted. The memory of her mother's torture replayed in Faith's mind, but now it was her own face she saw, her own screams echoing in that grim basement.

She had never felt more lost or afraid.

The lantern flames flickered erratically, casting large, distorted shadows on the stone walls. In the dancing light, every carved figure seemed to watch them with hollow eyes. Faith felt the talisman's energy pulse around them like a protective heartbeat, offering temporary sanctuary from the cruel world beyond.

She moved closer to her mother, longing to curl up and never leave the safety of these time-worn walls.

Her father's blood infused the air, a reminder that nowhere was truly safe anymore. Not for them. Not for her. The dark spaces between the stone columns seemed to whisper of all the ways she could break.

"I don't want to be special," she whispered into the darkness. "I just want to be your daughter."

Nell's arms tightened around her, and her father's hands found hers, squeezing gently. Right then, she wasn't the union of ancient bloodlines or the subject of prophecy. She was just a girl, held by parents who loved her, while their world crumbled around them.

Chapter 14

Hours passed. Dark veins crept up her father's body like poisonous ivy. Faith watched in helpless dread as the tendrils spread beneath his pale skin, creating intricate patterns that writhed in the flickering lantern light.

The wound from the hexed blade gaped, angry and raw, oozing a fluid with a sickly-sweet scent completely unlike vampire blood. The heady smell filled her nostrils, constricting her throat.

Christopher sat heavily on the stone bench, leaning back against the rough wall. Though he tried to suppress his grimace of pain, Faith noticed every subtle change in his expression, every spasm, every tremor running through his weakening body.

Water continued to drip in the darkness beyond their circle of lamplight, each drop echoing through the vast underground space with the steady rhythm of a heartbeat. The dancing flames from the wall-mounted lanterns cast multiple shadows across the historic stones. The air carried the musty scent of centuries — earth, stone and decay — now tainted by the sickly tang of her father's illness.

Faith traced her fingers along the uneven stone walls, seeking comfort in their ancient strength. But even the sanctuary's power felt weak and uncertain now — like her father's once-steady hands and her mother's faltering smile.

Everything solid in her world was crumbling, and she couldn't stop it. Perhaps the corruption infesting her father was also battling the Talisman, slowly sapping its strength in the same way it was draining Christopher. The thought sent a cold shiver down her spine. Had they unwittingly brought an evil force into this sacred space? Was their very presence breaking down the protection that had endured for centuries?

Nell paced between the towering columns, her boots clicking against the worn stone in an agitated rhythm. The sound echoed off the vaulted ceiling, mixing with the steady drip of water.

"Someone must have told Mary where to find us in Scarfskerry. We were careful — no contact, no traces, nothing to lead them to us."

"Jiangshina." Christopher's bitter laugh turned into a grimace that made Faith's heart clench. "Who else? The Magisters were never going to leave Faith alone. We should have known better. Jiangshina knew precisely where we were. Their claim to be mere watchers and chroniclers was bullshit. She was terrified of that damned prophecy, and it looks like it forced her hand."

"Is that the prophecy about me being the Eminence of Abominations?" Faith asked, though she instinctively knew the answer. "What did it say?"

Silence. The drip of water. Tiny rodent feet scuttling in dark corners. Flames flickering. Shadows dancing.

"Oh, come on," Faith insisted. "It's a bit late in the day for secrets now."

Nell halted her pacing, her shoulders visibly slumping.

"The prophecy speaks of a final apocalypse," she said reluctantly. "And you're somehow connected to it."

Faith took a moment to absorb those words.

"Connected to it... or am I the one who causes it?" she asked pointedly.

More silence followed.

CHAPTER 14

"We don't know anything," Christopher said, throwing up his shaking hands. "The prophecy is old and cryptic, and it's already deceived us once."

He shot Nell a knowing glance.

As he spoke, the black veins pulsed beneath Christopher's skin, each word seemingly fueling the spread of the corruption. Faith watched as another tendril slithered up to his collar, marking its territory like an invading army. Her keen vision picked up every detail of its advance — how it branched and spiraled, how it turned the surrounding flesh gray and lifeless.

A fat rat scurried past Faith's feet, its tiny heart beating a frantic rhythm that her sensitive hearing detected all too clearly. It reminded her of their meager sustenance since taking refuge — surviving on rodent blood, each small body barely enough to dull their hunger.

"The sanctuaries," Nell said abruptly, her face suddenly a mask of apprehension. Her words echoed around the stone chamber. "Magisters… they're the keepers of the knowledge, as they so smugly remind everyone, so…"

"Fuck," Christopher interrupted. "I hadn't even made the connection. They know the locations of the sanctuaries."

Nell gazed into a corner, as if searching her memory.

"In northern Scotland, there's Castle Semple Church, Dunkeld Cathedral and Fearn Abbey, as well as St Machar's," she said. "Seeking sanctuary was the obvious move for us. They must know that."

"Fearn Abbey is closest to Scarfskerry, but St Machar's is next," Christopher added. "If they stopped at Fearn Abbey, it might have bought us some time, but we need to move. Now!"

Chapter 15

They emerged into the pre-dawn darkness of Aberdeen's streets. Christopher staggered, the black corruption visibly spreading toward his neck. Faith moved to support him, but he gently pushed her away.

"Stay behind me," he ordered, his voice rough with pain. Even in his weakened state, he placed himself between her and any potential danger.

The rain had finally stopped, yet the air remained heavy with moisture and the promise of more storms to come. The cobblestones were slick beneath Faith's feet, reflecting the meager moonlight filtering through the heavy clouds.

The city's smells assaulted her heightened senses — wet stone, rotting seaweed from the nearby harbor, smoke from a dying fire, and beneath it all, the myriad mingled aromas of humanity.

Then she caught another scent: cold, dead flesh. Her hearing picked up footsteps moving with eerie synchronization through the surrounding alleys. The sound made her skin prickle with ancient instincts.

She remembered the unnatural flickering flames inside the crypt. The protective talisman was trying to warn them.

"They're herding us," Christopher said through gritted teeth, one hand pressed against his side.

"Faith, stay between us," Nell whispered, taking up position behind

CHAPTER 15

her daughter.

They moved as a unit, her parents forming a protective barrier despite Christopher's weakened state. Faith felt like a child again, sheltered by their love even as guilt gnawed at her.

Dark figures glided through the shadows with predatory grace. Mary's vampires had found them, moving like a coordinated pack, each step mirroring the others as if they shared one mind.

A blade whistled through the gloom.

Nell pulled Faith down just as the weapon embedded itself in the wall behind them.

"Not my girl," her mother snarled, her maternal instincts overpowering her usual gentle nature.

Faith's heart pounded against her ribs as they were forced down narrower streets. Her father's movements grew more labored with each turn, but he didn't slow, refusing to stop protecting them. The walls seemed to press closer, the weathered brick sweating centuries of grime in the damp air.

"Dad, please," Faith whispered as Christopher stumbled again. "Let me help you."

He managed a weak smile despite the pain etched on his face.

"My job is to help you, Little One."

The childhood nickname made tears sting her eyes.

Faith's sharp vision captured every detail of their prison — moss growing between cracked stones, rusted pipes snaking up the walls, broken windows staring down like empty eyes. The sky above had reduced to a thin ribbon of darkness, choked by overhanging eaves and centuries of encroaching architecture.

Another turn forced them deeper into the maze of backstreets, each passage narrower than the last. The walls bent inward overhead, old buildings sagging together like weary old men sharing secrets. Faith heard the scrape of boots on stone echoing from multiple directions, the sound bouncing around until she couldn't discern where the pursuit was coming from.

Nell grabbed Faith's hand, squeezing it briefly.

"We stay together," she said firmly. "No matter what."

The words bore the weight of two decades of unity.

Suddenly, a vampire lunged from a doorway.

Christopher shoved Faith back while Nell pulled her away, their movements synchronized even now.

They were forced into an even tighter passage, the walls barely an arm's length apart. Faith felt her mother's hand on her back, guiding her forward as her shoulder scraped against the rough stone.

"I'm slowing us down," Christopher gasped as they rounded another corner. The corruption had visibly spread in just a few minutes.

"We're not leaving you," Faith and Nell said in unison.

They flanked him, supporting his weight despite his weak protests. The family moved as one, just as they always had. But the narrow alleys betrayed them.

Another vampire appeared, teeth gleaming in a feral grin.

They spun around, only to find their retreat blocked by a dead end.

Christopher pushed Faith behind him while Nell stepped in front of them both, forming a desperate barrier between their daughter and the advancing vampires.

"Stay close to me," Christopher ordered, though his voice trembled with effort.

Faith could smell the sickly-sweet poison running through his veins, could hear the strain in his voice. Yet he still stood firm, still fought to protect her.

The alley ended in a sheer brick wall too high for even vampire abilities to scale. The aged stone loomed like a tombstone, sealing their fate.

The attackers spread out in a semicircle, with Mary now emerging

CHAPTER 15

at the center, pressing closer in the constricted space.

Rusty fire escapes creaked overhead, threatening to collapse under decades of neglect. Faith's enhanced hearing caught every groan of stressed metal, every crack of ancient mortar. The city itself seemed to conspire with their pursuers, offering no refuge, no escape.

"You had your chance." Mary's voice dripped with contempt, echoing off the close-pressed walls. "No more bargaining. No more mercy. I will take the girl, along with your lives." Her grin widened as she looked at Faith's mother and father.

The pack began to approach down the narrow alley.

Faith glanced at her parents, her stricken father and her panicked mother.

This was the end.

Their little family had only ever sought peace and solitude. Now it would only know pain and death.

Chapter 16

A shadow detached itself from the sheer wall above, dropping to land between Mary's forces and Faith's family.

The figure slowly rose to its full height — a broad-shouldered man well over six feet tall. He appeared well-muscled beneath a long black trench coat that nearly brushed the ground. Two swords were crossed on his back, their hilts worn smooth through years of use, the leather wrappings darkened with age.

The man turned to face the huddled family.

Faith's keen eyes took him in.

Then her breath caught.

This couldn't be... it didn't seem real.

His dark skin gleamed like polished mahogany. A clean-shaven face bore the marks of experience — a thin scar traced from his left ear to his jaw, another crossed the bridge of his nose. Despite these marks, he couldn't have been much older than thirty. Close-cropped black hair showcased hints of silver at the temples, and his eyes were a deep shade of brown. He wore a tactical belt laden with weapons, and fingerless leather gloves adorned his hands. A pair of shades peeked out from the breast pocket of his coat.

Faith found it hard to believe her eyes. Having grown up devouring vampire comic books and movies to understand the myths surrounding her kind, this stranger looked exactly like... Blade.

CHAPTER 16

"Sorry to crash the party." His rich baritone resonated with authority, filling the narrow space. A slight West African accent colored his words, adding an exotic edge that stood out to Faith's sheltered ears. His full lips curved into a confident smile. "But I've got strict orders regarding this one."

He noticed Faith's wide-eyed stare as she looked him up and down. "Name's Isaac," he said. "And yeah, I know who I look like — keeps things interesting!" His smile was fierce in the darkness.

Mary's grin vanished, replaced by a snarl that revealed her sharp teeth.

"Hunter!" She spat the word like a curse. "Kill him."

Her minions surged ahead, blades raised.

Isaac moved with precision, ducking to one side and drawing both swords in a single fluid motion. The steel sang as it cleared the scabbards, the sound echoing off the close-pressed walls. Faith's sensitive ears caught the whisper of well-oiled leather and the subtle ring of perfectly balanced blades cutting through damp air.

The first vampire lunged at him, teeth bared in a feral snarl.

Isaac pivoted on his back foot, allowing the attacker to slide past him by mere inches. His left blade swept up in an arc, catching the moonlight on its edge before severing the vampire's neck. The sound was like a cleaver cutting through wet wood, followed by the distinctive hiss of flesh turning to ash. The acrid smell hit Faith's nostrils, making her gag in the confined space.

Two more attackers charged at him simultaneously, moving in perfect sync.

Isaac dropped into a crouch, both swords extended outward. As the vampires closed in, he spun like a deadly top, his blades creating a whirlwind of silver. Blood sprayed in twin arcs, splattering the cobblestones with a sound like rain. The coppery scent filled the alley, mingling with the ash of dissolving bodies.

Faith's stomach lurched as she watched him in action. Each kill was precise, efficient and devoid of hesitation or mercy. Her hands trembled against the rough brick wall, seeking a grip on its solid reality. This wasn't the desperate, clumsy execution she'd managed earlier.

Isaac may have looked like a superhero, but reality was anything but neat. More vampires came at him with a coordinated brutality that quickly shattered any illusion of an easy victory.

Two vampires struck simultaneously from different angles, their blades moving in impossible synchronization. Isaac's initial dodge was more desperate than graceful, narrowly avoiding decapitation and sending him into a spin.

His left sword deflected one blade. However, the second attacker's weapon sliced a deep gash across his forearm.

Faith saw his muscles tense and the flash of pain in his eyes — he wasn't untouchable. This wasn't a movie. He was human. Vulnerable.

"Shit," Isaac muttered, the first crack in his confident façade.

The vampires pressed their advantage.

Where Isaac had once seemed like a dancer, he now looked like a man fighting for his life. His coat whipped around him as he moved, no longer a stylish flourish but a desperate shield against his multiple attackers.

One vampire slipped past his guard, its blade sliding between Isaac's ribs. Faith watched in horror as he staggered, red blood blossoming across his tactical shirt. For an instant, she feared he was finished.

But Isaac wasn't done. With a roar that combined pain and fury, he reversed his grip on his sword and drove it backward into his attacker's chest, then across the vampire's neck. The creature dissolved, but the move left Isaac exposed.

Another blade whistled toward his unprotected neck.

"Behind you!" Faith's warning made Isaac duck just in time. The

CHAPTER 16

blade missed his throat by millimeters, slicing through the collar of his coat.

Faith's heart thundered. This wasn't an effortless massacre set to dance music like in the Wesley Snipes movies. This was a real fight — brutal, messy, with death lurking at the slightest mistake.

Isaac was bleeding now. Multiple cuts covered his arms and side. His movements grew slower, each strike more deliberate. He didn't possess supernatural healing abilities. The smile had vanished, replaced by a grim determination that spoke of survival, not theater.

Faith realized she was holding her breath. One wrong move, one moment of weakness, and he would die. Then nothing would stand between her family and Mary's forces. But Isaac continued to fight with grim determination.

Faith's senses captured every detail: the wet sounds of blades slicing through flesh, the subtle differences in pitch as steel met bone or sinew, and the individual notes in the symphony of death surrounding her. Her vision registered the blood spray patterns on the brick walls and the way ash swirled through the night air like gray snow.

The metallic tang of blood mixed with the acrid scent of vampire ash made her fangs extend involuntarily. She tasted copper on her tongue and realized she had bitten her own lip. Every muscle in her body was coiled tight, caught between the urge to flee and the darker impulse to join the violence. This brutality was part of her heritage too.

A blade whistled past Faith's ear, close enough that she felt the rush of air.

Isaac spun to intercept the next attack, but she could see the strain in his movements. Even skilled Hunters had their limits. The thought sent chills through her veins — if he fell, her family would be next.

Chapter 17

The cobblestones grew slick with blood and ash, creating a treacherous dark paste. The acrid smell of decay filled the narrow space, making Faith's sensitive nose burn. Her heightened hearing discerned the subtle differences between the sounds of bodies collapsing and the softer whisper of ash settling. She could hear the wet scrape of boots on stone and the keen slicing of blades through the air.

A vampire slipped past Isaac's guard, a knife flashing in the darkness. Faith recognized the strike coming but couldn't move quickly enough.

In a desperate move, Nell shoved her aside. The weapon opened a deep gash in her mother's shoulder rather than Faith's throat.

"Mom!" Faith cried as she caught Nell, holding her mother tightly while glancing back up the alley.

The attackers had fled, forming a protective circle around Mary as they retreated. Isaac rushed back to tackle the one who had injured Nell.

The vampire lunged at Isaac with the long knife. The Hunter quickly severed the vampire's arm, the blade clattering to the ground still attached to the hand. He then deftly reversed his swing and decapitated the foe. The body crumpled to the ground and dissolved into dust on the cobbles.

Isaac gave a curt nod to Faith, who turned back to look at her parents. Her father was barely standing, and her mother clutched her wound.

Then Faith saw something horrifying.

Dark veins began to spread from her mother's cut, mirroring the poison slowly consuming Christopher. The same sickly-sweet odor tainted the air.

Another hexed blade.

Something inside her broke.

The two pillars of her world were crumbling, and it was all because of her — because of what flowed in her veins, because of what she was.

"I did this," she whispered, her voice trembling. "You're both dying because of me."

Her mind flashed back through the years — every training session with her father, every quiet moment spent reading with her mother, every time they had sacrificed their own happiness to keep her safe. They had given up everything to protect her, choosing isolation in the furthest corner of Scotland. And how had she repaid them? By bringing destruction to their door.

"I'm nothing but a curse," Faith continued, watching her mother press a hand to her infected wound. The words felt like broken glass in her throat.

She glanced at Christopher, recalling how he had thrown himself between the blade and her back in Scarfskerry. Always the protector. Even now, dying from dark magic, he tried to hide the extent of his pain.

"All those years of hiding," Faith said, her voice cracking. "All that sacrifice. And for what? To watch you both die because I wasn't worth protecting."

The guilt weighed heavily against her chest, making it hard to breathe. Every childhood memory now felt tainted — their quiet life had never been a gift, but a prison her parents had willingly entered to keep her safe. And she had failed them.

"You both deserved better," she continued, tears spilling down her cheeks. "A normal life. A chance at happiness. Instead, you got me — this thing. This abomination that brings nothing but pain."

Nell reached for her daughter despite her own suffering, but Faith stepped back. She couldn't bear her mother's touch right now or the gentleness in those eyes. She felt unworthy. Tainted.

The weight of it all — the prophecy, the bloodlines, the destiny she had never asked for — pressed down on her like a vice. But watching her parents suffer was worse than any other burden. Their love for her would be their death sentence.

Faith clenched her fists so tightly her nails cut into her palms. The physical pain was almost welcome — a small penance for what she had brought upon them. Blood welled in her palms, and she stared at it with hatred. This cursed blood that made her special, that made her hunted, that was now costing her everything she held dear.

The guilt threatened to drown her, but beneath it, something else was building — a rage so pure it felt like fire in her veins.

She looked at Isaac, who stood still, swords in hand, guarding them, still panting from his exertion. Faith saw the determination in his set jaw. She recalled his bravery, relentlessness, sacrifice, and his impulse to do the right thing. The fire inside her blazed suddenly brighter.

Faith felt something fundamental shift within her.

The sheltered girl who had hidden from the world was burning away, replaced by something harder, forged in guilt, shame and desperation. Her parents had sacrificed everything to protect her. Now it was her turn to protect them — whatever the cost.

No more running. No more hiding. No longer a little girl afraid of the world. Her parents needed help — real help, not just a temporary refuge. That meant one thing: America. The Vampire Council. It also meant finally accepting whatever fate awaited her. The time for

CHAPTER 17

lurking in the shadows was over.
"Ready to move?" Isaac asked, glancing nervously down the alley.
"Ready," Faith replied. "Let's go."

Chapter 18

The steering wheel vibrated under Isaac's grip as he took another corner at breakneck speed, the car's tires shrieking against the rain-slick cobblestones.

Mary and her forces had retreated long enough for the four of them to pile into Isaac's black SUV, with him carrying Christopher and Faith supporting her mother.

As always, Faith's hearing picked up every excruciating detail: the rubber fighting for purchase, her father's ragged breathing, her mother's soft whimpers and, beneath it all, the synchronized footfalls of Mary's forces. The sound resonated like a military drumbeat echoing through the parallel streets of Aberdeen, growing closer with each passing second.

"They're trying to cut us off from the north," Isaac said, his voice tight as he wrestled with the wheel. "To force us toward the harbor."

Lightning split the sky, momentarily transforming the granite buildings into looming giants. In that stark illumination, Faith caught glimpses of dark figures moving with inhuman speed through the maze of streets, slipping like shadows between the ancient structures. The storm that had followed them from Skarfskerry seemed to travel with them, as if nature itself had aligned with their pursuers.

Faith's nose detected an array of scents: wet stone, rusted metal from old drainpipes, the salt tang of the nearby harbor and, most hauntingly, the sickly-sweet corruption emanating from her parents' wounds. The smell was fundamentally wrong, like meat left too long in the summer heat.

"Hold on!" Isaac called out as he yanked the wheel hard left. The car fishtailed, sending them into a controlled spin.

Faith caught individual raindrops whirling past the windows, the determined set of Isaac's jaw in the rearview mirror and her father's head lolling against the leather seat. The world tilted around them.

Christopher convulsed beside her, his body jackknifing with such force that his head cracked against the window. Black veins spread up his neck like dark lightning, creating patterns that seemed to writhe beneath his pale skin. Faith watched as they branched and multiplied; his skin burned with fever — normally an impossibility for a vampire.

"Dad?" She grabbed his hand, trying to anchor him. His flesh felt like hot coals against her palm. "Stay with me … please, Dad."

His eyes fluttered open, but they were clouded and unfocused.

"Gabriel?" The name escaped Christopher's lips as a barely-heard whisper, thick with confusion and grief. "Is that really you, little guy? Gabriel? I'm so sorry I failed you, buddy. Gabriel?"

Faith's heart clenched. That name, whispered during Christopher's darkest moments or called out in nightmares. Gabriel. The brother he couldn't save, dead at six from leukemia — a lifetime before Faith's existence.

"It's Faith," she said softly, squeezing his burning hand. "Your daughter. You haven't failed anyone, Dad."

"They're gaining," Nell warned from the front passenger seat. Her voice was thick and slurred, as if she were speaking through molasses. Dark tendrils began creeping up her arm from the wound, spreading with alarming speed.

Isaac reached into his coat with his free hand, pulling out small silver spheres that caught the dim light.

"Cover your nose and mouth," he ordered. "This might get messy."

Faith pulled her shirt over her face just as Isaac's arm shot out, sending the spheres flying through the open window. They exploded on impact with the wet street, releasing a fine mist that Faith's sharp eyes tracked as it spread through the air like morning fog. The vapor engulfed their pursuers an instant later.

The screams that followed pierced through Faith's superhuman ears painfully. It was a sound like hot metal against her eardrums — raw, primal shrieks of agony as vampire flesh sizzled and burned. She slammed her palms against her ears, trying to block out the horrific chorus.

"What was that?" she gasped when the screaming finally subsided.

"The vapor of blessed water from Torre della Bell'Alda," Isaac replied, his eyes fixed on the road. "Mixed with a healthy dose of silver nitrate. It burns like acid for you vamps." He glanced at her in the mirror.

Her expression was tense. She didn't know how to react. The tactic had bought them time, but she didn't condone weapons intended to harm her kind.

More shapes emerged from the shadows ahead, moving with that same terrifying speed and synchronization. Isaac cursed in a language that sounded like Yoruba, then reached down beside his seat. He emerged with a handful of wicked-looking caltrops, their points glinting in the intermittent lightning.

"These might wake the locals," he warned before scattering them across the street behind them. The metallic clatter of their landing was quickly followed by more screams as vampire feet were shredded on the silver spikes.

"Where... where are we going?" Christopher's voice was barely audible over the engine and rain. "Have to... have to get Gabriel to his appointment... he needs his medication... poor Gabriel..."

CHAPTER 18

"The airstrip, Dad," Faith said, fighting back tears. "To the Council. Just hold on a little longer."

"The hospital... for Gabriel." He tried to sit up but fell back, his body trembling. "They said... said the new treatment might help... radiation therapy... have to get him there... the chemo just makes him worse... his hair was so soft... he was too small..."

"How much further?" Faith asked Isaac, her voice trembling.

"Ten minutes. Maybe less once we clear Aberdeen and hit the open road." He tightened his grip on the steering wheel. "If we make it that far."

They took another corner sharply, the car's chassis groaning in protest. This part of Aberdeen was a maze of narrow streets, dating back to the 18th century, if not earlier.

Out of the corner of her eye, Faith caught a glimpse of movement — dark shapes darting across the rooftops, keeping pace with their vehicle. Her keen vision picked out horrifying details: elongated fingers, razor-sharp claws, faces twisted in feral snarls and eyes reflecting streetlights like those of wild animals.

"They're above us!" she shouted.

Isaac didn't respond, only pressed down harder on the accelerator. The engine screamed as they sped down the narrow street, brick walls closing in on either side.

Moments later, they burst onto the open road.

Faith glanced at a sign ahead — 'A92 via Dundee, Arbroath, Aberdeen' — and looked back through the rear window. The vampires had been left behind, standing on the rooftops.

Chapter 19

They drove in silence, Nell clutching her father's hand tightly.

"Almost there," Isaac announced after about ten minutes.

Nell looked up and saw the sign — 'Netherley Private Airstrip'.

Christopher had gone completely rigid beside her, his skin burning hotter than ever. The black veins pulsed visibly beneath his skin, spreading intricate patterns across his face, reminiscent of a Māori tattoo. His eyes had rolled back, revealing only the whites.

Isaac sped over grass, pavement and gravel, bypassing the squat airport building and heading straight for the runway behind it. He screeched the car to a stop.

Faith spotted a small blue and white aircraft just ahead, its side emblazoned with 'Cessna Golden Eagle'.

"We have to carry him," Faith said, fighting down a wave of panic.

"I've got him." Isaac appeared beside her with the door already open, moving with almost inhuman speed.

"Get your mother." He nodded toward the sleek private jet, its engines already spinning up. "Don't stop for anything."

Faith helped Nell to her feet while Isaac lifted Christopher's weight. They rushed toward the plane, their feet splashing through puddles that mirrored the stormy sky. Her hands shook as she assisted her mother up the metal steps and into the cabin. The enclosed space felt suffocating after a lifetime spent in the open expanse of northern

CHAPTER 19

Scotland.

"Strap them in," Isaac ordered as he maneuvered Christopher into a seat and reclined it as far back as it would go.

"C… co… cold…" Christopher said. "So cold, Gabriel… The doctors said… said to keep you warm…"

"It's the fever, Dad," Faith said, securing his seatbelt. "Just hold on. Please."

"Get us in the air!" Isaac shouted toward the cockpit.

The whine of the engines rose to a pitch that made Faith's sensitive ears ache. She felt the aircraft shift as it began to move, accelerating down the runway and pressing her back into her seat. Her stomach lurched as they left the ground, the pressure change causing her ears to pop painfully.

"The poison spreads differently in each vampire," Isaac explained. "Age matters. Older ones can resist it better."

"How do you know so much about vampire physiology?" Faith asked, nervously glancing at her parents, trying to distract herself from the way the cabin walls felt increasingly constricting.

Isaac's expression darkened.

"I had to learn. After my sister…" He trailed off, forcing a smile that didn't reach his eyes. "She was…"

A scream from Nell shattered the moment.

Faith rushed to her mother's side as Nell thrashed in her seat, trapped in what seemed to be a nightmare.

"No," Nell gasped. "No more… no, please… not again… no…"

As Faith grabbed her mother's shoulders to calm her, a vision accosted her with terrible clarity.

***

Shackled to an iron post protruding from the ground.

The cavernous room was lit by two flickering torches on the far side, their moving flames casting ominous shadows across the expansive space.

Underground. The air was fetid.

Unconscious, but breathing — barely.

Bruises and bite marks covered every inch of her flesh. She resembled a mistreated animal, all the fight stripped from her, her survival instinct extinguished.

Just a bag of bones wrapped in paper-thin skin that burned like fire…

***

Faith jerked back with a cry, breaking contact. Her heart hammered.

Her visions were so unpredictable, but one thing was clear: the poison was breaking down her mother's mental barriers, allowing memories to bleed through unfiltered. The guilt hit Faith like a punch to the stomach — this was her fault.

She looked to her mother, then to her motionless father, feeling utterly bereft. An idea struck her.

"I can help," she said desperately, pulling up her sleeve. Her fangs extended automatically, ready to tear into her own flesh. "My blood… it's supposed to be powerful, right? Special? That's why they're hunting us."

Isaac caught Faith's wrist before she could bite into it. His grip was firm, his skin warm against her cold flesh.

"The hex doesn't work that way," he said softly. "It has to be cured at the source. This kind of dark magic…" He shook his head. "It requires specific counter-spells. Blood alchemy could only make it worse. We don't know where that could lead us."

"Then what good am I?" she pleaded. "What's the point of being special if I can't even save my own parents?"

Christopher stirred at the sound of her distress.

"Gabriel?" His hand reached out blindly, trembling in the air between them. "Don't cry, little man. I'll always be here… I promised Mom, didn't I? I promised I'd take care of you…"

Faith took his hand, feeling the tremors ripple through him. The black veins had spread across his face, turning the skin around them gray and lifeless.

"Tell me about him," she whispered, her throat tight. "About Gabriel."

Christopher's fever-bright eyes fixed on a point in the distance, and he seemed to calm slightly.

Isaac nodded in approval.

"He loved trains," Christopher said softly. "Had this little wooden one he carried everywhere. Even… even in the hospital." His voice cracked. "Blue and red. Dad painted it for him. He was so brave. Never complained. Not once. Just asked me to tell him stories about the adventures we'd have when he got better…"

Faith sensed Isaac's presence behind her as Christopher slipped back into delirium, his words dissolving into fevered mumbling. Then he grew quiet and still.

Nell was still now too. They both appeared to be in a trance state.

"Leave them be," Isaac said gently. "If they can descend into a trance, it might help them fight the disease, or at least slow its spread."

He took a seat opposite Faith.

"You need to do the same," he said. "You're no good to them when you're depleted. If you want to help them, then prioritize helping yourself first."

She was about to protest when he cut her off.

"If anything happens, I promise to wake you. You have my word — as a Hunter, as a friend, and even as a pretend superhero." He gave a sly wink.

Faith smiled weakly. She didn't want to admit it, but he was right: they weren't likely to face any threats at 37,000 feet. She should use the time to recuperate and heal.

She reclined her seat and shifted her weight before clearing her mind and taking a few deep breaths. The familiar pull of her restorative trance drew near. The events of the night were finally catching up with her.

As her consciousness began to drift, she noticed Isaac retrieving a med kit from one of the overhead compartments. Through her increasingly heavy eyelids, she watched him gingerly strip to the waist and tend to his various cuts and gashes with practiced efficiency.

Even in her fading awareness, Faith couldn't help but notice the stories etched into his ebony body — old scars mapping a life filled with battles fought and survived. His lean, muscled physique spoke of years of training and combat, not mere aesthetics.

Her last thought before the trance took over was one of deep gratitude — not just for his fighting prowess, but for the dedication and sacrifice that had shaped him into someone willing to risk everything to protect strangers.

A Hunter shielding vampires. How strange the world could be. With that final thought, she slipped into the void.

Chapter 20

Faith jolted awake, disoriented by her surroundings. A mechanical droning noise filled her ears, while recycled air flooded her nostrils. Rows of plush leather seats inside a narrow tube filled her vision.

Then reality came crashing down. Hard.

"Mom... Dad," she called, panic rising in her voice.

"Easy there," came a baritone voice.

Isaac appeared before her, dressed in fresh black fatigues but lacking his trademark coat and longswords. He looked markedly less threatening — almost gentle.

"Nothing's changed," he reassured. "The spread hasn't receded, but it hasn't gotten any worse, either. That's something."

Faith needed to see for herself. She bolted from her seat and rushed to Nell and then Christopher. Isaac was right: the black tendrils still snaked across their skin in that horrible fractal pattern, but it seemed like it hadn't progressed. Yet. She kissed both of them gently on the forehead before returning to her seat.

Isaac sat across from her. The silence of the cabin pressed in around them, broken only by the steady drone of the engines.

For the first time since their desperate escape, Faith truly studied Isaac. In the dim cabin light, weariness was etched into his features. Though his tactical gear was fresh, she could see the bandages beneath, evidence of the wounds he had sustained while defending them. Who was this man who had risked everything for her family?

"I never properly thanked you," she said softly, adjusting her chair back to an upright position. "You saved us back there. I was so caught up in everything..."

Isaac looked up, his gentle expression a stark contrast to the fierce warrior she recalled from the fight.

"No thanks needed. It's what we do."

A memory surfaced suddenly — something that had nagged at her.

"Back in Scotland, just after Mary appeared on the beach... I felt like someone was watching me from the cliffs." She studied his face carefully. "Was that you?"

Isaac shook his head.

"No. That was probably one of the Council's observers."

"What?" Faith straightened in her seat. "The Council was watching us?"

"Kavisha never stopped keeping an eye on your family," Isaac explained. "She maintained a small network of trusted observers."

"So, they knew about the attack?"

"Yes, but not in time to prevent it," Isaac said grimly. "By then it was too late. The Council sent Hunters to the known sanctuaries, hoping you'd escape. That's why I was alone. The others went to Castle Semple Church, Dunkeld Cathedral and Fearn Abbey. I was assigned to St Machar's." His eyes met hers, steady and sincere. "I'm sorry we couldn't do more, sooner."

"You did more than we could have hoped for," she replied, remembering how close some of those blades had come. "You didn't even know us, but you put yourself between us and... them... without hesitation."

"It's in the job description." Isaac's deep voice was warm despite his matter-of-fact tone. "Though I have to admit, you did me a solid with that warning about the attack from behind. You saved my neck,

CHAPTER 20

literally." He touched his collar where a blade had sliced through the fabric.

"The least I could do," Faith replied with a small smile. "I couldn't believe my eyes when you suddenly appeared. You don't look like any of the Hunters I read about." Her smile widened.

Isaac responded with his own grin.

"Let me guess. You were expecting someone less theatrical… less Black?"

"Something like that, I have to admit — rather shamefully." Faith returned his smile hesitantly. "Though the swords are a nice touch. Very cinematic."

"I had to put my own spin on it," he replied. "I loved the Blade movies when I was a kid. He was the only Black superhero we had for a long while."

Faith stared out of the window, captivated by the wispy clouds and the burning red sun settling on the horizon. The sky seemed ablaze. After countless solitary walks along Scarfskerry's gray beach, where she often stared up at the vast heavens, it felt surreal to be soaring through the skies in a droning metal tube.

She turned her gaze back to Isaac, who was observing her with keen interest.

"Can I ask you something?" Faith inquired. She shifted in her leather seat, the constant hum of the engines filling the pressurized cabin with a white noise that her hearing transformed into an orchestra of mechanical rhythms. "Why did you become a Hunter?"

The question caught Isaac off guard. His broad shoulders tensed, and his jaw clenched. Faith watched him swallow, his throat working as he stared past her through the small window. Outside, the sun was setting, painting the clouds in shades of blood red.

"My sister," he said, his rich voice tense and barely audible over the roar of the engines. "Imaani."

The plane hit a pocket of turbulence, causing the overhead compartments to rattle. Faith steadied herself against the seat as Isaac's fingers tightened on the armrests.

"She was turned during the first wave, twenty years ago," he continued, his fingers curling into fists, tendons standing out beneath his dark skin. "Forced to become one of the Red Claws. We searched for her everywhere, but..."

He trailed off as the cabin lights flickered, casting eerie shadows across his face. Faith caught every micro-expression that crossed it — pain, grief, barely contained rage.

"By the time we found her again, she wasn't my sister anymore. She was one of them."

The setting sun broke through the clouds outside, flooding the cabin with blood-red light. Isaac turned to stare out the window, his reflection a spectral crimson against the darkening sky.

"She was in San Luis when it happened," he continued, his voice taking on a hollow quality. "It was the first mass swarming of vampires in America." He closed his eyes, as if trying to push back the memories. "When they..." His voice faltered. "When they killed everyone. The whole town. Men. Women. Children. Babies." Each word seemed to inflict physical pain on him.

Faith remembered the shocking footage that had surfaced on YouTube — piles of bodies and streets running with blood. Her own mother had been there, though Faith knew Nell hadn't participated in the slaughter.

The plane banked, the engines changing pitch.

Faith glanced at her unconscious parents across the aisle, their skin marred by the creeping black corruption. When she looked back, Isaac had hunched forward, his imposing frame seeming smaller.

"The screams..." He swallowed hard. "They said you could hear the screams for miles — until they just... stopped."

CHAPTER 20

The cabin pressurization system cycled with a soft hiss. Faith noticed Isaac's heart rate accelerating and his breathing growing labored as he struggled against the memories.

"When Zachariah was killed and the blood connection broke, most of the horde reverted to human," he said, his knuckles tensed as he gripped the armrests. "Some were fortunate — protected by their minds blocking out what they'd done. But Imaani…"

He paused, turning to gaze out the window once more. Faith could see the muscles in his jaw working as he fought for control.

"The memories returned slowly, like a poison dripping into her mind. First came flashes — faces, screams, the taste of blood. Then more. And more." His voice cracked. "She started waking up screaming. Couldn't sleep. Couldn't eat. She would just sit there, rocking, muttering descriptions of people she'd… of people they'd made her…"

A tear slipped down Faith's cheek. Instinctively, she reached across and placed her hand over Isaac's clenched fist. Thankfully, no visions came to her.

"Then she remembered the children," Isaac continued, each word choked as if painful to speak. "A daycare center. They found it during the rampage and…" He couldn't finish.

Faith's imagination filled in the horrific details. She sensed the slight catch in Isaac's breathing, the way his heart pounded with remembered trauma.

"She couldn't live with it." His voice was flat, stripped of emotion. "It was the final straw that broke her — the memories of the kids. One morning, I found her in the bathtub. She'd…" He shook his head sharply. "The Red Claws might as well have killed her that first day. But this was worse. She died twice — once when they turned her, and again when she remembered what they made her do. The second death was slower, more painful, more cruel. I had to watch her fall

83

apart piece by piece. I was just a kid, not even thirteen. She was my big sister. My second mom, you could say. My rock."

Faith felt something shatter within her at the sight of this warrior reduced to such raw grief. The fierce Hunter had vanished, leaving behind a brother who had lost everything. She thought of her father and poor little Gabriel.

Isaac hunched forward. Tears traced down his cheeks, catching the red light from the setting sun.

"When the existence of Hunters became public knowledge, I knew what I had to do." His voice strengthened slightly, though his hands still trembled under Faith's touch. "I couldn't save my sister. But maybe I could save others from the same fate. Stop other families from being torn apart like mine."

Faith felt a pang of grief as she thought of her parents, corrupted and cursed just feet away.

"We're not so different," she said softly, squeezing his hand. "Both trying to protect people we love from forces we barely understand."

Isaac turned his hand over to grasp hers, his warm fingers intertwining with her cold ones. The simple contact seemed to ground them both.

"Your sister," Faith said softly after a long pause, "what was she like? Before?"

A faint smile flickered across Isaac's lips, though his eyes remained haunted. He fumbled with a chain around his neck, sliding it between his thumb and forefinger.

"She used to create these silly songs about everything. There was one for doing homework and another for brushing teeth..." A slight tremor entered his voice. "But her masterpiece was the 'Isaac's Being a Pain in the Butt' song. She'd sing it every time I annoyed her — which was often. By the end, it had about twenty verses."

He pulled out a small pendant from beneath his shirt — a tarnished

CHAPTER 20

brass whistle.

"She gave me this when I was seven. She said as long as I had it, she'd always hear me if I needed her." His thumb traced the worn metal. "Even after... everything... I couldn't take it off. Stupid, right?"

"No," Faith whispered. "Not stupid at all."

Faith squeezed his hand tighter, offering whatever comfort she could. In that moment, as the sun dipped below the horizon and darkness spread across the sky, the Hunter and the vampire found common ground in their shared grief. The ancient enmity between their kinds seemed insignificant — both understood what it meant to watch helplessly as darkness consumed those they loved.

"It's clear how you feel about Red Claws," Nell said. "But what about the rest of us? Do you agree with the truce the Hunters made with the Council of Elders during the war?"

He paused, considering his response.

"I've learned that there's more to this world than simple good and evil," he said eventually. "Monsters and heroes." His gaze met hers. "Sometimes the hardest part is figuring out which is which. Often, the lines blur until you can't tell anymore."

"And what am I?" Faith whispered, voicing her deepest fear. "A monster or a hero?"

For some reason, his opinion mattered to her.

"You're neither," he said firmly. "You're just a girl trying to save her family. That's the most human thing in the world."

Before she could respond, a scream pierced the cabin.

Chapter 21

Faith watched in horror as her mother's body twisted, her spine arching at an unnatural angle. The black veins around her throat pulsed and contracted like living things, spreading upward toward her face.

"Mom!" Faith bolted from her seat and reached for her mother. Nell's skin burned like fire beneath her fingers. "No, please... please don't leave me..."

Isaac checked his watch.

"We're still two hours out," he said. His voice held a note of fear that made Faith's stomach clench. "Maybe less if we push the engines."

He rushed to the cockpit to speak to the charter pilot.

Faith felt her mother's body go rigid beneath her hands. The dark veins around Nell's throat constricted like a noose, and her lips began to turn blue. Faith could see the tissue dying and smell the corruption spreading through her mother's body.

"Mom?" Faith's voice cracked. "MOM!"

Nell didn't respond. She remained still.

Panic flooded through Faith as she watched the black veins pulsate beneath Nell's skin, spreading their poison with each passing second.

Isaac rushed back to her side. "An hour and a half, at least. That's at full throttle," he said grimly.

"We don't have that much time," Faith implored.

CHAPTER 21

She focused on the black veins continuing to pulse under her mother's skin, spreading like ivy. The same corruption was taking hold of her father.

The impulse she had felt earlier surged again. Perhaps her blood could save them — or damn them. The power surging through her was an unknown force, part blessing and part curse, just like her.

She recalled Mary's transformation and how her blood had twisted the vampire, awakening something primal and dark. She remembered the way those black eyes had burned with unnatural hunger. Would the same fate befall her parents? Would her attempt to save them only corrupt them further?

But doing nothing meant watching them die. Each second brought them closer to an end she couldn't bear to face. Her hand trembled as she raised her wrist to her mouth.

Isaac's fingers closed around her arm, warm and steady against her cold skin.

"Don't even think about it," he said firmly. "We discussed this. Your blood is too unpredictable."

Faith locked eyes with him, seeing the genuine concern there. But she also detected something else — fear. He had witnessed his sister transformed by vampire blood. Now he might have to see it happen again. The thought terrified him.

"I've alerted the Council. They've summoned someone who can help," Isaac explained, though uncertainty tinged his voice. "We just need to get them to base."

"They're dying, Isaac. We don't have the luxury of time," Faith replied, her voice resolute even as doubt gnawed at her insides. "What else do we have to lose at this point?"

The words felt hollow as she spoke them. They had everything to lose. Her blood might turn her gentle mother into something like Mary — a creature of hunger and malice. It could strip away everything that defined her parents, leaving only shells filled with darkness. The same darkness that had haunted her bloodline since Vlad Tepes birthed their kind over five hundred years ago.

But wasn't darkness better than watching the light fade from their eyes completely? At least darkness meant survival. And maybe, just maybe, her father's noble bloodline would balance out the corruption. Light and dark, forever warring in her veins.

"I'm sorry," she whispered, to both Isaac and her parents.

Then, with supernatural strength and speed, she yanked her arm free and bit down hard. Blood welled up, glistening like black pearls on her pale skin.

She held her bleeding wrist over her mother's parted lips, watching the first drops fall. She did the same to her father. Each drop felt like a terrible promise — salvation or damnation; there would be no going back from this choice.

For a moment, nothing happened. Then Nell's body went rigid, every muscle locking tight. The black veins froze their pulsing pattern, as if two poisons were battling beneath her skin. The corruption seemed to retreat for a fraction of a second before surging back with renewed vigor.

A sound built in her mother's throat, starting as a low vibration that Faith felt more than heard. It grew into something between a hum and a growl, entirely inhuman. The noise made the hair on Faith's neck stand up, triggering instincts she didn't know she possessed. This wasn't the gentle voice that had read her bedtime stories, soothed her fears and whispered "I love you" every night of her life. This was something ancient and wrong.

Nell's back once again arched at an impossible angle, her spine bending until Faith heard vertebrae crack. Her fingers splayed wide, tendons standing out like cords as her hands twisted into claws. The growl morphed into a keening wail that threatened to shatter the

CHAPTER 21

airplane windows.

"Mom?" Faith's voice trembled. Her throat constricted around the word that had once meant safety, comfort and unconditional love. "Mom, please..."

The black veins began to move again, but differently now. Instead of their previous spiderweb pattern, they coalesced into thick lines that ran straight up Nell's neck. Faith watched in shock as they reached her face, spreading beneath the skin like ink in water.

Her mother's features contorted — cheekbones sharpened, jaw elongated slightly and teeth visibly lengthened behind pulled-back lips.

Then Nell's eyes snapped open.

Faith recoiled.

Where warm blue irises should have been, there were only pools of absolute darkness. Not just the iris and pupil; the entire eye had turned to shadow. Faith saw her own terrified reflection in those obsidian mirrors as black veins began to spider across her mother's forehead.

A new sound emerged from Nell's throat — a noise that contained fragments of laughter but was fundamentally wrong, like broken glass grinding together. Her lips pulled back further, revealing teeth that had definitely grown longer. When her mother turned toward her, there was no recognition in those black eyes — only hunger. Ancient. Endless.

The thing masquerading as her mother smiled.

Faith stumbled backward, her legs hitting the seat behind her. Her mind reeled with the enormity of what she had done. In trying to save her mother, had she instead erased her? Replaced her with something from her darkest nightmares?

"What have I done?" she whispered. "Oh God, what have I done?"

II

One of tainted blood

Chapter 22

The vast American landscape blurred past the tinted windows of the van as they sped through the darkness of North Carolina.

Faith pressed her forehead against the cool glass, her extra-sensitive eyesight absorbing every overwhelming detail of this alien world rushing by. The familiar gray emptiness of rural Scotland had been replaced by an onslaught of sensations that made her head spin.

Even at night, this new country pulsed with artificial life, relentlessly pushing back the darkness — endless streams of headlights slicing through the gloom, glowing billboards turning the clouds orange, sprawling towns spreading like luminous spider webs across the blackness.

Her ears picked up fragments of countless lives unfolding along the highway — snippets of music from passing cars shifting from country twang to hip-hop beats, heated arguments from distant houses that made her flinch with their intensity, televisions blaring game shows and news reports, dogs barking at unseen threats, babies crying in the night, and the endless hum of electricity rushing through power lines. Each sound pierced her heightened awareness, impossible to ignore. A police siren wailed in the distance, its shrill cry cutting through her thoughts like shards of glass.

The air here felt different, heavy with unfamiliar scents that assaulted her sensitive nose — exhaust fumes leaving a metallic taste on her tongue, fast food grease turning her stomach, industrial chemicals stinging her nostrils, and underneath it all, the mingled blood-scent of millions of humans crammed into vast cities.

Everything was too bright, too loud, just overwhelming since they landed at Charlotte-Monroe Executive Airport and were whisked away in two blacked-out Mercedes vans. Her parents were in the other vehicle just behind them.

Faith closed her eyes, trying to block out the sensory overload, but that only allowed guilt to resurface. Memories of what had happened on the plane flooded her mind — her mother's black eyes and elongated teeth, the way Nell's spine had arched at that impossible angle, the inhuman sounds that tore from her throat. Most haunting of all was the ancient hunger flickering in her mother's once-warm blue eyes. That image replayed over and over: her gentle mother transformed into something else entirely, before going limp and silent again.

"Hey." Isaac's warm hand squeezed her shoulder, pulling her from her spiraling thoughts. "They're fighters. Both of them."

It seemed he could read her mind — but perhaps that wasn't so difficult right now.

Faith managed a weak smile, grateful for his steady presence. Since their conversation on the plane, he had become an anchor in this overwhelming new reality. She noticed how frequently he glanced at the rearview mirror, and his other hand never strayed far from his weapons.

"You think she'll follow us here?" Faith asked.

Isaac's jaw clenched.

"Mary?" He checked the mirrors again before continuing. "I don't think she's on our heels right now. She's not the immediate threat. But she'll soon find out that you're no longer in Scotland, and then she'll have no reason not to come back. But we'll deal with that when

CHAPTER 22

the time comes. Try to rest now."

But rest was impossible. With every mile, her senses were assaulted anew. They passed a truck stop where the combined scents of diesel, coffee and human sweat nearly made her gag. A group of motorcycles roared past, the engines so loud that she had to cover her ears.

As they drove through a small town buzzing with Friday night activity, Faith's acute hearing registered laughter from a bar, the crack of pool balls and the thump of bass from speakers. Waves of beer, deodorant and desire rolled off the crowd. Her fangs emerged involuntarily before she could rein herself in. She caught Isaac watching her and quickly turned away, embarassed.

Nearly four hours after leaving the airport, the van turned onto a winding road that climbed into the Blue Ridge Mountains. Faith sensed the change in altitude; the air grew thinner and sharper. Ancient trees pressed close to the road, their branches forming dark tunnels overhead.

This felt more familiar — nature's domain rather than humanity's. She glimpsed the valley falling away below them, with twinkling lights resembling earthbound stars.

The van rounded another bend, and Faith's breath caught in her throat. Lightning split the sky, illuminating their destination in stark relief.

There, rising from the mountainside like something out of a gothic horror novel, stood Vhik'h-Tal-Eskemon. Turrets and spires pierced the night sky while gargoyles peered down from elaborate cornices, their stone faces locked in eternal snarls.

More lightning flashed, briefly revealing stained glass windows that seemed to glow with their own inner fire. Shadows shifted across the façade as clouds scudded past the moon, making the entire building appear to writhe.

But it wasn't just the imposing architecture that captured Faith's attention. She sensed something — a subtle vibration in the air, like the hum of a tuning fork pitched too low for human ears. Old Magick, she realized. A talisman. The same energy she had felt in the sanctuary of St Machar's Cathedral, but magnified at least tenfold. The very stones seemed to pulse with quiet power.

As they rolled up to the entrance, Faith caught movement in her peripheral vision. A massive shape detached itself from the shadows of the trees — something impossibly large yet fluid in its movements. Even in the darkness, she could make out the powerful silhouette, a form that seemed to absorb the scant moonlight filtering through the branches.

The shape moved with the grace of a predator, muscles rippling beneath its bulk as it emerged from the treeline. For a heartbeat, it just stood there — a living patch of deeper darkness against the night, radiating raw power and wild cunning.

Then Faith realized what she was seeing — a werwulf. The creature stood nearly ten feet tall, its curved claws glistening in the moonlight, each one as long as her hand. Its yellow eyes met hers for a brief moment, and Faith felt the weight of centuries in that gaze. Then it melted back into the gloom, leaving only the lingering scent of wet fur and wild places.

The encounter left her shaken, emphasizing just how far she was from her sheltered life in Scotland. This was a place where creatures of the night roamed freely, where ancient powers still held sway.

The van came to a stop before huge wooden doors carved with unfamiliar symbols. She steeled herself, aware that whatever waited inside could either save her parents or seal their fate. She just hoped she hadn't already sealed it with the reckless use of her blood.

Thunder rumbled overhead as Isaac and the two drivers carried her parents from the second van. Faith noticed the Hunter's eyes constantly scanning their surroundings. Even here, in this supposedly

CHAPTER 22

safe place, he remained on guard. She wondered what threats he expected to find in this sanctuary of the supernatural.

Her sharp eyes caught more movement in the shadows around them — shapes slipping between the trees, yellow eyes watching from the darkness. More werwulfs? Or something else? The weight of their unseen observation made her skin prickle.

An owl's cry pierced the night, but Faith recognized the unnatural undertone. It wasn't an owl at all, but something mimicking its call.

She stared up at the building's façade, trying to gather her courage. The entrance was dominated by an imposing wooden door with a black iron knocker shaped like two intertwining serpents. Their ruby eyes seemed to follow her movements, and she could have sworn she saw their metal coils shift slightly in the moonlight. As Isaac reached for the knocker, Faith noticed how he positioned himself in front of her, shielding her with his body. The protective gesture touched her.

Suddenly, her mother convulsed in the arms of one of the black-suited drivers. When her eyes fluttered open, they were completely black again. Her lips pulled back from elongated teeth as she spoke in a voice that wasn't her own: "The circle comes full round. Blood calls to blood."

It made no sense to Faith. Nell had to be delirious.

The sound of the knocker striking wood echoed like a death knell in the night air.

Faith held her breath, waiting to see who — or what — would respond from within the imposing fortress. Thunder crashed overhead, and heavy drops of rain began to fall, as if the storm had followed them across the ocean and finally caught up.

Chapter 23

As lightning illuminated the building again, Faith glimpsed movement at one of the higher windows — a face watching them. But before she could focus on it, it vanished, leaving her to wonder if she had imagined it. The rain fell harder now, and somewhere in the darkness, a wolf began to howl.

The huge doors swung open almost silently, though Faith's sensitive hearing detected ancient mechanisms turning within the thick wood, reminding her of St Machar's. Her vision pierced the murkiness beyond, revealing details that would elude ordinary eyes — elaborate carvings that seemed to shift with her gaze, gems embedded in the walls pulsing with inner light and gentle shadows cast by flickering firelight.

In the doorway stood a tall, thin man in an impeccable suit. His heartbeat confirmed his humanity before he spoke. He appeared to be around seventy, with a full head of white hair slicked back. Something about his scent was slightly off — not entirely normal, yet not entirely wrong.

"Welcome to Vhik'h-Tal-Eskemon," he said with a slight bow, his cultured accent difficult to place. "I am Sanford. You are expected."

He stepped aside to let them enter, and Faith noticed him subtly inhaling as she passed — testing her scent, categorizing her. His eyes widened slightly, and she found herself curious about what he detected.

The entrance hall was expansive, its ceiling shrouded in shadows overhead. Ornate chandeliers cast flickering light over marble floors laced with what appeared to be real gold. Mahogany surfaces and rich red rugs adorned the space. The air was thick with the musty scent of centuries mingled with something else — herbs and incense that made her nose tingle. Beneath it all, Faith detected the metallic tang of copper. Blood. Old blood. Soaked into the very stones.

Portraits lined the walls — stern-faced vampires whose eyes seemed to follow her as she moved. Faith noticed subtle movements in the paintings, like ripples in still water. One portrait, in particular, captured her attention — a woman in medieval dress whose features bore an unsettling resemblance to Mary Redclaw. She quickly looked away.

Her father groaned as Isaac assisted him across the marble floor, the sound echoing in the vast space. The black corruption stained his skin. Her mother remained silent, but Faith could smell the wrongness spreading through her body — her blood altered by Faith's desperate attempt to save her.

"This way," Sanford instructed, leading them toward a sweeping staircase. "The spellcaster is waiting."

Lightning flashed outside, casting eerie shadows through the stained glass windows. Faith picked up whispers from within the walls, scratching noises in the ceiling and a distant rhythmic chanting that set her on edge. The air around them felt thick with preternatural energy.

A woman appeared at the top of the grand staircase, her arrival announced by the melodic clinking of jewelry. As she descended, multiple necklaces jangled together, and Faith glimpsed glimmering stones — not merely decorative, but points of energy. The woman's olive skin and dark eyes identified her as Middle Eastern, while intricate henna patterns adorned her hands, hinting at Roma heritage. Her robes were a vivid blend of colors that shifted with the changing light.

"Come... come... I am Serafin," she proclaimed, her accented voice imbued with both warmth and authority. Her gaze swept over Faith's parents, lingering on the visible black veins beneath their skin. Faith noticed her sharp intake of breath and the way her fingers tightened around the banister. "Bring them. Quickly. This way."

They followed her down a corridor lined with tapestries illustrating scenes of supernatural warfare — vampires and werwulfs locked in combat, spellcasters wielding energy auras that Faith could hardly comprehend. Beneath their feet, the floor bore faintly glowing symbols that responded to their presence.

As they walked, Faith overheard snippets of conversation from behind closed doors:

"...the prophecy speaks of blood..."

"...Mary's forces are gathering..."

"...the hybrid child could be the key..."

Her mother convulsed in Isaac's arms. When her eyes opened again, they briefly appeared normal before the darkness engulfed them. "The circle," she whispered in a voice that wasn't her own. "It *must* be completed."

Serafin's bracelets jingled as she swiftly guided them into a room that assaulted Faith's sensitive nose with the strong scent of herbs and potions. The space was cramped with books and bottles on wooden shelves, while bundles of dried plants hung from the ceiling and littered the floor. A brass brazier burned in one corner, emitting sweet-smelling smoke that made Faith's head swim. Her eyes caught movement among the bottles — things floating in preserved liquids that should not have been able to move.

The spellcaster directed them to place her parents on two ornate

CHAPTER 23

beds, their frames carved with protective symbols. As soon as they were laid down, the carvings began to glow with a soft purple light. Faith noticed that the symbols twisted and reshaped when she wasn't looking directly at them, freezing in place when her gaze returned.

Serafin leaned over Faith's parents, her fingers tracing the patterns of corruption beneath their skin. Her bracelets jingled with each movement, the sound an odd discord in the charged atmosphere.

"Interesting," Serafin murmured, her eyes flickering to Faith. "Your blood fights the hex. You carry the Old Magick. Very old. It sleeps, but it dreams."

Faith's stomach tightened. She had no idea what Serafin meant or how she knew that Faith had given them her blood.

"Can you help them?" she asked, focusing on the only conversation that mattered to her right now.

"Perhaps." Serafin's rings caught the lamplight as she reached for a bottle filled with swirling silver liquid. "But first, you must tell me exactly what happened after you gave your blood. Every detail matters. The smallest thing could mean the difference between restoration and... something else."

With Isaac's help, Faith recounted the events of their journey in as much detail as she could muster.

"Leave me now," Serafin instructed once the story was told. "I have work to do."

Before Faith could respond, Isaac touched her arm. "Let her work. Come on."

Faith hesitated, reluctant to leave her parents behind. But Serafin had already turned away, her hands moving in intricate patterns while she muttered words that sounded foreign to Faith. The air in the room thickened, charged with an energy that made the hairs on Faith's arms stand on end.

"You can trust her," Isaac said softly. "She knows what she's doing."

They exited the room, and the door shut with a heavy thud behind them. Faith heard Serafin's chanting mingled with the steady drip of liquid.

Suddenly, a scream echoed from behind the thick wood, a sound that was neither human nor vampire. Faith rushed forward, but Isaac's firm grip held her back.

"Trust the process," he said with conviction. "They named you Faith. Now is the time to have a little."

But she noticed that his other hand had moved to rest on his weapons belt. Whether it was an old habit or something else, she could not tell.

Chapter 24

Isaac guided Faith down an expansive corridor leading to a drawing room filled with leather-backed chairs and towering bookshelves. Ancient tomes lined the shelves, bound in skins that Faith felt hesitant to identify. She glimpsed titles written in unfamiliar languages. The air was thick with the scent of aged leather and history.

Her keen ears picked up the rustle of Serafin's robes as she moved around Faith's parents, along with the clinking of bottles and murmurs of incantations.

These sounds were muffled by a gentle whirring that signaled another arrival. Faith noticed the mechanical noise before she saw its source: an electric wheelchair gliding into the room, guided by a delicate hand on the joystick.

Seated in the chair was a woman who, despite her physical limitations, radiated an authority that made Faith instinctively straighten her posture.

Though small in stature, she commanded attention through her bearing and elaborate attire. A stunning sari of deep purple and gold was draped elegantly around her slight frame, the luxurious fabric catching the light as she maneuvered. Her jet-black hair was neatly parted and woven into a plait that cascaded down her back, adorned with an intricate gold chain woven through its strands.

Faith noticed the array of precious stones around her throat, the colorful bangles that chimed softly as she moved her hands on the controls and the delicate gold chain connecting her left ear to her nose ring. Her dark brown skin seemed to radiate an inner glow, and when she smiled, her strikingly white teeth created a stunning contrast against her dusky complexion.

Her deep brown eyes appeared to harbor centuries of wisdom, and Faith felt an intriguing mix of respect and intimidation toward this exotic woman, who exuded both vulnerability and authority.

"Welcome, Faith," she said warmly, her Indian accent lending her words a melodic quality. "I am Kavisha Devi, High Chancellor of the Council of Elders."

She turned to Isaac, adding, "And to you, Isaac. I knew you wouldn't let us down."

The Hunter responded with a curt nod.

Kavisha moved her chair closer, and Faith sensed a gentle pressure in her mind, like fingers exploring. Her heightened perception detected something else — a wave of energy reminiscent of St Machar's and Vhik'h-Tal-Eskemon itself. It was that same low hum of strength and protection, but it now took on a physical form.

"Your parents are in good hands," Kavisha continued, her eyes fixed intently on Faith. "They are heroes, you know. They helped save us all — the world, you could say. And now here you are, their miracle child. The first of your kind." She reached out, taking Faith's hand in hers. "You've come so far from that little girl in Scotland. But I sense the changes in you are just beginning."

The moment their skin touched, Faith felt it — that same thrumming energy that filled the building, concentrated and controlled. Yet, there was something else too — layers of secrets, some dark, some desperate. Decisions made in shadow that could never see the light.

Faith pulled her hand back, overwhelmed by the contact. Part of her ached to trust this woman, who spoke so warmly of her parents.

CHAPTER 24

Another part recalled her mother's warnings about the Council's intricate politics and plots.

"You must have so many questions," Kavisha said softly. "About who you are. What you are. What you might become." Her gaze seemed to pierce straight through Faith's defenses. "What your blood truly means, and where we all find ourselves now."

"The only question I care about," Faith replied, struggling to keep her voice steady, "is whether you can save my parents. Everything else — who I am, what I might become — none of that matters if they..." She couldn't finish the sentence.

Kavisha's expression softened with what seemed like genuine sympathy. But before she could respond, a sudden change in the air made Faith's skin tingle. She sensed a shift in the building's energy — that same low thrum she'd felt since arriving, but now it was discordant, like an orchestra gradually falling out of tune.

A sound reached her from Serafin's workroom — not quite a scream yet, but a low keening that made her teeth ache. The old tomes on the shelves seemed to shudder, their spines creaking as if they sensed something amiss.

"Something's happening," Faith said, alarmed.

She picked up the rustle of Serafin's robes as the spellcaster moved frantically around the room and heard the subtle crack of glass as bottles began to vibrate.

Isaac was already on his feet, one hand on his sword hilt. His trained instincts had caught the change too.

"The hex," he said grimly. "It's fighting back."

Kavisha's bangles chimed as she gripped the arms of her wheelchair.

Then Nell's scream sliced through the air — a twisted, inhuman sound that Faith had hoped she'd never hear again. This time it bore harmonics that felt impossible for a human throat, layers of ancient voices intertwining with her mother's pain.

Without hesitation, Faith dashed to the door. Behind her, she heard Isaac curse and Kavisha call out, but she was already racing down the corridor. The magical symbols in the floor blazed to life as she passed, responding to her urgency.

Chapter 25

She burst into Serafin's workroom to find her mother thrashing against restraints that held her to the bed. The black veins beneath her skin writhed angrily while her eyes fluctuated between normal and deep darkness. Her father lay still on the other bed.

"The infestation fights your blood," Serafin said grimly, her hands moving in intricate patterns over Nell's convulsing form. Sweat beaded her brow. "But there is something else. Something awakening." Her piercing gaze locked onto Faith. "Your blood carries echoes — whispers that have slept for centuries."

The magical symbols on the bed frames flared blindingly bright before shattering into a cascade of purple fire and sparks. The bottles on the shelves began to vibrate, their contents swirling like mini hurricanes. Faith sensed a shift in the very air, as if reality itself was holding its breath, anticipating something significant.

Then the room erupted into chaos.

Glass shattered as bottles burst open on the shelves. Their contents mingled in the air, forming impossible patterns before dissipating into clouds of multicolored smoke.

Isaac instinctively moved to shield Faith from the flying shards. She caught his subtle wince as pieces sliced into his arm — wounds he willingly endured to protect her. The gesture struck her deeply; here was a Hunter, someone meant to destroy her kind, putting himself between her and danger without hesitation. Again.

He grabbed her arm and pulled her behind a heavy oak cabinet. In one fluid motion, he drew his sword, scanning the room with trained precision while tension mounted in his shoulders, revealing his unease at the crackling energies surrounding them.

"The magic's destabilizing," he shouted to Serafin.

The brass brazier tipped over, spilling burning coals across the floor and igniting the scattered herbs. The flames shifted into unnatural colors as they consumed the plants. Twisted faces appeared in the smoke — morphing into a dragon breathing fire, then into a longsword arcing through darkness.

Serafin raised her hands, her bracelets clashing as she chanted words that made Faith's ears ache. The spellcaster's henna tattoos began to glow with an inner light that matched the intensity of her eyes. Yet whatever magic she wielded seemed to have little effect on Faith's parents.

Suddenly, her father's body went rigid, arching off the bed. When his eyes opened, they were filled with that same terrible darkness. In unison, both parents spoke, their voices overlapping in horrid harmony: "The dark regent rises again. The circle opens. Blood will flow."

Faith felt Isaac position himself in front of her, trying to block her view.

"Stay back," his voice was firm. "These are not your parents speaking."

She pushed past him, desperate to reach them. "I have to help them!"

"Wait— " Isaac's warning came too late.

Her mother struck with astonishing speed, seizing the Hunter's wrist in a grip that crushed bones. Faith smelled the blood vessels bursting beneath his skin and heard the grinding of bone, yet he did

CHAPTER 25

not cry out.

Instead, he shifted his stance, positioning himself between Faith and danger despite his now damaged wrist. The gesture brought a sting to her eyes — this Hunter, who had every reason to hate her kind, was still fighting to protect her.

"Mom, please!" she cried out. "Let him go! He saved us! He's good. He's kind." Her words felt childish, but in the moment she couldn't think of anything else.

Her mother's head snapped toward her voice. For a brief instant, Faith thought she saw something flicker in those shadowy depths — recognition, love, fear?

Nell released Isaac's wrist and turned to face her daughter. Her black eyes fixed on Faith with terrifying intensity. When she spoke again, Christopher joined her, along with hundreds of discordant voices echoing in unison:

"He awaits, child of two bloods. Centuries behind the veil. Out of light comes darkness. Out of love comes hate. The blood of destruction. The blood of creation."

Both of her parents collapsed onto the beds and lay still. Faith rushed forward, her heart pounding against her ribs.

"Mom? Dad?"

No response. Their bodies were motionless, skin waxy and deathly pale beneath the writhing black veins. The room fell into an unnatural silence, broken only by the soft patter of liquid dripping from shattered bottles.

Then her father's hand twitched.

Faith caught the subtle movement of his fingers — not random spasms, but deliberate motions, as if he were writing something. Her breath hitched as she deciphered the message his index finger traced against the sheets:

R U N

Chapter 26

Faith pressed her palm against the rough granite of Vhik'h-Tal-Eskemon's outer wall, feeling the subtle vibrations of Old Magick humming through the stone.

Dawn painted the sky in hues of amber and rose, transforming the gothic nightmare of her dusk arrival into something almost beautiful. Sunlight caught the edges of gargoyles' wings and glinted off stained glass windows, softening harsh angles into graceful curves. Before her lay the grounds — carefully manicured lawns that gave way to wild forests ascending the surrounding mountains.

Her hearing picked up the whisper of Serafin's robes as the spellcaster moved between her parents' beds, still working whatever magic she hoped would save them. The sound tightened Faith's chest. Three days had passed since their arrival, yet there was still no change. The black corruption continued to paint abstract patterns beneath her parents' skin, leaving them suspended between life and death.

Her father's warning echoed in her mind. But where could she run? How could she abandon them?

A groan of pain filtered through an open window — Isaac, whose wrist was still healing from where her mother had crushed it during that moment of dark possession. The sound conjured memories of how inhuman Nell's eyes had appeared, how wrong her voice had become. Faith's heart clenched. She needed to move, to do something

CHAPTER 26

instead of waiting helplessly while others suffered.

Her feet carried her away from the oppressive weight of the mansion, past crumbling stone markers inscribed with vampire script so old that she couldn't decipher it. Protection wards, perhaps, or warnings to those who might threaten this sanctuary. The musty scent of history filled the air — old stone, ancient trees and lingering Old Magick.

The morning air also offered a symphony of other scents: the tang of pine needles, loamy earth still damp from yesterday's rain and the metallic undertone of mountain springs feeding the Toccoa River somewhere ahead. Everything was so different from the salt-laden winds of northern Scotland. Here, everything felt bigger, wilder, more intense. The sheer vastness of America overwhelmed her, making her realize just how sheltered her existence had been.

She passed between towering oaks, their branches forming natural archways overhead. Her vampire vision caught subtle symbols carved into the bark — more wards, their magic faded but not entirely gone. The trees themselves seemed to watch her progress, their leaves whispering secrets in a language she couldn't quite grasp.

A crow's harsh call drew her attention upward, just as the bird's tail feathers dissolved into wisps of dark smoke before reforming, as if reality itself was becoming unstable at the edges. Or was she simply imagining things?

A broken sundial attracted her attention, its face carved with hours that didn't exist in the mortal realm. The shadow it cast moved against the sun's natural path, serving as another reminder that she didn't belong here and couldn't grasp the rules of this world from which her parents had tried so hard to shelter her.

The snap of a twig drew her attention. Her senses heightened instantly — her ears straining for any sound, her nostrils flaring to catch unfamiliar scents.

There — a flash of russet fur darted between the trees, moving swiftly. She focused on the moving shape.

With lean muscle, powerful legs, and sharp eyes, it was a wolf. Yet something about its movements suggested intelligence beyond mere animal instincts. There was a grace, an allure she couldn't quite explain, compelling Faith forward despite her better judgment.

She found herself tracking the creature. Using her vampire stealth, she moved silently across the dry leaves, staying downwind as she followed the animal deeper into the forest. The trees closed in around her, ancient growth untouched by human hands. Bands of sunlight broke through the canopy like spotlights, illuminating patches of mist hanging in the still morning air.

The wolf's trail led her toward the sound of running water — the Toccoa River carving its way through the forest. Faith registered the subtle changes in the current as it flowed over rocks, the flickers of fish darting beneath the surface and the soft pads of the wolf's paws on the muddy bank ahead.

Crouching behind a wide oak, its rough bark pressing against her palm, she peered around to watch the wolf wade into the shallows. Sunlight danced on the water's surface, creating shifting patterns independent of the current. The wolf moved with grace, muscles rippling beneath its brown coat as it tested the water's depth.

Then something extraordinary happened.

It began with a subtle ripple beneath the wolf's fur. First, its spine lengthened and straightened, the sound of bones shifting and realigning like distant wind chimes. The wolf's front legs trembled, then began to stretch and reshape — muscle and sinew flowing like liquid beneath skin, digits elongating from paws into toes.

Fur receded in waves, like watching a time-lapse of the tide ebbing from the shore, revealing olive skin that seemed to glow in the dappled sunlight. The wolf's skull underwent the most dramatic

CHAPTER 26

transformation — its muzzle softened and retreated, the forehead rose, and ears migrated and reshaped themselves. Sleek black hair cascaded down like a waterfall, replacing the last patches of fur. The final transformation was in the eyes — shifting from lupine yellow to clear hazel while still holding a wild, untamed depth that made Faith's breath catch.

Where the wolf had once stood, a young woman now lingered in the shallows, water droplets cascading down her naked body like liquid diamonds. Every movement exuded a primal grace — neither entirely human nor fully animal, but something far older than either. Her high cheekbones and sharp nose lent her face an almost feline appearance, while her full lips and oval features softened what could have been harsh characteristics. Her long black hair hung down her back like a straight curtain, with beads of river water catching the sun. Her lithe, sinewy form was as captivating as the sleek wolf she had just been.

Faith found herself unable to look away, although she knew she should. There was something magnetic about the way the woman moved. Every gesture blurred the lines between civilized and wild, controlled and instinctual.

Suddenly, the woman grew still, tilting her head in a manner that eerily mirrored her wolf form. She turned, those hunter eyes scanning the treeline and honing in on Faith's hiding spot.

Faith's breath paused — not out of fear, though it perhaps should have been. Something else stirred within her, an unnamed sensation that quickened her pulse.

"I know you're there, bloodsucker," the woman called, her voice betraying a steely undertone beneath its calm surface. "Show yourself before I'm forced to come find you. Trust me, you don't want that."

Faith remained frozen, muscles tensed for either fight or flight. Realization struck her: she had made a grave mistake by following this creature into its territory. She sensed that something was about to go terribly wrong.

"Last chance, walking dead," the woman said, her voice sharpening. "Either you step out now, or I'll treat you as a threat... and that usually doesn't end well."

Faith hesitated, weighing her options.

She could run — her vampire speed might offer her just enough of an edge to return to the safety of Vhik'h-Tal-Eskemon. Yet, that intangible feeling in the air compelled her to stay. Perhaps it was curiosity. Perhaps it was sheer exhaustion from fleeing everything that frightened her, including her entire life.

She stepped out from behind the tree, hands raised to indicate she meant no harm.

"I'm sorry," she called. "I didn't mean to intrude."

The woman's nostrils flared as she caught Faith's scent. Her eyes widened momentarily before narrowing dangerously.

Without warning, the woman's body began to shift again. Bones cracked and reformed beneath her skin, expanding as her frame soared in height. Muscles writhed and thickened, tendons stretching and transforming. Dark fur erupted from her skin in waves, like spilled ink smoothing across her changing body. Her jaw elongated as teeth lengthened into gleaming fangs, while her nose and mouth morphed into a lupine muzzle. Her eyes glowed, shifting from hazel to a feral amber.

Fingers transformed into massive paws tipped with curved black claws. The creature's shoulders broadened until they were wider than a doorway, packed with corded muscle that rippled beneath its thick pelt. Its chest expanded, releasing a growl that seemed to shake the very air. Where a slender young woman had stood moments before now loomed a monster straight out of humanity's darkest nightmare.

The werwulf rose to its full height — nearly ten feet of primal fury

CHAPTER 26

made flesh. Its eyes locked onto Faith with predatory intelligence, exhibiting both bestial hunger and a chillingly human calculation. Every movement radiated barely contained violence, a power capable of tearing a person apart as easily as breathing.

Faith had just enough time to register its muscles coiling before the werwulf lunged at her.

Even with vampire reflexes, Faith barely managed to dodge the attack, but her foot caught on an exposed root, sending her crashing to the ground.

The werwulf was on her instantly, large paws pinning her shoulders while its hot breath washed over her face.

Faith's heart pounded against her ribs. She could feel the power in the paws holding her down and knew that a single swipe of those claws could rip her open.

The werwulf's face lowered, bringing its fierce yellow eyes inches from hers. Faith caught the wild scent of its breath — a mix of earth, storm winds and the very essence of nature itself.

Chapter 27

A low growl built in the creature's chest. Yet there was something more in those intelligent eyes — not just aggression but curiosity. The werwulf was studying her, assessing her in a way that hinted at human reasoning beneath its terrifyingly feral exterior.

"You're the hybrid child," it rumbled, its voice a throaty growl. "I can smell it. You're not like the others."

The pressure on Faith's shoulders eased slightly. She watched in awe as the creature morphed above her, shrinking and reshaping until the young woman now crouched over her. The woman maintained her dominant position but no longer appeared actively threatening.

Faith became acutely aware of every point of contact between them, feeling the warmth radiating from the woman's skin in stark contrast to her own vampire coolness.

She tried to keep her eyes focused on the woman's face but found her gaze betraying her, drawn to the graceful line of her neck, the elegant curve of her shoulders and the way her long black hair fell around them like a curtain.

Heat rushed to Faith's cheeks as she realized she was staring. She quickly looked away, but her keen senses remained traitorously aware of her assailant's proximity, the sound of her heartbeat and the lingering scent of wild places clinging to her skin.

Faith found her gaze drawn back to the woman's face — those sharp cheekbones, the determined set of her jaw and eyes that echoed the forest.

"You're either very brave or very stupid to follow a werwulf through its territory," the woman said, her body remaining tense. "Do you really know nothing? Is it true you've lived under a rock your entire life?"

"Under several rocks," Faith replied, trying to keep her voice steady despite being pinned down. "Northern Scotland is basically a giant collection of rocks."

A flicker of surprise crossed the woman's eyes at Faith's attempt at humor. The pressure on Faith's shoulders eased slightly, though the woman maintained her grip. She seemed to notice how Faith's gaze was fixed intently on her face, refusing to let her eyes drift down. With a smirk, she finally released her hold and shifted her weight off Faith.

"When you're raised in the wild, nakedness isn't shameful; it's natural," she explained.

Faith sat up and brushed soil from her palms.

"When you're raised in the United Kingdom, nakedness is absolutely shameful," she retorted. "Also not something you generally come across in public."

This brought a reluctant smile to the other woman's face. "I'm Leona," she said.

Faith remained still, unsure whether any sudden movement might provoke the werwulf's aggressive instincts.

"Faith," she responded cautiously. "Though it seems you already know who I am. Or at least what I am."

"Only by reputation," Leona said, her posture relaxing slightly. "They say you're either salvation or destruction, but no one seems quite sure which."

"That makes two of us," Faith muttered, surprised by the bitterness in her own voice.

Leona tilted her head, much like her wolf form, and her expression shifted from hostility to curiosity.

"You really don't know what's happening, do you?" she asked, her voice softening.

Faith shook her head.

Leona walked over to where she had left her clothes in a heap by the shore, her movements still carrying that predatory grace. Faith tried to avert her gaze.

"You might want to look away," Leona said, glancing back with a hint of amusement. "Since you're so proper and British about these things."

Faith turned her head, her cheeks warming.

"Scottish," she corrected. "There's a difference."

"Is there?" Leona responded, her tone dripping with sarcasm as she dressed. "Never noticed."

"Spoken like a true American," Faith replied dryly, surprised to find herself engaging in something resembling banter with someone who had been threatening her just moments ago.

When Leona returned, dressed in green combat pants and a white tank top, her posture was more relaxed but still wary. She settled cross-legged on a fallen log, maintaining enough distance to react if necessary.

"So," she said, studying Faith with sharp eyes. "Tell me about Scotland, and why someone like you was hiding there of all places."

They talked. It wasn't exactly friendship, but the hostility had evolved into cautious curiosity. Faith wondered if this was how all supernatural relationships began — with the threat of violence giving way to something more complicated.

A crow's harsh caw pierced the air, prompting both women to look up. The bird circled high above, joined by others that wheeled in

CHAPTER 27

patterns that seemed unnatural. Faith noticed subtle details — their wings moved too stiffly and they were perfectly in sync, more like a cluster of mechanical drones than living creatures.

Then, one by one, they began to plummet. Their bodies dissolved into black smoke before reaching the ground, leaving behind only the acrid scent of ash. The display sent a chill down Faith's spine.

"That's been happening more often lately," Leona said grimly. "Nature itself seems to be reacting to something. That's part of why we were summoned here."

"We?"

"My parents," Leona looked almost exasperated. "You really don't know anything about the wider world, do you?"

Faith shook her head. "I grew up far away from any of this. Protected." The word tasted bitter on her tongue. "Fat lot of good that did anyone, in the end."

Something in her tone must have pierced Leona's defenses. She studied Faith for a long moment, her head tilted in that familiar lupine manner.

"You're not what I expected," she finally said.

"Sorry to disappoint," Faith replied.

"I didn't say it was disappointing." Leona's lips curved into a hint of a smile. "Just unexpected."

A sound reached Faith's ears: footsteps on the mansion grounds, moving with inhuman uniformity. Council guards on patrol. Both women instinctively pressed closer to the trees, though Faith couldn't quite understand why.

"There are rumors," Leona said quietly, her earlier hostility replaced by something closer to concern. "Talk of ancient powers stirring, of blood magic awakening. The kind of magic that can turn birds to smoke and make wolves act against their own nature."

Faith's throat tightened as she recalled her mother's black eyes, her father's warning traced in the sheets.

"Is that why you're all here? Because of me?"

Fresh guilt washed over her. How many others was she drawing into her chaos?

"Not everything is about you!" Leona exclaimed harshly.

Faith felt as though she had been slapped.

Then Leona's face broke into a laugh.

"Hey, just kidding. I seem to have inherited my dad's sense of humor. It's an acquired taste."

A twig snapped in the distance, making both women tense. Leona's head tilted, nostrils flaring as she tested the air. Her entire body coiled with sudden alertness, reminding Faith that the beast lay just beneath that human exterior.

"Just a deer," Leona said, though her shoulders remained tense. "Sorry, I get jumpy sometimes. I guess it's an inherited trait, much like my terrible sense of humor." She let out a hollow laugh. "My mom used to map out three escape routes wherever we went. Dad tried to convince her to relax, but... well, trauma leaves its marks."

"My parents were the same way," Faith replied softly, recognizing the familiarity in Leona's words. "Always watching, always ready to run. I used to think they were just overprotective."

"Until you realized they were actually protecting you from something?" Leona's eyes locked onto hers with unexpected understanding.

Faith nodded. The tension between them shifted into a shared recognition of their experiences.

"My mom lost her brother in the last war," Leona said, absently tracing patterns in the dirt with a stick. "Uncle Lupo. I never met him, but I grew up in his shadow. I'd see how she'd go quiet sometimes when looking at old photos, and how Dad would put his hand on her shoulder, both of them carrying a weight I didn't understand."

CHAPTER 27

Suddenly, she snapped the stick, the crack echoing through the trees.

"They tried to give me a normal life — as normal as it can be when you're running with wolves. But I could always feel them watching, waiting for something to go wrong again."

"Like they're trying to protect you from a danger you can't see," Faith finished. "But it follows you anyway."

Leona looked up sharply.

"Yeah, exactly like that." She regarded Faith with newfound interest. "Is that why you were in Scotland? Hiding from whatever this is?"

Faith thought of Mary, of her parents lying corrupted and motionless in the vast building just up ahead.

"Not sure why we even bothered," she said bitterly. "It caught up with us, anyway. You can't outrun fate, I guess. Or prophecies. Or whatever madness this is."

The weight of unspoken history hung between them. Faith could almost visualize it — Lupita's parents bearing their grief into the wilderness, attempting to forge something new from the ashes of their loss. Just as her own parents had fled to Scotland, believing distance could stave off the darkness.

But the darkness, it seemed, had a way of finding you no matter how far you ran.

As if on cue, a scream pierced the morning air.

Chapter 28

The shriek was something between a scream and a chant. Faith's head snapped towards the mansion as her enhanced hearing picked up Serafin's voice rising in a crescendo that made the air itself vibrate.

Without a moment's hesitation, Faith moved, her speed blurring the forest around her. Trees morphed into indistinct streaks of green and brown.

As she approached the mansion, its walls seemed to pulse with an otherworldly rhythm, synchronized with Serafin's incantation.

Faith burst through the doors, her momentum propelling her to her parents' room in an instant. Serafin stood between the beds, arms raised and fingers spread wide.

Dark tendrils of corruption — the black patterns that had been slowly consuming her parents — writhed like living shadows, resisting the spellcaster's magic. This infection was not merely a disease; it was a sentient force unwilling to be expelled, unwilling to lose its hosts.

"Autrud hadha alshara almuzlim watruk hawula' alnaas salimin!" Serafin's voice cracked like thunder. The words sounded Arabic to Faith's ears.

Faith watched, transfixed, as Serafin's magic pulled the darkness from her parents' bodies. The black corruption coalesced into a massive, roiling mass, twisting and screaming just above the two

CHAPTER 28

bodies — a sound that embodied pure malevolence and raw pain.

Isaac now stood in the doorway, his bandaged wrist forgotten, eyes wide with a mixture of terror and hope.

The windows began to vibrate, first with a subtle tremor and then a building resonance. Hairline fractures spread across the glass like spider webs.

The corruption screamed — a sound that transcended mere sound, a psychological assault that made Faith's ears ring and her senses reel. It was the sound of ancient malevolence being torn from its moorings.

Suddenly, the windows exploded outward. Shards of glass flew like crystalline daggers as the black mass was violently expelled, steaming and hissing, fighting against its banishment.

Serafin wobbled on her feet.

Isaac lunged forward, catching the spellcaster just before she hit the ground. He thought nothing of his injury as he took her weight in his arms.

Nell and Christopher lay still, the remnants of dark magic dissolving into nothingness on their skin.

Morning light poured through the shattered windows, illuminating a room that had just witnessed a miracle — at least in Faith's eyes.

Her parents drew a simultaneous, ragged breath.

Their eyes flew open.

The darkness was gone.

Chapter 29

Shattered glass hung suspended in the air like frozen rain, each jagged shard catching the morning light. Faith watched as a single droplet of her father's blood slid down one of the larger pieces. The crimson bead reached the tip of the shard and hung there, trembling as if waiting for permission to fall.

Time felt stretched thin in the aftermath of Serafin's spell. The air crackled with residual magic that made Faith's heightened senses resonate like plucked strings. Her sensitive nose detected the acrid scent of banished darkness — notes of charcoal and decay mingling with the metallic tang of spilled blood and the sweeter undertone of spent power.

As more sunlight streamed through the ruined windows of Vhik'h-Tal-Eskemon, the suspended glass began to shift and dance, casting prismatic reflections across the room's ancient stones. Some shards rotated slowly, their edges casting rainbow fractals across the walls, while others vibrated to rhythms only they could perceive. Each piece seemed to retain an echo of the dark force that had been torn from her parents' bodies just moments before.

Faith knelt between her parents' beds, every supernatural sense focused on detecting signs of recovery. Her eyes followed the last traces of black corruption as they faded from their skin, leaving behind strange silvery patterns that resembled frost on a winter window. The marks seemed to shift and change when she wasn't looking directly at them, as if they retained some fragment of the sentient darkness that had nearly claimed her parents' lives.

She heard the subtle harmonics of power dispersing — like the ring of crystal being struck. Beneath that, she could hear Serafin's labored breathing and the soft rustle of her robes as she moved to sit against a wall.

Isaac remained close to the door, watching, guarding, protecting.

Nell's fingers twitched first, a movement so slight that only Faith could catch it. Then her mother's hand spasmed, fingers curling like claws before slowly relaxing. When her eyes opened again, they were normal but unfocused, holding the lost look of someone waking from a century of dreams.

"M-mom?" Faith's voice cracked on the word.

Nell's lips moved, trying to form words, but only broken sounds emerged. Her face contorted with effort and frustration. Faith caught her mother's flailing hand, squeezing gently. Nell's skin felt cool beneath her touch — vampire cold, familiar and safe.

"It's okay, Mom," she soothed. "Take your time. You're safe now. Both of you are safe."

Christopher's recovery was painfully slow, and watching it was even more difficult. His body remained rigid, his face locked in a grimace that made Faith's chest ache. Silvery marks, remnants of the corruption, traced elaborate patterns across his skin — both beautiful and terrifying, like scars carved by lightning. His fingers twitched erratically against the sheets, as if still fighting against bonds only he could feel.

Faith sensed Serafin's uneven heartbeat as the spellcaster observed with fierce concentration. The henna tattoos on her hands glowed faintly. Her eyes remained fixed on Faith's parents, as if her will alone could keep them tethered to the world of the living.

"The corruption..." Serafin's voice was rough with fatigue. "I've never seen anything like it. It fought back fiercely. It was alive. It wanted them."

As more light filled the room, Faith began to scrutinize her parents with fresh eyes. She noticed every subtle detail — Nell's hands still trembled slightly and Christopher's movements were uncharacteristically hesitant as he attempted to sit up, as if he no longer trusted his own body.

"You should rest," Faith said, the words feeling foreign as they left her mouth. How many times had they told her the same thing over the years? Now, here she was, the roles having reversed.

"We've rested enough," Christopher mumbled weakly. His attempt at a wry smile didn't quite reach his eyes.

Faith caught the flash of fear that crossed his face when he tried to stand — her father, her pillar of strength, uncertain of his own balance. She moved to help him, but he waved her away. Some patterns, it seemed, were too ingrained to break.

"Dad," she said softly. "Let me help."

Something in her voice made him pause. Their eyes met, and Faith saw the moment he realized she wasn't just his little girl anymore. She had made choices, faced dangers and saved their lives. The dynamic between them had shifted in irrevocable ways.

Nell watched them from her bed, her face a complex mix of emotions. When she spoke, sorrow edged her voice.

"I'm so sorry, sweetheart," Nell whispered. "We tried so hard to protect you from all of this. And now..."

"Mom," Faith interrupted, moving to sit beside her. "You gave me everything — love, safety, a childhood free from fear. But I'm not a child anymore. I can't hide in Scotland forever, pretending the world doesn't exist. And neither can you."

Nell's cold fingers found hers again, intertwining.

CHAPTER 29

Christopher gave a weak laugh that turned into something closer to a groan.

"We thought that if we ran far enough... remained quiet enough..." He shook his head. "You're not our little girl anymore."

"I'll always be your little girl," Faith said fiercely. "That won't change. But maybe... maybe now we can protect each other. We can face whatever's coming together."

She observed her parents exchanging a look — one of those silent conversations they had perfected over decades. An understanding passed between them, easing Nell's shoulders and unclenching Christopher's jaw.

"When you were small," Nell said slowly, "you used to have nightmares. Do you remember? You'd wake up screaming about darkness and blood. We thought they were just dreams, but now..." She touched one of the silver marks on her arm. "Now I wonder if you were seeing this. If some part of you always knew what was coming."

"I still have nightmares," Faith admitted. "But they're different now. They're about losing you both. About not being strong enough to protect the people I care about."

Briefly, her thoughts flickered to Leona and Isaac, but she pushed them aside for the moment.

Christopher reached out and took her free hand, forming a circuit between the three of them. The silver marks on their skin seemed to pulse in unison, a reminder of the blood they shared and the destiny that bound them together.

"We can't promise we'll always be here," he said quietly. "No one can make that promise. But we can promise to stop trying to shield you from who you are. You've earned that much."

"And maybe," Nell added, "you can promise to be patient with us while we learn to let you grow up. It's not easy watching your child become stronger than you."

Tears pricked Faith's eyes.

"I'm not stronger," she said. "I'm just... different. And I still need both of you. Just not in the same way as before."

Rapid footsteps echoed in the corridor, multiple sets moving without the uniformity of vampires. A couple appeared in the doorway, and Faith's breath caught as she recognized them from her mother's old sketches.

Chapter 30

Devan and Lupita. A quick glance at Lupita confirmed her as Leona's mother; the resemblance was uncanny.

But the drawings had captured them in time from two decades ago, failing to show how age had marked them — silver threading through Devan's dark hair, fine lines around Lupita's eyes that deepened when she smiled, and a slight limp in Devan's left leg from an old injury. Their movements exuded the easy synchronization of a couple who had spent decades together.

"Nell?" Devan's voice cracked slightly. "My God…"

Faith watched her mother's face transform at the sight of her old friend. Tears spilled down Nell's cheeks as Devan crossed the room in three quick strides and embraced her fiercely. The gesture carried decades of history — battles fought together, losses shared, a bond transcending the boundaries between mortal and immortal.

"You don't seem to have aged a day," Devan said with a forced lightness. "You must tell me your secret — some kind of face cream?"

The attempt at humor fell flat as the weight of reality settled in. Faith watched the realization wash over her mother: others would age and die while she remained forever young. The immortal and the mortal, divided by time's relentless passage. The subtle crow's feet around Devan's eyes, the silver in his hair, the slight stiffness in his movements — all signs of a clock that had stopped for Nell but continued its steady march toward mortality for her old friend.

Faith's stomach twisted with a stark realization — she was the only one in the room whose future was uncertain. Would she continue to grow older while her parents remained eternally young? Would they have to witness their only child age, become infirm and die while they remained unchanged? Or would her vampire blood eventually freeze her in time too? The questions pressed against her chest like weights.

"Devan..." Nell's voice was raw with emotion. "I'm so sorry... we never..."

"Hey, none of that," he said firmly, though Faith detected a slight tremor in his voice. "We all knew what we were doing when we chose our paths."

"Wolf-man," Christopher said, extending a hand toward Devan.

Devan brushed it aside, wrapping his arms around Christopher instead.

"Fang-banger," Devan replied. "I see you're still a stiff, in more ways than one."

Christopher's grin was wide and genuine.

Lupita moved to stand beside her husband, one hand resting on his shoulder. Her sharp eyes found Faith's, brimming with unexpected warmth.

Faith sensed the subtle shift in energy the moment Leona entered the room. It was Isaac's reaction that caught her attention — the tightening of his shoulders, his fingers brushing instinctively against his sword hilt, the slight elevation of his heartbeat that only a vampire's keen hearing could detect. But why? Had he witnessed Leona's earlier attack on her? Was he always watching?

Chapter 31

Leona's nostrils flared as she picked up Isaac's scent, her head tilting in that distinctly lupine way. Her lips curved into what might have been amusement or challenge.

"Hunter," she acknowledged, the word laden with history and tension.

"Werwulf," Isaac replied, his voice carefully neutral, though his body language conveyed much more. He shifted his weight almost imperceptibly, positioning himself between Leona and Faith — a move that could have seemed coincidental, but wasn't.

Leona narrowed her eyes. She prowled further into the room, each step bringing her closer to Faith and forcing Isaac to either step aside or make his protective stance clear. The air was heavy with unspoken challenge.

Faith felt trapped between their conflicting energies — Isaac's controlled power and Leona's wild vitality.

"Breathe," Leona whispered, finally reaching Faith's side after Isaac stepped away. Her voice had an undertone that felt almost like a growl — not threatening, but grounding. Her hand found Faith's shoulder, warm and steady, while her gaze remained fixed on Isaac.

Faith noticed the Hunter assessing them, his bandaged hand tightening almost imperceptibly around the hilt of his sword. A flicker of something dark crossed his eyes before he looked away.

Concern? Jealousy? A warning? She couldn't quite decipher his emotions.

Turning her gaze back to Leona's parents, who were chatting animatedly with her own, Faith again observed the subtle effects of time on Devan's face — the soft creases at the corners of his eyes, the slight softening of his jaw and the almost imperceptible stiffness in once-fluid movements. Even Lupita, still striking with her olive skin and clear hazel eyes like her daughter's, showed the gentle changes brought by two decades. They wore their aging with dignity, but the sight tightened Faith's chest with apprehension. Each mark served as a reminder of her own uncertain future.

She glanced at Leona, imagining the day she might witness the young werwulf's fierce vitality slowly fade, those sculpted contours softened by age and that wild spirit dimmed by the heavy hand of mortality.

"Are you okay?" Leona whispered, close enough that her breath stirred Faith's hair. The warmth of her body, so alive and vital, only emphasized the cold uncertainty gnawing at Faith's core.

"I don't know what I am right now," Faith whispered back, her voice catching. Her response carried multiple meanings.

Across the room, Isaac caught her eye, his expression softening with understanding. How many times had he witnessed this particular tragedy unfold in his line of work? How many immortals had he seen broken by the burden of outliving everyone they cared for?

Christopher struggled to stand, his movements unsteady. Faith moved to help him, but Isaac was there first, supporting her father with his good arm.

"Easy," the Hunter murmured. "The corruption's gone, but your body needs time to heal."

"How long?" Christopher asked, his voice rough as if he had been screaming. "How long were we...?"

CHAPTER 31

"Three days," Faith answered, hating the tremor in her voice. "You were both gone for three days."

Her father's hand found hers, squeezing gently. The silver marks on his skin seemed to pulse where they touched.

"We weren't gone, Little One. Just… lost. There was darkness, but something kept calling us back. Your blood, I think. Fighting the corruption. You guided us back, Faith."

"Or damned you in the first place," Faith whispered, guilt clawing at her throat.

"No." Serafin's voice held unexpected strength despite her exhaustion. "Your blood saved them. The darkness tried to use it, to twist it for its own purpose, but there was light mixed with the shadow. The joining of bloodlines created something new. Something neither fully dark nor fully light."

"Like me," Faith said softly.

"Exactly like you." Leona's hand remained on Faith's shoulder, warm and steady. Faith could feel the subtle thrum of power beneath her skin, the wolf nature barely contained in human form. "Taking action is not weakness, Faith. It's strength."

"It's reckless," Isaac interjected, his voice tight with emotion he struggled to control. "We still don't understand what her blood can do. The risk— "

"The risk was letting them die," Leona snapped, her eyes flashing with something distinctly wolflike. Faith sensed the muscles tensing beneath Leona's touch, a sign of an impending transformation. "Sometimes you have to trust your instincts."

"Instincts get people killed." Isaac's jaw clenched, his knuckles hard around the hilt of his sword. "Or worse."

Faith detected the old pain in his voice; he was thinking of his sister.

"So does being afraid to act." Leona's fingers tightened protectively on Faith's shoulder, her skin fever-hot, another sign of her wolf nature rising. "She saved them. That's what matters."

Faith felt caught between them — Leona's wild certainty and Isaac's careful control. Both were trying to protect her in their own ways, each making her pulse quicken for different reasons. Leona's touch ignited something primal within her, a yearning for freedom and raw honesty. Meanwhile, Isaac's steady presence offered anchor points in a world that increasingly felt chaotic.

As the sun shifted outside, the suspended glass shards caught more light, sending rainbow refractions dancing across the walls. Faith noticed the subtle movement as they began to vibrate in response to some unseen force — perhaps a remnant of the corruption's rage? The air thickened with potential, like the moment before lightning strikes.

Faith felt Leona and Isaac draw closer to her, their shoulders brushing against hers. Static electricity crackled where they touched, heightening her senses with conflicting sensations — Leona's vital heat on her right and Isaac's steady warmth on her left. Without thinking, she reached out and grabbed both their hands for support.

Sensations slammed into her.

***

No visions, but intense emotions — chaos, hot and cold, wild and contained, primal and disciplined. These opposing forces created a maelstrom.

Feelings crashed through her mind like storm waves: anger, guilt, desire, rage, longing, remorse, grief, need, nothingness.

Chapter 32

Faith yanked her hands away, gasping.

Both Leona and Isaac stared at her with matching expressions of concern. Leona's body tensed for action while Isaac instinctively reached for his weapon.

"What did you see?" Leona asked softly, her voice carrying undertones of a growl.

But Faith couldn't respond. How could she convey that she had just experienced heartbreak, rage, death — perhaps even her own.

"Faith?" Her mother's voice brought her back to the present. "What was it? What did you see?"

Faith shook her head, trying to clear the heat of emotion clouding her thoughts. "Nothing clear. Just... fragments."

Leona's eyes scrutinized her face, sensing the deception. The werwulf opened her mouth to speak, but a sudden gust of wind swept through the broken windows, carrying an unnatural chill.

The fierce wind caught the suspended shards of glass, making them dance through the air like deadly wind chimes. Faith's acute hearing registered their subtle song — a discordant melody that spoke of breaking points and shattering certainties.

"The barriers are thinning," Serafin remarked grimly. "Between what should be and what was never meant to be."

A sound like distant thunder rolled across the sky, even though

Faith's senses detected no storm. The suspended glass shards vibrated in response, their deadly dance growing more frantic. Suddenly, one larger piece broke free, shooting across the room like a thrown dagger. Faith's reflexes kicked in, allowing her to track its trajectory as it hurtled toward her mother's exposed throat.

Three things occurred simultaneously: Leona's body began to shift, bones cracking as she started her transformation; Isaac's hand moved toward his sword, though he would never reach it in time; Faith's body reacted purely on instinct, moving faster than she ever had before.

Her hand shot up and caught the glass shard inches from Nell's neck. Blood welled from her palm where the sharp edges had pierced her flesh. Looking down, Faith saw her reflection in the shard — a face half in shadow, half in light. She yanked the glass from her skin and let it drop to the ground.

She felt Leona and Isaac flanking her once more, their presence both comforting and complicated. She couldn't help but wonder which of them she had seen falling apart, which one would be forced to make an impossible choice, and whose world would ultimately shatter.

A murder of crows gathered on the glass-strewn windowsills outside, their movements unnaturally synchronized as they observed the scene within the room with unnervingly intelligent eyes. Faith noticed the subtle wrongness in their forms — the way their feathers sometimes seemed to dissolve into smoke at the edges, how their shadows fell in impossible directions.

Then, the birds took flight as one, their wings beating in perfect unison. They spiraled upward into the morning sky, a living tornado of black feathers and shadows. With movements that defied nature, they began to arrange themselves against the pale blue canvas of the sky.

CHAPTER 32

Faith's skin went even paler as a face emerged from the living darkness — precise features, cold eyes and a cruel smile composed of wings, beaks and writhing shadows. The image loomed for one terrible moment, massive and malevolent against the heavens, before the birds fractured and scattered like ash in the wind.

Faith sensed the heavy weight of prophecy and destiny pressing down on her. But this time, she refused to run. Whatever lay ahead, she would confront it head-on. Even if it meant she would be the one to shatter.

Chapter 33

Faith's fingertips traced the gouges and scratches on the surface of the ancient oak desk, each mark a silent testament to hours of frantic research and desperate note-taking. Scattered papers blanketed every inch of the workspace, their edges curling with age, the handwriting hurried and intense. Her sharp eyes picked up every detail: coffee ring stains, tear drops that had warped the ink and spots where a pen had pressed so hard it nearly tore through the page. She tried to decipher the scrawls:

Find connection between blood magic and prophecy
Trace historical records of the Griffenrougue clan
What's in Alaska?

More notes spiraled across the margins, with arrows linking seemingly random thoughts, as if the writer's mind raced faster than their hand could keep up.

Faith felt drawn into the frantic energy of the research, experiencing an unexpected kinship with whoever had occupied this space before her, seeking answers within the vast underground library of Vhik'h-Tal-Eskemon.

The air carried the stale scent of old leather bindings and age-yellowed paper.

CHAPTER 33

Faith's hearing captured the subtle sounds of the library around her: the gentle settling of old wood, the whisper of pages shifting in distant stacks and the soft skittering of mice in the walls. The space felt alive, as if centuries of accumulated knowledge had granted it a kind of sentience.

Faith's fingers paused on a thin volume of historical portraits. The crude printing technique of the era rendered the images as collections of black dots, but something about one particular portrait made her pause. The caption identified the woman as Justina S., and despite the primitive reproduction method, Faith felt an odd sense of familiarity looking at the face.

Perhaps it was just fatigue after hours of research, but she could have sworn the woman's features echoed her own in some way. She shook off the strange feeling and turned back to her primary research, pulling the massive tome toward her.

The book was titled *'Emissary of Darkness: Vlad Tepes, Voivode of Wallachia (1431-1477)*. The pages were so thin and delicate that she barely dared to breathe on them. The book chronicled the reign of her ancestor in excruciating detail, and Faith's stomach churned as she forced herself to read yet another disturbing account:

The Feast of St. Bartholomew, 1459
"Today I witnessed an atrocity that shall haunt me until my dying day. Our gracious host, Voivode Tepes, had arranged a great feast for the local boyars and their families. The tables were laden with delicacies, and the wine flowed freely. But when the nobles were deep in their cups, Tepes' men sealed the hall."

"I tire of your soft hands and silk clothes," the Voivode announced, his eyes blazing with terrible glee. "Let us see how you stomach honest work."

"The elderly and children were impaled first, stakes driven through their bodies as their loved ones watched. The rest were marched to the castle

work site, forced to labor until they collapsed. Those who fell were impaled where they lay. The screams continued for days."

"I write this now in secret, praying I will live to bear witness. The death toll rises hourly. This morning I counted eight hundred stakes..."

Faith slammed the book shut, her hands trembling. The motion stirred up a cloud of dust, which her acute eyesight transformed into a galaxy of dancing motes. She struggled to steady her breathing, grappling with the horror of realizing that this monster's blood coursed through her veins.

Her fingers landed on another page, this one detailing how Vlad had received Turkish envoys who refused to remove their turbans in his presence. He had ordered the turbans to be nailed to their heads, the spikes driven deep into their skulls. The writer described Vlad laughing at their screams.

The page featured an image of Vlad in his regal attire. The man had an intensity that seemed to leap from the page, despite the primitive reproduction in clusters of black and sepia dots. Dark, wavy hair framed a face that was angular and sharp, with pronounced cheekbones and piercing eyes that seemed to look directly through time. A carefully trimmed mustache and beard gave him an almost aristocratic appearance, belying the brutal history she had just been reading.

Something about his gaze made Faith shiver. The eyes held a calculating coldness, a predatory intelligence that seemed to echo the horrific accounts she had just read. This was not just a man, but a creature of calculation and cruelty, someone who could order hundreds impaled without feeling a moment's remorse.

Each revelation struck her like a slap to the face. Faith had known abstractly that her ancestry was dark, but reading these firsthand accounts and seeing the brutality laid out in precise detail made it

CHAPTER 33

viscerally real. This wasn't just history; it was her heritage, her very blood.

A single drop of moisture fell onto one of the scattered papers. Faith reached up, surprised to find tears on her cheeks; she hadn't even realized she was crying.

"Not pleasant reading, is it?"

The voice made Faith jump violently — she should have sensed someone approaching. Her kind was designed to hide in the shadows, to hunt and survive.

Chapter 34

Faith turned to see Kavisha's wheelchair gliding between the towering shelves, her bangles catching the dim light. She wore a deep green and gold sari, with intricate paisley patterns woven into the material in metallic thread that seemed to shift and dance in the library's low light. A wide gold border framed elaborate designs of peacocks and lotus flowers along the sari's edge.

"I'm sorry," Faith said quickly, scrambling to gather the scattered papers as if caught prying into someone else's affairs. Her hands shook slightly as she attempted to organize the chaos of research. "I was just trying to understand…"

"No need to apologize." Kavisha's warm smile radiated centuries of wisdom, but Faith detected a shadow behind it. "You're sitting exactly where another seeker of knowledge once sat — Amara."

Faith's hands froze over the papers.

"The librarian? The one who helped save my mother during the war?"

"The very same." Kavisha maneuvered her wheelchair closer, her sari rustling softly. "She spent countless hours at this desk, searching for answers that could help us win the war. In doing so, she also helped me answer an important question."

The High Chancellor's eyes grew distant. "She showed me that humans could be just as remarkable as vampires. Perhaps more

CHAPTER 34

so, given that their brief lives burn so much brighter. Their very mortality drives them to be fierce and determined, unwilling to waste a single moment. They don't have the luxury of time."

Faith observed the emotions playing across Kavisha's face — fondness, admiration, and something darker: guilt.

"And now she pays the price for that lesson," Kavisha continued, her voice tight with barely suppressed anguish. "She and Haiden, the Hunter, are in hiding, pursued by those clinging to outdated prejudices. Some members of the Council of Elders have never forgiven me for elevating a human to their ranks. Dragos Vacarescu, the Speaker of the Council, Gustav Nielsen and Loshua Dascălu are among those who see my actions as an affront to immortals."

These names meant little to Faith, but it was clear Kavisha needed to unburden herself.

"They're hunting Amara?" Faith felt a tightness in her chest at the thought of someone targeting the woman who had helped save her mother — and indeed, the world. "But why? After everything she did to help?"

"Because she represents change." Kavisha's fingers fidgeted with her bangles, causing them to chime discordantly. "And I am the one who put a target on her back."

The weight of guilt in Kavisha's voice was unmistakable. Faith noticed the catch in her words and how her shoulders drooped beneath her elegant sari.

"You couldn't have known," Faith said softly.

"Couldn't I?" Kavisha's laugh was humorless. "I've lived for centuries. I've seen how the fear of change can twist people and make them cruel. I knew there would be resistance to putting a human on the Council, but I thought..." She shook her head. "I thought if they could see her value, her dedication to the common cause, they would understand. Instead, I ruined the life of someone I had come to think of as a daughter."

The confession hung in the air between them. Faith sensed the weight of unfallen tears — tears that Kavisha was too proud to shed.

"I can still see her face," the High Chancellor continued, her voice low. "She didn't want to leave her library, her books, her life. But they were already moving against her. Some of the oldest, most powerful vampires in the world, all because I dared to suggest that a human could be our equal."

Faith absorbed this, feeling the weight of responsibility and consequence radiating from the High Chancellor. While Faith grappled with her own heritage, Kavisha navigated the larger conflict between progress and tradition, between change and stagnation.

"Do you think they've sided with Mary?" Faith asked, suddenly alarmed by the implication. "Those who left the Council?"

"That remains to be seen," Kavisha replied, meeting Faith's gaze. The High Chancellor paused, seemingly reluctant to continue.

"Go on. Please," Faith encouraged.

Kavisha rested her hands on her lap. "If someone were to present an opportunity to return to the old ways — where vampires hold onto their sense of superiority and humans are seen as a subspecies, mere cattle — it would be easy for those unwilling to change their mindset to see the appeal. Many of our kind have rallied behind Mary, captivated by the Red Claws' rhetoric of immortal supremacy."

Faith recalled the history books she had read as a child. Some tendencies seemed universal, regardless of immortality. Fanaticism, hate and prejudice were unfortunate truths of the world.

Before Faith could delve further, footsteps echoed across the library's stone floor, quick and purposeful. She picked up the subtle difference between these steps and the more uniform movements typical of vampires.

Chapter 35

Leona emerged from the stacks, her presence starkly contrasting with the library's somber atmosphere. She was dressed in combat gear that accentuated her athletic build, her black hair pulled back in a practical braid, highlighting her angular features. Faith caught her scent — damp earth, storm winds and something feral that stirred her vampire instincts, evoking both alertness and intrigue.

"There you are," Leona said, her voice carrying a slight growl that seemed intrinsic to her being. "It's a perfect day for training ... and you definitely need it after your last performance. The forest is calling, girl." She flared her nostrils slightly, catching the scent of old books, and Faith noticed her suppress a small shudder.

"Maybe later. I really should finish..." Faith gestured to her research, torn between her desire to understand her history and the magnetic pull of Leona's vibrant presence.

"Books?" Leona's expression twisted in genuine distaste. "You can't learn about life from dead trees, Faith. Come run with me. Feel the wind. Life is out there, not confined to this paper dungeon."

The temptation was almost overwhelming. Faith could vividly imagine the crisp forest air and the exhilaration of running freely. She sensed traces of the outside world clinging to Leona — pine needles, fresh earth, morning dew. It called to a primal part of her, urging her to leave behind the burdens of dark history and simply exist in the moment.

Yet the weight of her past bore down on her like iron chains. She couldn't escape who she was, no matter how much she might wish to. And knowledge was power, as Amara had demonstrated before her.

"I need to know who I am," she said softly. "I need to understand my origins."

Something flickered in Leona's gaze as she glanced at the open books — concern, fear, perhaps even a hint of revulsion. The werwulf's posture shifted subtly, becoming more alert and defensive. Faith noticed the slight tension in her muscles and the way her fingers flexed as if preparing for action.

"You're not them," Leona said firmly, her voice laced with that low growl. "You're not bound by their choices."

"Aren't I?" Faith replied, tracing a finger along a passage detailing another of Vlad's atrocities. "What if — "

"What if you stop letting the dead define you?" Leona interrupted, her tone sharp enough to trigger Faith's defensive instincts. "You are alive — sort of. You're here. That's what matters. Focus on the here and now."

Faith noticed how Leona's gaze lingered on the books, her body tense as if bracing for an unseen threat. The werwulf sensed something dark within those pages, something that made her wild nature retreat.

"Another time," Faith said gently, hoping to soften her refusal.

Leona's jaw tightened, the muscles standing out briefly before she managed to steady herself. "Your choice." She turned to leave but paused. "Just… don't lose yourself in there."

Faith watched as Leona faded back into the stacks.

"She fears for you," Kavisha said softly. "She sees how these histories draw you in. Perhaps she's right to be concerned. History is just that — history. Even prophecies don't define the future in black and white.

CHAPTER 35

Your life's course is not set in stone, or ink."

Before Faith could respond, another figure emerged from the shadows.

Chapter 36

Serafin approached with careful steps, her usual grace hindered by exhaustion. The spellcaster's face was drawn, dark circles under her eyes from the effort of saving Faith's parents.

Faith sprang to her feet, instinctively moving to support Serafin. She reached her side just as the woman's knees threatened to buckle.

"I'm fine… I'm fine," Serafin protested, though she leaned heavily on Faith's arm. Her robes rustled with movement, releasing a scent of herbs and ancient magic. "I just need to find a specific grimoire. The incantation I used on your parents… it wasn't optimal. Like trying to sing a harmony with only half the notes."

Faith guided Serafin to a chair, noticing how the spellcaster's hands trembled slightly. Without thinking, she reached out to steady them. The moment their skin touched, the vision rushed in.

***

Two little girls lay in a sun-dappled garden, their matching faces turned toward an endless summer sky. At six years old, they mirrored each other perfectly — every freckle, every eyelash, even the way their chests rose and fell in perfect synchronization. Their small hands were clasped tightly together, as if afraid of even an inch of separation.

As clouds drifted overhead, their shared imagination breathed life

CHAPTER 36

into the shapes above with bursts of magic that danced between their fingers. Tiny fireworks of pure energy painted the air in cascading colors, each spark carrying the pure joy of their connection.

"For ever and ever?" one girl whispered, her voice imbued with the fierce love and unshakeable trust that only a child can possess.

"For ever and ever," the other sister vowed solemnly, squeezing her sister's hand tighter.

Their destiny was inscribed in historic texts and whispered legends.

In each generation of spellcasters, a sacred pair was born — always twin sisters, their names echoing with each other like their magic. Nalindra and Darlinna, the first and most powerful, whose benevolent deeds still resound through history. Then came Rosalie and Erilosa, followed by Yansa and Sanya. Now, Serafin and Farsine were destined to carry that revered tradition forward, their shared power both a gift and a burden.

But the idyllic scene of the garden suddenly fractured like breaking glass.

The sisters faced each other across a circle carved in dark earth, their childhood innocence stripped away by teenage fury. Ancient trees loomed above them like silent judges as their once-perfect harmony splintered and cracked. Their combined magic, meant to shine like a star, now sparked and sputtered.

"You're holding us back!" Farsine screamed, her voice tearing through the forest. Anger twisted her face, revealing something darker lurking behind her eyes — something ravenous. "We could be gods if you weren't so weak, so afraid!"

"Please," Serafin pleaded, reaching for her other half with trembling hands. "Can't you feel what these shadow arts are doing to you? To us? Each spell leaves another mark on your heart. I'm losing you piece by piece."

"They make us stronger!" Magic crackled around Farsine's fingers, no longer the pure light of their childhood. "Why can't you see that? Why do you insist on keeping us chained to these... limitations?"

The vision shattered again before reforming.

The sisters stood back to back, their magical bond stretched between them like a thread of light about to snap. Waves of pain radiated from their impending separation — physical agony, emotional devastation and magical entropy all coalescing into one overwhelming torment.

"If you walk away now," Serafin's voice faltered into a sob, "we'll never be whole again. Our magic, our souls — everything we are will be broken, forever."

"Then let it break." Farsine's words fell like stones shattering calm water. "Better broken than bound by your weakness."

The severing struck like a thunderclap.

Serafin crumpled to her knees as blood poured from her nose, her magic spiraling out of control in her grief. Farsine's responding scream echoed through the trees, raw with shared agony. The very air trembled as their twin bond — meant to last a lifetime — shattered into irreparable fragments.

Yet Farsine continued to walk away, each step leaving drops of her own blood on the forest floor, choosing power over love, ambition over sisterhood.

Chapter 37

Faith jerked her hand back as if it had been burned, her body trembling with the anguish of what she had witnessed. The phantom pain of the severed twin bond echoed through her nerves like aftershocks.

She gazed at Serafin, truly seeing her for the first time. The permanent shadows beneath her eyes were not merely a sign of exhaustion; they revealed the weight of an irreparable loss.

"I'm so sorry," Faith whispered, her voice thick with shared grief. "Your sister…"

For a brief moment, Serafin's face crumpled before she steadied herself, her shoulders sagging as if the memory were a physical weight.

"The ability of sight," she murmured, a bittersweet smile touching her lips. "Sometimes, I forget you carry that particular 'gift.'"

Pain etched deep lines around her mouth as she continued. "Magic between twin girls is sacred — a bond meant to last forever. But sometimes…" Her voice cracked. "Sometimes we make choices that shatter everything we're meant to be."

"Is that why healing my parents nearly broke you?" Faith asked gently. "Because your magic is…"

"Crippled. Unstable." Serafin's fingers traced patterns in the air, but the light they created flickered and faded like dying stars. "Magic craves balance — light and dark, creation and destruction. Two halves. Much like you, child." She gripped the nearby bookshelf, her knuckles turning white.

"Your blood carries echoes of ancient power," she continued. "When I was healing your parents, I felt something stir — something that has been asleep for a very long time."

Faith glanced back at the oak desk where she had been reading about unimaginable horrors from the past.

"Vlad's legacy? The Omni-Father, as they call him." Faith's stomach churned at the thought.

"Perhaps." Serafin studied her intently. "The union of your bloodlines — light and dark, creation and destruction. The potential there… like mine and Farsine's, like Nalindra and Darlinna's." She trailed off, lost in thought.

"But will it heal or destroy?" Faith pressed, desperate for answers.

"That choice belongs to you alone." Serafin's voice carried the weight of bitter experience. "Power simply exists. Our choices give it meaning." Her eyes grew distant. "Though sometimes those choices cost more than we could ever imagine."

"Thank you," Faith said softly. "For saving my parents. I understand now what it truly cost you." She took Serafin's hands in her own again. This time, no visions came.

Serafin's smile was gentle yet haunted. "Your parents were heroes once. They saved us all. This was the least I could do. I owe it to Sanya, also." She reached out, her cool fingers brushing Faith's cheek. "Remember this, child — darkness lives in all of us. Your ancestor chose cruelty. Your parents chose love. Now you must forge your own path."

The weight of those words settled on Faith's shoulders like a heavy mantle. As she looked across at the scattered research, each page brought to mind the themes of blood and destiny. Thoughts

CHAPTER 37

flooded her mind: Leona's wild heart, Isaac's unwavering strength, her parents' sacrifice, Kavisha's guilt, Serafin's tragic loss, Amara's unfair burden, Vlad's unrestrained cruelty, and Mary's dark depths.

In the end, who would she choose to be?

Chapter 38

Faith stood at the edge of Vhik'h-Tal-Eskemon's manicured grounds, where centuries-old protective magic met the wild forest. The air was filled with an array of scents — pine resin, loamy earth, mountain laurel.

She needed to escape the oppressive weight of what she had discovered in the library. Serafin's heartbreak lingered, while Vlad's atrocities replayed endlessly in her mind — *eight hundred stakes, nails driven into skulls, screams that lasted for days.*

A flash of movement drew her gaze.

Leona emerged from the treeline in her massive werwulf form, muscles rippling beneath dark russet fur as she loped across the grounds. The morning sun highlighted amber tones in her coat, making her appear to be a creature of living flame.

As Leona approached, her form shimmered and flowed, bones and sinew reshaping themselves until she stood before Faith in human form, naked as the day she was born.

Faith quickly looked away, cheeks burning. Yet her eyes betrayed her, stealing furtive glances at the bronzed, lithe figure in front of her.

Leona chuckled and swiftly donned the clothes piled at the edge of the grounds. Within moments, she was back in her close-fitting training gear.

CHAPTER 38

"It's okay; you can look now. My shame is covered," she quipped. Faith turned her head.

"Finally crawled out of that dank old crypt?" Leona's sharp features softened as their eyes met. "Sometimes you need to stop reading about life and start living it."

Faith inhaled the subtle spice-and-earth scent that always clung to Leona's skin, stronger now after her run through the forest. Leona radiated vitality, making Faith acutely aware of her own cold, undead flesh.

"Reading is safer," Faith replied, hating how small her voice sounded. Twenty years of isolation had left her ill-equipped for even basic interaction. "Books don't…" She trailed off, unsure how to explain her fear of connection.

"Don't what?" A new voice joined them, rich and controlled. "Don't challenge you? Don't make you face what you're capable of?"

Faith spun toward the sound.

Isaac emerged from the house, his movements precise and deliberate. Both swords were strapped to his back. His long coat flowed behind him.

Had he been watching her all along? The thought was both unsettling and oddly comforting. Faith caught his subtle scents — weapon oil, leather and something muskier that made her throat tighten with thirst. She swallowed hard, forcing back her vampire instincts.

"How long have you been lurking there?" Leona asked, her tone edged with irritation. Her hazel eyes narrowed slightly as she studied the Hunter.

"Long enough." Isaac's hand rested casually on his thick utility belt. "Someone needs to keep watch. There are still threats, even here."

"You mean me?" Leona asked, raising her eyebrows.

"I mean many things." The Hunter glanced at Faith before turning back to Leona. "The world isn't divided into neat categories of friend and foe. It never has been."

Faith noticed the charged glances among the three of them. The complexity of their dynamic made her dizzy. In Scotland, her relationships had been limited to her parents; she had no framework for navigating this kind of tension.

"Well, since you're here, Hunter," Leona said, a feral grin spreading across her face, "why not make yourself useful? Faith needs to learn to fight, not hide."

Isaac paused for a long moment.

"Combat training requires discipline," he replied. "Structure. It's not just about raw instinct."

Faith felt an urge to retreat to the safety of the mansion, but the memory of Vlad's cruelty echoed in her mind.

"I'm always up for learning," she ventured, hoping that focusing on physical activity would distract her from her thoughts.

"Now you're talking!" Leona exclaimed, excitement bubbling over as she dropped into a fighting stance. "Show me what you've got, vamp girl. Don't think — feel!"

Without warning, she launched herself at Faith.

Faith's heightened reflexes screamed at her to move; however, years of careful restraint made her hesitate. Leona's shoulder struck her midsection, sending both of them tumbling across the damp grass.

They landed hard, with Leona on top. Her face was inches from Faith's, her hazel eyes blazing with something wild. Faith felt paralyzed by the intensity of the moment — the heat radiating from Leona's skin against her cold flesh, the subtle spice of her scent and the rhythm of Leona's heartbeat thundering against Faith's chest.

"I'm still in human form," Leona chided. "You're much stronger than me. Faster, too. But you're afraid of your own power." She shifted her weight. "Stop thinking so much. Trust your instincts.

CHAPTER 38

Act."

Faith caught Isaac watching them, his expression carefully neutral, yet his body coiled with tension. He tracked their every movement. What had she gotten herself into?

"That's enough." Isaac's voice sliced through the air like one of his blades. He stepped forward, drawing a sword in one smooth motion. The steel sang as it cleared the scabbard. "Getting knocked to the ground won't teach her anything useful."

Leona rolled off Faith and sprang to her feet, offering Faith a hand up.

"Sometimes the best lessons come from getting knocked down." Leona held Faith's gaze a moment longer than necessary before turning to Isaac with a challenging smirk. "But by all means, show us your 'disciplined' approach." She pretended to yawn.

The sun glinted off the silver scars on Isaac's dark skin as he assumed a fighting stance. Faith noted every detail — old blade wounds, burn marks and smaller nicks that spoke of battles survived. He began demonstrating basic forms, each movement precise and controlled.

"Watch my footwork," he instructed. "Balance is key. Power is meaningless if you can't stay on your feet. Your strength comes from your legs. You must remain grounded."

Faith tried to focus on the lesson, but her senses betrayed her. She noted every subtle shift of muscle beneath his shirt, the steady rhythm of his heartbeat and the way sweat glistened on his skin. His scent enveloped her — a mix of leather and steel combined with something uniquely human that made her fangs ache. She swallowed hard, fighting back her predatory instincts.

"Your turn." He offered her the sword, hilt-first.

The weapon felt foreign in her hands — awkward and unfamiliar. She tried to mirror his movements but stumbled on the first swing, nearly losing her grip on the blade.

"Here." Isaac moved behind her, his chest pressing against her back as he covered her hands on the sword grip. "Like this." His touch was gentle yet firm, positioning her grip with careful precision. Faith felt warmth seep into her cool flesh, causing her breath to catch.

A low growl made her snap her head up.

Leona stood at the edge of the training area, visibly trembling as she fought against transformation. Her hazel eyes shifted to amber, pupils elongating. The growl deepened.

"Enough with the technical procedures," she snarled. "She needs to learn how to actually fight, not dance a waltz. You don't have time for choreographed moves in the heat of battle."

"As opposed to charging in like a feral maniac?" Isaac retorted. "That's sure to keep her safe."

Bones cracked and reshaped as Leona's transformation took hold. Her training clothes shredded as her body expanded, dark fur erupting in waves from her skin. In moments, she became a creature of muscle and fury, claws extended.

The beast charged.

Isaac shoved Faith aside, raising his sword in a defensive arc.

But Leona was ready.

She caught the blade between her massive paws, using Isaac's momentum to throw him off balance. They collided in a blur of motion — sword against claws, technique versus raw instinct.

Faith moved backward, overwhelmed by the sudden turn of events and the sensory overload. She heard every snarl, every impact of flesh against steel. Her nose filled with the tang of blood as claws found flesh and blade bit into fur. It was a chaotic blur of fury, rage and resentment.

"Stop!" she cried, but neither seemed to hear her, or perhaps neither wanted to.

CHAPTER 38

Isaac had lost his sword and struggled to deflect Leona's huge claws with his forearms. Blood trickled down his skin from fresh cuts as the werwulf pressed her advantage, driving him toward a tall oak.

Something shifted within Faith. The careful restraint instilled by her parents began to crack. Dark, untamed power surged through her dead veins like lightning.

Moving instinctively, her vampire speed carried her between the combatants faster than human eyes could follow. She caught Leona's descending claw with one hand while pressing the other against Isaac's chest to hold him back.

"I said STOP!"

The force of her shout seemed to shake the very air.

Both Leona and Isaac froze, staring at her in shock.

Faith realized she was effortlessly holding back several hundred pounds of enraged beast.

Leona's enormous form shuddered, bones cracking as she began to shift back to her human shape. Moments later, she stood before them naked, her olive skin gleaming with sweat. New scars marked her flesh where Isaac's blade had struck. She lacked the luxury of vampire healing, but none of the wounds seemed too deep.

Isaac quickly averted his gaze, a flush creeping up his dark skin. Faith noticed his pulse quickening, though she couldn't tell if it was from exertion or Leona's nudity.

"Really?" Leona spat, making no attempt to cover herself. Instead, she placed her hands on her hips and gulped in air. "You try to gut me with a sword but can't handle a little skin?" She stretched languorously, seemingly enjoying his discomfort. "The body is natural. Nothing to be ashamed of."

"Some of us were raised with different values," Isaac muttered, still not looking back.

"Some of us were raised in cages," Leona countered, her voice carrying a hard edge. "I prefer freedom." Her eyes locked onto Faith's. "In all things."

"We should move to more challenging terrain," Isaac suggested, eager to shift past the moment. "The protected grounds won't prepare you for real combat. It's unlikely you'll find yourself fighting on manicured lawns."

Leona's lips curved into a predatory smile. "Finally, something we agree on." She shifted back to her werwulf form, her immense body easily dwarfing them both. "Try to keep up," she growled, then raced off.

Chapter 39

They ventured deeper into the wilderness, leaving behind the mansion's protective wards. The terrain rose sharply into the Blue Ridge Mountains, forcing them to navigate fallen logs and loose scree. Faith observed how sunlight fractured through the leaves overhead, creating ever-shifting patterns on the ground. The air was thick with the complex scents of decomposing leaves, animal tracks and mountain springs, accompanied by a symphony of birdsong and rustling branches.

"Focus," Isaac cautioned, noticing her distraction. "Your enhanced senses are an advantage, but you need to learn to filter out what's unimportant. Always be alert to potential threats."

Suddenly, a big paw swept his feet out from under him. Isaac rolled with the impact, springing up into a fighter's stance with both swords drawn. His left wrist was still bandaged, but he held the sword firmly.

Leona's deep voice came with a hint of amusement: "Always be alert to potential threats."

"Lesson two," Isaac replied, his blades glinting in the sunlight, "never let your guard down."

He lunged forward and executed a series of precise strikes, each movement measured and controlled — a lethal dance honed by years of training. Yet Leona countered his calculated assault with raw, primal strength. The colossal werwulf wove between his swords with the grace of smoke, moving with a fluidity that belied her size.

When Isaac feinted left, telegraphing a killing stroke, Leona didn't take the bait. Instead, she dropped low and spun, her leg sweeping in a wide arc that would have taken out Isaac's legs if he hadn't anticipated it.

He leaped over the attack, his blades creating a cross-cut that should have caught her exposed flank, but he held back. He didn't want to injure her.

Leona dodged, her large figure flowing around his swords like water around stone.

Before Isaac could adjust his stance, she was inside his guard. Her hot breath washed over him as her huge jaws snapped shut mere inches from his throat — a stark reminder that in a real fight, a large part of him would be missing right now. Instead, she placed a paw on his chest and pushed him away with ease.

Isaac went flying but managed to turn the fall into a controlled tumble down a short slope, springing up ready to fight again. However, Faith noticed the slight tremor in his hands and the fresh scratches on his dark skin.

"Your turn," Leona bellowed, fixing her fierce amber gaze on Faith. "Show us what you've got, hybrid child."

Faith stepped into what she hoped was a defensive stance. Her body thrummed with energy, but she had no idea how to wield it.

Leona charged.

Faith's speed allowed her to dodge the initial attack, but she wasn't ready for the subsequent strike. A paw caught her midsection, sending her crashing into a young tree. The impact would have been fatal for a human.

"Get up," Isaac called from his position, frustration evident in his voice. "You're stronger than you realize. Use it!"

Faith rolled to her feet, spitting out bits of vegetation.

CHAPTER 39

Although her body was already healing, her pride was bruised. She struggled to remember Isaac's lessons on form and balance while also considering Leona's advice about instinct. The result was a confused hesitation that left her wide open.

Leona took her down again, pinning her with one large paw. The werwulf's hot breath washed over Faith's face as she growled, "Stop fighting yourself. Your body knows what to do if you let it."

"Easy for you to say," Faith gasped. "You've had your whole life to learn this. I've spent twenty years being taught to hide who I am."

The pressure on her chest eased as Leona stepped back, her fierce features softening slightly. "Then it's time to unhide."

Isaac approached and offered Faith a hand up.

"She's right, though her methods are... unconventional." His fingers lingered against her cold skin. "You have gifts: strength, speed, sharp senses. But they're worthless if fear holds you back."

"I'm not afraid," Faith protested, though her words sounded hollow even to her ears.

"Aren't you?" Leona's voice was gentle despite her fearsome appearance. "Afraid of your power? Of losing control? Of becoming like him?"

The last question hit Faith hard. Vlad's atrocities echoed again in her mind — a legacy of blood and cruelty she could never escape. Her hands began to shake.

"Hey." Isaac's warm fingers caught her chin, forcing her to meet his eyes. "You aren't any of that. The choices of a long-dead tyrant don't define you."

"Precisely." Leona nudged Faith with her massive muzzle, surprisingly gentle for such a fierce creature. She glanced at Isaac, something unspoken passing between them. "We all carry darkness. The trick is learning to use it without letting it use you."

Faith looked between them — Leona's primal power and Isaac's controlled strength — two different approaches to the same fundamental truth. Both had found ways to embrace their nature without losing themselves.

"Show me," Faith said softly. "Show me how."

The next hour was brutal. They ran her through drill after drill, pushing her vampire abilities to their limits. Faith lost count of how many times she hit the ground, how many trees she accidentally shattered with poorly controlled strength, and how many times her senses overwhelmed her at crucial moments.

But slowly, painfully, she began to improve. Her body started recalling the movements, her supernatural instincts aligning with conscious action. She managed to dodge one of Leona's charges completely and even landed a solid hit that made the werwulf grunt in surprise.

"Better," Isaac approved, though his arms bore fresh bruises from demonstrating blocks. "You're learning to think and react simultaneously instead of letting one aspect override the other."

"Time to put it all together," Leona declared, her imposing figure casting long shadows in the dense undergrowth. "Three-way spar. No holds barred."

The idea sent a shiver of dread down Faith's spine.

She glanced at Isaac, expecting disapproval, but instead, the Hunter offered a half-smile.

Chapter 40

They arrived at a relatively flat area next to a rushing mountain stream. The terrain added an extra layer of challenge, with loose rocks, exposed roots and patches of slippery mud lurking to trip the unwary. Faith's stomach clenched. She had managed only a few hits during practice, and the prospect of taking on both opponents sent her anxiety spiking.

"Remember," Isaac said softly, sensing her apprehension. "You have advantages over both of us. Use them."

The stream babbled over the rocks, its steady flow contrasting starkly with Faith's racing thoughts. She attempted to center herself, seeking the delicate balance between thought and instinct that had brought her fleeting moments of success in their sparring session.

"Hunter ready! Werwulf ready! Vampire ready! FIGHT!" Leona shouted, mimicking the soundtrack of a video game.

The werwulf surged at Faith with terrifying speed. While her vampire reflexes allowed her to dodge, she was caught off guard by Isaac's quick follow-up attack. The flat of his blade struck her shoulder, sending her stumbling toward the stream.

She managed to turn the stumble into a roll, recovering just in time to see Leona and Isaac engage in combat. Primal fury clashed with precise skill, power collided with practiced control — a visceral dance of blade and claw.

Faith tried to maneuver around them, searching for an opening. She heard every impact, every grunt of exertion, every shift of muscle and bone. The sound of their heartbeats filled her ears — Leona's heavy with effort, while Isaac's remained steady amidst the chaos. When they separated for a brief moment, she saw her chance.

Faith darted in, attempting to replicate Leona's throwing technique, but her execution was awkward; she telegraphed the move clearly.

Leona caught her arm effortlessly, using Faith's momentum to hurl her past. She tumbled into the stream, the cold water shocking her system. By the time she regained her footing, soaked and shaken, Isaac and Leona were already locked in combat once more.

The werwulf's deadly claws scraped against Isaac's crossed blades as he fought to hold her back. Faith could smell fresh blood from the new cuts marking both fighters. The tension that had simmered all day now seemed to fuel their conflict, intensifying every clash.

Determined, Faith tried again, this time focusing on speed rather than strength.

She landed a solid kick to Isaac's side, but the moment of triumph was short-lived. He turned at the impact, his blade sweeping in an arc that she narrowly ducked under — thankfully, it wasn't aimed at her neck.

Leona seized the opportunity, swiping at Isaac's legs. However, he anticipated the move. Rolling with the impact, he quickly rose behind Faith, using her as a shield against the werwulf's next assault.

Caught between them again, Faith felt the heat radiating from both their bodies and inhaled the intoxicating mix of their scents. Her senses threatened to overwhelm her at the worst possible moment.

She attempted one of the combination moves they had practiced, trying to blend her speed and strength. Instead, her feet became tangled, and she fell hard. Only her supernatural reflexes saved her, allowing her to roll instead of face-planting.

CHAPTER 40

"You're still thinking too much," Leona growled.

"And not watching your footwork," Isaac added, offering her a hand up.

Faith accepted his assistance, feeling the warmth of his skin against her cold flesh. But before she could regain her balance, Leona swept both their legs out from under them. They crashed together in a tangle of limbs before the werwulf pounced on them.

Pinned between them, Faith felt Isaac's solid warmth beneath her while Leona's imposing, furred form pressed against her front. The physical contact sent her senses into overdrive. She felt the steady thrum of Isaac's heartbeat, took in the wild, spicy scent of Leona's fur, and registered the warmth radiating from their bodies against her skin.

"Always be alert to potential threats," the werwulf said playfully.

A twig snapped somewhere in the forest, and all three sprang to their feet, instinctively shifting into survival mode. They moved with unconscious synchronization, forming a defensive triangle.

Faith strained to identify the threat, but filtering the input proved difficult. The forest was filled with stimuli — creaking branches, rustling leaves, small animals scurrying through the underbrush. Any sound could signal something significant or merely an innocent noise.

"Just a deer," Leona said after a moment, her large head turning to track the animal moving through distant trees.

"We should head back," Isaac suggested, suddenly hyper-aware of their surroundings as he sheathed his swords. "You've had enough for one day."

Faith was shaking with exhaustion, her clothes torn and muddy from repeated falls. The training had pushed her well beyond any limits she had previously tested.

"Rest," Leona said calmly. "Learn. Grow stronger." Her muscles rippled beneath her dark fur. "Because next time, I won't go so easy on you."

    Faith managed a weak smile, though her chest ached with confused longing. This day had awakened something in her — not just combat skills but deeper hungers she didn't know how to process. Her keen senses remained focused on both of them, catching every subtle move, quick glance, hitched breath.

    For Faith, what had started as a training session had evolved into something much more complex. As they walked back toward the mansion's protective walls, she couldn't shake the feeling that she was teetering on the edge of both liberation and recklessness — much like her bloodline.

Chapter 41

Days passed within the walls of Vhik'h-Tal-Eskemon. Faith had learned to interpret the mansion's moods as one would read the weather, sensing the ebb and flow of Old Magick pulsing through its foundation. The energy possessed its own personality — sometimes dormant like a sleeping cat, and other times restless like storm winds.

The protective wards etched into the floor had become familiar companions, their soft glow a constant reminder of the sanctuary that still existed in this shadowy world.

But this morning felt different.

Faith first noticed it when the ever-present magical hum shifted to a discordant note, as if a symphony had unraveled into chaos — every note wrong, every harmony jarring.

The air thickened, pressing against her skin like wet velvet. New scents invaded her nostrils — old parchment, grave dust and something else, something that hinted at carefully contained power and knowledge sealed away in forgotten tombs.

Then they appeared, as if birthed from shadow itself — five robed figures materialized in the entrance hall with movements so precise they seemed choreographed. Their boots made no sound against the marble floor, despite Faith's attuned hearing. Even the whisper of their robes seemed muted, as if reality itself bent around them.

The leader lowered her hood with deliberate grace, revealing features as if carved from alabaster — flawless white skin, sleek black hair pulled back sharply and oriental features that revealed no emotion as she surveyed the space. Faith recognized her from her parents' descriptions: Jiangshina, leader of the Magisters.

The reaction was explosive.

"YOU!" The word erupted from Christopher's throat as he lunged at Jiangshina, his face contorted in a snarl that revealed elongated fangs. "You betrayed us! You told Mary where to find us!"

Faith had never seen such fury on her father's face. This was not the controlled dad who had protected her, nor the gentle soul who had taught her guitar. This was something else — an intense fury born of two decades of fear and rage.

The other Magisters moved faster than even Faith's vision could track. One moment, her father was charging forward; the next, he was slammed against the wall with enough force to crack the stone. Two of them pinned his arms, their grip making the tendons stand out on Christopher's forearms.

"Dad!" The word escaped Faith's lips as she instinctively rushed to help him.

Strong hands seized her from behind, their grip like iron bands around her biceps. The overpowering scent of old parchment and cemetery soil made her gag slightly. She struggled, but the one holding her might as well have been made of granite.

"Let her go!" Isaac's voice cut through the chaos like the strike of a sword.

Faith sensed the soft whisper of steel being drawn and felt Isaac shift his weight into a fighter's stance. His heartbeat remained steady, anchoring her amidst the supernatural chaos with his unwavering human determination.

A low growl sent a chill down Faith's spine, bypassing conscious thought and tapping directly into her primal instincts. Before she

CHAPTER 41

could see Leona, she felt the beginning of her transformation. The air around the werwulf rippled and distorted as the change took hold.

Fabric tore as Leona's clothes split at the seams. Bones cracked and reformed while muscles twisted beneath skin that sprouted dark fur. Her face elongated into a lupine muzzle filled with sharp teeth as her body expanded, towering nearly ten feet. Curved claws scraped against the marble floor, and her amber eyes blazed with protective rage.

"No!" The word erupted as a throaty snarl, Leona's voice thick with the transformation. "You don't come here and threaten my friend."

Devan and Lupita followed suit, transforming into their werwulf forms in perfect synchronization. The sounds of their reshaping bodies filled the hall — bones cracking, muscles reforming and primal power unleashed. Now, three enormous werwulfs stood ready to face the robed figures, their lips curled back to reveal teeth longer than Faith's fingers.

The building's magic responded to the escalating violence. The protective symbols carved into the floor flared bright, casting intricate patterns of light across the marble. The temperature dropped, and Faith saw her breath misting in the air; the very stones vibrated with a warning.

Isaac moved to position himself between Faith and the newcomers, but Leona was faster, her colossal body flanking Faith, ready to attack the Magister still gripping her. The werwulf's fur brushed against Faith's arm, radiating heat that contrasted with the unnatural cold in the room.

Caught between Leona's wild protective fury on one side and Isaac's controlled rage on the other, Faith felt disoriented. Perhaps it was the magic filling the air, pressing against her heightened senses like a storm poised to break.

"STAND DOWN!"

Kavisha's voice sliced through the tension, exuding an authority that froze everyone in place. The soft whir of her wheelchair's motor sounded unnaturally loud in the ensuing silence as she entered the hall. The amethysts at her throat pulsed in rhythm with the symbols on the floor.

"There will be no bloodshed in this sanctuary," she proclaimed, her tone resolute. The gems in her jewelry flared brighter, matching the intensity in her dark eyes. "Magisters, release them. Now."

The robed figures turned to Jiangshina, who gave the slightest nod before they released Faith and Christopher.

Faith stumbled as the iron grip fell away, bracing herself against Leona's flank. Her fingers sank into the thick fur, soft as raw silk. The werwulf emitted a reassuring rumble, yet her fierce eyes remained locked on the Magisters. Faith could sense the tension radiating through Leona's body.

The air crackled with competing energies — the ancient power of the Magisters, the primal force of the werwulfs and the mansion's protective magic all converging toward an imminent clash. Faith absorbed every detail of the volatile atmosphere: Leona's thundering heartbeat, Isaac's steady breaths and the way Christopher's hands clenched into fists.

More profoundly, she felt the weight of destiny pressing down on them, as if reality itself held its breath, waiting to see what would unfold.

"Jiangshina." Kavisha's voice, though softened, held a steely edge. "You will explain yourself."

The Magister straightened her shoulders, gathering her composure. When she spoke, her voice was soft and musical, clear as cut glass, imbued with centuries of carefully maintained control.

"We are the watchers," she began, each word deliberate and measured. "We are named such that we are the keepers of lore and

CHAPTER 41

heritage, we are among the…"

"Bullshit!" Christopher's voice snapped like a whip, raw with decades of pent-up fury. "You don't just watch. You're terrified of the prophecy and what Faith represents." His fists clenched again as long-buried rage surged to the surface. "You led Mary right to us! You made that choice!"

The temperature plummeted further, frost patterns creeping across the windows like reaching fingers. Faith felt a shift in the building's protective magic — changing from a warning to a state of readiness, as if the very stones of Vhik'h-Tal-Eskemon were bracing for violence.

"We did no such thing," Jiangshina replied sharply. After a moment, her rigid composure faltered slightly. "But you're not entirely wrong. The truth, as always, lies in the shadows between."

"Then illuminate those shadows," Kavisha commanded, her wheelchair edging forward. "Now."

Chapter 42

Faith noticed Leona's muscles tense beneath her fur, poised to spring at the slightest provocation. Isaac's hand rested firmly on his sword hilt. The air thickened with clashing powers — primal, ancient and controlled — pushing against one another like storm fronts on the brink of collision.

"You speak of choice," Jiangshina said, locking her gaze with Christopher's. Something flickered within the depths of her stare — regret? Fear? "But choice is an illusion when destiny pens the tale. The blood of creation flowing in her veins..." She turned her gaze to Faith. "...could damn us all. Mary seeks to wield it for darkness. We seek to prevent that darkness from rising."

"By killing her?" Christopher's voice trembled with rage. "That's what you implied twenty years ago when you showed up on our doorstep. That we could save the world by murdering my daughter."

Faith felt her father's pain as if it were a tangible presence, observing his hands shake with suppressed rage. Two decades of running, fear and the struggle to protect her culminated in this moment.

"It was one option," the Magister replied, avoiding eye contact with Faith. "What is one death compared to an apocalypse?"

Faith sensed Isaac moving closer on her left side.

"And who granted you that authority?" Isaac's controlled voice carried edges as sharp as his sword. "Who gave you the right to decide

CHAPTER 42

who lives and who dies based on prophecies and possibilities?"

"We are the keepers of knowledge," the Magister intoned, straightening. "The guardians of — "

"The guardians of nothing!"

Nell's voice sliced through the air like lightning. Faith hadn't realized her mother had arrived until she saw her standing at the sweeping staircase, her face a mask of anger that stole Faith's breath. This wasn't the gentle soul who had read her bedtime stories; this was a woman who had endured torture and trauma, someone who had faced true darkness and survived.

"You hide in your ivory towers while others fight and die," Nell continued, her words heavy with firsthand pain. "You cloak yourselves in neutrality while the world burns."

"You know nothing of sacrifice," Jiangshina snapped, her composure cracking for the first time like lightning through storm clouds. "Nothing of the price we've paid to maintain balance."

Faith studied the Magister's face, noticing the mask slip just slightly. Sensing an opportunity and driven by instinct — or perhaps destiny itself — she reached forward and brushed her fingers against Jiangshina's hand.

It worked.

Faith felt momentarily disoriented, as if reality had tilted on its axis. Then the sounds and images flooded into her mind.

***

The metallic scent of blood assaulted her senses first — coating her tongue and flooding her nostrils until she tasted copper at the back of her throat. The scent was so thick and overwhelmingly human that her vampire instincts screamed in response.

The scene crystallized around her with horrifying clarity: Jiangshina kneeling in a pool of cooling crimson that soaked through her once-pristine robes. In her arms lay a broken body — a mortal man whose kind eyes stared sightlessly upward, the laugh lines around his mouth now frozen in a final expression of terror.

Jiangshina's perfect composure, maintained over centuries of calculated neutrality, shattered like glass. Tears carved glistening paths through the mask of blood that covered her alabaster face.

"I'm sorry," she whispered to the corpse, her voice cracking with emotions buried deeper than any tomb. "I'm so sorry, Tobias. I should have protected you better. I should have known he would discover us..." Her fingers trembled as they traced the contours of his face one last time.

A shadow fell over them like a shroud, bringing with it the stench of decay and corrupted power. Zachariah's laughter slithered through the air, sharp like broken glass ground underfoot.

"Consider this a lesson in staying neutral." His voice dripped with cruel amusement. "Next time, don't let your heart rule your head. A Magister, infatuated with a mortal?" He clicked his tongue, the sound obscenely loud in the death-laden silence. "How... very disappointing."

Faith caught a glimpse of his face in the flickering torchlight — severe features twisted into a smile devoid of warmth, eyes burning with a madness masked by certainty.

"The next time you or your Magisters try to stop me," he continued, savoring each syllable like fine wine, "I won't be so quick or so... merciful... in my lessons."

Jiangshina tightened her arms around Tobias's body, pulling him closer as if she could shield him even now. Her tears fell silently onto his still face, mixing with his blood.

"Chronicle this moment, Magister," Zachariah sneered, his voice thick with satisfaction. "Record it well. And remember — neutrality protects you only as long as you maintain it. Break that neutrality again…" He let the threat linger in the air like poison.

The vision began to fade at the edges like burning parchment, but not before Faith caught one final, searing detail — Jiangshina's expression as she looked up at Zachariah.

Beneath the grief and fear, something else burned in her eyes with an intensity that matched his own: hatred. Pure and eternal as darkness itself, promising a vengeance that would outlive empires.

Chapter 43

Faith pulled her hand away with a gasp, reality rushing back in a flood of sensation — the chill air of Vhik'h-Tal-Eskemon, the lingering scent of werwulf musk, the soft whir of Kavisha's wheelchair. But most of all, she felt the weight of Jiangshina's eyes on her.

"I saw exactly what price you paid," Faith said quietly. "I saw Tobias. I felt your pain. Your guilt. Your fear." She swallowed hard, tasting phantom copper on her tongue. "I understand now — why you choose neutrality. Why you would do anything to prevent that cruelty from touching the world again."

The Magister took an involuntary step back, her face crumbling like a mask finally giving way after centuries of wear.

"How did you..." Her voice trembled. "How could you possibly..."

"I saw it in your memories," Faith continued, her own voice trembling slightly. "When I touched you, I witnessed what Zachariah did to punish you. I felt how it shattered you — how you would choose any alternative rather than risk experiencing that pain again."

For a moment, Jiangshina seemed both ancient and youthful — a girl who had lost everything, trapped within centuries of carefully constructed walls.

Faith noticed her mother flinch at the mention of Zachariah's name, and she observed Christopher instinctively move closer to Nell, as if to shield her from even the memory of her tormentor.

CHAPTER 43

"Then you understand," Jiangshina whispered. "You understand why we can't let the darkness rise again."

"We are doing everything we can to track Mary and sto— " Kavisha began.

"NO!" Jiangshina's scream shattered her centuries of composure like glass. Terror seeped through the cracks in her façade. "You don't understand!"

The other Magisters turned to their leader, shocked by this unprecedented display of emotion. The building's magic responded to her outburst; the protective symbols in the floor pulsed erratically, while more frost patterns spiraled across the windows at dizzying speed.

"The blood magic..." Jiangshina's voice trembled as she fought for control. "It isn't about power. Mary isn't trying to become like her brother." Her eyes locked onto Faith with desperate intensity. "She's trying to bring him back."

Chapter 44

The ensuing silence was absolute. Even the mansion's ever-present magical hum seemed to pause.

Faith felt Leona stiffen beside her. The werwulf's fur bristled against her arm as a low growl built in her chest. On her other side, Isaac's breath caught.

"That's not possible," Christopher whispered. Yet Faith could hear the tremor in his voice as he clasped Nell's hand. "Even the darkest magic can't— "

"It can," Jiangshina said, her words falling like lead in the frozen air. "With the right blood. With your daughter's blood." She turned to Faith, her face a mask of barely contained terror. "The corruption that nearly killed your parents? It was a test. Proof that your blood can bridge the gap between life and death itself."

Nell made a sound — between a gasp and a sob — that broke Faith's heart. She watched as her mother's hands began to shake, pressing against her neck and chest as if the phantom pain of past torment had awakened anew.

"The prophecy…" Jiangshina continued, her voice hollow. *"'Yet the Eminence of abominations will rise again.'* We were all wrong. The prophecy wasn't speaking about Faith. It was about him. About Zachariah."

Faith felt the temperature plummet further as the mansion's magic

CHAPTER 44

responded to the mere mention of such darkness. The air grew ice-cold.

"The blood of destruction. The blood of creation. A new Family is born," Jiangshina recited. Each word resonated like a death knell in the stillness. "Your blood won't just create new Red Claws, Faith. It will resurrect their master — their creator. The darkness we thought we had finally cast out from the world."

Faith felt the ground tilt beneath her. Her acute hearing picked up her mother's ragged breathing — an echo of her humanity — and she noted how tightly her father's jaw was clenched, the grinding of his teeth audible.

"Mary doesn't want to rule," Jiangshina whispered, her voice barely discernible, even to vampire ears. "She wants her brother back. To restore what was taken from her. And she will burn the world to ashes to achieve it."

The revelation struck Faith like a physical blow.

All those years hiding in Scotland, believing they were fleeing from Mary — the final Red Claw. The truth was far worse. Faith wasn't just a weapon to be wielded; she was the key to unleashing the very evil her parents had sacrificed everything to escape.

Suddenly, Nell collapsed, her legs buckling as two decades of buried trauma surged to the surface. Christopher caught her, but Faith could see the raw terror in their faces, reminiscent of that first night in Scotland when Mary's forces had finally tracked them down.

"Mom!" Faith rushed toward her mother, but Nell instinctively flinched away, lost in memories of her captivity under Zachariah.

"No, no, no…" Nell's whispered denials shattered Faith's heart. "He can't… I can't…" Her hands pressed against her throat as if Red Claw fangs were tearing at her flesh.

"We won't let that happen," Leona snarled, her formidable presence moving closer to Faith protectively. "He doesn't get to rise again.

None of us will allow it."

"You don't understand," Nell's voice broke. "You didn't see what he was capable of. What he did... what he forced others to do..." She looked at Faith with eyes filled with old terror. "He'll never stop hunting you. He won't rest until he gets what he wants."

"Then we fight," Isaac asserted, stepping beside Faith. "We protect Faith. We stop Mary. We ensure that monster Zachariah stays in whatever hell he's rotting in."

But Faith barely registered their words. Her mind spun with the implications. Every drop of her blood carried the potential for apocalypse. Every beat of her heart pumped destruction through her system. She stared at her hands, questioning how something so fundamental to her existence could also contain such terrible power.

"You're not alone in this," Leona's voice softened. "Whatever comes, we face it together."

"All of us," Isaac added.

Faith felt the conflicting energies surrounding her. Yet, for the first time, instead of feeling torn, she felt... anchored. Protected. Maybe even loved, in two very different ways.

As she watched her mother tremble in her father's embrace, saw the fear in Jiangshina's eyes and felt the very stones of Vhik'h-Tal-Eskemon vibrate with unease, one unsettling truth came to her mind: love alone might not be enough to avert the impending disaster.

Her blood had the power to bridge the gap between life and death. Somewhere in the darkness, Mary was waiting, poised to wield that power and resurrect the greatest evil the world had ever known.

The words of the prophecy echoed in her mind with renewed intensity: *"Blood connects all. Blood is the liberator. Blood is the destroyer. Blood is the answer."*

Chapter 45

Faith's back slammed into an ancient oak with enough force to splinter its bark, sending a shower of wood fragments cascading around her. Despite her preternatural constitution, pain radiated through her body as her bones knitted themselves back together with a series of delicate snaps. The sensation made her wince — healing quickly didn't mean healing painlessly.

The rich scents of crushed vegetation and split wood filled her senses. Sweet sap oozed from the damaged tree, its aroma blending with the earthy scent of the ground and the metallic scent of her own blood, where splinters had pierced her skin.

She barely had time to register these sensations before Leona's bulky mass charged through the cloud of debris. The werwulf's muscles rippled beneath her dark russet fur as she moved with astonishing speed. Each of Leona's powerful paws left deep gouges in the earth, sending small tremors through the ground that Faith felt beneath her boots.

Curved claws raked the air where Faith's head had been just a moment before. Only her supernatural reflexes allowed her to duck and roll, the wind from Leona's strike stirring her hair. She came up in an awkward crouch as fragments of dry bark rained down around her, peppering her shoulders and getting caught in her clothes.

This impromptu training session had been Faith's idea, sparked by witnessing her mother crumpled and broken at the prospect of Zachariah's return. Faith wanted to be strong enough to protect those she loved — to fight and defend them. But now, as she sat on the cold ground, she questioned the wisdom of the sparring session.

A blade whistled through the air — the unmistakable sound of honed steel slicing through the atmosphere. Faith twisted away from Isaac's attack, but not quickly enough. His sword punctured her shoulder with surgical precision, drawing a thin line of blood.

"Too slow," Isaac called out, frustration and concern evident in his voice. "You're still hesitating."

Faith rose to her feet, trying to focus and apply the techniques they had spent hours drilling into her. But her senses overwhelmed her — the thundering of Leona's outsized heart, the controlled rhythm of Isaac's breathing, the way sunlight fractured through the leaves above, creating ever-shifting patterns. Even the breeze carried too much information, wafting hints of deer paths and distant mountain streams.

A low growl rumbled from Leona's chest, emitting frequencies too deep for human ears to detect. Faith felt it in her bones, triggering ancient defense instincts. The werwulf's amber eyes blazed as she pressed her advantage, each step deliberate and measured despite her size.

Faith attempted to dodge again, trying to remember Isaac's lessons about footwork and center of gravity. But her attention was divided among too many distractions: the way Leona's weight shifted for her next move, the subtle changes in air pressure as Isaac circled to her blind side and the persistent chorus of birdsong that her ears insisted on cataloging. Her foot caught on an uneven patch of ground, and she fell hard, soil filling her mouth.

"Get up!" Isaac's voice was sharp. She saw him exchange a loaded glance with Leona. "How many times? You're stronger than this.

CHAPTER 45

Better than this."

But was she? Memories of her mother's broken form resurfaced — Nell crumpled on the floor of Vhik'h-Tal-Eskemon, decades of buried trauma overwhelming her at the thought of Zachariah's return. Faith had spent twenty years being protected. Now it was her turn to protect others. But how could she do that if she couldn't even handle a simple training session?

Thunder rolled overhead, despite the absence of a forecasted storm; the sound resonated deep within her. The sky darkened ominously as heavy clouds gathered quickly. Faith felt the pressure change against her skin, the fine hairs on her arms standing on end. Her eyes caught subtle movements in the forest as animals sought shelter, sensing the approaching tempest.

Yet something else seemed to lurk among those ominous clouds — a sleeping power that whispered of darkness and strength, growing louder with each thunderclap. It called to her blood like an echo across centuries, promising the means to protect those she loved, if only she dared to answer.

She recalled the surge of power from their previous training session — how it had flowed inside her like liquid lightning when she finally let go of her restraint. How she had sped between Leona and Isaac, holding back the werwulf's massive body with just one outstretched arm.

Mary's words from Scotland echoed in her mind: "Can you feel it? It's calling to you."

She had felt it then, the seductive whisper of untamed power. The sensation had alarmed her then, but now, lying in the dirt while Leona and Isaac circled her fallen body, she reconsidered her fear.

Faith made a choice.

She was done being afraid.

Done being weak.

Done being protected.

Chapter 46

Faith closed her eyes and reached for the dormant force within her. Instead of recoiling as she had her entire life, she opened herself to the power that had begun with the Omni-Father, Vlad Tepes, centuries ago.

It began as a cold spark deep in her chest, like swallowing frozen lightning. The sensation radiated outward in waves of dark fire, transforming her once lifeless flesh. Each wave brought heightened awareness — nerves igniting with newfound sensitivity, muscles coiling with predatory strength and senses expanding beyond anything she had previously experienced.

Her hearing sharpened, allowing her to distinguish the individual wingbeats of birds circling overhead. She could hear the sap flowing through the trees, the subtle shifting of roots deep underground and the minute sounds of insects boring into dead wood. The forest transformed into a symphony of life and decay.

Next, scent overwhelmed her, revealing complex layers of information. She could detect the adrenaline flooding Isaac's system, tracking the chemical changes in his sweat that betrayed his underlying frustration. Leona's wild musk carried primal vitality that made Faith's predatory instincts awaken. She even caught faint traces of her own scent — akin to grave dirt and winter storms.

But it was more than just heightened senses; this power reshaped her fundamentally. Her bones felt denser, stronger. The very air against her skin seemed different, as if reality itself had gained new texture.

The sensation was intoxicating.

For the first time, Faith felt whole — as if she had been living only half an existence until that moment. The careful restraint instilled by her parents fell away, like heavy chains clattering to the ground. A dark, exhilarating vitality surged through her, heady like fine wine.

When Faith opened her eyes, both Leona and Isaac took involuntary steps back. She observed their reactions in perfect detail — the bristling of Leona's fur, the dilation of Isaac's pupils. His heartbeat quickened slightly, echoing like a drum in her heightened perception.

"Your eyes," Isaac said softly. "They've changed."

Though she couldn't see her reflection, she felt the difference. Everything was sharper, clearer, more immediate. Colors appeared more vivid yet darker, as if shadows possessed an unfamiliar depth. Each moment unfolded in crystalline detail, stretching out with perfect clarity.

She moved without conscious thought, her body flowing like smoke on the wind. One moment she was on the ground; the next, she materialized behind Isaac. Her cold hand wrapped tightly around his sword wrist before he could react.

The Hunter was skilled, but Faith's newfound strength rendered his resistance feeble, akin to that of a child. She could feel the delicate bones grinding beneath his skin and caught the scent of pain and fear in his sweat.

She twisted, sending him crashing into a young pine with enough force to snap the trunk. The sound of splintering wood mingled with his grunt of pain, creating a harmony that made her dark blood sing. Part of her was horrified at hurting him, but that feeling receded into the background. The entity flowing through her demanded more.

CHAPTER 46

Leona blurred toward her, claws extended.

But Faith perceived the attack with preternatural clarity. Time seemed to slow as she tracked every ripple of muscle beneath dark fur, every subtle shift in weight that signaled the werwulf's intentions.

With deft grace, Faith stepped inside Leona's guard, catching one paw and using the werwulf's momentum to throw her forward effortlessly.

Leona's heavy body carved a furrow in the earth as she tumbled to a stop.

Before Leona could recover, Faith was on her, cold hands finding pressure points on the giant beast's neck that her heightened senses revealed with perfect clarity. She could feel Leona's pulse pounding beneath her fingers and smell the blood rushing just beneath the skin. The dark power streaming inside her thrummed with possibility.

"Faith, stop!" Isaac's voice seemed to echo from a great distance. "You're hurting her!"

But Faith was intoxicated by the rush. How easy it would be to squeeze a little harder, to feel that thundering heart gradually falter and cease. The darkness in her blood craved that moment of ultimate dominance — the ability to hold life and death in her hands.

Chapter 47

Strong arms wrapped around her from behind, trying to pull her away. Faith snarled, a sound void of any humanity, and threw her head back. The impact connected with Isaac's face, a satisfying crunch reverberating through her. She felt his nose break and caught the scent of fresh blood. The smell sent an electric thrill down her spine, making her dead heart flutter in her chest.

Spinning to face him, she kept Leona pinned with one hand.

Blood streamed from his broken nose, soaking his fatigues. The sight should have horrified her, but instead, it ignited something ancient and hungry within her.

Then she caught his eyes. Not fear, as she had expected, but something else. Concern. Empathy. For her. The expression mirrored how her father looked at her mother during her darkest moments, cutting through the frenzy enveloping her.

"This isn't you," he said softly, his hands raised in a non-threatening gesture despite the blood dripping down his chin. His voice carried the same gentle tone he used when helping her practice sword forms — patient and understanding. "Come back to us, Faith."

His words hit her like punches to the gut, breaking the dark shell she'd wrapped around herself.

Faith looked down at her hands, still pressed against Leona's throat. The werwulf's pulse fluttered beneath her fingers like a trapped

CHAPTER 47

bird. When had she transitioned from simple nerve strikes to actual strangling? The presence whispering in her veins had made it feel so natural, so right.

Horror pulsed through her as she realized how close she had come to killing someone she cared about. The darkness receded slightly, allowing rational thought to return. Yet, she could still feel it beneath the surface. Waiting. Ready. Hungry. Not banished, merely restrained — for now.

Faith released her grip and stumbled backward.

Leona immediately shifted back to her human form, gasping for air while massaging her throat. Angry red marks stood out against her olive skin where Faith's fingers had pushed down, making Faith's stomach lurch.

"I'm so sorry," she whispered, the words feeling wholly inadequate. "I didn't mean to... I never wanted..."

But the words felt hollow because part of her *had* wanted it, had reveled in the power of having a creature so strong completely at her mercy.

Thunder crashed overhead, closer now. Fat raindrops pattered through the canopy of leaves and branches. The water felt shockingly icy against Faith's skin, grounding her in the moment. But it couldn't wash away what she had just done — or almost done.

Faith tilted her face up, allowing the rain to cleanse her skin, hoping it would wash away the intoxicating force still humming in her veins.

"We need to talk about what just happened," Isaac said, his voice slightly nasal from a broken nose. He had produced a cloth from somewhere and was trying to stem the bleeding.

"I lost control," Faith admitted, hating how small her voice sounded. She wrapped her arms around herself, feeling suddenly cold in a way that had nothing to do with the weather.

"No," Isaac replied firmly, despite his injury. He took a step toward her but stopped when she flinched away. "You found control — but let it morph into something else. That wasn't blind rage I saw. Your movements were precise, calculated. You knew exactly what you were doing."

The words stung because they were true. When she embraced the darkness, everything had become clear. Each move and attack felt perfectly natural, as if she had been fighting for centuries rather than days. The power revealed not just strength but skill — generations of combat knowledge ingrained in her very blood.

"It felt…" Faith struggled to articulate her feelings. "It felt right," she conceded. "Like I was finally becoming what my blood demanded."

"And that's what scares you," Leona said, her voice rough from the damage to her throat. She had pulled on a spare set of clothes from her pack. "Because you think that what you were 'meant to be' comes from him. From Vlad."

Faith flinched at the name.

Images from the history books flashed through her mind. Did Vlad experience this same dark clarity when he committed those atrocities? Did it feel as natural to him as it had to Faith just moments before?

"I can't be like him," Faith whispered. "I won't."

"Then learn to control it," Isaac said, approaching her slowly, as if afraid to startle her. "What happened today wasn't just about power; it was about choice. You chose to embrace that darkness, which means you can also choose how to use it. You have to be the one in control. Always."

Faith remembered the moment she had decided to awaken the sleeping force within her. It had been a conscious choice, born from frustration and a desperate need to protect those she loved. But the power quickly spiraled out of control, transforming protection into domination.

CHAPTER 47

A flash of lightning illuminated the forest, immediately followed by booming thunder. The storm now roared overhead, its wild energy mirroring Faith's inner turmoil. Rain fell harder, beating against leaves and branches with increasing intensity.

She was drawn to a puddle that had formed from the rain. The surface had settled enough to reveal a reflection, and what she saw made her breath catch.

Chapter 48

Her face looked sharper, the angles more pronounced. And her eyes... they had taken on a darker hue, as if shadows danced in their depths. For a second, she could have sworn she saw Vlad's features superimposed on her own — the elongated face, the defined nose, those harsh lines, the same capacity for cruelty igniting her gaze.

She jerked back from the puddle, but the image felt seared into her mind. Was this her destiny? To become like him, no matter how fiercely she fought against it?

"But what if I can't control it?" The question that had haunted her day and night finally emerged. "What if it controls me?"

"Then we'll stop you," Leona replied matter-of-factly, inching closer despite Faith's earlier actions. "That's what friends are for. That's what pack is for."

The simple declaration hit Faith harder than any physical blow. Friends. Wolf pack. After twenty years of isolation, after nearly killing her, Leona still considered her a friend, closer even. The realization made her eyes sting with unshed tears.

"Besides," Leona continued with a slight smirk, though Faith noticed she was keeping her distance more than usual, "you're not the only one who walks a line between control and chaos. You think it's easy being a werwulf? Always feeling the wild calling, always anticipating the thrill of the hunt. Your body demands prey. It

CHAPTER 48

demands fresh flesh."

"Or being a Hunter," Isaac added. "Carrying generations of hatred and violence, but choosing every day to protect instead of destroy." He gave Faith a meaningful look. "We all have darkness in us. The trick is learning to use it without letting it use you."

Faith studied both Leona and Isaac with fresh eyes as they walked back toward Vhik'h-Tal-Eskemon.

Leona maintained a careful distance — not so obvious as to appear intentionally fearful, but far enough away that she could react if Faith lost control again. Her lean muscles were tense, primed for action. Each time Faith moved suddenly, Leona's heartbeat quickened, and her fingers twitched — an early sign of potential transformation. The bruises on her throat were deepening to an angry purple.

Isaac kept one hand relaxed near his utility belt, a subtle indicator of his true level of comfort.

As they crossed back onto the mansion's grounds, the protective wards hummed around them. Faith noticed how both Leona and Isaac visibly relaxed within the Old Magick's influence. They seemed to trust the wards more than they trusted her now.

"Faith," Leona said, breaking the heavy silence. Her usual confident swagger was replaced by a measured tone. "What you did back there… it wasn't just a loss of control. It was something else. Something darker."

"You weren't just fighting," Isaac added. "You were hunting." His grip on his belt tightened. "I've seen that look before — in the eyes of the worst kind of vampire. The ones who relish the kill."

"I wouldn't have…" Faith began, but the denial faltered. She couldn't truthfully claim what she would or wouldn't have done if Isaac hadn't stopped her.

"Maybe not," Leona said. "But you wanted to. We both felt it and saw it in your eyes." She inhaled deeply, wincing at the pain in her throat.

Faith sensed the distance that had formed between them. These two people, who had begun to mean so much to her, now looked at her with barely masked wariness. The easy camaraderie they had shared earlier felt like a distant memory.

She had wanted to prove she could protect those she loved, but instead, she had revealed precisely why they needed to protect themselves from her.

"We're not giving up on you," Leona said, noticing Faith's expression. "But we'd be fools to ignore what just happened. We know what you're capable of."

Trust, Faith realized, was like glass — easily shattered and painfully difficult to mend. She had broken something precious today. Only time would reveal if it could be repaired.

As they approached the mansion, its shadows seemed to reach for her, acknowledging the darkness flowing within her. She caught a glimpse of her reflection in one of the windows — her eyes still holding remnants of that former power, that former tyrant. Just then, she barely recognized herself. Perhaps that was what terrified all three of them the most.

Before she could flee inside, Isaac stopped her.

"What happened today doesn't have to define you," he said. "But you need to make a choice about how to move forward."

"He's right," Leona added, though Faith observed that she still kept a careful distance. "That power isn't going away. You need to learn to live with it and control it, or it will control you."

The rain began to ease, although thunder continued to rumble in the distance. Faith felt the subtle shift in air pressure, a sign that the storm was moving on. Yet, she could still sense that other storm within her, a force waiting to be called upon again.

What frightened her most was how much she craved to summon

CHAPTER 48

it. The memory of that perfect clarity, the sense of everything falling into place, tugged at her like an addiction. Even now, a part of her yearned to embrace that darkness once more.

Faith took a deep breath and squared her shoulders. She would learn to control this power — not just for her own sake, but for those she needed to protect. The darkness was merely a tool; she had allowed it to become something more today, awakening feelings inside her that she wasn't ready to confront. But she could no longer afford to fear it, especially with Zachariah's possible return looming.

Thunder rumbled one last time, as if nature itself acknowledged her decision. Faith could still feel that coiled potential rippling in her veins like living shadow. But this time, she would be its master, not its slave. She just hoped she was strong enough to keep that promise.

Chapter 49

Faith's thoughts weighed heavily as she stepped back into the protective embrace of Vhik'h-Tal-Eskemon.

Navigating the labyrinth of corridors, a scent reached her nostrils — old parchment and grave dust, timeworn ink and the stuffy air of buried catacombs. Her nostrils flared as she caught the distinct aroma of Jiangshina wafting up from somewhere deep within the mansion.

There was something Faith needed to do, and it involved the Magister. She followed the invisible scent trail.

With each step down the stone staircase, the air grew colder. Flickering shadows from oil lanterns mounted in iron brackets danced across the weathered walls. Faith took note of the stone's erosion; each groove and crack seemed to tell stories from centuries past.

The silence pressed against her ears, broken only by the subtle crackle of flames and the whisper of her own movements. As she descended deeper into the mansion's foundations and entered the grand library, the texture of the darkness shifted. It became thicker and more tangible, carrying a weight and presence that made her skin tingle with ancestral memory.

The power she had embraced during her training still hummed within her body like a slumbering dragon, resonating eagerly with

CHAPTER 49

the library's accumulated Old Magick.

Faith's eyes adjusted to the gloom, revealing towering shelves packed with books bound in animal hides. She moved deeper into the stacks. Her sensitive nose detected layers of scent that narrated the library's history — centuries of dust settled in corners, the sweetness of aging paper, the metallic tang of ink, possibly mixed with blood, and beneath it all, the indefinable smell of time itself.

She found Jiangshina alone among the deepest stacks, her usually perfect posture bent with exhaustion as she pored over an ancient tome bound in cracked brown leather. Other volumes lay scattered across the broad oak table, their pages filled with cramped writing. The wood bore the scars of centuries — gouges from frustrated researchers and in one corner, what looked suspiciously like bloodstains.

Faith noticed the strange diagrams on the pages — concentric circles drawn in substances she didn't want to identify, symbols that seemed to writhe and change when she tried to focus on them and illustrations of rituals that were beyond her comprehension. The dark power she had embraced earlier stirred in response, reaching for secrets that perhaps should remain buried.

Her body still vibrated with that intoxicating strength, making her acutely aware of how easily she could cross the distance to the Magister. Her amplified faculties cataloged every detail: the subtle movement of dark blood beneath Jiangshina's pale skin, the slight tremor in her hands as she turned pages and the vulnerability of her exposed, slender neck. Faith found herself calculating how quickly she could reach the Magister and the ways she could end her life before she could even cry out.

These thoughts horrified her, yet a part of her processed them with chilling precision. Was this what Vlad had felt? This constant awareness of power and dominance, of how fragile others were? Had he experienced this same automatic assessment of weaknesses, this predatory instinct that turned everyone into potential prey?

Faith forced the dark impulses aside, redirecting her focus to why she had sought out the Magister.

"I know you're there," Jiangshina said without looking up, her voice laden with centuries of careful control. Each word was precise, as if she had spent lifetimes learning how to modulate her speech to conceal her true feelings. "Your heartbeat gives you away."

The Magister paused, tilting her head slightly as if listening to something beyond normal perception. "No... not just your heartbeat. Something else. A... resonance." Her fingers tightened around the edges of the book. "Like the echo of a song that was never meant to be sung."

Faith stepped into the circle of lantern light, watching how the flames cast shifting shadows across Jiangshina's face, revealing the subtle signs of stress that her perfect skin couldn't quite mask.

"I wanted to apologize," Faith said, suddenly unsure if this was a good idea. "For earlier. For seeing... him. For sharing your private life without permission."

The memory of Jiangshina's overwhelming grief still burned in her mind, making her own chest ache with borrowed heartache.

Faith took another step forward.

Jiangshina's head snapped up, her eyes widening.

Panic flickered across her features before she could suppress it. She recoiled slightly as Faith drew closer, an instinctive flinch that brought Faith to a halt. The Magister's fear felt palpable; she didn't want to be touched, didn't want her wounds reopened.

But there was something else, too.

Jiangshina's nostrils flared as she caught Faith's scent, and her composure began to fracture. The subtle shift in her posture, the way her muscles contracted beneath her robes, hinted at ancient instincts

CHAPTER 49

recognizing a predator.

"You've been summoning it," she hissed, her voice a mix of disapproval and fear. Each word seemed to extract something vital from her, as if merely acknowledging the darkness was perilous. "I can smell it on you. The hunger." As she gripped the edge of the table, her hands trembled slightly. "You have no idea what you're dealing with."

Faith was taken aback; this was unexpected.

"I need to become stronger," she finally replied, irritated by how defensive and childish her words sounded. "To protect my parents. To fight Mary. To prepare for Zachariah's return."

"Protect them?" Jiangshina's laugh was humorless, shattering the library's quiet like breaking glass. "The power in your blood doesn't protect, child. It destroys. It corrupts. It— " She abruptly halted, pressing her lips together as if suffocating a more profound truth. Her gaze seemed to penetrate Faith, revealing something terrible overlaid on her form. "I can sense it even now, evaluating my weaknesses. Calculating how quickly you could end my life."

Faith flinched, recalling her earlier thoughts about the Magister's fragile neck. Was she that transparent? Was Jiangshina truly that perceptive? The darkness in her blood stirred once more, whispering of how effortless it would be to silence this woman who knew too much.

She buried the thought deep within herself.

"Old blood recognizes its own," Jiangshina continued, her voice low. "I can feel it reaching out from you, testing the air like a serpent's tongue. Tasting for weakness. Searching for prey." She shivered slightly. "Just like him. Just like Vlad."

The temperature in the cavernous room seemed to plummet at the mention of his name.

"We call him the Omni-Father because he is the progenitor of our kind, the source of our lineage," Jiangshina explained, her tone less harsh now. "His barbaric experiments birthed the blood-borne infection that lives within us. We are spawned from cruelty, from brutality, from suffering, from darkness itself."

Faith noticed the tremor in Jiangshina's hands as she began to gather scattered papers into neat piles, as if imposing order on her desk could somehow restore her world to balance.

"But that is our legacy, not our destiny," the Magister continued, a note of resolve in her voice. "We have the free will to choose another path. A more enlightened one. I see that very battle taking place within you. You are the embodiment of the war between light and dark. Radu and Vlad. Compassion and cruelty. Bonded by blood."

Jiangshina turned to face Faith directly.

Faith forced herself to remain utterly still, battling both her instinct to flee and the darker urge to attack. She kept her voice steady.

"Then help me understand it. Help me control it."

A flicker of surprise crossed Jiangshina's eyes at Faith's plea for help. The Magister studied her intently, as though she could see right through flesh and bone.

"You want to understand?" Jiangshina's voice was laden with bitter knowledge as she gestured to the books spread across the table, their pages filled with arcane wisdom. "This is what I've been researching: blood magic, ancient rituals, the price of power and the cost of resistance."

Her fingers danced over a weathered page, tracing diagrams that seemed to shift beneath her touch.

"Your blood is unique — not only because of Vlad's darkness but also because it carries Radu's light. This combination has created something unprecedented." She locked eyes with Faith, an intensity in her gaze that made the air crackle. "Something that could either save us all, or destroy us all. Just like your mother before you."

CHAPTER 49

"My mother," Faith echoed, pausing to reflect. "Is that how Mary found us?" She voiced the question that had haunted her for weeks.

Jiangshina's shoulders slumped slightly.

"Most likely. If Zachariah gave her a vial of your mother's blood before his fall, a spellcaster could use it to locate Nell. Blood calls to blood — it's one of the oldest magics, even predating vampires."

Faith's thoughts flashed back to Scotland. First her home in Scarfskerry and then St Machar's in Aberdeen. Had her mother's blood acted as a tracking device for Mary? It certainly sounded that way. The implications were frightening.

Chapter 50

The Magister looked shaken after mentioning Zachariah, revealing a weariness and vulnerability that was rare in her. The usually composed woman seemed to crumple inward, centuries of control giving way to expose a wounded soul beneath. She looked tired. Vulnerable. Hurt.

"You loved him very much, didn't you?" Faith asked softly, careful to keep her tone gentle. "Tobias?"

Faith was suddenly worried that she had overstepped, pushing too hard against old wounds. But then the Magister's rigid posture softened, like ice melting under spring's first warmth.

"He brought fresh colors to my long, long existence," Jiangshina whispered, her voice thick with memory and unshed tears. "I saw how loving a mortal could make even an immortal's dead heart feel alive again."

Faith thought of Isaac — his steady heartbeat anchoring her during training, the warmth that thawed the cold of her undead flesh. Then she remembered Leona's wild vitality, that primal heat that made her feel almost alive again.

Conflicting desires surged within Faith. Both offered different kinds of salvation. Both threatened different kinds of damnation. But how could she trust herself with either of them when the power sweeping through her blood whispered of dominance and

CHAPTER 50

destruction? How could she choose between such contrasting forms of warmth when her own nature felt so cold?

"Was it hard?" Faith asked. "Letting yourself care for someone so... mortal?"

"Terrifying," Jiangshina replied. "Every moment was precious because I knew it was fleeting. Each touch felt heavy with the knowledge of impending loss." She studied Faith's face. "But you understand that fear, don't you?"

Silence enveloped them, punctuated only by the soft crackle of flames.

"I see how you look at them," Jiangshina said gently, her tone shifting to something softer, almost maternal. "The Hunter and the wolf woman."

Faith's hands clenched involuntarily as memories flooded back of how easily she had hurt them both during training, how the darkness in her blood had yearned for worse.

"It's not just about mortality," Faith said, the words spilling out before she could stop them. "Everything I feel seems... dangerous now. Caring for anyone feels like handing the darkness more weapons to use against me." She swallowed hard. "And when there's more than one person..."

"Ah." Jiangshina's voice was filled with understanding, not judgment. "The heart rarely follows straightforward paths, especially for beings like us, who exist between worlds."

"I could hurt them," Faith whispered. "I already have. And they're so different — one tied to nature's wildness, the other sworn to destroy our kind. How could I possibly..." She trailed off, lost in the impossibility of her situation.

"Tobias used to say that the heart wants what it wants, no matter what fate demands of us," Jiangshina reflected, her voice tinged with memory. "Perhaps your unique nature means you aren't bound by traditional choices. Tobias taught me about finding balance," she continued, her voice thick with emotion. "He showed me how to find joy in simple moments — watching sunsets, sharing meals I couldn't taste but enjoyed through him, and learning to laugh at the small absurdities of life. He also taught me that rigid neutrality without compassion is just another form of cruelty."

Faith inched closer, drawn in by the raw pain in Jiangshina's voice.

"Neutrality without compassion," Faith echoed softly. "Is that why you suggested..." Her words faltered, caught in her throat like thorns.

"That your mother should end her pregnancy?" Jiangshina's smile turned bitter. "It was out of fear. After watching Tobias die, after experiencing that loss..." She shook her head, her impeccable composure finally unraveling. Tears glistened in her eyes. "I convinced myself that preventing one death was better than risking another war. I thought sacrificing an unborn child was preferable to allowing that darkness to spread again."

The confession lingered in the air, heavy and tangible, pressing down on both women. Faith should have felt anger, should have recoiled from the woman who had advocated for her death before she was even born. Instead, she discovered an unexpected kinship. They both had been shaped by forces beyond their control and carried burdens that others could not understand.

Tears began streaming down the Magister's face.

Without thinking, Faith wrapped her arms around Jiangshina's trembling shoulders. The Magister stiffened at first, unaccustomed to such contact. But then, she seemed to collapse inward, centuries of restraint finally yielding to grief long suppressed.

"I miss him," she whispered into Faith's shoulder, her words muffled. "Every day, every moment, I miss him, I miss him, I miss him. And I hate myself for suggesting your death, for allowing fear to drive me to advocate the same cruelty that took him from me." Her hands

CHAPTER 50

clutched at Faith's shirt, seeking anchor points in the emotional storm. "I became what I despised most — someone willing to sacrifice innocence for the supposed greater good."

Faith held her tightly as sobs wracked Jiangshina's slender frame, feeling each tremor ripple through her. The scent of old grief filled the air — salt tears mingling with bitter regret and the library's musty atmosphere. Faith could pick up the subtle hitches in Jiangshina's chest, hear the nearly silent mantra of "I'm sorry" whispered against her shoulder over and over again.

"I forgive you," Faith said softly, holding her even closer.

The words surprised her even as she spoke them, yet she knew they were true. They carried their own kind of power. "You were trying to protect others in your own way, just like my parents tried to protect me by hiding in Scotland. Just like I'm trying to protect them now by learning to control this power."

Faith's voice caught as the parallels struck her.

"We're just imperfect souls doing our best with impossible choices."

Jiangshina pulled back slightly, studying Faith's face with red-rimmed eyes. The lantern light highlighted the tear tracks on her cheeks, making them glisten like silver rivers.

"You're nothing like him, you know. Nothing like Vlad." She reached up to brush Faith's cheek with trembling fingers, the gesture both tentative and tender. "You have his power, yes, but you also have something he never did — the capacity to forgive, to understand, to care, to love."

Faith felt something fundamental shift between them; the careful distance of Magister and subject transformed into something closer to mentor and student, or perhaps even friends. The air itself seemed to change, becoming warmer and less oppressive, as if the library approved of their newfound understanding.

"Will you help me then?" Faith asked, her voice carrying both hope and trepidation. "Help me understand what I am, what I could become?" She gestured to the books surrounding them, their spines gleaming in the flickering light. "Help me learn to control this power without losing myself to it, to avoid becoming like... him."

Jiangshina's face softened with understanding.

"Power doesn't corrupt instantly," she said. "It seduces slowly, one small choice at a time. Each decision to embrace the darkness seems reasonable in the moment — to protect those you love, to prevent greater evils, to prepare for future threats." Her eyes grew distant. "Until one day, you look in the mirror and barely recognize yourself."

Faith thought about how natural it had felt during training — the urge to squeeze just a little harder on Leona's throat, to feel Isaac's bones break.

"I'm afraid," she whispered. "Not of the power itself, but of how much I want to use it. Of how good it feels." She met Jiangshina's gaze. "What if I can't stop myself from becoming like him? What if it's inevitable?"

"Nothing is inevitable," Jiangshina said firmly, taking Faith's hand. "You have something Vlad never did — people who will fight for your soul, who will stand between you and the darkness, even at the cost of their own lives." Her voice softened. "The question is, are you willing to let them?"

Faith reflected on Isaac and Leona, who continued to support her despite knowing the monster lurking beneath her skin. She thought about her parents, who had sacrificed everything to give her a chance to be more than what her bloodline dictated. She considered Jiangshina, who had lost everything to darkness yet still chose to guide Faith toward the light.

In that moment, she no longer felt alone. And sometimes, that was all you needed.

Chapter 51

Faith's bare feet pressed against the damp earth. The rich forest carried layers of scent — decomposing leaves, mushroom colonies and tiny organisms breaking down matter into new life. Nature's cycle of birth and death. Like her own existence, caught between those two states.

Leona emerged from behind a wide tree trunk, already in her imposing werwulf form. Faith's keen senses picked up the heady mix of spice and earth that always clung to the shapeshifter's fur, along with subtle pheromones that spoke of excitement and anticipation. The beast's amber eyes were fixed on Faith with predatory intensity.

Faith felt the darkness stir in her veins, responding to the primal challenge. But this time she didn't fight it or try to suppress it.

Instead, she remembered Jiangshina's words about control and balance. She let the power flow through her dead flesh like liquid shadow, but kept it carefully leashed. No more losing herself to bloodlust. No more letting the darkness decide how far things went.

Her hearing caught every subtle sound — Leona's thundering heart, the scrape of claws against soil, the whisper of branches stirring in the morning breeze. The werwulf's breath came in controlled pants, releasing small clouds of steam in the cool air. Faith cataloged each detail automatically, using her enhanced senses to track potential threats while maintaining focus on her opponent. A key lesson from

Isaac.

The Hunter's absence felt like a physical thing. He had left three days ago, following new leads about Mary's movements. Faith missed his steady presence, the anchor point of his controlled strength. But she couldn't deny that training felt simpler without him here — no competing impulses or confused emotions to cloud her judgment.

Leona struck without warning, her huge form blurring forward at breakneck speed.

But Faith was ready.

She let the darkness sharpen her reflexes while maintaining firm control over its more destructive urges. Her body flowed like water around the attack, each movement precise and measured. No wasted energy, no blind fury. Just pure, disciplined energy.

The werwulf's claws carved furrows in the earth where Faith had been standing a heartbeat before.

Faith used her momentum to slide between Leona's legs, one hand trailing across the soft fur of her underbelly. She could have struck a killing blow. The darkness whispered of how easy it would be. But Faith was in charge.

"Getting slow in your old age," Faith teased as she sprang back to her feet.

Leona's answering growl carried undertones of amusement along with a predatory edge.

"Old age is something you might get to know, in time," she rumbled back. "Then we'll see who's getting slow."

The werwulf spun with that smooth grace that still amazed Faith — her huge body moving like a dancer despite its size — and charged again.

This time Faith stood her ground.

They met in a blur of motion. Cold flesh against hot fur. Supernatural strength against primal power. Faith matched Leona's raw force

CHAPTER 51

with calculated precision, using techniques Isaac had drilled into her.

When Leona swept low with one large paw, Faith vaulted over it while simultaneously blocking the follow-up strike she knew would come.

Her body hummed with the thrill of controlled combat. This was nothing like the blind rage that had possessed her before. She felt every moment with crystal clarity, each movement a conscious choice rather than an instinctive reaction. The darkness enhanced without overwhelming, sharpened without consuming.

They grappled and spun across the forest floor, leaving deep gouges in the soil. Faith registered the tang of their exertion — Leona's wild musk mixing with her own cold scent. Her ears caught the subtle changes in the werwulf's breathing, the way her colossal heart pounded with both effort and excitement.

Then Leona did something unexpected.

As they tumbled together, she suddenly shifted form.

Faith found herself pinned beneath a very human, very naked Leona. The transformation had happened so quickly that their bodies were still pressed together, skin against skin. Faith's heart seemed to stutter in her chest.

Time stretched like honey, thick and golden in the morning light.

Faith became acutely aware of Leona's fever-hot flesh against her cool skin, the press of soft curves, the way their breath mingled in the narrow space between their faces. This close, Leona's scent was overwhelming to Faith's sharper senses — earth and spice and wild places, with feral undertones that made Faith's throat tighten with unfamiliar hunger.

She recorded the slight flush coloring Leona's olive skin, how her pulse fluttered visibly in her throat like a butterfly, the way her hazel eyes darkened with something that wasn't quite predatory anymore. Or perhaps this was a different kind of hunting altogether. Faith caught the subtle dilation of Leona's pupils, heard the quickening of her heart, smelled the spike of pheromones that spoke of desire rather than combat.

For once, Faith didn't immediately look away from the naked form. She had spent twenty years avoiding connection, hiding from intimacy, afraid of what might happen to anyone who got too close. But here, pinned beneath Leona's vital warmth, that careful distance felt difficult... no impossible... to maintain.

Leona's lips curved into a knowing smile. Then she leaned down, closing the distance between them with deliberate slowness. Her eyes fixed on Faith's. Her breath ghosted across Faith's mouth, carrying promises of freedom. The wolf woman radiated heat like a living flame, chasing away the perpetual cold of Faith's undead flesh.

But even in this moment of connection, Isaac's face flashed through Faith's mind — his steady dark eyes, the careful way he touched her during training, how his guarded tenacity offered a different kind of sanctuary. One promised liberation through the embrace of nature's chaos, the other through mastery of the self.

Leona must have sensed her hesitation. She paused, her lips a whisper away from Faith's. Their eyes met, and Faith saw understanding dawn in those fierce hazel depths. The werwulf recognized the war being waged in Faith's heart — not just between different kinds of wanting, but between the concept of wanting itself and the darkness that threatened to corrupt it.

Just before their lips could meet, everything changed.

Chapter 52

Faith's supernatural senses screamed a warning.

The very air seemed to curdle, carrying the smell of the grave and corruption. Her hearing cataloged multiple feet moving with unnatural synchronization through the trees.

"Mary," Faith whispered, the name falling like lead between the two women.

Leona's eyes went wide, ears pricked up, nostrils flared. She sprang to her feet and began shifting. Bones cracked and fur sprouted as she returned to her towering werwulf form.

The intimate moment between them shattered like crystal, leaving behind only the stark reality of impending violence. Faith felt the darkness coil tight in her veins, ready to be unleashed — but this time with purpose and control.

The attack erupted from all directions at once.

Dark figures materialized from the shadows between trees. Blades glinted in the filtered sunlight. The air filled with the subtle wet sound of fangs extending.

Faith's senses went into overdrive. Her hearing caught every footfall, every whisper of cloth. Her nose filled with the cold smell of undead flesh and ancient malice. Her vision tracked multiple threats simultaneously, catching the subtle tells that telegraphed incoming attacks.

The first vampire reached her with unnatural speed.

But Faith moved faster.

The darkness flowed through her like arctic wind, making time seem to stretch and slow.

She caught the attacker's blade arm and twisted.

Bones snapped.

Steel clattered against tree bark.

Faith snatched the falling sword from the air.

More vampires converged.

Faith's borrowed blade sang.

The sound of steel meeting flesh filled the air.

Bodies dissolved to ash.

Black blood sprayed in graceful arcs.

The rich copper scent filled the air.

But she kept control. No blind fury. No losing herself.

She wove between attacks like smoke, letting Isaac's training guide her blade while Jiangshina's words helped her maintain balance between power and restraint.

Leona fought beside her, a whirlwind of fur and fury. Her claws tore through vampire flesh. Her jaws crushed undead bones. The sound of her snarls mixed with the clash of steel and the whisper of bodies turning to ash.

Faith's hearing caught the change in Leona's breathing first — a sharp intake of air followed by a pained growl. She spun toward the sound just in time to see a tall vampire drive his blade deep into the werwulf's side. The scent of Leona's blood hit Faith's nose like a physical attack, rich and vital and terrifyingly abundant.

The darkness surged in Faith's veins, demanding vengeance. But she kept it leashed, using its power without letting it use her.

Three swift strikes left the offending vampire in pieces, his flesh crumbling to ash before he could even scream. Faith's blade moved

CHAPTER 52

with careful finesse, guided by the countless hours of Isaac's patient instruction.

But more attackers pressed in.

Faith found herself trying to protect Leona while fighting off multiple opponents. Her senses picked up the sound of blood dripping from the werwulf's wound, the way Leona's heart had started to labor. They were badly outnumbered, and now one of them was injured.

Then Faith felt it — a subtle vibration in the air, like the first tremors before an earthquake. Leona had sent out a silent call through the pack bond, summoning aid.

More vampires circled them, blades raised.

Faith moved to protect Leona, who was struggling now, her breaths ragged and labored.

Faith's sensitive ears caught the sound of massive bodies moving through the forest at speed. The attackers registered the sound a few moments later, turning their heads in the direction of the rumble.

Devan and Lupita burst from the trees in their werwulf forms, colossal bodies launching into the fray with earth-shaking impact. The sound of their snarls filled the forest as they carved through Mary's forces with savage efficiency. Faith caught the subtle differences in their fighting styles — Devan's raw fury contrasting with Lupita's precision, yet both equally lethal.

Moments later Christopher and Nell materialized from the shadows like avenging spirits. They moved with perfect synchronization, decades of partnership evident in every motion. Nell picked up the sword of a fallen vampire. The blade left trails of silver in the air under her determined hand, while Christopher's bare hands dealt death with terrifying efficiency. He snapped bones, twisted heads and tore through flesh with his teeth.

The battle became a dance of death.

Faith found herself fighting alongside her parents. But the dynamic had shifted fundamentally. She was no longer the helpless child they needed to protect. Instead, she moved to cover their flanks, her borrowed blade intercepting attacks meant for them.

She caught their reactions — Nell's wide eyes when Faith seemed to move in the blink of an eye, almost as if she was teleporting. The way Christopher's muscles tensed when she unleashed controlled bursts of immense power, slicing through their assailants. They had spent twenty years trying to suppress her bloodline, and now they watched as their daughter embraced it with terrifying skill.

Faith's blade sang through the air.

Vampires crumbled to ash.

Blood painted abstract patterns on tree bark before hissing to ash.

The sound of combat filled the forest accompanied by the roar and snarls of the three huge beasts.

Then, as suddenly as it had begun, the attack broke.

The remaining vampires melted back into the shadows, leaving only the acrid smell of dissolution and the copper scent of spilled blood. The forest fell into an eerie silence, broken only by the sound of Leona's labored breathing and the drip of blood from various wounds.

Faith moved to check on the injured werwulf, but her perceptive ears picked up something that made her freeze.

Footsteps moving through the damp ground, but not away from them.

This wasn't a retreat.

This was a regrouping.

The real battle was about to begin.

Chapter 53

Faith felt it first — a chilling sense of wrongness that made her flesh crawl. The forest had fallen into an almost supernatural silence, as if nature itself was holding its breath. Even the ever-present mountain winds faded away, leaving a strange stillness.

Small animals fled through the underbrush in panic, their tiny hearts racing with terror. Birds took flight en masse, their wings beating a frantic rhythm against the darkening sky. Every instinct Faith possessed — both vampire and human — screamed danger.

The ground beneath her seemed to grow colder, frost patterns spiraling across fallen leaves despite the warm afternoon. Faith's fangs grew of their own accord, reacting to threats her conscious mind had not yet grasped.

"Something's coming," she whispered, her voice too loud in the unnatural silence. She noticed her parents exchanging loaded glances — they felt it too.

Then the scents hit her — ancient corruption and ancestral menace, like tainted blood and rotting flesh mingled in the air.

They emerged as if created from shadow, the darkness coalescing into solid forms. Three figures materialized, each radiating power that made the very air crackle with malevolence. Unlike Mary's soldiers, who moved with militaristic precision, these beings each possessed their own distinct gravities.

The first glided forward with serpentine grace, her white-blonde hair floating as if suspended in liquid. She wore an ornate Victorian gown of midnight blue silk and black lace, the high collar adorned with intricate silver embroidery. The air crystallized around her with each step, delicate frost patterns blooming beneath her feet only to shatter with her next movement.

"The hybrid child," said the stranger, her voice a harmony of frequencies. Some tones resonated below even vampire hearing, causing the ground to vibrate in response. "In the dead flesh." Her accent hinted at Eastern Europe, from an era long past. "I expected someone... taller."

"Come now, Magda," rumbled the massive figure beside her. He stood nearly seven feet tall, with shoulders broad as castle gates. His ebony skin bore ritual scars and multiple necklaces of carved bone and ivory hung from his neck. Faith caught the scent of savannah winds and exotic herbs that clung to his emerald green and gold robes.

"Size means little," he thundered, his voice echoing like African drums. Each word struck with physical force, causing the nearby leaves to tremble. "I sense the old power in this one."

"She is mine, Essien," snapped Magda. "I'll drag her back to Mary myself."

"Patience," said the final figure, and Faith sensed the others subtly yielding to his authority. Reality seemed to bend around him like a heat mirage, making it difficult to look directly at his form.

He appeared to be the youngest among them — perhaps thirty when turned — but power radiated from him like warmth from a furnace. His fine features bore an unsettling resemblance to Faith's own, marking him as one of Vlad's direct descendants. He wore an impeccably tailored black suit that seemed from another century, its perfect lines appearing out of place against the forest backdrop. A

CHAPTER 53

signet ring gleamed on his finger, depicting two snakes devouring their own tails.

"We are not common flesh peddlers," he said, each word precise and measured. "We are the Ancients. The True Blood. We have certain... standards to maintain."

"As you command, Dragomir," Magda replied, her tone humble. Ice crystals danced in the air around her mouth as she spoke.

Faith sensed their unique menace — Magda's cold precision reminiscent of a scientist studying an interesting specimen; Essien's barely contained strength, centuries of warrior discipline enveloping primal power; Dragomir's aristocratic disdain cloaking a keen hunger.

"You'll be coming with us, hybrid child," Dragomir stated, addressing Faith. His smile revealed an array of sharp teeth, and the energy around him writhed eagerly. "Mary was right. You have grown strong." He took a step forward, the air rippling around him like water. "But are you strong enough to face those who helped forge the very night itself?"

"Get back to the mansion!" Christopher ordered, his voice tight with barely controlled fear. "Now!"

But retreat was no longer an option.

The Ancients closed in, forming a loose triangle, their power pressing against Faith's senses like a physical weight. She could hear more movement in the trees — dozens of feet moving in synchronization. Mary's soldiers were re-emerging from all directions, boxing them in completely.

They were surrounded. Outnumbered.

Leona's body pressed against Faith's back, blood still seeping from her earlier wound. The werwulf's heart pounded with pain and effort, yet her muscles remained coiled and ready. Faith could feel the heat radiating from Leona's fur and smell the wild musk of her nature mingled with the metallic aroma of fresh blood. Devan and Lupita moved to flank them, while Nell and Christopher shifted into defensive positions.

The darkness awakened in Faith's veins, responding to the power surrounding them. It recognized something in these beings — a kindred malevolence that reached back to Vlad himself. Faith felt it reaching out like smoky tendrils, yearning to connect with that greater darkness.

But she kept her emotions in check, recalling Jiangshina's lessons in the library: *"Power doesn't corrupt instantly. It seduces slowly, one small choice at a time."*

Chapter 54

Magda was the first to strike, her movements fluid and swift. One moment, she was yards away; the next, she had materialized behind Nell with a blade raised. Faith's extraordinary vision could barely track the attack — it was as if Magda didn't move through space but simply ceased to exist in one spot and reappeared in another. The air crystallized in her wake, leaving delicate trails of frost patterns.

Nell managed to partially deflect the strike, but Magda's blade still cut a deep gash across her shoulder. The scent of Nell's blood reached Faith's nostrils — sweet yet familiar and wrong. The Ancient vampire followed up with terrifying speed, each cut precise and calculated. While Mary's soldiers fought with brute force, Magda moved like a surgeon, each strike aimed at tendons and vital points. Ice formed in her blade's wake.

Christopher attempted to assist Nell, but Essien intercepted him. The Ancient relied solely on overwhelming power, dismissing weapons entirely and casually batting aside Christopher's attacks. When he struck, the impact sent Faith's father crashing into a big oak tree, cracking its trunk with the force. Christopher crumpled to the ground, dark blood trickling from his mouth.

Meanwhile, Dragomir entered the fray with composed finesse, distorting reality around him with each movement, making it difficult to track his true position. He seemed to glide across the battlefield.

When Devan charged at him, Dragomir caught the beast's claws with his bare hands. There was a sickening crack, like branches snapping in winter, as he twisted, causing Devan's roar of pain to echo through the forest as bones crunched. Birds that hadn't yet fled took flight at the sound.

Faith attempted to reach the fallen werwulf, but Mary's soldiers pressed in, forcing her back. Her borrowed blade sliced through their ranks, but for each one she struck down, two more took their place.

The cacophony of combat filled the forest — steel meeting flesh with wet thuds, bones breaking like brittle branches, bodies turning to ash with sounds reminiscent of sand falling on stone. The acrid aroma of vampire dissolution mingled with the metallic tang of werwulf blood hung in the air.

Lupita launched herself at Dragomir, striving to protect her fallen mate. However, the Ancient vampire moved like smoke, impossible to pin down. His counter-attack struck her across the face with a sound like a thunderclap, the force spinning her immense figure through the air. She crashed into the underbrush with a whimper that made Faith's heart clench.

Leona fought with desperate fury despite her injury, but blood loss was beginning to take its toll. Faith could hear the werwulf's heartbeat growing increasingly erratic, and her movements became slower and more uncoordinated. When Magda disengaged from Nell and turned her cold gaze toward the injured werwulf, Faith realized with horrifying certainty what would come next.

The Ancient's blade flickered out with inhuman speed, frost patterns spiraling along its length as it moved. Leona attempted to evade, but her injury made her a fraction too slow. The steel cut deeply into her side, just below her ribs. Her legs buckled as more of her vital blood soaked into the forest floor. Ice spread from the wound, prompting a cry of doubled agony from Leona.

CHAPTER 54

"No!" Faith screamed, fighting to reach Leona. But Essien's enormous frame blocked her path. His fist struck her in the stomach like a battering ram, driving the air from her lungs. The follow-up blow took her legs out from under her. She hit the ground hard enough to crack ribs, feeling the bones break only to begin healing, then shattering again under another devastating strike.

Through the pain, she looked up to see her parents trying to reach her. But Magda and Essien moved to intercept them, their centuries of experience evident in every motion. Nell went down under a flurry of precise strikes, while Christopher struggled futilely against Essien's overwhelming strength.

The forest floor soon became a canvas of blood, both werwulf and vampire. Faith's sharp hearing picked up the labored breathing of the werwulfs, who struggled against injury and exhaustion. The coppery aroma of spilled blood filled her nostrils, mingling with the acrid scent of vampire ash. Every heightened sense provided damning evidence of their defeat and impending end.

Dragomir loomed over her, his mouth twisted into a smile devoid of warmth, the shadows around him writhing with eager anticipation.

"You see now the difference between borrowed power and true strength?" he sneered, reaching down with fingers curled toward her throat. "Perhaps Mary will allow us to teach you what that really means."

Faith looked around wildly. She saw her loved ones broken and bleeding around her — Leona barely conscious, Devan and Lupita struggling to rise with their fur matted in blood, and her parents battered and beaten down. The very people who had sacrificed everything to protect her were now lying broken on the forest floor.

Jiangshina's words echoed in her memory once again: *"Power doesn't corrupt instantly. It seduces slowly, one small choice at a time."*

The darkness churned in her veins, reminiscent of how it had felt during training — that perfect clarity, that intoxicating strength that made her want to squeeze harder on Leona's throat and feel Isaac's bones shatter beneath her hands. The memory of their fear and pain twisted in her chest like a knife.

Faith watched as Magda's blade sliced into Leona again, drawing fresh blood from the werwulf who had somehow forgiven Faith, who still believed in her despite the monster lurking beneath her skin. She could hear Isaac's voice echoing in her memory: "You have to be the one in control. Always."

But what if control meant death? What if restraint led to the destruction of everyone she loved?

The darkness beckoned her, promising the strength to save them. Yet she remembered how quickly protection had turned to cruelty during training, how easily noble intentions had twisted into a hunger for dominance. If she let go now, would anything remain of her when the darkness receded? Would she still be Faith, or would she become something else entirely — something closer to Vlad, something that could never again be trusted around those she loved?

Another cry of pain from Leona pierced the air. Lupita screamed in anguish. Faith caught the sound of Nell whimpering on the ground, witnessed her father's futile struggle against Essien's overwhelming strength.

She made her choice.

"I'm sorry," she whispered, though whether to her parents for becoming what they feared, to Leona and Isaac for proving their trust misplaced, or to herself for surrendering, she couldn't tell.

The careful control she had maintained began to crack. The darkness in her blood roared to life, demanding release. This time, Faith didn't fight it. She didn't try to control or contain it.

She embraced it.

She let go.

CHAPTER 54

She simply let go.

Chapter 55

The darkness exploded outward from her like a physical force, causing even the Ancients to stumble back. The very air seemed to snap and fracture as power rolled off her in waves. Her eyes turned black, twin wells of darkness. When she spoke, her voice carried harmonics that should not have been possible from a human throat.

"ENOUGH!"

The word echoed through the forest like thunder. Trees creaked and swayed as if caught in a fierce wind, though no breeze stirred the air. Faith felt the darkness surge through her veins like liquid fire. She did not resist or attempt to tame it. Instead, she directed it, channeling centuries of power toward a single purpose: protecting those she loved.

Her borrowed blade began to glow with dark energy, shadows coiling around the steel like serpents. The metal acquired an obsidian sheen as magic infused it.

In an instant, she sprang to her feet, power surging through her lifeless flesh like an arctic storm. Now, her movements left trails of shadow in the air, each strike infused with the weight of generations.

Magda was the first to recover from the shock. She darted toward Faith with astonishing speed, frost patterns spiraling in her wake. But this time, Faith noticed the subtle distortions in reality that hinted at where the Ancient would appear. She could sense the areas

CHAPTER 55

where reality bent to accommodate such movement. When Magda materialized by her side, Faith's blade was already poised to meet her.

Steel clashed with steel, producing a sound reminiscent of shattering ice, as if worlds were colliding. Supernatural cold met bygone darkness as their blades locked. Magda's perfect features twisted in disbelief as Faith matched her otherworldly speed. Where the Ancient vampire had previously seemed to manipulate time and space itself, Faith now moved with equal fluidity, the darkness guiding her along paths between moments that eluded the naked eye.

"Impossible," Magda hissed, her accent thickening with fury. Ice crystals formed in the air around them, responding to her anger.

She unleashed a flurry of strikes so swift they were blurred even to vampire vision, each cut aimed with precision at vital points.

Yet Faith's weapon intercepted every attack, guided by a power older than herself. Dark energy crackled where their weapons met, sending shadows spiraling through the air like smoke. Each impact generated a discordant symphony of ice colliding with shadow, cold clashing with darkness. For the first time, uncertainty flickered in Magda's ice-blue eyes.

Essien charged in like an avalanche, his mammoth body moving with an agility that belied his size. The ground trembled beneath his approach. However, Leona met his onslaught, undeterred by her injuries. The vampire and the werwulf collided with earth-shaking force, raw power clashing against primal fury.

"You dare challenge one who crushed the bones of Nyamwezi, the king of wolves?" Essien's voice boomed as he grappled with Leona. The air vibrated with the force of his words, making the leaves quiver on their branches.

This time, however, he faced not just one werwulf, but three. Devan and Lupita flanked him, their bulky forms attacking the vampire from multiple angles. While he focused on blocking Leona's huge claws,

Devan's teeth sank into his shoulder. As he turned to dislodge Devan, Lupita's strike brought his legs collapsing beneath him.

Essien crashed down with enough force to crack the earth beneath him, sending tremors through the forest floor. His roar of anger resonated with deep tones, producing frequencies that defied the natural order. Though he was down, he was far from defeated.

Amid the chaos, Dragomir moved like a dancer, seemingly untouched by the violence around him. Reality bent and warped in his wake, making it difficult to pinpoint his true location. Now Christopher and Nell faced him as one, their decades-long partnership evident in every synchronized movement.

When Dragomir struck at Christopher, Nell was there to parry with her blade. When he attempted to circle behind her, Christopher's counterattack forced him back. They moved like well-rehearsed dancers, each anticipating the other's needs.

"Mere children," Dragomir sneered, his hawkish features twisted into a smile that did not reach his eyes. Shadows writhed around him like living entities. "I was there when the Omni-Father bestowed the gift upon us. When the seas ran with— "

His boasting was abruptly cut off by a grunt of pain as Faith's darkness-infused blade opened a deep gash across his chest. The Ancient vampire staggered back, genuine shock replacing his carefully composed façade as black blood welled from the wound. The liquid moved with an unnatural slowness.

"You talk too much," Faith said.

Magda saw an opening and struck, her body seemingly folding through space as she reappeared behind Faith. Ice crystals formed in her wake, creating deadly yet beautiful patterns in the air. But Faith was no longer merely a spectator; she could anticipate Magda's movements. When Magda reformed, Faith's blade was already arcing toward her throat.

CHAPTER 55

The Ancient vampire's eyes widened in disbelief as her head was severed cleanly. For a brief moment, she remained intact — an alabaster statue caught in eternal surprise. Then her flesh began to crack like ice, dark energy leaking from the fissures. She had just enough time to whisper, "How…" before her body exploded into a cloud of frozen ash, centuries of existence reduced to crystalline dust that sparkled momentarily in the air before dissolving.

The death of one so old sent a shockwave through the battlefield. Even Dragomir paused, his aristocratic features betraying genuine fear for the first time. The remaining vampires shifted uneasily, their harmony of movement faltering as old certainties crumbled around them.

Essien roared in fury at his companion's death, his huge body blurring toward Faith with singular intent. Any thoughts of capturing Faith alive to take back to Mary vanished from his frenzied eyes. However, his rage made him careless. The three werwulfs moved as one, forcing him off balance as he charged. Their immense bodies became a coordinated dance of fur and fang, each attack precisely timed. As he turned to face them, Faith struck.

Her blade plunged into his back, finding its mark in his heart. The giant's ritual scars flared brightly with defensive magic, striving to protect his flesh. Colors that defied nature blazed from the markings as centuries-old protections activated. Yet Faith's power, drawn from both light and dark bloodlines, proved stronger. Cracks spread across his ebony skin like lightning bolts, each fissure leaking his life force. His bulky body seemed frozen in time, trapped between existence and dissolution.

"No," he rumbled, his voice fading into frequencies beyond hearing. "We are the True Blood… we cannot…"

With lightning speed, Faith whipped her blade back out, shadows trailing in its wake. The steel sang with dark harmonics as she swept it across his neck in a blur.

His enormous form began to crumble, flesh turning to ash from the outside in. As his body disintegrated, Faith sensed tribal battles, forgotten rituals and ceremonies older than civilization itself through the cracks in his flesh. His final expression was one of utter incomprehension before he completely dissolved, leaving behind only a great pile of dark ash and the lingering electric scent of magic. The very air seemed to exhale as his power dispersed.

Dragomir stared at the remnants of his fellow Ancients, his once careful composure shattered. Where he had moved with inhuman grace, he now stumbled backward like a newborn fawn. Reality ceased to bend around him as his concentration faltered.

"RETREAT!" he commanded, his voice cracking like thin ice. The shadows that had eagerly served him scattered like startled birds.

The remaining vampires needed no further prompting. They melted into the trees, racing to follow their master in desperate flight. Their once-perfect synchronicity dissolved into barely controlled panic as they fled.

Chapter 56

The forest fell silent, save for the sounds of labored breathing and the steady drip of blood onto leaves. Faith sensed the darkness beginning to recede, its purpose fulfilled. It settled back into her veins like a sleeping dragon, no longer demanding release. She turned to check on the others, her keen senses registering their conditions.

Leona appeared to be in shock, her substantial form trembling as the battle fury faded. Devan and Lupita supported their daughter, concern etched across their tired faces. Faith's own parents moved to her side, their movements still echoing the harmony of their fighting.

The forest around them bore the scars of supernatural combat — shattered trees, scorched earth and frost patterns slowly melting in the returning warmth. The air crackled with residual power as esoteric magics dissipated like smoke on the wind. The heavy scent of dissolution lingered, a reminder of how close they had come to destruction.

Faith kept her guard up until her heightened hearing confirmed that the attackers were truly gone and the sounds of the forest began to return. Her eyes gradually returned to their normal state, though the borrowed blade still held traces of shadow.

The forest seemed to exhale alongside her. Birds cautiously resumed their songs and insects began their chorus anew. The natural world was reasserting itself, a magic and wonder of its own kind.

When she turned, Faith found everyone staring at her. It was her parents' reactions, however, that tightened her chest.

Christopher stood frozen, his hands trembling slightly at his sides. He appeared caught between instinctive fear and desperate hope. This was the man who had spent twenty years teaching her control, instilling restraint in her from her earliest moments of awareness. Now, he was watching his daughter embrace the very power he had feared would consume her.

"Faith," he whispered, her name catching in his throat like a prayer. "That was..." He took a halting step forward, then another. "I've never seen anything like it. It..." His words faltered.

Nell's reaction was even more profound. Silent tears streamed down her face, glimmering in the returning sunlight like diamonds. This was the woman who had endured unimaginable torture at Zachariah's hands, who understood all too well the corruption that power could bring. She had spent two decades trying to shield Faith from that darkness.

"I understand now," Faith said, meeting their gazes. The darkness pulsed gently, like a second heartbeat. "I see why you were so afraid. Why you tried to protect me from this." She looked down at her hands. "But I'm not just Vlad's blood. I'm not merely the legacy of corruption and cruelty. I'm your daughter too. You taught me compassion, control, love. That is as much a part of me as any darkness."

Nell's breath wavered, possibly on a sob. She stepped forward and pulled Faith into a fierce embrace. Faith felt her mother's tears against her neck and heard the subtle catch in her breathing. Christopher wrapped his arms around them both, and for a moment, they were simply a family — no longer vampires or prophecy or destiny, just parents and child holding each other in an unforgiving world.

Chapter 57

Faith's knuckles hovered inches from the door, her fist clenched yet unable to complete the motion of knocking. The rich scent of Serafin's healing herbs wafted through the thick wood, mingling with subtler notes of antiseptic and bandages, all underlined by the smell of blood. Muffled voices drifted from within; Serafin murmured incantations as she worked, her tone tinged with exhaustion, interspersed with Leona's pained groans.

Since the battle, the spellcaster had tirelessly tended to the injured, first stabilizing Leona's wounds and then moving on to Devan and Lupita, before returning her focus to the young werwulf. Faith's sensitive nose detected the lingering traces of herbs and magic in the hallway, invisible footprints marking Serafin's path between patients.

Faith chastised herself for not having acted faster during the battle. She should have anticipated Magda's strike. Been quicker. Stronger. She should have protected them all more effectively. Once again, others had suffered because of her.

Her fingers traced the ornate carvings on the door frame — protection wards humming with Old Magick. The symbols seemed to writhe under her touch, responding to the darkness still lingering in her blood after the fight. Startled, Faith quickly pulled her hand back, unsettled by how readily the wards recognized her nature.

"Faith."

Kavisha's voice echoed down the corridor, making Faith's shoulders tense. The soft whir of the High Chancellor's wheelchair grew louder as she approached, clad in a deep crimson sari threaded with gold, a color reminiscent of fresh blood. The gems at her throat pulsed rhythmically with Vhik'h-Tal-Eskemon's protective magic.

"The emergency council has gathered," Kavisha said, her tone gentle yet firm. "They are waiting."

Faith cast one last glance at Leona's door before following Kavisha down the corridor toward the mansion's grand drawing room. Each step felt heavier than usual, burdened by the weight of impending judgment.

Her senses captured every detail around her — the afternoon light slanting through stained glass windows, casting colorful shadows across the marble floors; the whisper of Kavisha's sari as she maneuvered her wheelchair with practiced skill; and the subtle vibration of protective magic pulsing through the stones.

The drawing room doors stood open, revealing the assembled group inside. The space felt smaller than usual, crowded with tension and unspoken fears. Dark wood paneling absorbed the scant natural light filtering through the heavy curtains, while a massive fireplace cast dancing shadows across bookshelves and the worried faces of those gathered.

Faith's parents sat together on one of the leather-backed sofas, their postures revealing the lingering pain from the battle. Christopher's jaw was clenched tight, while Nell nervously worried the hem of her sleeve — a habit Faith hadn't seen since their days in Scotland. A mark from Magda's ice blade marred Nell's neck, although the wound was slowly healing.

Devan and Lupita occupied another couch, their bodies displaying similar signs of combat. Faith noticed how Lupita leaned away from her left side, where Dragomir's strike had landed, while Devan's right

CHAPTER 57

arm hung stiffly after Essien had nearly torn it from its socket. Their wild scents merged with the undertones of Serafin's herbs and healing magic.

Jiangshina stood by the fireplace, her usually perfect posture slightly bent from either exhaustion or worry — perhaps both. The other Magisters were arranged around the room like dark sentinels, their robes absorbing the shadows. Faith noticed that one was missing.

As Faith entered, all eyes turned to her. She felt the weight of their attention pressing against her skin. The darkness in her blood stirred in response, but she kept it carefully leashed, determined not to give them any reason to fear her.

"Please, sit," Kavisha said softly, gesturing to an empty armchair.

Faith sank into the plush seat, noticing how everyone else subtly looked away from her — movements her sharp awareness registered with painful clarity. Only Jiangshina met her gaze directly, conveying understanding rather than fear.

The fire crackled in the hearth, its light catching the gems in Kavisha's jewelry and making them pulse like captured stars. The flames cast twisting shadows on the walls, their dance mirroring Faith's inner turmoil as she braced for the judgment that was about to come.

"The Ancients' attack changes everything," Kavisha began, her bangles chiming softly as she adjusted her position. The sound felt loud in the tense silence. "Mary isn't just gathering followers anymore. She's mobilizing forces we hadn't even considered." Her eyes found Faith's. "And she's becoming increasingly desperate to capture you."

"Then let her come," Devan growled, his human voice resonating with the undertones of his wolf nature. "We killed two of her precious Ancients. Let her send more."

"At what cost?" Kavisha's reply was sharp, making the gems at her throat pulse with a responding energy. "Look at yourselves. Look at what this battle has already cost us." She gestured toward the door, beyond which Leona lay recovering under Serafin's care. "How many more will be hurt or even killed before this ends?"

Faith again felt the weight of guilt pressing down on her chest.

"What are you suggesting?" Christopher asked, although his tone indicated he already knew the answer. He gently squeezed Nell's hand.

Kavisha's hands paused on the arms of her wheelchair, her sudden stillness capturing everyone's attention. When she spoke, her voice bore the weight of centuries of difficult decisions.

"Faith must remain within Vhik'h-Tal-Eskemon's protective walls," she stated firmly. "At all times. No more training sessions on the grounds, no more risks." She raised a hand as protests began to rise. "This isn't a suggestion. The Council has already made its decision."

The words settled heavily in the silence. Faith felt a deep shift within her, as if the very air had become harder to breathe.

"No," she said.

The word escaped as a whisper, yet it held enough power to make the protective wards in the floor pulse in response. "You can't just lock me away again."

"It's not imprisonment," Kavisha replied hastily — perhaps too hastily. "It's protection."

"It's the same thing!"

Faith shot to her feet, her movements infused with unnatural speed. Several people flinched, and she noticed the subtle shift in posture from the Magisters, their hands inching forward as if preparing to attack or defend. Their fear only fueled her desperation.

"Faith," Nell began, reaching for her daughter.

But Faith stepped away, unable to bear her mother's touch at that moment. The gesture of rejection made Nell's face crumple, amplifying Faith's own anguish.

CHAPTER 57

"You don't understand," Faith continued, her voice trembling. "I've just started to live. Really live." Her hands shook as she struggled to convey her feelings. "I know what it means to embrace my nature instead of hiding from it. To exist in the world rather than merely watch it through windows."

"Your courage is admirable," Kavisha said. "But courage without wisdom leads only to destruction."

"And wisdom without action is just cowardice," Faith retorted, her words sharper than she intended. The darkness inside grew, resonating with her escalating emotions.

Jiangshina exchanged a knowing look with her, while Devan nodded in approval.

Faith took a slow breath, recalling Isaac's teachings about control. The memory of his calm presence ached in her chest; he should be here, offering his quiet strength and unwavering support. Instead, he was out there, hunting Mary's forces while Faith faced the threat of imprisonment.

"I understand why you're trying to protect me," Faith said, her voice softening. "But locking me away won't save anyone. It will only ensure that Mary eventually wins." She met Kavisha's gaze directly. "She's not afraid. She's not hiding. She's out there right now, gathering forces and spreading her poison. Every moment we spend cowering behind these walls is another moment she grows stronger."

Her eyes met Jiangshina's. "You taught me that control comes from choice and that power must be mastered, not suppressed." Turning to her parents, she added, "And you taught me about sacrifice — about fighting for what matters, no matter the cost."

The hearth fire crackled, casting flickering shadows over worried faces.

"There has to be another way," Nell said softly, her voice echoing old fears. "Some compromise between freedom and confinement."

"There isn't," Devan replied, his tone heavy with certainty. "Not anymore. Mary made sure of that when she sent the Ancients. That's a declaration of war in my book."

Faith knelt before her mother, taking her cold hands in her own. "I know you're scared. I am too. But I can't go back to living in fear. I won't."

The sound of running feet in the corridor made everyone sit up. Faith detected the urgent rhythm of the footsteps, causing a prickle of foreboding on her skin.

Chapter 58

The missing Magister appeared in the doorway, his robes disheveled.

"High Chancellor," he gasped, "we've just received confirmation. Mary's forces... when they were in Scotland... they took St Machar's Cathedral."

Faith felt her mother's fingers tighten almost painfully around hers. Her own legs weakened, forcing her to grip Nell's hands tighter for support.

St Machar's — where they had sought sanctuary in those terrifying first days after fleeing Scarfskerry. Where her father had lain bleeding from Mary's hexed blade. Where her mother had held her while she trembled with fear.

The memories washed over her with vivid clarity — the way the talisman's energy had wrapped around them like a mother's embrace. She remembered tracing her fingers along walls that had sheltered their kind for centuries, feeling the accumulated power of countless vampires who had given a part of themselves to strengthen those wards. The sacred space had given them precious time to heal, to plan, to hope.

"The sanctuary..." Kavisha whispered, genuine fear lacing her voice. "How did they breach the wards?"

"They didn't need to," the Magister replied, speaking faster now. "Certain Council members have sided with Mary — Gustav Nielsen and Loshua Dascălu. They disabled the protections from within." His voice faltered. "The talisman... Mary Magdalene's tear... they've taken it."

The words triggered something in Faith's mind — that terrible vision from the beach in Scarfskerry when Mary had reached for her. Like a key turning in a lock, the fractured images suddenly aligned with crystal clarity: a woman kneeling at the foot of a rough wooden cross, her tattered shawl unable to contain the cascade of dark hair beneath. Those distinctive features — high cheekbones, prominent nose — twisted in grief as tears carved paths down her face. Not just any woman's tears, but Mary Magdalene's, shed as she watched her savior die.

That vision hadn't just been of the past — it had been a warning of this moment, of Mary seizing an artifact sanctified by perhaps the most profound grief in human history. A tear that had fallen at the very intersection of divine and mortal, of death and resurrection. The symbolism was shattering.

"Then it's begun," Kavisha said softly, glancing at Jiangshina, who gave the briefest of nods. The High Chancellor's bangles chimed as her hands trembled. "Mary isn't just gathering forces. She's collecting the artifacts of power — items needed for the resurrection ritual." Her eyes locked onto Faith's, holding no hint of compromise. "The decision is final. You will remain within these walls where we can protect you. Where Mary cannot reach you."

Faith's gaze dropped to the protective wards pulsing in the floor — so similar to the ones that had failed at St Machar's. The ones breached not by force, but by betrayal.

"You think these walls will protect me?" she asked, her voice hollow. "St Machar's stood for centuries. Its magic was anchored in hope and sacrifice. And it fell." She looked up, meeting Kavisha's eyes. "How long before that happens here?"

CHAPTER 58

The silence that followed held no answer, only the weight of history repeating itself — sanctuaries becoming prisons, protection turning to confinement, safety purchased at the cost of freedom. Just as the Old Magick had crumbled in St Machar's walls, Faith felt her own walls closing in.

"You can't do this," she whispered.

"We can, and we must." Kavisha's voice was gentle yet unyielding. "Our wards will be strengthened. Guards will be posted. You will be safe here."

Chapter 59

Safe. The word echoed in Faith's mind as she stood, her legs feeling unnaturally heavy. She moved to the window, needing to glimpse the outside world. The grounds where she had trained with Leona and Isaac stretched before her — the torn earth, scattered leaves and broken branches all testament to moments of freedom she could not reclaim.

Her vision captured every detail she was now denied: the way sunlight danced on the forest beyond the grounds, the subtle movements of creatures in the undergrowth and the endless sky that once promised a world of possibilities. Now, it all mocked her from a distance that felt insurmountable.

As she turned back to the room, the protective wards pulsing in the marble floor appeared transformed. Where they had once offered sanctuary, they now resembled prison bars. The gentle vibration of protective magic gliding through the stones was no longer comforting; instead, it felt suffocating.

The darkness in her blood recoiled at the thought of confinement, but there would be no escape this time. No distant shore to offer refuge, as it had in Scotland.

As she passed another window, she stopped and pressed her hand against the cold glass. The training grounds blurred behind a film of tears she could not shed. She recalled the wild energy of Leona

CHAPTER 59

during their sparring matches, Isaac's steady guidance as he taught her blade work, and the simple joy of testing her limits beneath a vast open sky.

All of that was gone now, reduced to memories she would have to cling to behind these old walls.

"I understand this is difficult," Kavisha said softly from behind her. "But in time—"

"No," Faith interrupted, her voice raw. "You can't understand. None of you can." She turned to face them, allowing them to see the truth in her eyes. "I spent twenty years watching the world pass me by in Scotland. Twenty years learning to make myself smaller, quieter, less than I am. And just when I finally learned to stop being afraid of my own shadow…"

She trailed off, her heightened senses overwhelmed by the reality of her new prison — the pulsing wards, the thick walls blocking out most outside sounds, the curtains dimming the natural light in the room.

"This isn't just about protection," she continued, her voice barely above a whisper. "This is about fear. Your fear. My fear. The same fear that kept me hidden in Scotland."

Jiangshina stepped forward, her composure faltering slightly. "Sometimes fear exists for a reason," she said softly, her voice melodic. "It's a natural instinct designed to keep us alive."

"But is it living?" Faith asked, letting the question linger in the air. "Or is it just existing?"

She surveyed the grand drawing room — the ornate furniture, towering floor-to-ceiling curtains and countless rows of books lining the shelves.

"This place…" she gestured to their surroundings, "is beautiful, filled with knowledge, history and power. But it's still a cage. A bigger one than Scotland, perhaps. A more elegant one. But still a cage."

"A cage that will keep you safe," Kavisha insisted. "It will prevent you from becoming Mary's tool for Zachariah's resurrection."

"Safe," Faith echoed, the word bringing no comfort. "Like St Machar's was safe? Like anywhere is truly safe while Mary grows stronger?" She shook her head. "You're not protecting me. You're just delaying the inevitable."

"Faith," her mother began, but Faith couldn't bear to hear whatever justification was coming.

"Don't," she whispered. "Please. Don't try to make this better. Don't tell me it's for my own good, or that I'll understand someday, or that time will ease the pain." Her voice cracked. "Because we both know those are lies. We both know what imprisonment does to the soul — how it twists you inside until you can barely remember who you used to be. I saw that in you. I felt it."

She watched as the truth of her words struck her mother like blows. Nell's face crumpled as memories of her own captivity resurfaced. Christopher moved to support her, but his gaze remained fixed on Faith's face. She recognized the conflict in him — his instinct to support his child clashing with his understanding of the impact Faith's words were having on Nell.

"The Council's decision is final," Kavisha said. "I'm sorry, Faith. Truly. But this is how it must be."

The darkness in her blood roiled with helpless fury.

Her thoughts turned to Isaac, out there somewhere, hunting Mary's forces while she remained confined behind these suffocating walls. She thought of Leona, recovering from wounds sustained while protecting her — wounds that Faith could never repay with anything but absence. Every connection and possibility felt like it would wither behind these ornate gothic walls.

As Faith faced the bitter truth, she felt the salt tears burning her

CHAPTER 59

eyes finally fall. She had ended up right back where she started: a prisoner.

Chapter 60

Faith's bare feet made no sound on the cold marble floor as she approached the door. The familiar scents of herbs and tinctures intensified with each step — sage and yarrow, lavender and wintergreen.

The protective wards of the mansion pulsed beneath her feet, their glow seeming to mock her with promises of safety that felt more like chains. She forced her darker thoughts down. She hadn't come here to dwell on her captivity. She had come to see her friend.

Faith picked up movement behind the heavy oak door — the rustle of Serafin's robes, the clink of glass vials and, most importantly, the steady rhythm of Leona's heartbeat. It was stronger than it had been after the battle, though still not quite its usual thunderous pulse.

She raised her hand to knock but hesitated, recalling how the werwulf had fallen to Magda's blade. The image was burned into her memory: Leona's towering body crumpling, blood soaking into russet fur, ice spreading from the wound — all because of Faith. Because of who she was, and what she was.

Before she could retreat, the door swung open, revealing Serafin's exhausted face. Dark circles shadowed the spellcaster's eyes, and her usually pristine robes were stained with herbs and blood. Nonetheless, she managed a wan smile at the sight of Faith.

"I thought I sensed someone lurking," she said softly, her voice

CHAPTER 60

rough with fatigue.

Faith noticed the henna patterns on her hands glowing fitfully, like dying embers — a sign of depleted magic, Faith reasoned.

"How is she?" Faith asked.

"Healing." Serafin stepped aside, allowing Faith to enter. "Though not as quickly as she'd like. Werwulfs are stubborn patients."

"I heard that," came Leona's voice from within, laced with a hint of her usual growl despite being in human form.

As Faith stepped past Serafin into the chamber, her keen eyes adjusted instantly to the dim light. Candles flickered in wall sconces, their flames reflecting off countless glass vials and brass instruments. Bundles of dried herbs once again hung from the ceiling, filling the air with their pungent aromas. Yet Faith's attention was immediately drawn to the figure on the wide bed.

Leona lay propped up on pillows, her olive skin several shades paler than usual. Bandages wrapped her torso, stark white against her dusky complexion. Her long black hair was tied back in a messy braid, revealing the sharp angles of her face. Despite her condition, her hazel eyes retained the wild light that made Faith's breath catch.

"You look terrible," Faith said, trying to use humor to mask her concern.

"You should see the other guys," Leona replied with a weak smirk. "Oh wait, you can't. They're ash."

Faith noticed Serafin swaying slightly by the door, her hands trembling as she arranged vials on a nearby shelf. The spellcaster's exhaustion was evident in every movement.

"When was the last time you rested?" Faith asked her gently.

"There hasn't been time," Serafin murmured, her shoulders slumping at the question. "The wounds from the Ancients cut deep. It takes me… extra effort."

Faith understood what that meant — Serafin was working twice as hard to compensate for her fractured magic, the missing half of her power that had walked away with her twin sister. Remembering the harrowing vision of Serafin's past made Faith's chest ache.

"Go," she said softly. "I'll stay with her. You need to rest."

"But the bandages need changing, and the pain salve—"

"Can wait an hour," Faith interrupted. "You're no good to anyone if you collapse."

Serafin hesitated before nodding. "One hour," she agreed. "Try to keep her from doing anything stupid."

"Hey!" Leona protested from the bed. "I'm right here!"

"Yes," Serafin replied dryly, "that's exactly why I said it."

With that, the spellcaster gathered her robes and slipped out, leaving Faith alone with Leona.

The candles flickered briefly in the draft from the closing door, casting dancing shadows across the walls. Faith stood awkwardly by the bed, suddenly unsure of herself.

"So," Leona said, breaking the silence. "Are you going to hover there like a vampire bat, or are you going to sit down and tell me what's wrong?"

Faith carefully perched on the edge of the bed, hyper-aware of every movement. Her senses cataloged details automatically — the slight catch in Leona's breathing as she shifted, the subtle increase in her heart rate at Faith's proximity, the lingering scent of her blood beneath the herbal poultices.

"What makes you think something's wrong?" Faith attempted to keep her voice light.

Leona's expression softened. "Because I know you, bloodsucker," she replied. "And because you're doing that thing with the hem of your sleeve."

Like mother, like daughter.

Faith forced her fingers still.

CHAPTER 60

"The Council met today," she finally said, the words feeling heavy. "They've ordered me to remain within the mansion. At all times. I'm effectively trapped."

"What?" Leona attempted to sit up straighter but winced as the movement pulled at her wounds. "They can't do that!"

"They already have." Faith's voice cracked slightly. "After what happened with the Ancients… they say it's too dangerous for me to be outside the wards."

"Bullshit," Leona growled, her eyes flashing amber — a sign of her wolf nature rising, despite her injuries. "That's not protection, that's imprisonment."

The word hung heavily in the air between them.

Faith felt something inside her crack as she heard her own thoughts echoed back to her.

"Sometimes I wish…" she began, then paused.

"What?"

"Sometimes I wish vampires were more like werwulfs," Faith admitted. "You're so… free. Wild. Untamed." She gestured vaguely. "Your father back at the meeting — even injured — his first instinct was to fight, to face the threat head-on, instead of hiding behind walls."

"Yeah, well, look where that got us," Leona replied, gesturing to her bandaged torso with a weak attempt at humor. Seeing those pristine white bandages twisted something in Faith's chest. The guilt she'd been suppressing crashed over her like a wave.

"I'm so sorry," she whispered, her voice breaking. "This is all my fault. If I hadn't—"

"Stop." Leona's hand found hers, fever-hot against Faith's cool skin. "Don't you dare apologize. It was my choice, and I'd make the same one every time."

"But you almost died!" Faith's words tore from her throat. "I saw you fall. I saw the blood. I saw—" She broke off, unable to continue.

"Hey." Leona's fingers tightened around hers. "Look at me."

Reluctantly, Faith raised her eyes to meet Leona's fierce gaze.

"You're pack," Leona said simply, as if those two words explained everything.

"What?"

"Pack," Leona repeated. "Family. The highest honor a wolf can bestow." Her thumb traced patterns on Faith's palm, sending shivers up her arm. "We protect our own. No matter what. You're my own, now... and you don't get a choice in that. "

A warm feeling bloomed in Faith's chest, pushing back against the cold guilt that had taken root there. Leona's words carried a weight beyond simple comfort — they were a declaration, a promise, an offering of belonging that Faith had never dared hope for.

The candlelight caught the sharp planes of Leona's face, softening her fierce features. Her hazel eyes glowed with an inner fire that had nothing to do with her wolf nature. Faith found herself leaning forward unconsciously, drawn in by the gravity of that gaze.

"There's something I should have done," Faith whispered. "Back in the forest, before..."

"You don't need to thank me, dufus," Leona interrupted. "I told you, that's what pack—"

Faith didn't let her finish. Instead, she leaned in and pressed her lips to Leona's.

Chapter 61

The kiss was gentle, almost hesitant — nothing like their nearly moment in the forest. Faith felt Leona freeze for a heartbeat, surprised, before melting into the contact. Her lips were incredibly warm against Faith's cooler ones, tasting of wild places.

Faith's acute senses went into overdrive, cataloging every detail of the moment: the way Leona's heartbeat hammered in her chest, the subtle change in her scent as desire mingled with her usual wild musk and the slight catch in her breath as Faith cupped her cheek.

Leona's hand tangled in Faith's hair, drawing her nearer. The kiss deepened, growing more urgent. Faith experienced sensations she had never felt before — a warmth that lessened her perennial cold, a lightness in her chest that made her feel almost fully alive again.

Time stretched like honey, thick and golden in the candlelight. Faith lost herself in the kiss, in the bliss of finally connecting with someone without fear. Her usual careful restraint melted beneath Leona's touch, replaced by a different kind of hunger.

She could sense the pulse rushing just beneath Leona's skin, rich with life and vitality. The darkness in her veins stirred hungrily, reminding her of what she truly was — a predator, no matter how carefully she tried to hide it.

Faith started to pull back, memories of the training session flooding her mind — how easily she had pinned Leona's throat, how natural it had felt to squeeze just a little harder. The darkness had felt so right then, so perfectly aligned with her nature. What if she lost control now, in this intimate moment? What if the hunger for blood merged with this new hunger for connection?

"Hey," Leona whispered against her lips, sensing her withdrawal. "Stop thinking so much."

"I could hurt you," Faith breathed, the words carrying all her fears. "You've seen what's... inside me."

Leona's hand came up to cup her cheek. "You won't."

"How can you be so sure?"

"Because I know you," Leona replied simply. Her hazel eyes held absolute certainty. "Because I know you."

As Leona's thumb traced patterns on her cheek, Faith made a choice. She was tired of letting fear rule her life. Tired of holding back, of making herself smaller, of denying what she felt. The darkness in her blood hummed, but this time she didn't fight it. Instead, she let it merge with the warmth blooming in her chest, creating something new — something that wasn't quite human, wasn't quite vampire, but was entirely Faith.

She leaned forward again, letting her cool lips brush against Leona's warm ones. The kiss deepened, and this time Faith didn't pull away.

Some distant part of her registered footsteps approaching in the corridor, but the sound seemed insignificant compared to the sensation of Leona's fingers trailing down her neck and the thrum of the werwulf's heartbeat beneath her palm. The world shrank to this moment, this connection, this perfect understanding between two souls straddling the line between human and other.

Then the door swung open.

Faith pulled away from the kiss at the sound of a sharp intake of breath. She turned to see Isaac standing in the doorway. His usually steady heartbeat had turned erratic. His eyes wide.

CHAPTER 61

"I… brought new bandages," he said quietly, his voice tightly controlled. "Serafin asked me to…"

His words trailed off as his gaze shifted between Faith and Leona. Faith witnessed the moment his careful composure shattered — a flash of raw emotion flickered in his eyes before his Hunter training regained its grip. His jaw clenched so tightly that she could hear his teeth grinding.

"Isaac," Faith began, though she had no idea what she could possibly say.

He stepped back into the corridor, his movements suddenly stiff and formal.

"I should go," he said, still maintaining that carefully measured tone that did little to disguise his emotions from Faith's heightened senses. "Clearly, I'm interrupting something."

"Wait—" Faith started to rise, but Isaac was already gone, his footsteps echoing down the corridor with military precision.

The room fell silent, save for the soft crackle of candle flames and Leona's slightly elevated breathing. Faith remained frozen, caught between the warmth of what had just happened and the cold reality of what it might cost.

"Go after him," Leona said with a sigh.

Faith turned back to her in surprise. "What?"

"Go." Leona's voice was soft, though Faith could see the tension in her shoulders. "We both know you need to."

"I don't…" Faith trailed off, unsure of how to finish the sentence. She didn't what? Want to leave? Know what to say to him? Understand her own heart?

The darkness in her blood stirred fitfully, echoing her emotional turmoil. She had spent so long fearing connection, afraid to let anyone close enough to be hurt by what she was. Yet now, she had managed to hurt them both at the same time. Just typical of her. A walking curse."

"Faith." Leona's hand found hers again, squeezing gently. "It's okay. I'm not going anywhere." A slight smirk touched her lips despite the gravity of the moment. "Well, not like I could right now anyway."

Tears she couldn't shed burned behind Faith's eyes. "I never meant…"

"I know." Leona's thumb brushed across her knuckles. "But he needs to hear whatever you're going to say more than I do right now."

She settled back against her pillows, though Faith noticed the tremor in her hands that revealed her exhaustion. "Besides, Serafin will be back soon to torture me with more of her herbal slime. You don't want to be here for that." She sounded tired now.

Faith stood slowly, her legs feeling unusually unsteady. She paused at the door, looking back at Leona. The werwulf's crisp edges were softened by the candlelight, but her hazel eyes held that familiar wild certainty that had drawn Faith to her from the beginning.

"Thank you," Faith whispered, unsure whether she meant for the kiss, the understanding, or something deeper.

Leona's smile was gentle despite the fierce light in her eyes. "That's what pack is for." She looked exhausted now.

Faith lingered in the doorway, watching the steady rise and fall of Leona's chest as slumber finally claimed her. The werwulf's face had softened in sleep, losing some of its fierce edges, though her fingers still twitched occasionally as if reaching for something in her dreams. The candlelight caught the sheen of sweat on her brow, a reminder of the fever still burning through her body as she healed.

Faith felt restless as she stood between Leona's room and the corridor where Isaac had disappeared. Two paths stretched before her – one blazing with wild heat, the other offering steady warmth. Yet standing there, knowing she was now forbidden to leave these walls, both paths seemed to lead nowhere.

CHAPTER 61

As she finally stepped into the corridor, Faith's ears caught two distinct sounds: Leona's steady heartbeat behind her, and the distant rhythm of Isaac's measured footsteps ahead.

She touched her lips, still warm from Leona's kiss, and took her first step down the corridor. A few candles guttered in their sconces as she passed, casting her shadow in multiple directions, as if even her silhouette couldn't decide which way to go.

Chapter 62

Faith's feet glided across the marble floor. She picked up Isaac's scent trail with painful clarity — weapon oil and leather layered over his natural aroma, now tainted by a sharp tang of controlled anger mixed with something deeper and more wounded.

A distant rhythmic sound reached her ears — steel slicing through the air with deadly precision. Each strike carried barely contained fury that even Isaac's rigid Hunter training couldn't fully mask. The sound grew louder as she approached the east wing, where a training room had been established during the battle of the night creatures two decades ago.

Her lips still tingled from Leona's kiss, the warmth already fading, leaving her in her usual cold state.

Faith paused at the entrance to the training hall, her sensitive nose registering layers of scent — fresh sweat mingling with old blood that seemed permanently absorbed into the wooden floors, along with steel, leather and exertion. Usually, these familiar aromas brought her comfort, reminding her of hours spent learning control under Isaac's patient hand. Now, they only deepened her confusion.

Through the partially open door, she watched Isaac execute his forms. His long coat hung on a nearby rack, exposing a fitted black shirt that revealed the controlled power in each movement. Twin swords traced lethal arcs through the air, their steel singing with

CHAPTER 62

every precisely aimed strike. Faith recognized the sequence — a series of killing blows designed specifically for hunting vampires. Each cut could have severed a head or pierced an undead heart. The symbolism was not lost on her.

His execution was flawless as always, but Faith noticed the subtle signs — the slight tremor in his hands between strikes, the way his jaw clenched tight enough to make the tendons stand out in his neck, how his usually steady heartbeat carried an unstable undertone.

"I know you're there," Isaac said without breaking his rhythm. Sweat gleamed on his dark skin in the lamplight as he continued his deadly dance. "We're trained to sense you."

The words carried an edge she'd never heard from him before, reminding her with brutal clarity of what he was — a Vampire Hunter.

Faith hesitated before stepping into the room. She caught how Isaac subtly adjusted his stance — a shift that kept his blades between them while maintaining an appearance of casual movement. The unconscious gesture felt combative.

"Isaac," she began, then faltered. What could she possibly say? Sorry you caught me kissing someone else? Sorry for feelings I don't understand? Sorry for being what I am — this mongrel creature trapped between worlds?

"No need to explain." His tone remained carefully neutral as he initiated another sequence of strikes. The steel of his swords whispered through the air. "What happens between you and the wolf girl is none of my business." He executed another precise cut, one that would have decapitated a vampire. "I'm sure you have more important matters to worry about than a Hunter's... opinion."

The last word carried an edge as sharp as his blades. Faith again noticed the tremor in his hands that his training couldn't quite suppress. She remembered how those same hands had steadied her during countless practice sessions. How they had bandaged her wounds without hesitation, despite her being what he was sworn to destroy.

"That's not fair," she whispered. "You know you're more than just—"

The clash of steel on steel cut her off as Isaac's swords collided with enough force to send sparks dancing through the air. The sound echoed off the high ceiling like thunder, making Faith's sensitive ears ring.

"Spar with me," he said abruptly, tossing her one of his swords. The weapon spun through the air in a perfect arc.

Faith caught it instinctively; her enhanced reflexes made the action look effortless. The familiar weight settled into her palm like a missing piece clicking into place. She recognized this blade — the one he had used to teach her control and balance. Small nicks in the guard marked their countless training sessions together.

They circled each other slowly, their bare feet silent on the worn floorboards. Faith noted how Isaac favored his right side slightly — an old injury that never quite healed. Her keen eyes saw every detail of his controlled movements, the way his muscles coiled beneath his shirt, how his throat worked as he swallowed.

He struck first, the blade whistling toward her ribs. Faith parried instinctively, muscle memory kicking in. Steel met steel with a sound like breaking ice. They moved together in a deadly dance, one they had performed countless times during training. But this felt different — each strike was laden with emotions neither dared voice.

"You're holding back," Isaac said through gritted teeth as their blades locked.

His face was inches from hers, close enough for her to feel the heat radiating from his skin. Sweat beaded on his forehead, carrying complex scents that made her fangs ache.

"Like you always do," he added. "Afraid of what might happen if

CHAPTER 62

you let go?"

Faith disengaged with supernatural speed, quickly putting distance between them. A stirring darkness filled her veins, responding to his challenge.

"You know why I have to maintain control," she said.

"Do I?" He pressed forward, his attacks becoming more aggressive. Each strike forced her back a step. "Or is that just what you tell yourself? What everyone has been telling you your whole life?"

The taunt shocked her — it was so unlike Isaac, whose patience and steady control had been constants in her training. She had never heard this edge of bitterness in his voice before.

Their swords clashed repeatedly, the impacts sending shockwaves up Faith's arms. She caught the scent of his blood as she opened a small cut on his hand, eliciting an involuntary extension of her fangs. This stark reminder of her identity — of the hunger that always lurked beneath the surface — made her stumble.

Seizing the opportunity, Isaac swept her legs out from under her.

Faith hit the floor hard, the impact driving the air from her lungs. Before she could recover, his blade was up against her throat.

Chapter 63

"You see?" Isaac said sternly, his eyes reflecting something that wasn't quite anger. "Always pulling back. Always afraid." The steel was cool against her skin, but his hand still trembled slightly where it gripped the hilt. "Even now, you could throw me across the room like a rag doll if you wanted to. But you won't."

"Because I don't want to hurt you," Faith said, the words carrying more weight than she intended.

Something flickered in Isaac's expression — a mix of pain and longing. The blade wavered against her throat before withdrawing entirely. He offered her a hand up.

Faith took it, feeling his fever-warm skin against her enduring cold.

"We need to talk," he said as she regained her feet, his tone shifting to one that carried new gravity. "About defending yourself, about security measures. About…" He hesitated, choosing his words carefully. "About things that have come to light."

Faith caught the subtle change in his heartbeat — a slight acceleration that betrayed the anxiety beneath his controlled exterior. "What things?"

Isaac moved to replace his swords on the rack, his movements precise and deliberate. She noticed how his fingers lingered on the hilts, as if drawing strength from the familiar weapons. "The wards have been acting strangely lately, fluctuating in ways they shouldn't."

CHAPTER 63

Faith remembered how the protective symbols had writhed under her touch earlier. "I thought that was because of me. Because of what happened during the battle with the Ancients."

"That's what we assumed at first." Isaac began methodically cleaning his blades, though Faith noted how his movements lacked their usual grace. "But I've been talking with Kavisha and Jiangshina. The patterns don't match typical power interference."

He paused, testing the edge of one sword with his thumb. A drop of blood welled up, its sharp scent flooding Faith's nostrils. "Someone might be probing the defenses."

Faith's stomach dropped as memories of the ward failure at St Machar's resurfaced. "Could Mary's forces breach the mansion's protection?"

"No." Isaac's tone was firm, but Faith sensed an undercurrent of tension. "The Old Magick here is too strong, too deep. Not from the outside…" He trailed off, leaving the implications hanging heavily in the air.

Faith instinctively thought about those in the mansion right now: her parents speaking softly in their room, Devan and Lupita checking on Leona, Serafin preparing additional healing potions. Kavisha and the Council members planning strategy. Various functionaries and staff members going about their business. They all believed they were safe behind ancient magic. Magic that could potentially be undone — from within, like St Machar's.

"There's more," Isaac continued, setting down his cleaned blade. He turned to face her fully. "We think we know where Mary plans to perform the resurrection ritual." His gaze was intense. "The mansion outside Angel Falls in Gerogia. The place where the Red Claws slept for a century. Where your father served as caretaker."

Faith felt weak in the knees. She sank onto a nearby bench, the wood creaking beneath her. "The ceremonial casket," she whispered, horrors aligning in her mind. "Where Zachariah slept for a hundred years."

"Yes." Isaac's voice was grave. "That vessel, which contained him for so long, holds his essence — his power." He paused to gauge her reaction. "It makes the perfect conduit for resurrection."

The vision from Scarfskerry beach crashed over her anew — Zachariah rising from a stone vessel, his dark eyes burning with malevolence. She recalled Mary Magdalene's tears from that same vision, realizing it had proven true. The thought sent a chill through her. This had to be true, as well. She had seen it.

"That's why your weapons training means so much now, why I was being so hard on you," Isaac said, stepping closer. His scent enveloped her — weapon oil and exertion mingling with something uniquely him. "You need to have the killer instinct, Faith. The wards. If they fail… if they are compromised from within…"

"What are you saying?" Faith asked, though a deep instinct already knew the answer.

Isaac leaned closer, his voice barely above a whisper. "There's talk of a spy within Vhik'h-Tal-Eskemon."

The words seemed to drop the room's temperature several degrees.

"We think that's how the Ancients knew when to attack," Isaac went on, his eyes locked onto hers. "How they knew exactly when you'd be outside the wards, in the forest. Someone here was likely feeding that information to Mary."

Horror washed over Faith as the implication sank in. If a traitor lurked within these walls, someone capable of disabling the wards… The weight of guilt pressed down on her chest like a tangible weight. Her earlier worries about kisses and confused feelings felt absurdly trivial now. Everyone she cared about was in danger.

"They'll all die because of me," she whispered.

"Faith— " Isaac began to approach her, one hand reaching out.

CHAPTER 63

But she backed away, wrapping her arms around herself. The dark force tossed and turned, responding to her emotional turmoil. "Don't," she said. "Please. I can't… I can't bear anyone else being hurt because of what I am."

She turned and fled the training room, her supernatural speed propelling her through the corridors in a blur. But she couldn't escape the haunting truth that shadowed her every step — while she remained within these walls, everyone she loved was at risk. The very sanctuary meant to protect her had become a trap, not just for her, but for all of them.

Chapter 64

Faith watched Leona test her body across the training room, where Faith had spoken to Isaac two days before. Unlike the mansion's other chambers, with their gothic grandeur and ornate decorations, this room was sparsely functional. Scarred wooden floorboards, worn smooth by decades of combat drills, creaked beneath Leona's feet. Faith's keen hearing picked up the subtle shifting of old timber and the whisper of countless battles absorbed into the wood grain.

Weapons racks lined the walls, their steel reflecting the light from iron lanterns mounted in brackets overhead. High windows of leaded glass cast diamond patterns across the floor.

The werwulf moved with dexterity, each motion a careful exploration of her restored muscles and sinews. Although in human form, her movements still retained a wild, natural freedom.

"Serafin may be heavy-handed with those stinking poultices," Leona declared, rolling her shoulders experimentally, "but I have to admit — the woman knows her stuff." She executed a perfect backflip, landing with predatory precision. "Good as new."

Faith registered the subtle sounds of healed tissue stretching and flexing — definitely not as "new" as Leona claimed, but far better than the devastating wounds inflicted by Magda's blade. The memory of that moment still haunted Faith: Leona's vast form crumpling, blood soaking into russet fur while ice spread from the wound like creeping

CHAPTER 64

death. She shuddered, then tensed as familiar footsteps approached — measured and precise, much like their owner.

Isaac appeared in the doorway, his eyes assessing the scene. Faith noticed the slight acceleration of his heartbeat when he saw her, followed by another uptick as he noticed Leona.

"You wanted to see me?" he asked, his tone carefully neutral. His gaze flickered between Faith and Leona, noting their proximity.

Faith extended her supernatural senses, scanning for anyone nearby who might overhear. She detected Serafin in her workroom two floors above, Kavisha consulting with Council members in the drawing room and her parents speaking softly in their chambers. No one was close enough to listen in.

"Close the door," she said softly.

Isaac's hand moved instinctively to his belt, an unconscious gesture revealing his Hunter training. "What's going on?"

"Scared, Hunter?" Leona's smile held a predatory edge. She stretched languidly, making no effort to hide how her tank top rode up to reveal toned ab muscles. "This is just a chat… between *friends*."

Faith noticed the tension in Isaac's jaw and the way his fingers tightened around his weapons belt. The air was charged with unspoken rivalry. She recalled the taste of Leona's kiss, but also remembered the training sessions with Isaac, his steady presence teaching her control when she feared her own nature. The contrast between the memories was stark.

"I have a plan," Faith said, forcing herself to concentrate. "And I need both of you."

Isaac raised an eyebrow. "Both of us?"

"She already has my support," Leona replied, stepping beside Faith. "The question is, Hunter — can you be trusted to help?"

"That depends entirely on the plan," Isaac replied evenly, although Faith could sense the irritation in his voice. "And whether it genuinely helps or is just another reckless impulse." He stared at Leona.

Faith took a deep breath. There was no point mincing words at this point. "We're going to destroy Zachariah's tomb. The stone vessel located in the mansion outside of Angel Falls." She watched as Isaac's eyes widened. "Before Mary can use it to bring him back."

Silence enveloped them. Faith caught the subtle increase in Isaac's heartbeat and the way his breath hitched. She noticed how his grip on his belt tightened, tendons standing out on his wrist.

"You can't be serious," he said, finally.

"Deadly serious." Faith met his gaze. "Kavisha confirmed Mary is gathering the 'items of power', as she called them, for the ritual. That means she isn't ready, yet. We have a window of opportunity, but it's closing fast."

"A window of opportunity for suicide, maybe." Isaac ran a hand over his close-cropped hair — a gesture that signaled agitation. "Even if we could overturn the Council's decree keeping you here, which we can't— "

"They don't need to know," Leona interrupted, her expression resolute. "Unless you plan to run off and tell mummy Kavisha?"

Isaac clenched his jaw. "You have no idea how many of Mary's forces could be guarding that mansion — or what other defenses might be in place. This isn't just reckless; it's insane."

Faith felt the darkness stir in her veins. She forced it back, maintaining control even as frustration threatened to overwhelm her. "What's insane is doing nothing while Mary grows stronger. While everyone here is at risk because of me."

A sound in the corridor made them freeze.

Faith extended her senses, tracking the movement — the footsteps faded into the distance. But the moment underscored the precarious nature of their meeting.

"Someone's always watching," she whispered, though she couldn't

CHAPTER 64

pinpoint the source of her certainty. The darkness within her pulsed in agreement. "We can't trust anyone else with this plan, not with a potential traitor among us."

"That's even more reason to avoid something this dangerous," Isaac countered, but Faith detected a slight tremor in his voice. "Faith, consider what you're suggesting. Your parents—"

"Would try to stop me," she finished. "Just as they tried to keep me hidden in Scotland. Just like the Council is trying to confine me now." Her hands clenched into fists. "I'm tired of others making decisions about my life and my destiny. This is my responsibility. My fight. But I can't do this alone."

"It's not just about you anymore," Isaac said softly, his gentle tone stirring memories of their training sessions, his patient guidance. "There are larger considerations to— "

"Like the whole world being at risk if Zachariah rises again," Leona interjected, moving closer to Faith. "But I guess Hunters only care about following orders instead of actually protecting people, saving countless actual lives."

Isaac's composure cracked slightly. "You know nothing about what Hunters care about," he snapped. "Or what we sacrifice."

"I know you're afraid," Leona taunted, her hazel eyes glinting with something wild. "Afraid of taking action without permission. Afraid of trusting your instincts." She paused, the weight of her words palpable. "Afraid of losing her."

The tension hovered like drawn blades.

Faith caught Isaac's sharp intake of breath and saw the moment his training clashed with raw emotion. She recalled the look etched on his face when he discovered her kissing Leona, how quickly he tried to mask it.

"Stop it," Faith said quietly. "Both of you. This is about more than just… us." Even as she uttered the words, she felt the tug of their conflicting natures — a reflection of her own internal battle. "This is about stopping Mary before she can resurrect a monster who would enslave humanity and kill those we hold dear."

She turned to Isaac, letting him see the conviction in her eyes. "I saw it in my vision back in Scotland when Mary touched me. I saw Zachariah rising from that stone box, his power reaching out like shadows coming to life." The memory sent a shiver down her spine. "But I'm hoping visions aren't absolute destiny; that they're warnings, chances to change what's coming. We have to try, at the very least."

"And if we fail?" Isaac asked, yet Faith sensed his resistance wavering. "What if we're caught, or killed? Or worse — what if Mary captures you?"

"Then at least we fought," Leona said, intertwining her fingers with Faith's. "Instead of hiding behind walls and waiting for the end to come to us."

Faith felt the weight of Isaac's gaze as he studied their joined hands. But there was something else — a subtle shift in his posture that hinted at an internal conflict.

"You actually think this is possible?" he asked, glancing up. "With just the three of us?"

"We're the perfect team," Faith replied, hope flickering in her eyes. "Your Hunter stealth, Leona's raw power, and…" She hesitated, feeling the darkness stir within her. "Whatever I am now."

"A force of nature," Leona said fiercely, squeezing her hand. "You proved that against the Ancients. You're a fucking force of nature, girl."

Isaac hadn't witnessed that battle, but he'd seen firsthand what she was capable of.

"Someone's coming," Faith whispered, stretching her supernatural senses. Footsteps approached in the corridor, moving with vampire grace and getting closer.

Chapter 65

They sprang apart. Leona immediately dropped into a series of stretches that resembled a legitimate workout. Isaac moved to the weapons rack, pretending to inspect the blades. Faith's didn't know what to do with herself. So she just stood there.

The footsteps passed without stopping, yet the moment left them all a little shaken. The constant threat of discovery hung over them like a dark cloud.

"This is what I mean," Faith said softly once she was sure they weren't overheard. "We're not safe here. None of us are. If the wards fail like they did at St Machar's…"

"They won't," Isaac insisted, though the doubt in his voice was palpable. "The Old Magick here is substan—"

"Magic is only as strong as those maintaining it," said Leona, interrupting him once again. "And if there's really a traitor…" She let the implication linger.

Faith watched the conflict play across Isaac's features. His Hunter training battled with the truth of their words and his growing suspicions about their security.

"I can't just sit here waiting for everything to fall apart," Faith said, her voice cracking slightly. "Watching everyone I care about put themselves at risk because of what I am. Because of what my blood could do, to the world." She met Isaac's gaze. "Could you live with that? Knowing we might have prevented it, but chose to do nothing?" The question struck home.

Faith saw the moment Isaac's resistance crumbled, even as he tried to maintain his composed exterior.

"Even if — and I mean *if* — we attempted this," he said carefully, "we would need a solid plan. Intelligence about the mansion's layout, defensive measures—"

"Already working on it," Leona interrupted with a predatory smile. "Unless you're not up for a real challenge, Hunter? Maybe you should stay here where it's safe and let the grown-ups handle it."

Faith saw the flash of anger in Isaac's eyes before he managed to suppress it. She also noticed how his spine straightened and his jaw set with determination. Leona's taunt had clearly hit its mark.

"You really think you can handle this without my input?" he asked, his tone deceptively mild. "Your solution to everything is to charge in, teeth and claws flying. This requires actual strategy."

"Then prove you're more than just talk," Leona challenged. "Show us what the mighty Hunters can really do." Her smile turned sharp. "Unless you don't care about Faith as much as I do."

The words hung in the air like drawn daggers. Faith felt the tension spike between them — primal versus disciplined, wild versus controlled. Their rivalry crackled with something deeper than mere antagonism, something that centered on Faith with uncomfortable intensity.

Time was running out. She could feel it in her bones, in the darkness flowing in her body, in the way reality itself seemed to fray around the edges.

"I'm doing this," she said firmly, meeting both of their gazes in turn. "With or without you. But I'm asking for your help." She paused, letting her words sink in. "Both of you."

The silence stretched between them, heavy with unspoken emo-

CHAPTER 65

tions.

"You know I'm with you," Leona said, her usual fierce demeanor softening. "Pack is pack. We stay together." The words echoed with memories of their kiss and promises made by candlelight.

They both turned to Isaac. He stood perfectly still, his body reflecting the rigid control of his Hunter training.

"This is suicide," he said finally, his voice rough. "But…" He met Faith's eyes, and she saw something crack in his careful composure. "I can't let you face it alone."

Relief washed over Faith. But before she could respond, movement caught her vision — a shadow passing behind the high windows, too fluid to be natural. A scent that didn't belong flashed through her nostrils, so fleeting she wondered if she had imagined it.

"Someone's watching," she whispered, though she struggled to locate the source. The darkness in her blood stirred anxiously, reacting to the potential threat.

Leona flared her nostrils, scenting the air, while Isaac's hand moved instinctively to the hilt of his sword. They formed a triangle, backs turned inward, scanning for danger from every direction. The position felt natural — right — as their differing natures complemented each other, despite their rivalry.

Nothing. Only silence.

"We need to move fast," Faith said, her voice barely above a whisper. "Before Mary collects what she needs. Before the wards fail. Before…" She trailed off, unable to articulate her fear — that she might lose either of them before she could untangle the complex emotions they created within her. Her feelings seemed trivial in light of the imminent threat, yet they intertwined with everything else, complicating each decision she faced.

"We'll need supplies," Isaac said, slipping into tactical mode. His voice held a forced calm. "Weapons, maps of the region around Angel

Falls, transportation."

"Mere details," Leona interrupted yet again, her fierce grin returning.

Isaac didn't look impressed.

"The question is, when do we move?" asked Leona.

"Tonight," Faith replied firmly. The word hung between them. "During the changing of the guards outside. I've memorized their pattern — there's a gap in coverage just after dawn"

"That doesn't leave much time for logistics," said Isaac.

Leona rolled her eyes.

"We have to act fast." Faith met his gaze steadily. "Since St Machar's fell, there's nowhere truly safe anymore." She paused to allow them to see the weight of responsibility in her eyes. "I won't watch another sanctuary fall. I won't see more people hurt because of what I am."

The darkness in her veins stirred, responding to her resolve. But this time, she didn't resist it. Instead, she let it flow through her dead flesh like a savage wind, accepting it as part of who — and what — she was becoming.

She glanced between the two who meant so much to her in different ways. "This is your last chance to back out."

"Not going to happen," Leona said immediately, her hazel eyes fierce. The werwulf's loyalty made Faith's chest swell.

Isaac's response came slower, more measured. "Someone needs to keep you both from getting killed." His attempt at dry humor didn't quite mask the emotion in his voice. "Besides, I've already broken about every Hunter protocol since I've known you. Might as well go all in."

Faith reached out and gripped both of their hands.

"Go," she whispered urgently. "Before we're discovered. And remember — trust no one else."

They separated quickly. But as Faith moved through the mansion's

CHAPTER 65

corridors, she felt eyes on her that she couldn't locate. The sensation raised the fine hairs on her neck. She paused at a window, watching storm clouds gather above Vhik'h-Tal-Eskemon's gothic spires. The thunderheads moved with unnatural purpose, as if nature itself was being twisted by darker forces. Lightning flickered within their depths.

Conflict was coming, whether they were ready or not. Faith could feel it in her bones, in the darkness flowing inside of her, in the charged air. Their only hope lay in reaching Angel Falls before Mary completed her collection of sacred items — before Zachariah could rise again.

Faith's fingers traced the cold glass, leaving trails in the condensation. Beyond her reflection, she caught a glimpse of movement in the gathering storm — a murder of crows wheeling against the dark clouds, their wings beating in perfect synchronization. As she watched, they began to arrange themselves into a familiar pattern — a face.

Chapter 66

Faith moved silently through her sparsely furnished room. After nearly a month in the ancient mansion, the space still felt temporary, just like everywhere else they had hidden since fleeing Scotland.

There were no personal belongings or mementos — nothing that couldn't be abandoned at a moment's notice. The only constants in her life were the sounds reaching her sensitive ears from the next room: her father's low murmur and her mother's gentle replies.

The familiar cadence of their conversation sent waves of guilt crashing through her chest. For twenty years, they had given up everything to protect her, living like ghosts on the fringes of the world. Their dreams, their freedom, any chance at a normal life — surrendered without hesitation or regret.

She remembered her mother's anguished face that terrible night in Scotland, twisted with desperate fear as Mary's forces closed in. She recalled her father throwing himself between Mary's blade and her back, willing to die rather than see his family harmed.

A soft sound from the corridor made her freeze. Her senses stretched out, noticing every whisper of movement and every subtle shift in the air. Just someone passing, she realized, but the moment of panic left her trembling. Discovery now would mean doom.

Faith pressed her forehead against the cool window glass, watching storm clouds gather in the sky. The darkness inside stirred restlessly,

CHAPTER 66

responding to the brewing tempest.

Very shortly she would shatter what little security her parents had managed to rebuild since Scotland. Their careful plans, their desperate protections, their endless vigilance — all of it undone by her decision to act.

More footsteps in the corridor made her tense again. She recognized Leona's quick rhythm in the strides. The werwulf passed without stopping, maintaining their careful pretense of normalcy.

Another wave of guilt swept over her.

She was using Leona's loyalty, her fierce devotion to pack, to drag her into terrible danger. The werwulf would follow her into hell itself without hesitation, it seemed — and Faith was taking advantage of that trust, that bond, that love. Just as she was exploiting Isaac's protective instincts, letting Leona's taunts manipulate his Hunter pride into agreeing to help them.

She heard her mother's voice again, softer now: "I worry about her, Christopher. She seems so... distant lately."

"She's finding her own way," her father replied gently. "We have to trust her."

The irony of his words twisted like a knife.

She was about to prove that trust tragically misplaced. They would wake tomorrow to find her gone — their greatest fear realized. Would they believe she had been taken? Or would they suspect the truth — that their daughter had chosen to walk away willingly?

Faith's fingers traced the rough stone walls, feeling the grooves and imperfections that had borne witness to centuries of supernatural history. The protective wards hummed beneath her touch, the Old Magick recognizing a kinship in her nature — or perhaps sensing the darkness inside her, the same power that had enabled her to destroy two Ancient vampires.

A distant rumble of thunder pulled her gaze back to the window.

The storm clouds had thickened and become more ominous, with lightning flickering within their depths like trapped souls yearning for escape.

She could hear Devan's unrestrained laughter echoing through the mansion, his tone carrying a blend of strength and gentleness reminiscent of her father. She imagined Devan's reaction upon discovering his daughter was missing, and thought of Lupita, who had already lost her younger brother, now facing another devastating blow.

"I'm sorry," Faith whispered to the empty room, unsure who she was apologizing to. Her parents for shattering their trust? Leona's family for enabling their daughter's reckless loyalty? Isaac for manipulating his protective instincts?

The bare stone walls of her temporary chamber seemed to press in on her, as if the mansion itself judged her guilty.

She caught a shift in her parents' conversation next door — her mother's voice had grown softer, more intimate. Faith recognized that tone from countless quiet moments she had witnessed between them. Their love had endured decades of impossible odds, marked by trauma but finding healing in each other's arms, in those muted, undramatic moments.

Would she ever experience that kind of love? The thought sent an unexpected pang through her chest. Her gaze drifted back to the window, recalling Leona's fierce kiss and how the werwulf's wild heat eased her persistent cold. Then Isaac's face flashed through her mind, remembering how carefully he had touched her despite knowing what she was.

Both had breached her carefully constructed walls. Both had offered her warmth and liberation. And now she was dragging them into terrible danger, using their feelings for her as weapons to achieve her goals. That's how it felt, anyway.

CHAPTER 66

A soft scraping sound overhead made her freeze. She instinctively tracked the noise, concluding it was just mice in the attic after a moment of tension. But the spike of fear left her trembling; one mistake, one moment of carelessness, and everything would unravel.

She pressed her hand against the wall that separated her room from her parents' chamber, letting their familiar voices wash over her. "Please forgive me," she whispered, her words catching in her throat. "Sometimes love means making impossible choices. You taught me that."

The harsh truth settled over Faith like a heavy mantle — she would rather break their hearts than watch them die because of what she was. It was better for them to hate her for leaving than to face that possible future: Mary's forces breaching the mansion's defenses, the wards failing just as they had at St Machar's, everyone she loved cut down while trying to protect her.

Faith recognized the parallels. Like mother, like daughter — both choosing to walk into the unknown to protect those they loved. Would this realization break Nell? Or would she see herself in her daughter's actions?

Faith recalled the stories of her mother's captivity, how she had endured unimaginable torture to keep others safe. That same blood flowed through Faith's veins, intertwined with Vlad's darkness and Christopher's light.

"Blood connects all," her mother had recited as they came under attack in Scotland. "Blood is the liberator. Blood is the destroyer. Blood is the answer."

A sudden gust of wind rattled the windows, making Faith jump. The storm intensified, lightning flickering more frequently within the roiling clouds. Her sharp eyes caught movement in the courtyard below — guards patrolling, their steps perfectly synchronized. Soon, that same precision would create a brief gap in their coverage — their only chance to escape.

She thought of Isaac then: his planning, precision. His nobility. His selflessness.

Now Faith was using his own nature against him, allowing Leona's taunts and his own benevolence to guide him toward a mission that went against his Hunter instincts. The guilt tore at her. But what choice did she have? She needed both Leona's strength and Isaac's tactical skills if they had any hope of stopping Mary.

Another roll of thunder shook the mansion's very foundations. Faith sensed the protective wards pulsing within the stone, heightened as if reacting to some unseen threat — or perhaps they too sensed her impending betrayal.

She again put her palm up against the cold wall, feeling the ancient Old Magick thrumming beneath its surface. Her parents were just on the other side of the stone. The urge to run next door nearly overwhelmed her — to hug her mother one last time, to thank her father for his endless patience, to try to explain why she had to do this. But she knew that seeing them would shatter her resolve. Some goodbyes were better left unsaid.

Chapter 67

Faith sensed the subtle shift in the air that heralded the approaching dawn. The night's protective darkness would soon give way to vulnerable twilight. Time was running out. She moved silently to her window, watching the storm clouds churn above Vhik'h-Tal-Eskemon's gothic spires, lightning illuminating the ground below in stark relief.

Faith tightened her grip on the windowsill, leaving small indentations in the wood. The dark force in her body shifted uneasily, responding to the storm. Was she leading Leona and Isaac to their deaths? The thought sent ice sweeping through her veins. She could still stop this — wake her parents, confess everything, find another way.

But deep down, she knew it was impossible. The vision of Zachariah rising from his stone vessel was burned into her mind, along with the horror that would follow.

She picked up a change in her parents' voices next door — they were saying goodnight before going into trance, their routine unchanged despite the new setting. Faith's chest heaved as she realized these might be the last words she would ever hear them speak.

"I love you," her mother whispered, the words carrying clearly through the wall.

"You too, always," her father replied softly.

Faith pressed her face against the cold stone separating their rooms, committing the moment to memory. Everything she had ever learned about love and sacrifice was contained in those simple exchanges — in the way her parents had chosen each other despite impossible odds, and in their unwavering devotion to Faith.

She took one last look around the bare chamber that had briefly been her home. The emptiness felt fitting as she prepared to leave everything behind once again.

Turning back to the wall separating her from her parents, she whispered, "I'm so sorry," knowing they couldn't hear. "Please understand... someday."

The darkness in her veins surged with anticipation as she eased her door open. There would be no turning back after this moment. She was choosing to walk willingly into the unknown, just as her mother had done twenty years before. But this time, she wasn't alone.

Chapter 68

She crept through the darkened corridors of Vhik'h-Tal-Eskemon. The pre-dawn air was thick with tension, pressing against Faith's skin like wet velvet. She detected the synchronized footsteps of guards patrolling outside — twenty-three seconds until a shift change created their narrow window for escape.

Her nose registered complex layers of scent: sage and yarrow from Serafin's workroom, the oily aroma of weapons being cleaned in the armory, and beneath it all, the musty smell of centuries-old stone. The wards hummed beneath her feet, a steady reminder of what she was about to leave behind. Protection. Safety. Family.

Thirty seconds.

Faith noticed movement in her peripheral vision — Leona emerging from the shadows, her lithe figure clad in form-fitting combat gear that highlighted each movement. The etched lines of her face were tense with focus as she assumed her position as lookout, hazel eyes shimmering with anticipation. Faith's keen hearing picked up the rapid thundering of Leona's heart, quickened by excitement rather than fear. Faith envied her sometimes.

Twenty-five seconds.

Isaac appeared from the other direction, his Hunter training evident in every precise movement. His gaze met Faith's briefly, conveying volumes without words. The van keys gleamed dully in his hand, acquired through means Faith hadn't inquired about, but knew involved planning and stealth. Like everything the Hunter did.

Twenty seconds.

The guards' footsteps began to fade as they moved toward the back of the expansive mansion for their shift change. Faith tensed, ready to sprint. She just needed three seconds to—

Footsteps. New ones. Coming from the wrong direction. Faith froze as the sound registered — the whisper of robes against marble, the gentle jingle of multiple necklaces containing healing crystals.

Serafin.

They hadn't accounted for this.

Pressing herself against the wall, Faith willed her body to blend with the shadows.

Across from her, Leona went preternaturally still.

Isaac had vanished — a testament to his training.

Serafin's footsteps grew closer. The scent of herbs and incense intensified. Faith could distinguish the individual crystals chiming together now and smell the traces of herbal ointment clinging to the spellcaster's robes. Faith picked up something else too — exhaustion, bone-deep weariness in her languid steps that spoke of too many patients and too little rest. Bless her good heart, thought Faith. But right now, Serafin was an obstacle.

Ten seconds.

The spellcaster paused at the corridor junction, mere meters away from where they hid. Faith didn't dare breathe, though she technically didn't need to. The darkness in her veins stirred uneasily, responding to her rising tension.

Five seconds.

Serafin sighed heavily, the sound echoing with days upon days of accumulated fatigue. Mercifully, she turned down another corridor and the rustle of her robes faded into the distance.

CHAPTER 68

Two seconds.

Faith exploded into motion, her vampire speed propelling her to the large front door faster than human eyes could track. She threw it open. Isaac sprinted outside towards the parked Council vans. Leona was hot on his heels, her athletic form seeming to glide along the ground.

One second.

They converged on the vehicle just as the guards disappeared into the back of the building and the new patrol had yet to step foot outside. Faith registered fragments of casual conversation — complaints about early shifts and jibes about their seniors. It felt so normal, so human. The banality of it warmed her in a way she couldn't put her finger on.

The van's engine hummed to life, its sound deafening to Faith's sensitive ears. She froze, bracing for shouts of discovery. Yet the guards' conversation continued uninterrupted as Isaac steered the vehicle towards the gates.

Faith and Leona piled in. Faith taking the passenger seat while Leona leapt into the back. Faith watched Vhik'h-Tal-Eskemon quickly shrink in the side mirror, its gothic spires reaching toward the sky like grasping fingers.

Somewhere in there, her parents slept in trance, unaware that their greatest fear had just come true — their daughter was gone. The darkness within stirred again, responding to her guilt. Faith forced it back, focusing instead on the road ahead. They had chosen this path. There was no turning back now.

283

III

Eminence of abominations

Chapter 69

"Well," Leona said. Her tone was light. "That was fun. A bit anticlimactic though. I was hoping for at least one dramatic fight."

"The best missions are boring ones," Isaac replied tersely, gripping the steering wheel tightly as he guided them towards the I-26 West. "Drama gets people killed."

"Says the man who carries two swords on his back," Leona shot back. "Because that's not dramatic at all."

"They're tools, not theater props."

"Right, and I suppose the long coat is practical too?"

Faith caught the tightening of Isaac's jaw in the rearview mirror. "The coat provides protection and concealment for— "

"Oh please," Leona interrupted, rolling her eyes. "You wear it because it looks cool, and you know it. Just admit you have a flair for the dramatic, Hunter."

"I admit nothing of the sort."

Issac glanced at Faith and raised a conspiratorial eyebrow.

Despite everything, Faith felt a smile tugging at her lips. Their banter offered a welcome distraction from the weight of their actions. She looked in the mirror again, watching the mansion disappear around a bend. The sight sobered her instantly.

"I'm sorry," she whispered into the night.

"Hey." Leona leaned forward, her hand warm on Faith's shoulder.

"No apologies. We're in this together."

"Some of us more willingly than others," Isaac muttered, though Faith noticed the slight upturn of his lips.

"Oh, I'm sorry," Leona said with exaggerated concern. "Is this too exciting for you? Would you prefer a nice, quiet evening polishing your dramatic coat collection?"

"I don't have a collection."

"The three identical black coats suggest otherwise," she replied. "You think we haven't noticed?"

"They're not identical. They're optimized for different— "

"Drama levels?"

Faith let their voices wash over her as the van ate up the miles, as she once again left her safe world behind. The sky continued to lighten, dawn approaching like an unstoppable tide. She thought of her parents waking to find her gone, imagining their fear, pain and desperation.

"I love you," she thought towards the now distant mansion. "Please understand."

The darkness in her veins churned once more, but this time she didn't fight it. She would need every weapon, every advantage, every ounce of power to ensure their sacrifice wasn't in vain. To stop Mary. To prevent Zachariah's return. To save them all.

"For the love of all that's holy," Leona groaned from the back, "can you please drive faster than my grandmother? And she's been dead for thirty years."

Isaac's hands tightened on the wheel. "The speed limit exists for a reason."

"Yes, to piss me off, specifically." Leona's leg bounced with barely contained energy. "We're in a getaway car, not a freakin' golf cart!"

"This is *not* a getaway car," Isaac replied with forced patience. "This is an armored tactical— "

CHAPTER 69

"Boring-mobile?"

" — vehicle that requires— "

"Some actual speed?" Leona lunged forward, her foot shooting between the front seats toward the gas pedal.

Isaac swerved slightly as he blocked her attempt. "Will you stop that?"

"Then take a hint!"

Faith picked up the sound of Isaac's teeth grinding. The noise grated against her ears like metal on stone.

"In case you've forgotten," he said tightly, "we're trying not to draw attention. Getting pulled over for speeding would— "

"Be more exciting than watching you plod along, granddad."

" — compromise the entire mission."

Faith caught Leona's reflection in the side mirror — the werwulf's angular face twisted in a theatrical expression of agony as she flopped back against her seat.

"I'm dying," Leona announced to no one in particular. "Of boredom. Right here in this van. The world's most boring death during the world's most boring mission to save the damn world." She perked up suddenly. "Hey, I could shift and run alongside! That would be coo— "

"No," Faith and Isaac said in unison.

"You're no fun," Leona pouted. "Neither of you." She leaned forward again, this time reaching for the radio. "At least let me put on some— "

Isaac's hand shot out, blocking her. "No music."

"Are you serious?" Leona's voice rose an octave. "What kind of monster doesn't allow music on a road trip? You're worse than Vlad!"

"This isn't a road trip," Isaac replied through clenched teeth. "This is a covert— "

"If you say 'tactical operation' one more time, I swear I'll— "

"Guys." Faith's voice cut through their bickering. "Police car." Isaac straightened while Leona froze.

Chapter 70

The patrol car cruised by in the opposite lane, the driver oblivious to them. Faith registered every detail — the officer's bored expression, the half-empty coffee cup in the holder and the slight wobble in the vehicle's front tire that suggested alignment issues. They drove in silence for a few minutes after it passed.

"That," Isaac said finally, "is why we maintain proper protocol and—"

"Oh my god," Leona groaned, dropping her head into her hands. "You're actually going to turn this into a lecture about protocol, aren't you? You're physically incapable of not turning this into a lecture."

"If you'd just— "

"I'm going to die. Actually die. Death by Hunter lecture. What a way to go."

Faith chuckled, despite herself.

Though he kept his voice light during the bickering, Faith noticed how Isaac's eyes constantly scanned their surroundings. His casual glances at the mirrors weren't random — he was maintaining a precise schedule of surveillance, checking each angle at carefully timed intervals.

The van continued south, eating up miles as the sun climbed higher. Faith watched the landscape change outside her window — the Blue Ridge Mountains gradually giving way to gentler hills then thicker forests. She caught hawks circling overhead, deer moving through distant trees and small creatures scurrying through the underbrush. Everything was so alive, so vital.

Leona's wild laugh filled the van as she made another joke at Isaac's expense. The sound carried such warmth, such life. Faith's gaze shifted to Isaac. His eyes remained focused on the road, but she caught the subtle softening around his mouth when he thought no one was looking as Leona chided him.

"You're brooding again," Leona said, leaning forward between the seats. "I can practically hear your thoughts spiraling."

"I'm fine," Faith lied, the words ashen in her mouth. Another manipulation. Another careful deception. They didn't deserve that. The weight of guilt pressed against her chest; she had dragged them both into this insane mission. They deserved some truth.

"I just... feel guilty," she admitted. "For dragging the both of you out here." She turned to Isaac. "For letting Leona bait you about being afraid." She turned to Leona. "For playing on your pack instincts. What kind of choice did I give you?"

"The kind that comes from caring," Leona said after a beat, her hand warm on Faith's shoulder. "You think I don't know my own mind? That I'm some puppet you can manipulate with pack loyalty?"

"And do you think my Hunter training is so weak that a few taunts could force me to cave in?" Isaac added, a slight smile touching his lips. "Give us some credit here."

"But you're only here because I—" began Faith.

"Because you what?" Leona's voice carried an edge now. "Because you dared to let people care about you? To care back?"

"Because you trusted us enough to ask for help?" added Isaac. "I take that as an honor, not a burden, not a manipulation."

Leona raised her eyebrows. "That might be the only sensible thing you've said all day, bargain-bin Blade."

CHAPTER 70

Even Issac laughed at that one.

A realization struck Faith. It had been easier to believe she had manipulated them both than to accept the truth — that they had chosen this path, chosen her. That they were in fact pack. All three of them. And Faith belonged.

She felt wetness sting her eyes.

"Thank you," she whispered, the words carrying all she couldn't express.

They passed a sign for the Georgia state line.

They were getting closer. Soon they would reach Angel Falls — the place where everything had begun. Where her mother had worked as a waitress in the Tiger Diner, where her father had first come to town as caretaker of the Red Claw mansion, where their impossible love story had started.

"You okay?" Isaac asked softly, noticing her faraway stare.

Before Faith could respond, Leona's head popped up between the seats again. "She'd be better if someone wasn't driving like a sedated turtle."

"I'm maintaining a safe and reasonable— "

"I will literally pay you to stop saying things like that."

" — speed that ensures— "

"That's it." Leona began climbing into the front. "I'm driving."

"What? No!" Isaac protested, trying to fend her off while keeping the van steady. "Get back in your seat!"

"Then drive faster!"

"This is completely childish— "

"Your face is childish!"

"That doesn't even make sense — "

"Your mom doesn't make sense!"

"Will both of you please— " Faith began.

A horn blared as a truck passed them, its driver gesturing angrily at their erratic driving.

"See?" Isaac said triumphantly. "This is exactly why— "

"If you say 'protocol' one more time— "

Faith leaned her forehead against the cool glass of her window, letting their bickering wash over her. They still had hours to go before reaching Angel Falls, before facing whatever awaited them. For now, she would take comfort in this strange moment of almost-normalcy, even if it came with a soundtrack of:

"I will literally eat you."

"That's not even anatomically possible — "

"Want to test that theory? I will shift right now and stuff your cube of a head in my jaws then—"

Faith smiled faintly. They were either going to save the world together or die trying — probably while arguing the entire time.

Hours passed. Scenery blurred. The engine thrummed.

A sign reading 'Welcome to Angel Falls, GA: Population 2,670' suddenly appeared around a bend, its faded paint and slightly crooked wood betraying years of small-town budget constraints.

Her throat tightened as they passed it. This was where everything had begun. Where an immortal caretaker and a mortal waitress had defied all odds to find love. Where impossible choices had forged unbreakable bonds. Where her very existence had been set in motion.

It was as if her life had come full circle.

Chapter 71

The town emerged from the surrounding forest like a scene from another time. Peeling paint on storefronts, cracked sidewalks with weeds pushing through and the single traffic light swaying gently in the afternoon breeze. It all felt smaller than Faith had imagined from her mother's stories.

They cruised down East Main Street, passing Henrietta's Antique Furniture with its dusty window displays and a dress shop advertising alterations in faded gold lettering. Faith inhaled deeply, taking in the layers of scent — fresh bread from the bakery, motor oil from the garage and beneath it all, the complex aroma of lives unfolding in this quiet corner of Georgia.

As they continued, the Henry Freeman Memorial Library came into view, its imposing granite pillars and ornate wooden doors standing out among the more modest buildings. Faith recalled her mother's stories about Amara, the librarian who had been a hero in her own understated way, now in hiding due to the tangled politics of the vampire world.

"There it is," Faith whispered, her voice catching slightly. "Where they first met."

The diner looked just as her mother had described — peeling stucco exterior, faded sign and parking lot across the street. Faith could almost visualize it as it had been two decades earlier: her mother waiting tables, her father appearing like a dark angel in the doorway with his guitar case strapped to his back, their lives forever altered in this unremarkable small-town diner.

"We shouldn't really stop," Isaac said quietly, but his hands were already guiding the van into one of the thirty-minute parking spaces directly in front. He seemed to know her too well.

"Just for a moment," Faith replied, her gaze locked on the entrance. "I just want to see."

"I'll keep watch," Leona said, her voice unusually gentle.

Chapter 72

The bell above the door chimed as Faith stepped inside. The interior was a snapshot of small-town Americana, frozen in time — chrome-edged tables, vinyl booths, metal napkin holders that had likely been there since the fifties. Her keen ears picked up the soft hum of ancient refrigeration units, the sizzle of meat on the grill and the clink of silverware against plates. Other scents reached her — coffee and grease, sweet pie filling and burnt toast. Decades of meals served, lives lived and stories told.

"Be right with you!" a voice called from the kitchen window.

A man emerged from the back — mid-forties, with lines around his eyes that deepened as he smiled. The name tag on his grease-stained apron read "Dwayne" with "Manager" in smaller writing underneath.

Faith's breath caught. This had to be him — the young cook from her mother's stories, Dwayne Redmond, now grown into middle age.

"What can I get…" Dwayne trailed off, his smile faltering slightly as he studied her face. "Sorry, but… do I know you?"

Faith's mind raced. She hadn't considered the possibility that her face might betray her heritage.

"Don't think so, just passing through," she said quickly, forcing a casual smile. "Thought I'd grab a coffee, but I should really get back to my friends." She gestured vaguely behind her.

"You sure?" Dwayne's brow furrowed. "You look just like someone

I used to..." His eyes widened slightly. "Wait a minute."

"Sorry, I really need to go." Faith backed toward the door.

"Hold on," Dwayne called after her. "Are you related to— "

The bell chimed again as Faith pushed through the door, perhaps a bit faster than a human would. She slid into the van, her hands trembling slightly.

"Drive," she said, urgently

Isaac didn't question her.

The van pulled away from the curb smoothly, leaving the Tiger Diner — and twenty years of history — behind.

"You okay?" Leona asked softly, her hand resting on Faith's shoulder.

"He recognized me," Faith replied, watching the diner fade in the side mirror. "Some echo of my parents." She swallowed hard. "We need to hurry. If word gets back to Mary that someone matching my description was seen in town... Fuck! That was so dumb of me!"

Leona leaned forward. "I seriously don't think the Tiger Diner features in the plans of the forces of darkness," she said. "Don't sweat it, girl."

The words offered little comfort to Faith.

Isaac said nothing, just pressed down slightly harder on the accelerator.

Chapter 73

They followed the winding road out of town until they joined Martin Luther King freeway, the van's engine humming steadily as buildings gave way to cornfields and forest. Faith spotted movement among the trees — birds taking flight, small animals scurrying for cover. Even nature seemed to sense something coming.

The Red Claw mansion appeared suddenly through the trees, its grand architecture a stark contrast to the rural Georgia landscape. The top half of the house peaked over a tall stone wall that lined its perimeter. Dark windows loomed like empty eyes, while gargoyles crouched along the roof edge, their stone faces frozen in snarls.

Though imposing, the once-majestic mansion looked neglected and rundown from the outside. Its withered grandeur paled compared to the gothic grandiosity of Vhik'h-Tal-Eskemon.

"Well," Leona said quietly, "that's not ominous at all. You vamps don't exactly do understated when it comes to architecture."

Faith couldn't argue with that assessment.

Issac turned onto a dirt road that led up to the large gates of the property. Instead of stopping at the mansion, he drove a little further on then veered off the road into a cornfield, doing his best to hide the vehicle behind overgrown stalks.

"This will have to do," he said, killing the engine and turning to both women. "The tunnel entrance is located in the forest around the back, according to the plans."

"Lead the way Scoutmaster," said Leona. She seemed to be enjoying herself.

They exited the van and made their way into the dense forest behind the mansion.

They found the iron gate exactly where the Hunter had indicated, half-hidden by thick vegetation. The lattice pattern cast strange shadows on the ground as afternoon sun filtered through the metal bars.

"Ready?" Isaac asked, his hand resting on the rusty latch.

Faith nodded while Leona's eyes flickered with amber fire. Isaac pulled the latch. The gate opened with a screech of protest, revealing darkness beyond.

Chapter 74

One by one, they slipped inside, moving in perfect silence. The air in the tunnel was thick with the scent of damp and decay. Faith's sensitive eyes pierced the gloom, revealing damp stone walls and a floor layered with decades of debris.

The darkness in her veins hummed with anticipation as they crept deeper. Each step brought them closer to Zachariah's tomb, to Mary's plans.

The tunnel seemed to breathe around them, its ancient stone exhaling the fetid air of decades. Faith registered the subtle sounds of their progress — Isaac's measured footsteps, Leona's barely contained energy and the distant drip of water echoing in the darkness ahead. The air grew colder as they moved further, heavy with old secrets.

Faith's nose detected mineral-rich groundwater seeping through stone, the sweet decay of rotting wood supports and old mortar crumbling to dust. Yet, there was something else: a scent that hinted at power and corruption, at rituals performed in forgotten depths.

They reached a section where the ceiling dropped lower, forcing them to duck. Faith noticed the rough-hewn stone — tool marks left by long-dead hands, crude symbols carved into the walls and patches of phosphorescent fungus casting a sickly light in the gloom.

"I don't like this," Leona whispered, her voice barely audible even to Faith's sharp hearing. "It feels wrong. Like the walls are watching us."

Faith understood completely. There was an awareness here.

"We're getting close to the kitchen entrance," Isaac murmured. "According to the old blueprints, there should be a—"

He broke off as Faith's hand shot up in warning. Her senses had detected something — a change in air pressure, a shift in ambient sound, a presence that raised the fine hairs on her neck.

They froze, barely breathing.

Faith strained her hearing to its limits, filtering out the drip of water and the subtle settling of stone.

Nothing. No heartbeats. No breathing. No movement.

The mansion above them lay utterly, unnaturally silent. Yet there was something tangible she could feel. She noticed Leona's scent changing as the werwulf prepared to shift, while Isaac's hands moved with practiced silence to his sword hilts.

"This feels wrong," Faith whispered, the words escaping her lips barely above a breath. "There should be something — guards, patrols, some sign of Mary's forces. But there's just..."

"Nothing," Leona finished, her voice taut in the suffocating stillness.

They found the kitchen entrance about ten feet ahead, a massive granite boulder covering a large gap in the wall. Faith's vision highlighted the subtle groove marks that allowed it to be gripped, worn smooth by years of clandestine escapes.

"Ready?" she mouthed.

Her companions both nodded.

Faith pressed her hands against the cold stone. She heaved with all of her supernatural strength. The boulder ever-so-slowly shifted, rolling to reveal an inky darkness beyond. The stuffy air of the kitchen assaulted her sensitive nose — decades-old spices, more rotting wood and the metallic reek of rusted cookware.

One by one, they slipped through the narrow opening in silence,

CHAPTER 74

emerging into a large hearth.

Faith's eyes quickly adjusted to the gloom as she exited, unveiling a space frozen in time — copper pots hung from ceiling hooks, their surfaces green with age; cabinets stood open, their contents long used or decayed; a hefty wooden table bore the scars of countless knife marks.

"The atrium," Isaac whispered, his voice sounding loud in the oppressive stillness. "That's where they kept the hibernation caskets. Where Zachariah slept for a hundred years."

The silence pressed against them like a tangible force. Faith still detected no movement, no signs of life or undeath in the vast mansion. It was as if the entire building was holding its breath, waiting.

"We go on," she finally whispered. "Carefully. Together."

They moved into the blackness led by Faith, heading toward whatever destiny or damnation awaited them. The choice — and its consequences — would be on her head.

Chapter 75

Something felt off as they moved through the large kitchen. Each footstep faded too quickly, absorbed by something unseen. The darkness pulsing in Faith's blood stirred uneasily, responding to a threat she couldn't yet identify.

They emerged into a wide corridor. Dim light filtered through grime-covered windows, casting eerie shadows across the worn floorboards, which creaked beneath their careful movements. The scent of decay hung in the air.

"You okay?" Leona whispered in Faith's ear. Her usual wild energy seemed dulled, probably suppressed by the oppressive atmosphere.

"Something's off." Faith extended her senses to their limits. The mansion's peculiar acoustics swallowed her words. She noticed Leona's tension, the way the werwulf kept glancing behind them, as if checking for something — or someone — only she could sense.

They stood still. Three hearts beat in the darkness — Faith's slow and cold, Leona's quick with tension, and Isaac's steady and reliable as ever. Yet, beyond their presence, the vast mansion enveloped them in an unnatural silence, as if it consumed sound itself.

Isaac moved closer, his shoulder brushing against Faith's.

"It's too quiet," he murmured, his Hunter training evident in how he positioned himself between them and the kitchen's entrance. "Stay close. I'll take point."

CHAPTER 75

"Because you're expendable?" Leona's attempt at humor landed flat.

"Because I'm trained for this." He moved ahead of them, each step carefully placed to avoid the most damaged floorboards.

Faith followed, perceiving details with heightened clarity. Cobwebs stretched between rafters in geometric patterns, revealing decades of neglect. Wallpaper peeled away like dead skin. Floorboards warped beneath their weight.

This had once been her father's domain, before love and fate turned him into something more than a caretaker of the undead.

A sound from above made them freeze.

Scratch.

Scrape.

Scrabble.

Isaac gestured sharply toward a shadowed alcove. They pressed into the narrow space, bodies tight against one another. Faith found herself wedged between them — Leona's fever-hot form behind her and Isaac's steady warmth in front.

She felt Leona's heartbeat spike against her back, an irregular rhythm that seemed out of place for the usually composed werwulf. Her breath stirred Faith's hair, carrying those familiar notes of wild places. Faith's own cold flesh seemed to absorb their combined warmth like a flower turning toward the sun.

The scratching grew louder, now accompanied by high-pitched squeaks.

Just rats.

Faith's muscles remained coiled for action. She sensed Leona relax a little behind her, her body softening against Faith's. The intimate contact sent a jolt of electricity down Faith's spine.

"The coast is clear," Isaac informed. "We should keep moving. The atrium isn't far."

Faith pulled away from Leona's warmth, already craving the contact.

They ventured deeper into the mansion's shadowy core, following Isaac as he navigated the wide hallway. Her senses were on high alert, picking up more signs of decay: elaborate crown molding crumbling to expose the house's bones, rugs eaten away by insects and the march of time.

Her keen ears captured the subtle sounds of the building shifting — timbers creaking under their own weight and the wind whispering through cracks in the ancient stone. Yet still, there were no signs of Mary's forces. No indication of a trap. But it all felt wrong. A heavy sense of unease permeated the air.

They passed through an open set of doors that led to a grand dining room. A massive oval table dominated the space, its polished surface dull with decades of dust. Thirty leather chairs stood like silent sentinels, their once-rich upholstery cracked and faded.

Isaac's hand brushed against Faith's arm, drawing her attention.

"Look." He crouched to examine the floor, his fingers tracing through the dust to reveal cleaner wood beneath. "Someone's been here recently. Multiple someones."

Faith's skin prickled. "Then where are they now?"

The question hung in the stagnant air, unanswered.

The wrongness clung to her senses like a physical weight, making her flesh crawl. Leona's usual predatory grace was replaced by tense wariness. The werwulf's nostrils flared, constantly testing the air.

Isaac exited the room and moved further up the hallway, stopping at a narrow door. He eased it open, the old hinges protesting. After scanning the interior, he turned back to them.

"In here." His words carried an edge. "There's something you need to see."

Chapter 76

The small chamber beyond reeked of Old Magick and dark purpose. The scents assaulted Faith's senses — both fresh and dried herbs, incense with undertones of grave dirt, and beneath it all, the lingering memory of blood.

"Someone's been busy," Isaac said.

Ancient texts lay open on a rough wooden table, their pages covered in cramped writing. Ceremonial daggers caught the dim light, their blades inscribed with strange symbols. Brass bowls waited like hungry mouths, their surfaces etched with patterns Faith recognized from her vision in Scotland.

Leona moved to the books with uncharacteristic focus, her usual wild energy contained as she studied the yellowed pages. "Resurrection rituals," she murmured, fingers lingering on certain passages. "Bridging life and death." Something in her voice put Faith on edge.

"Then we destroy them." Isaac reached for the nearest tome.

"Wait!" Leona grasped his wrist. Faith noticed her fingers quivered against Isaac's skin. "We… we shouldn't disturb what's here."

A distant sound made them freeze. Wood creaked under weight, and movement whispered through the old corridors.

Faith strained her hearing.

Nothing.

Just the house settling.

"We should keep moving." Isaac's voice was tight. "The atrium isn't far now."

But before they could leave, Faith's acute vision caught something that made her pause: a small drawing tucked between the pages of one of the books. She pulled it free.

The sketch depicted a face she knew too well, although she had never seen it in person. Chiseled bone structure, dark eyes that seemed to burn even in simple charcoal strokes and a cruel mouth that spoke of calculated malice. Zachariah Redclaw, captured by an artist's hand.

"That's him?" Leona leaned closer, her warmth pressing against Faith's side and chasing away some of the chill that had settled in her bones. "He looks like a total douche."

Faith nodded, unable to find more elegant words. The face from her mother's nightmares, from her own visions, stared back at her with terrifying intensity. Even rendered in simple lines on paper, his gaze seemed to pierce through her.

"We need to keep moving," instructed Isaac. "I'll take point again and make sure the path is clear."

The mansion's peculiar acoustics continued to absorb sounds that should have echoed. Their path remained suspiciously devoid of obstacles. With every step, Faith felt they were drawing closer to something ominous. Every supernatural instinct warned Faith they were plunging into danger, yet she couldn't discern the threat. The sense of wrongness seemed to emanate from everywhere and nowhere simultaneously.

They ventured further down the expansive hallway until twin doors loomed before them like the gates of Hell — massive oak panels reinforced with black iron. This had to be it, the heart of the mansion, the atrium where the Red Claws had slumbered for a century.

Faith instinctively reached for the handles.

CHAPTER 76

"Wait." Leona's hand shot out to stop her, the gesture almost too quick, too forceful. The werwulf's eyes darted around the corridor, her muscles coiled. "Let me... let me check first. Something feels wrong." Her voice carried an edge Faith had never heard before. What had gotten into her?

"I've studied the blueprints," said Issac, levelly. "I know where the threats can emerge from. This is what Vampire Hunters do. I'll go first."

Leona looked angered.

Faith's mind raced, attempting to make sense of the sudden confrontation. She attributed it to fear — fear that made them act irrationally, fear that sowed doubt among them when they needed to trust each other.

Faith found herself unconsciously stepping closer to Isaac, drawing comfort from his unwavering focus on their mission. Something about Leona's erratic behavior since entering the mansion set her on edge, though she couldn't quite say why.

"Let's just get this over with," Faith said. "Together. Then we can get the hell out of here."

She grabbed the handles once more and flung the doors open.

Her sharpened vision took in every detail of the chamber beyond. The space where the Red Claws had rested for a century stretched out before them, expansive and imposing.

A grand staircase dominated the back area, its wooden railings rotted in places. Stone caskets lay in concentric circles around a central platform, their lids cracked or entirely missing. In the center stood a twisted metal machine, its dozens of tubes laying dry and cracked on the ground.

But it was the hook that captured Faith's attention — a large iron fixture embedded into the ceiling, its surface darkened with old stains that her nose identified as blood. A human skeleton hung upside down, its bones yellowed with age, one ankle bound with a leather strap that was tied to the metal hook. This was how the sleeping Red Claws were fed, through that elaborate machine.

Faith shuddered.

"It's too easy." Her voice was barely a whisper in the oppressive air. "Where are the guards? The protections? The wards? Anything?"

As if summoned by her words, movement erupted from every direction.

Chapter 77

Dark-robed figures swarmed from behind pillars, from within caskets, from doorways. They emerged from the deepest shadows of the atrium like nightmares taking form, their movements carrying an otherworldly fluidity.

Even amidst the chaos, Faith registered the unnatural pallor of their flesh, the predatory grace in each step the complete absence of mercy in their obsidian eyes.

The grand atrium transformed from a space of faded glory into a killing ground. Moonlight filtered through the high windows, highlighting exposed fangs that gleamed like silver daggers. An ancient chandelier above the staircase swayed overhead, its crystals casting fragmented patterns across walls that had witnessed a century of supernatural slumber.

They were everywhere: hidden behind towering columns, slipping through deep shadows beneath the sweeping staircase and emerging from doors Faith hadn't noticed in her initial scan of the room. Each new shadow seemed to give birth to another attacker until Faith lost count.

"No," she whispered.

They suddenly lunged from all sides at once.

Faith's reflexes kicked in, allowing her to twist away from grasping hands with preternatural speed.

But there were simply too many of them.

Cold fingers seized her arms, their grip like steel cables against her flesh. More hands grabbed her legs as she tried to kick free, immobilizing her with terrifying efficiency.

She caught glimpses of Leona, similarly restrained, with multiple attackers forcing her arms behind her back. Faith picked up the creak of straining muscles as Leona fought against their hold, a low growl building in her chest. But she didn't shift. Not yet.

The darkness in Faith's veins surged in response to the threat, begging to be unleashed. But before she could tap into that power, more attackers quickly pressed in. Their combined strength forced her to her knees, the frigid stone of the atrium floor biting into her flesh through her pants.

Then Mary emerged.

She stepped from the deepest shadows behind the staircase and moved with the fluid grace of old nobility. Her defined planes were reminiscent of portraits Faith had seen in history books from Vhik'h-Tal-Eskemon's vast underground library — that same Redclaw heritage written in the sharp cheekbones and prominent nose. But it was her eyes that commanded attention. They held none of the maniacal gleam Faith remembered from Scotland. Instead, they carried a weight of purpose that was somehow more terrifying.

"Welcome home, child." Her voice carried centuries of refinement. She studied Faith with an intensity that felt almost maternal — a dark mirror of Nell's loving gaze. "Finally, I can help you understand what you really are."

She moved closer, her regal crimson robes whispering against the stone floor. Faith noticed how her steps formed a perfect geometric pattern, like she was performing a ceremonial dance.

"Your mother and father never really understood," Mary continued, something like regret coloring her tone. "They saw only the darkness

CHAPTER 77

in the bloodline, never its true purpose. But what is within you has the power to reshape reality itself." Her eyes softened with what looked disturbingly like genuine concern. "You've been taught to fear your nature, to cage it behind walls of guilt and restraint. But I can show you how to embrace it. How to become what you were always meant to be. A catalyst. For a new dawn."

The offer held such conviction, such absolute certainty, that Faith felt its pull despite herself. This wasn't just some power-hungry monster in front of her. This was someone who genuinely believed in her cause — who saw herself not as a villain but as a savior. That made her infinitely more dangerous.

A shift in rhythm caught Faith's attention — a heartbeat quickening with emotion. Her gaze snapped to Isaac, and the world tilted on its axis.

Chapter 78

He stood there untouched.

No hands restrained him.

No assailants hovered nearby.

He was set apart from the chaos, his dark skin appearing ashen in the moonlight, his usually steady hands trembling slightly at his sides but not reaching for his weapons.

"Isaac?" The word escaped Faith's lips like a plea, begging for him to deny what her instincts already knew to be true. "Isaac..."

The name caught in Faith's throat, heavy with memories of gentle training sessions, of his strong hands guiding hers on sword hilts, of quiet moments when his human heat had chased away her incessant cold. Her mind rebelled against what her instincts were screaming. Not him. Not the protector. Not the savior.

"Isaac.. please...," she implored. "Tell me this isn't..."

But he wouldn't meet her eyes, and that hurt worse than any blow.

She had memorized those eyes — their warmth when he praised her progress, their quiet strength when her control slipped, their subtle softening when he thought she wasn't looking.

Now they were fixed on the floor, denying her even the comfort of understanding why.

Mary's laughter shattered the moment, ringing out like breaking glass in the vast space. "Your Hunter friend has been quite...

CHAPTER 78

accommodating," she said, each word landing heavily in the silence.

The betrayal crashed through Faith's defenses like a tidal wave. Part of her wanted to scream, to rage, to let her darkness tear him apart for this treachery. But another part, the part that remembered his patient teaching and unwavering support, just wanted to understand. How could the same hands that had so carefully bandaged her wounds now deliver such a devastating blow? How could someone who had helped her control her darkness now plunge her world into shadow?

"You led us here." Faith's voice broke on the words, emotion fracturing each syllable. "The escape plan, the route, the mansion's layout… it was all…"

"A trap," Leona finished, her voice thick with rage. "I sensed something was wrong out there, I could feel it. You fucking pathetic, jealous coward!" Her hazel eyes blazed as she glared at Isaac. "You couldn't stand the fact that she chose me, could you? That she'd never be yours?"

Isaac flinched as if struck, but still wouldn't meet their gaze. Faith noticed his fingers tracing the scar on his face — that same nervous gesture. The sight made her feel for him, despite everything.

"I'm sorry," he whispered, the words barely audible across the distance. "I never wanted… I didn't…"

"Save your bullshit!" Leona's voice rose to a roar that echoed off the high ceiling. "You self-righteous bastard! You weak, pathetic excuse for a—"

"Enough." Mary's command sliced through Leona's outburst. "You've played your part adequately, Hunter. You may leave."

Isaac's head snapped up, real fear flickering across his features. "But you… you promised—"

"Leave," Mary's smile was cruel. "Now. Unless you'd prefer to stay and witness what comes next?"

Isaac took a hesitant step backward, his carefully maintained composure crumbling.

Faith's keen hearing picked up the thundering of his heart, its rhythm screaming with fear and indecision. His eyes finally met hers, filled with a depth of anguish that made her breath catch.

"Faith, I—" He stretched out one hand, then let it drop. "There are things you don't understand. Things I had to—"

"Just go." Faith's voice emerged as a whisper, the words tasting like ash in her mouth. "You've done enough, Isaac. Just go."

He stood frozen for a few moments, his expression haunted. Then he turned and walked away, each step echoing in the vast space. Faith watched him vanish into the shadows, capturing every detail of his retreat — the rigid set of his shoulders, the slight stumble in his usually precise stride, the way his hands clenched into fists at his sides.

"Running away again, coward?" Leona's voice carried a tone that was almost inhuman, but Faith detected something beneath the fury — a tremor that spoke of deeper wounds. She caught the subtle catch in Leona's breath, the way her heart stuttered between thunderous beats of rage.

"That's right, traitor — crawl back to whatever stinking hole you came from, before I—" The threat dissolved into something raw and vulnerable. She had never heard Leona's voice crack like that before.

Faith registered the complex cascade of emotions emanating from the werwulf — not simply anger, but hurt, betrayal, and underneath it all, a crushing grief. This wasn't just about Isaac's betrayal. This was about bonds made, however much the Hunter and the wolf appeared to dislike each other. This was about pack, about family, about trust freely given and then brutally shattered. This was about what it meant to be wolf.

Faith sensed the shift in air pressure as Leona's control began to shatter. Her muscles tightened beneath her captors' grasp, and her

CHAPTER 78

body temperature surged dramatically. The scent of damp earth and primal fury emanated from her in waves, making even the vampires holding her hesitate.

"You're a fucking wimp!" Leona screamed after Isaac's retreating form, but Faith caught how her voice wavered, how her body trembled with more than just rage. "A jealous, weak excuse for a man who couldn't stand to see her happy."

The last word emerged as a sob before transforming into a howl that rattled centuries of dust from the rafters. Faith realized with stunning clarity that Leona was mourning. Mourning the loss of what they could have been, all three of them together. Pack. Family. More.

Chapter 79

Leona couldn't contain her emotions — and her body responded in kind.

Bones splintered and reformed with sounds like wet branches snapping in a storm. Muscles writhed and multiplied beneath skin that split and healed in rapid succession. Her spine arched as it elongated, vertebrae pushing through flesh before being engulfed by waves of dark fur that spread around her.

The vampires holding her suddenly found their grips filled with something that defied even their immortal strength.

Leona's shoulders expanded outward, tendons creaking like a ship's rigging as her frame doubled in size. Her elegant fingers twisted and lengthened into large paws tipped with pointed claws. The sound of her jaw dislocating and reforming echoed through the atrium — a wet, meaty crack followed by the soft whisper of new teeth sliding into place like daggers being drawn.

Where the lissome young woman had stood just moments before now loomed a beast. Russet fur rippled over thick, dense muscles. Her transformed skull held rows of teeth longer than Faith's fingers, gleaming dangerously in the dim light. But it was her eyes that truly marked the change — amber flames burned with both bestial fury and human intelligence, creating a terrifying combination.

The beast threw back her head and roared, a sound carrying all of

CHAPTER 79

Leona's primal rage. The very air seemed to vibrate with its force, causing the ancient chandelier to sway violently overhead while rats scuttled for deeper shadows.

Mary's vampires involuntarily recoiled, their predatory instincts recognizing a threat older than themselves. Older than mankind itself. From a time when beasts ruled the plains.

The first vampire fell before he could cry out, his head severed from his shoulders in one swift motion of curved claws. His body began disintegrating into ash, mingling with the layers of dust already littering the atrium floor. Another attacker found himself crushed between massive jaws, his flesh crumbling to nothing before he even registered his demise.

The sight of Leona's savage assault ignited something within Faith. The darkness in her veins surged to life, responding to the chaos around her. It flowed through her dead flesh like a storm, amplifying her strength beyond normal vampire limits. The grip of the attackers on her arms faltered.

With a surge of force, Faith wrenched herself free. She spun low, darkness coiling around her fingers like a living shadow. Her strike slammed into the nearest vampire's knee, shattering the joint and sending him staggering. Before he could regain his footing, she slipped inside his guard. Her strength propelled her hand through his chest, fingers closing around something vital before tearing outward. His body collapsed before her bloodied hand.

She moved instinctively, the darkness guiding her every action. Each strike landed with clinical precision — throats torn out, spines shattered, heads severed from shoulders. The air filled with the soft whispers of dissolving bodies, the ash accumulating on Faith's skin and clothes like a grim snowfall.

Leona's primal ferocity contrasted with Faith's precise strikes. Yet they were able to work in tandem. The werwulf's power scattered their foes, creating openings that Faith seized with lethal efficiency. Together, they moved in a deadly dance, their combined fury cutting down body after body after body.

Mary's confident smile had vanished, replaced by something closer to fear as she watched her forces crumble to ash. Her precise features twisted with barely concealed concern while Faith and Leona carved through her vampires with devastating efficiency.

"Stop them!" Mary commanded, but the order carried an edge of desperation.

More of her soldiers rushed forward only to be torn apart by Leona's unforgiving claws or shattered by Faith's darkness-enhanced strikes.

The tide of battle had turned.

Where Mary's forces had moved with perfect coordination before, now they fell back in disarray. Faith caught the flash of genuine fear in Mary's eyes as she realized she was losing control of the situation.

Victory felt tantalizingly close.

Movement near the grand staircase grabbed Faith's attention — a flutter of embroidered fabric that her heightened vision instantly recognized. Her body reacted before her mind could process what she was seeing, the familiar patterns of those robes triggering memories of healing and safety.

Then the figure stepped fully into the moonlight streaming through the high windows, and Faith's heart nearly froze in her chest.

Chapter 80

Serafin.

She stood at the top of the stairs, her silver-streaked hair coming loose from its usual neat braid. Faith picked out the intricate patterns on her robes, the delicate henna designs on her hands that had soothed so many wounds, the gentle face that had offered comfort after her training accidents.

Faith's mind searched for answers, to make sense of what she was seeing.

The spellcaster must have spotted them leaving Vhik'h-Tal-Eskemon in the shadows and followed despite her weakened state from healing the injured. Her selfless nature had compelled her to help. But that same benevolence now put her in grave danger.

Faith's protective instincts flared.

"Serafin!" Faith's shout echoed off the high ceiling. "Get out of here! Run!"

Without thinking, she raced forward, the darkness granting her supernatural speed as she rushed to protect the woman who had saved her parents. Behind her, Leona's snarls took on a desperate tone as she fought to clear a path through the remaining vampires.

Faith reached the spellcaster just as Serafin raised her hands. However, there was something unsettling about her movements — something that caused the darkness in Faith's veins to writhe in warning. She instinctively began to pull back, but the spellcaster's hand shot out with lightning speed, her fingers pressing against Faith's forehead.

The familiar features of the woman shifted into a smile void of the gentle healer Faith knew. When she spoke, her voice held no warmth. "Sleep abomination, curse of two bloods. The circle awaits."

Pain erupted behind Faith's eyes as magic rushed into her mind, feeling like molten steel poured directly into her skull. Her heightened senses spiraled out of control — sounds morphed into needles of agony, scents became overwhelming and colors swirled together like spinning paint, too bright and too quick.

Dimly, she was aware of her legs giving out and the cold stone floor of the atrium rushing up to meet her. The world tilted and spun as consciousness began to fade. In her last moments of awareness, fragmented sensations flooded her mind with stark clarity.

The coppery taste of her own blood filling her mouth, trickling from her nose as Serafin's magic ravaged her mind. Leona's huge outline launching at the spellcaster in a desperate act of fury, only to be repelled by a barrier of crackling energy that left scorch marks on her tan fur.

The darkness in Faith's veins struggled against the magic consuming her consciousness, but Serafin's power felt ancient and unyielding, like drowning in an ocean of thick mud. It dragged her down with relentless force.

Through the thickening shadows, Faith registered one final series of sensations:

Leona's howl of rage and grief carried all the fury of another betrayal she could no longer express in words. The sound seemed to shake the very foundations of the mansion. The soft whisper of Serafin's robes as she knelt beside Faith's paralyzed form, her fingers gently brushing hair from Faith's face — a gesture that felt like a

CHAPTER 80

mockery of maternal comfort.

Mary's voice faded into the distance as consciousness slipped away: "Make the preparations. When she wakes, we beg..."

The magic enveloped her completely, dragging her down into depths where even a vampire's senses could not reach.

Her last thought fractured like light through broken crystal: *I'm sorry, Mom. Sorry, Dad. I tried to be strong... I failed you... I failed everyone...*

Then there was nothing but complete and utter darkness.

Chapter 81

The chanting reached Faith before she fully regained consciousness, a rhythmic murmur that seemed to bypass her ears and scrape directly against her skull: "Rasie sufletul morților și aduc viață nouă." Over and over, the words echoed through her awareness like a corrupted heartbeat.

Pain followed — not the clean agony of physical wounds, but something deeper and more insidious. Her heightened perception spiraled in nauseating waves as the after-effects of the magic ravaged her nervous system.

Colors bled together, scents overwhelmed her nose in dizzying combinations and every sound carried jagged edges.

She forced her eyes open, fighting against magical vertigo. Her senses gradually stabilized enough to assess the situation.

She and Leona were bound near the massive entrance doors, shackled to the wall by their wrists and ankles. They were surrounded by Mary's forces. Their black robes made them appear more like shadows than solid beings.

The grand atrium had transformed in her absence.

Ritual circles carved into the stone floor pulsed with sickly energy, their arcane symbols seeming to writhe like living things. The big chandelier above swayed gently, though no breeze stirred the stagnant air.

CHAPTER 81

The chanting dominated her senses, but underneath it, Faith caught something — a whisper of movement beyond the atrium walls? The sound vanished before she could focus on it, lost beneath the cacophony.

Mary glided across the stone floor towards Faith.

"Time to witness what you've helped create," she said, her voice carrying an edge of reverent anticipation.

She brought her face uncomfortably close to Faith's.

Before Faith could respond, Mary's cold fingers reached up and caressed her chin, the touch unexpectedly gentle yet invasive.

"Your blood will open doors long sealed," she whispered.

The world around Faith fractured as Mary's touch connected them, reality splitting like thin ice as colors inverted and sounds distorted once again. She was suddenly elsewhere — pulled into memories not her own.

***

"You're being dramatic again."

The underground chamber was thick with the musty scent of damp earth and iron, clinging to the stone walls like forgotten memories.

Mary stood rigid beside a heavy oak table, her slender fingers digging into the aged wood grain so forcefully that her knuckles turned bone white.

Opposite her, Zachariah worked with methodical precision, arranging small glass vials in a wooden case lined with crimson velvet, each movement deliberate and controlled.

"Seventeen members of our Family butchered, and you call me dramatic?" Mary's voice was dangerously low, a thin veneer of control barely masking the fury beneath. "They had wolf trackers we weren't even aware of."

"And whose responsibility was that?" Zachariah didn't look up from his task, his fingers moving over the vials as if conducting a silent orchestra. In the half-light of the chamber, his profile appeared chiseled from marble — elegant yet utterly cold.

Mary pushed away from the table, the scrape of her movement echoing through the chamber. "I don't recall you mentioning those *dogs* in your intelligence reports."

Silence stretched between them, thick with unspoken accusations.

From a shadowed corner, Damien observed the exchange, his bald head faintly gleaming in the flickering lamplight. Delicate creases mapped his alabaster face like ancient rivers across a pale landscape. His Magister's robe hung loosely from his thin frame.

"You both presume to know the enemy's capabilities," Damien said, his voice betraying the faintest hint of an accent buried beneath decades of wandering. "That is your first mistake."

"I don't need philosophy lessons, Damien." Zachariah sealed the wooden case with a small brass key, the sharp click of the lock underscoring his irritation. "I need solutions."

Mary walked to the small, beveled mirror hanging on the stone wall, absently adjusting her hair as her reflection stared back with predatory intensity. "The beasts are working with the Council now. They've changed tactics."

"And so must we." Zachariah lifted one of the vials to the light, studying the ruby liquid within. His expression transformed, the hardness melting into something resembling reverence.

Mary watched his reflection in the mirror, her eyes narrowing. "You've taken more from her."

It wasn't a question.

"I've secured our future," Zachariah replied, the vial capturing the light like frozen fire.

Mary turned from the mirror. "Father would have called it hubris."

CHAPTER 81

"Father isn't here." There was an edge in his tone that brooked no argument. He extended his hand, the vial balanced between his long fingers. "Take it."

Mary hesitated. "Why?"

"Because I'm tired of your wounded pride," Zachariah said, though the words lacked their usual venom. "You've earned this."

Mary approached cautiously, as if Zachariah might snatch the vial away at the last moment — a cruel game he had played when they were children. When her fingers finally closed around the glass, she held it up, examining the contents.

"The captive's blood," Damien said, gliding forward from the shadows. "It resonates with itself. Blood calls to blood."

"A compass," Mary said, understanding dawning in her eyes.

"An insurance policy," snapped Zachariah. "If we're separated in what's to come. If anything happens to one of us."

The unspoken implication hung in the air between them, heavy as a corpse.

She slipped the vial into her breast pocket, feeling its weight against her ribs like a second heart. "You're expecting the worst?"

"I'm ensuring continuity," Zachariah corrected, his voice softening slightly. "The Red Claws must endure, regardless of any individual loss."

Mary's eyes narrowed. "Including yours?"

"No one is irreplaceable." Zachariah's gaze flicked to Damien, whose timeless face remained impassive, then back to Mary. "Not even me."

A lie. They all knew it.

Mary adjusted her collar, a practiced gesture that concealed the slight tremor in her hand. "I've lived in your shadow for decades. I've watched you rise while I remained forgotten."

Zachariah's expression softened. "You were never forgotten, sister."

"Overlooked, then," she countered, her words sharp as fangs.

"Protected," Damien interjected, his papery voice filling the spaces between their anger. The lamplight caught the web of fine veins across his bare scalp, making them appear to shift and dance. "Our sweet, precious, only sister."

Mary's laugh was unexpectedly sharp, slicing through the chamber like broken glass. "I didn't need protection when the Hunters came for us in Brussels. I didn't need it in Madrid, or Vienna, or when the sickness swept through London."

Zachariah studied her, something unreadable passing behind his eyes — perhaps pride, perhaps fear. "The Family needs you, Mary. Your patience. Your perspective. Your wisdom."

"Pretty words." But Mary's posture had shifted, the tension in her shoulders loosening almost imperceptibly, like ice beginning to thaw.

The distant sound of shouting filtered down from above, shattering the fragile moment between siblings.

Damien turned sharply toward the sound, causing the light to cascade across the contours of his ancient face, highlighting every crease and hollow.

"They've breached the eastern entrance," he said, alarmed.

"Go," Zachariah ordered Mary. He was already moving toward a narrow passageway. "We meet at the sanctuary in three days. If you're not there—"

"I'll find you," Mary finished, her hand instinctively touching the pocket where the vial lay hidden. "I always do."

Chapter 82

Faith gasped as the vision abruptly released her, the underground cavern dissolving like smoke. She blinked rapidly, disoriented as she returned to the present moment — to the cold shackles biting into her wrists and the pulsing ritual circles on the atrium floor.

Faith's mind reeled from what she had witnessed.

Mary had already moved away, returning to the stone casket that dominated the chamber — Zachariah's resting place for a century. And soon he would emerge from that very casket, no longer a memory or vision but flesh and blood, undead though it may be. The monster from her mother's nightmares would walk again, stepping from the tomb into a world that had only just recovered from his previous reign of terror.

A makeshift altar had been erected next to the casket, laden with objects — thorns, a simple cup and part of an age-worn scroll among them. Faith's keen vision picked out a small diamond-shaped item, its surface catching the light like a trapped star. Mary Magdalene's crystallized tear, she realized, taken from within the sanctuary of St Machar's Cathedral.

The darkness in Faith's veins stirred restlessly, responding to the magic saturating the air. But when she tried to move, cold metal cut into her wrists and ankles. Superhuman strength counted for little against these shackles.

She turned her head to Leona. Faith's chest tightened as she took in her friend's condition. The werwulf had reverted to human form, her powerful frame now diminished and vulnerable. Her naked body had been covered with one of the vampires' dark robes, but it couldn't hide her trembling. Her usually carved features were drawn with exhaustion, and her hazel eyes had lost their wild light.

"I can't shift," Leona whispered, the words carried a desolation that made Faith's heart crack. Leona's voice — usually so full of wild confidence — sounded hollow, diminished. "Whatever that bitch did to me…"

Faith watched Leona's fingers curl and uncurl, as if trying to feel claws that wouldn't come. She noticed the rapid flutter of her pulse at her throat, the way her muscles spasmed with phantom attempts to transform, a sheen of cold sweat on her olive skin.

"It's like…" Leona's voice caught. She closed her eyes and Faith saw tears gathering at the corners. "Like someone cut out part of my soul. The wild — it's always been there, since I was twelve. Even when I wasn't shifted, I could feel it. Feel her. My wolf. My true self."

Her breath hitched on a sob that she tried to swallow back. "But now there's just… silence. Emptiness. I reach for her and there's nothing. Like trying to grab smoke." A shudder ran through Leona's frame. "I can't feel the pull of the moon, can't hear the song of the wild."

Faith had never heard such raw vulnerability in Leona's voice. The werwulf who had laughed in the face of danger, who had tackled life with fierce joy, now sounded lost in a way that went beyond physical imprisonment.

"Even in human form, I could feel her strength. Her instincts. Her freedom." Leona's hazel eyes opened, and Faith saw they were filled with despair. "But this… this feels like someone reached inside and tore out everything that makes me… me."

CHAPTER 82

Leona twisted against the shackles, but the movement lacked her usual fluidity. It was jerky, purely human, and the wrongness of it shocked Faith.

"Without my wolf..." Leona's words dissolved into a sound of pure anguish — not quite a howl, not quite a sob, but something caught between. "I can't protect you, Faith. Can't fight. Can't even feel the truth of what I am anymore."

Faith longed to reach for her, to offer comfort, but the metal held her fast. She watched helplessly as Leona's shoulders shook with silent sobs — watched this proud, fierce creature brought low not by physical bonds, but by the theft of her essential self.

Leona's red-rimmed eyes found Faith's. She held her head up and seemed to regain some of her composure. "This world is truly evil," she said. "First Isaac betrays us, then Serafin..."

"That wasn't Serafin," Faith interrupted gently, piecing it together. "That was Farsine — her twin sister. The one who chose dark power over their bond."

The memory of Serafin's vision flickered through her mind: two little girls lying in a sun-dappled garden, their joint magic painting the air with cascading colors, before ambition and greed tore them apart.

"That explains the similar scent. But how..."

Before Leona could finish, movement near the altar drew their attention.

Chapter 83

Farsine approached, her colored robes brushing against the stone floor. In her hand, she held what appeared to be a simple branch, but Faith's eyes revealed its true nature — a wand carved from blackened bone. The spellcaster's face mirrored her gentle sister's, yet harder, as if years of dark magic had cost her something vital, something inherently good.

"Don't fight it. Trust me, you'll only hurt yourself," Farsine said, her voice cold.

The darkness within Faith coiled tight, recognizing a threat. But the metal shackles held firm as Farsine began to wave the wand in intricate patterns. Faith felt a strange tugging sensation beneath her skin, as if her very essence was being pulled toward the surface.

Then the pain began.

It started as a subtle itch, like thousands of needles pressing outward from within. The sensation quickly transformed into white-hot agony as her blood responded to Farsine's magic. Faith's heightened senses forced her to experience every excruciating detail — the way her skin prickled and stretched as the blood sought escape, how each pore dilated unnaturally to allow passage, the sharp copper scent filling her nostrils as her essence was literally torn from her body.

Faith's blood emerged in a fine crimson mist, each droplet carrying fragments of her hybrid nature — vampire strength, human vulner-

CHAPTER 83

ability, darkness and light suspended in perfect, terrible harmony. The cloud hung in the air like a grotesque halo, individual droplets catching the light like rubies. They quivered in response to Farsine's magic. The terrible beauty of her life force transformed into an instrument of resurrection.

This was violation on a cellular level, magic reaching into her very core and pulling out what made her unique. What made her Faith.

The bone wand moved again, and the cloud of blood streamed into a waiting metal bowl held in the spellcaster's other hand. Faith watched her essence pool in the vessel, thick and dark as wine, yet alive with terrible potential. Each drop that fell felt like a piece of her being stolen away, harvested for purposes that went against nature itself.

The sight chilled Faith as memories crashed over her — her mother's fear at Zachariah's torture, of blood used as a weapon, of power torn from unwilling veins. Now Faith truly understood that horror, felt it in ways that went beyond mere physical pain. This was violation of the deepest kind — the theft of something sacred, something that should never be taken by force.

Those vials in her vision — the ones Zachariah had so carefully arranged in the velvet-lined case, the ruby liquid that captured the light —that had been her mother's blood. The "captive" they had spoken of, whose blood resonated with itself, had been Nell.

The irony was almost too much to bear. For twenty years, her parents had hidden her away, trying to protect her from this very fate — only for her to walk willingly into the same trap that had once ensnared her mother. The same darkness, the same violation, now visited upon the child.

"Beautiful," Farsine whispered, studying the bowl's contents with unsettling intensity. "Such potential."

"Like the power you and Serafin once shared?" Faith's words made the spellcaster flinch. But Faith was furious at how she had just been treated. Like an animal. "Before you chose darkness over your own sister," she spat. "*Your* own blood."

Farsine's careful composure cracked slightly. "You have no idea what—"

"I saw it," Faith interrupted, forcing herself to hold the spellcaster's gaze despite the lingering pain pulsing through her body. "I saw your shared magic painting the air with light. I felt the bond between you — so pure, so perfect." She noticed the bowl in Farsine's hand beginning to tremble slightly. "And I felt it shatter when you walked away. I saw your sister shatter, also. Felt her heart break into a million pieces."

"Enough." The command emerged as a hiss.

"She loves you still," Faith pressed, sensing the spellcaster's vulnerability. "Even after everything. The pain eats away at her soul, but she can't stop loving you. Can't stop missing her other half."

"I said stop!" Magic crackled around Farsine's wand, making the air taste like lightning. But Faith caught the sheen of wetness in her eyes before she turned away.

"Was it worth it?" Faith asked softly. "Trading love for power? Leaving her broken and alone while you chased the shadows?"

Farsine's shoulders tensed as she turned back. When she spoke, her voice carried an edge of something that might have been regret. "You cannot understand. The choices I made…"

"I understand perfectly," Faith replied. "I understand choosing love over power. My parents chose love — chose me — even knowing the cost. Even knowing they'd spend their lives running and hiding, being nothing, seeing nothing. Because some things matter more than power. And you ruined that for us. You used my mother's blood to track us down, then hunt us to the cathedral, didn't you?"

The metal bowl shook in Farsine's hand now. Faith's hearing picked up the spellcaster's ragged breathing, the subtle catch that betrayed

CHAPTER 83

barely contained emotion.

"What did Mary promise you for your... services?" Faith pressed on. "One of the artifacts of power? Mary Magdalene's tear from St Machar's?"

Farsine's eyes widened. It seemed Faith had hit the mark.

"That tear was shed during the greatest grief known to a woman, so they say," said Faith, still holding Farsine's gaze. "But I've seen into your sister's soul. I think Serafin knows that kind of grief. And *you* did that to her."

Farsine looked stricken.

For a second, Faith glimpsed the girl from her vision — the one who had lain in the garden with her sister, their magic transforming sunlight into rainbows.

Chapter 84

"The blood, Farsine. Now," commanded Mary. The spellcaster's mask fell back into place. She straightened, though Faith noticed her movements had lost some of their grace. As she carried the bowl of blood toward the altar, her steps seemed almost uncertain.

"She's rattled," Leona whispered.

Faith nodded, watching Farsine begin to incorporate her blood into the ritual. The spellcaster's gestures had indeed lost their previous precision. Power sparked and crackled around her hands in unpredictable bursts, making the nearby vampires shift uneasily.

Faith caught another anomaly through the chaos — the subtle scrape of boots against stone, so faint even vampires might miss it. But when she tried to focus on the sound, it slipped away like smoke.

The chanting intensified: "Rasie sufletul morților și aduc viață nouă... Rasie sufletul morților și aduc viață nouă..." The words seemed to take on physical form, pressing against Faith's heightened senses like waves.

She watched Farsine combine her blood with other substances on the altar, each mixture producing reactions that sent shadows writhing across the walls.

Mary stood transfixed beside Zachariah's casket, her face trans-

CHAPTER 84

formed by anticipation. "Yes," she breathed as the magic built and built. "The hour approaches. Soon, brother. Soon you will walk among us again."

The ritual circles carved into the floor began to pulse with increasing intensity. Faith studied their arcane geometries — perfect circles nested within circles, each one inscribed with symbols that seemed to shift and change. Her vision from the beach in Scotland was manifesting before her eyes, yet she was powerless to stop it.

Something stirred within the stone casket. A sound like granite grinding against itself filled the atrium as the lid moved ever so slightly.

The massive chandelier swayed more violently now, its crystals catching and fracturing light into kaleidoscopic patterns. Faith heard the subtle creak of ancient chains that supported it, the metal protesting as supernatural energies built beneath. The sound merged with the endless chanting to create a discordant symphony.

"It's really happening," Leona whispered, her voice tight with barely controlled fear. "He's actually coming back." She tugged uselessly at her shackles, muscles straining against unyielding metal. "I'm sorry, Faith. I should have seen through Isaac's lies earlier. I should have acted when I confronted him in the hallway. I—"

"Don't," Faith replied firmly, though her own voice shook. "This isn't your fault. None of it is."

Leona's eyes softened momentarily. Even bound and powerless, she still tried to offer Faith strength through her gaze alone. The gesture made Faith's chest tighten with equal measures of tenderness and guilt — guilt for leading someone she was growing to care for so deeply into this trap.

Faith watched Farsine continue the ritual, noting how the spellcaster's movements had become increasingly erratic. Power sparked and sputtered around her hands like badly controlled electricity. The magical energies she commanded seemed to resist her will, creating feedback that made the very air crackle with instability.

Farsine was agitated, but she was also fractured from her twin sister, which affected both of their abilities.

Mary appeared not to notice, her attention fixed on the casket as it continued to stir. Her face held the fervent anticipation of a zealot about to witness a miracle.

"The power builds," she whispered. "Can you feel it, brother? The strength of blood calling you back?"

Faith's sensitive eyes caught subtle changes in the ritual circles — the carved symbols beginning to bleed into one another, their perfect geometries starting to warp. Dark energy pulsed through the floor in waves that seemed increasingly chaotic. Even Mary's vampires had begun to shift uneasily, their synchronization faltering as the magic grew more unstable.

"Something's wrong," Leona muttered. "The spell… it's not right."

Faith noticed it too. Like a symphony playing subtly out of tune. She watched Farsine's face carefully, catching the flicker of concern in her eyes as another surge of power escaped her control. Their earlier confrontation about Serafin had shaken something loose in the spellcaster — some crucial element of control had splintered.

The bone wand trembled in Farsine's grip as she attempted to channel the growing energies. Sweat beaded on her forehead, and her movements had lost all trace of their previous fluidity. She looked almost afraid now, though she tried to hide it.

"More power!" Mary commanded, oblivious to the mounting instability. "Push harder! Break through the veil!"

Farsine complied, but Faith saw the cost written on the spellcaster's face. Whatever darkness she had embraced by abandoning her sister was now slipping beyond her ability to control. The magic responded with increasing violence — sparks of wild energy that made the air

CHAPTER 84

itself seem to crack and burn.

As the ritual's energy writhed chaotically through the atrium, Faith's heightened senses again registered something beyond the immediate chaos. Her hearing pierced through layers of sound — past the endless chanting, past the grinding of stone against stone, past Farsine's increasingly labored breathing.

There — outside the atrium. Multiple heartbeats, their rhythms carefully controlled yet quickening with anticipation. The subtle scrape of boots against stone, so faint even vampires might miss it. Metal whispering against leather. A series of soft clicks.

Faith's nostrils flared, catching traces of scents that didn't belong — gun oil and Kevlar, adrenaline and determination.

She caught Leona's eye, wondering if her sharp senses had detected it too. But Leona remained focused on Farsine's deteriorating spellwork, her muscles trembling with the effort of fighting whatever magic had suppressed her ability to shift.

The sounds outside grew more distinct — whispered commands, the shuffle of multiple bodies taking position, the subtle crackle of radio static quickly silenced. Faith forced herself to keep her gaze on the ritual, not wanting to alert Mary's forces by staring at the walls. But her every instinct screamed that something was building beyond their prison of stone and magic.

The question was — friend or foe? In this nightmare of betrayal, she hardly dared to hope.

The lid of Zachariah's casket shifted again, drawing her attention back to the immediate threat. But even as she watched Mary's face glow with zealous anticipation, Faith's hyper-hearing continued to track the ghost-quiet symphony beyond the walls.

Whatever was coming, it was coming now.

Chapter 85

The first explosion shook the atrium like thunder, causing the ancient chandelier above to sway violently.

Faith's hearing discerned the precise sequence of detonations — multiple breaching charges perfectly synchronized. Her sensitive nose was flooded by the complex layers of scent: the sharp tang of cordite and gunpowder, the metallic aroma of weapons being drawn. But beneath it all, the ritual's magic saturated the air with the crisp smell of ozone and something darker.

The grand doors burst inward, splintering into a shower of wood and iron. Faith captured every detail with stark clarity — the centuries-old wood fracturing along its grain, the decorative metalwork warping and twisting, and dust particles swirling in the aftermath like snow.

From the debris cloud rolled small metal spheres, innocently gliding across the stone floor. The carved symbols flared brighter as the devices passed over them, as if the magic recognized the coming violence. Faith's instincts screamed a warning just seconds before the spheres detonated.

Pure UV light flooded the chamber, bright as a dozen suns. The vampires' agonized screams filled the air as the artificial light seared their vision. Faith squeezed her eyelids shut, but even then tears streamed down her face due to the after-effects.

CHAPTER 85

Amid the chaos, black-clad figures surged through the ruined doorway. Each stride was measured, each position calculated for maximum tactical advantage. Through squinted eyes, Faith counted six of them, their utility belts laden with weapons.

The ritual's pulse quickened in response to their presence, as if recognizing a threat to its completion.

The squad's leader moved like liquid shadow, his pale skin glistening with sweat as he leaped over a fallen column. He was well over six feet tall with long black hair worn in a ponytail and a distinctive Roman nose. Twin curved swords were drawn in a single fluid motion from his sides. His face bore the weathered confidence of a veteran warrior, a scar running from temple to jaw. As Faith's vision slowly recovered from the UV assault, she noted the way his muscles tensed beneath his tactical gear, how his eyes constantly assessed threats and the absolute authority he radiated.

"Pattern Omega!" he commanded. "Wire, now!"

The Hunters moved like one entity, producing what appeared to be simple spools of silver wire. But as they deployed the material, Faith caught the scent of holy water and blessed oil. The wires whistled through the air, wrapping around the still-dazed vampires with surgical precision.

The results were devastating.

Where the blessed silver touched undead flesh, it burned like acid. The acrid smell of seared tissue filled the air as Mary's forces writhed in their gleaming bonds, their attempts at defense shattered by pain and confusion.

"The ritual!" Mary shouted, her voice a mix of fury and desperation. "Protect the ritual — AT ALL COSTS!"

But her remaining forces were scattered, their defensive formations broken by the brutal efficiency of the Hunter assault. The UV grenades had worked effectively — even those vampires who had avoided the blessed wire moved sluggishly, their supernatural speed compromised by seared retinas still struggling to heal.

Faith strained against her shackles, the metal biting into her wrists. The darkness within surged in response to the violence, begging to be unleashed. She caught Leona's eyes and saw the same desperate need for action mirrored there. Her muscles trembled as she fought against whatever magic suppressed her ability to shift.

The Hunter leader reached them in a blur, his swords carving a path through Mary's defenders. His blades moved with terrifying precision — one stroke severed a vampire's spine while the other took off its head, the body crumbling to ash before hitting the ground.

He produced a strange tool from his belt — a modified bolt cutter with runes etched into the blades. The metal glowed faintly in the dim light, resonating with the same energy Faith had felt in Vhik'h-Tal-Eskemon's protective wards.

"Hold still," he ordered, positioning the tool against Faith's restraints. "These shackles are warded. One wrong move and they'll contract, severing your limbs."

Faith didn't need to be told twice. She stood as still as a statue.

The special cutters made quick work of her bonds, the metal falling to the ground with a crash. The moment Faith was free, she moved. The darkness powered through her veins like a tempest, amplifying her strength beyond normal undead limits. Her eyes caught the gleam of a fallen scythe — its wicked curve promising elegant death. She snatched it from the floor.

Chapter 86

Faith plunged into the fray, darkness swirling around her like a living shadow as she carved through Mary's remaining forces nearby. Each strike landed with flawless execution, guided by a power beyond herself.

A vampire lunged at her with desperate speed, fangs bared in a snarl.

Faith pivoted on her back foot, letting the attack slide past. The scythe's blade caught moonlight before shearing through undead flesh with terrible ease. The sound was like a cleaver through wet wood, followed by the distinct hiss of a body turning to ash.

Two more attackers came at her simultaneously.

Faith dropped into a crouch, the scythe extended outward. As they reached her, she spun like a deadly top. One of Isaac's signature moves. The blade became a whirlwind of silver, opening both vampires from hip to shoulder as she rose. Their flesh began to dissolve before they even registered the killing blows.

Faith moved through Mary's forces like a force of nature, each strike flowing into the next with sinuous dexterity. The darkness guided her movements, showing her exactly where to cut, how to move and when to strike.

Falling ash filled the air like an obscene snowstorm as bodies dissolved around her. The scythe's blade left trails of silver in the air as Faith moved between opponents.

She registered everything with crystalline clarity — the subtle shift of weight that telegraphed an attack, the whisper of cloth as blades swept past, the soft sigh of flesh parting beneath steel. The darkness amplified her senses until each moment stretched, giving her all the time she needed to position her blade for the killing strike.

The Hunters pressed toward the ritual circle where Farsine continued her dark work, their boots crunching through drifts of vampire ash. But before they could reach it, the spellcaster's hands moved in a complex pattern.

Energy crackled through the air like sheet lightning, coalescing into a shimmering barrier that encompassed her, Mary, the stone casket and the remaining vampires still maintaining their chant.

One Hunter charged the barrier, his blade raised high. The moment he struck the energy field, power surged through him. His body convulsed and spasmed beneath his tactical gear, his eyes rolled back in their sockets, the smell of burning flesh and melting Kevlar filled the air.

He was thrown backward like a rag doll, his body smoking as it hit the ground. After a few tense moments he managed to turn onto his front and crawl away. He was injured but alive.

"Fall back!" the Hunter leader commanded.

His forces immediately withdrew to defensive positions, their movements displaying the same precise coordination as their attack. Faith noticed how they maintained perfect spacing even in retreat — never presenting a clustered target, always covering each other's vulnerable angles.

"Keep your distance," shouted the lead Hunter. "Wait for a breach in the field."

A figure emerged from the shadows behind him — a woman Faith recognized instantly from her mother's sketches. Seeing her in

CHAPTER 86

person, though, was an experience no drawing could have captured.

Chapter 87

Dark skin, braided hair shot through with silver, eyes that held a soft, scholarly wisdom. She wore the same tactical gear as the Hunters but carried herself differently — less like a warrior and more like someone who had chosen this path out of necessity rather than calling.

Amara.

This woman had known Faith's mother when she was human — had shared coffee and conversation, had witnessed her fall in love with Christopher, had stood by her during the impossible choice that transformed a mortal waitress into something eternal. This woman had been there for all the moments Faith would never know or experience.

Amara's eyes widened as she took in Faith's features, filling with tears that caught the ritual circle's sickly light like trapped stars. The chanting grew louder, but for Faith, it seemed distant compared to this moment.

"Oh my god," Amara said, her voice thick with emotion. "You look so much like her. You have the same fire in your eyes." She stepped closer, one hand reaching out. "I'd know you anywhere — Faith... oh Faith..."

Before Faith could respond, Amara pulled her into a fierce embrace. The gesture carried two decades of history — of friendship and sacrifice, of battles fought and wounds sustained and healed.

CHAPTER 87

Faith inhaled Amara's scent: old books and gunpowder, herbal tea and weapon oil — an unlikely combination that somehow felt exactly right for this mortal woman in her arms.

"I was there, you know," Amara said softly as she pulled back to study Faith's face, to drink her in. Her soft fingers traced Faith's features with gentle wonder, as if mapping the echoes of her old friend. "The night your father turned your mother. Such a desperate choice, made from the purest love." Her smile was gentle despite the tears still trailing down her cheeks. "She was so afraid — not of dying, but of losing who she was. Your father promised to help her hold onto her humanity, to never let her new nature consume her soul. And now here you are — living proof that love can overcome darkness."

The ritual circles flared suddenly, their light casting Amara's face in sharp relief. Still, the Hunters watched and waited.

"I..." Faith struggled to find words past the lump in her throat. All her life, she had been intrigued by her mother's human past — the life she'd had before immortality claimed her. Now she faced someone who had known that Nell, had loved her, had watched her transform, but loved her still. "Mom's drawings didn't do you justice."

Amara's laugh was warm despite the dire circumstances. "Your mother always made me look far too heroic in those sketches. As if being stuck behind a library desk looking like I hadn't slept for a year made me some kind of revolutionary figure!"

She glanced down at her tactical gear with a self-deprecating smile. "Though I suppose trading those frumpy cardigans and sensible trousers for tactical gear is quite the character arc." Her eyes sparkled with humor. "They say the pen is mightier than the sword, but it turns out library cards can be surprisingly effective weapons, when you have an open mind."

The librarian studied Faith with the same keen intelligence that had once uncovered Zachariah Redclaw's secrets in historic texts. Her dark eyes held both wisdom and warmth, and Faith understood why her mother had trusted this woman with not just her life, but the fate of their entire world. In Amara's steady gaze, Faith saw the same quiet strength that had helped save her mother when everything seemed lost.

Faith glanced back at Farsine and Mary. The ritual continued. The assembled Hunters maintained their distance just outside the dome of energy. Magic rippled in the air.

The Hunter leader — Haiden, Faith now realized, remembering Kavisha's explanation — approached Faith and Amara. His swords were slick with dark blood that had yet to dissolve into ash.

"How did you know?" Faith asked, looking from Haiden to Amara.

"We've been watching this place, on the High Chancellor's orders," Haiden explained, his voice heavy with authority. "We have Hunter surveillance teams at various places of interest, trying to discern Mary's strategy. We saw the energy cloud from outside. It permeated through the building. Looked like the Northern Lights from out there."

Faith sent out silent thanks to Kavisha, whose foresight probably saved her life.

"The magical resonance is fascinating," added Amara. "The thaumaturgical readings went off the charts. The way it's affecting the local metaphysical field... the theoretical implications alone— "

A commotion by the doors interrupted her.

Faith's heart seized as two Hunters dragged a struggling figure into the atrium.

Chapter 88

Isaac.

Bright red blood trickled from a split lip, and his tactical gear was torn and dusty. The sight of him sent conflicting waves of emotion crashing through Faith. Part of her still wanted to rush to him, to protect him as he had once protected her. His steady hands had guided her, his patient voice had talked her through moments of doubt.

But those same hands had led them into this trap. That same voice had woven lies.

The darkness within her was agitated, offering the seductive simplicity of pure rage. How much easier it would be to just hate him, to let the betrayal burn away the lingering warmth. Yet her heart refused such simple categorization. The pain of his betrayal cut so badly precisely because his care was equally deep — she had felt the genuine concern in his touch, seen the real torment in his eyes when their gazes met.

"Found him trying to slip out through the kitchens," one Hunter reported.

He shoved Isaac roughly forward.

Leona's reaction was instant and visceral. "You coward!" she snarled, straining against the Hunters now holding her back. "This is all because of you! Your betrayal! Your weakness! You sold us out!"

Haiden's face hardened.

"Is this true?" he asked his fellow Hunter

Isaac remained silent.

"I expected better from you," Isaac said quietly. "We swore oaths. Vows to protect, to serve, to stand against the darkness." His grip tightened on his sword hilt. "You've broken trust with everything we represent."

Leona seemed to snarl and snap, even though she was in human form.

"There's only one way out of this for you, traitor," she shouted. "And I'm going to be the one to deliver justice!"

Faith watched Leona's fury build, a force so powerful it began to manifest physically. Muscles tensed beneath her skin as she fought against Farsine's suppression spell. Bones cracked and reformed, but she couldn't complete the transformation. She remained caught between forms — fangs elongated but not fully grown, patches of fur sprouting across olive skin, limbs partially reshaped into something bestial.

The sight was horrifying — nature itself refusing to be contained, but fighting against artificial constraints it could not overcome. Faith picked up the spice of Leona's rage, the thundering of her partially transformed heart.

Faith sprang forward to help her friend, but Amara's hand caught her arm and held her back.

"Wait," the librarian said. "Emotional extremes can break magical bindings. I've read about it. The stronger the emotions, the more it disrupts arcane matrices. Her anger might be exactly what she needs right now."

Faith's mind flashed back to Amara's desk in Vhik'h-Tal-Eskemon's cavernous library. Her frantic scribblings during days of painstaking research. Faith stood down, trusting the woman who her mother also had total faith in.

She watched helplessly as Leona's partially transformed body convulsed. The werwulf's fury seemed to gain physical form — waves of primal energy that made the very air ripple. Farsine's spell fought back, creating feedback that filled the surrounding area with crackling power. The two forces were fighting each other.

"You were supposed to be pack!" Leona's voice emerged as a mix of human speech and bestial roar, carrying all the betrayal of broken bonds and shattered trust. "We trusted you! I trusted you! We could have been—"

Something snapped.

The sound was like crystal shattering — pure, sharp and final. Farsine's magic broke under the weight of Leona's rage. Her transformation completed in an explosive surge of power that knocked two Hunters off their feet and sent Faith staggering backward.

Where a twisted, half-shifted creature had stood moments before now loomed ten feet of fury given flesh. Russet fur rippled over dense muscle as Leona's enormous figure lunged toward Isaac. Her claws carved furrows in the stone floor with each stride, carrying the unstoppable force of the wild itself.

Isaac didn't resist as massive paws slammed him to the ground. He lay beneath Leona's bulk, acceptance written on his features as knife-length teeth hovered inches from his throat.

Faith's acute hearing picked up his whispered words: "Go on, do it. Just do it."

Faith moved without thinking, her hand stretching toward them. The darkness inside her coiled tight with conflicting impulses — the lingering urge to protect Isaac warring with the need for bloody vengeance. "Leona, wait— "

She stumbled toward them, her fingers brushing Isaac's exposed arm as she fell forward. His walls were down, his emotions laid bare.

FAITH

The vision slammed into her.

Chapter 89

Steam curled from the rusted showerhead, enveloping the cracked bathroom mirror in fog. The ancient pipes groaned their familiar tune — a sound that, years later, Isaac would associate with safety, coconut oil and his sister's gentle hands working through his curls.

"Hold still," Imaani murmured, her fingers deftly navigating a stubborn knot. At seventeen, she moved with the poise of someone much older, each gesture measured and deliberate. The bathroom light caught a shadow beneath her collar — a bruise she hoped Isaac hadn't noticed. "Almost done."

The tiny bathroom barely accommodated them both. Isaac perched on the cheap plastic toilet lid while his sister worked, the cramped space forcing his knees nearly against the wall. Through the paper-thin walls, the artificial laughter of a game show filtered in from the neighbor's apartment, its forced cheer contrasting sharply with the steam and silence surrounding them.

"Marcus is having people over tonight," Imaani said quietly, her hands never pausing. "Remember what we practiced?"

"Stay in my room. Music on, but not too loud. Homework done before dark." The rules rolled off twelve-year-old Isaac's tongue with well-worn familiarity. He felt his sister's fingers still for just a moment.

"And?"

"Lock the door. Don't come out, no matter what I hear."

The pipes rattled suddenly, making them both jump.

In the small circle Imaani had wiped clear on the mirror, Isaac caught her expression — a fierce love battling with shadows no teenager should carry. She wore long sleeves despite the heat, but Isaac had seen the marks. He had heard the muffled sounds from their stepfather's room on nights when their mother worked late cleaning offices.

"Imaani?" His voice came out smaller than he intended. "I could fight him..."

"No." The word held a quiet steel. She resumed working the coconut oil through his hair, each touch a reminder of the gentleness their exhausted mother could no longer provide. "Your job is to study. To learn. To be the man your Daddy would be proud of."

Their father's absence loomed heavy in the tiny space — another ghost haunting their two-bedroom apartment, alongside their mother's fading smile and the echoes of better days. Before cancer stole him. Before Marcus moved in with his heavy hands and hungry eyes.

A police siren wailed past their building, and Imaani's hands stilled again. "Remember what else we practiced? For outside?"

"Yes." Isaac sighed but recited: "Keep my hands visible. Say 'sir' or 'ma'am.' Move slow. No sudden movements. But why, Ima?"

She exhaled. "Not because you've done anything wrong, but because of this." She picked up his hand and rubbed his dark skin gently. "Because they see this first, and the person second."

The words tasted bitter, but he had seen enough to understand. Like last week at the grocery store, wearing his favorite Apollo 11 t-shirt, when he had started toward an elderly white woman struggling with a high shelf. Imaani had caught his shoulder and drawn him back with gentle hands and careful words. "Some people might not

CHAPTER 89

understand that you're just trying to help, Isaac. They might be afraid, even though there's nothing to fear from a sweet boy like you."

At first, Isaac couldn't comprehend how offering to help could frighten anyone. But the moments of realization began to accumulate.

He noticed how his best friend Jason's mother watched him carefully during playdates as he grew older, despite his having visited their house since first grade. He noted how Imaani taught him to keep his hands visible in stores, to always request receipts even for small purchases. "It's a drag," she would say, "but these are things you need to know."

Or his first day of advanced math, when the teacher checked his schedule twice, as if a boy who looked like him couldn't possibly belong in that classroom. Never mind that Isaac had been helping their mama balance her cleaning service accounts since he was nine — "real-world calculus", as Imaani called it, pride warming her voice.

"It's not fair," he had complained at the time.

"Life isn't about fair," Imaani had explained. "It's about surviving. About keeping your dignity when they try to take everything else. Daddy used to say dignity isn't what they give you — it's what they can't take away. Remember that."

The pipes groaned again, a sound like weeping. Or maybe that was just how Isaac felt, understanding even at twelve what his sister sacrificed to keep him safe. To give him a chance at something better.

"Done," Imaani announced, her voice deliberately light. She wiped the mirror clear, meeting his eyes in the reflection. "Looking sharp, little bro. Now, did you finish that history homework?"

Isaac nodded, his throat too tight for words. He wanted to tell her everything — how he heard her crying in the shower when she thought everyone was asleep. How he wished he were bigger and stronger, able to protect her the way she protected him. How he understood exactly what she endured to keep Marcus's attention away from him.

    Instead, he leaned back against her, letting her warmth chase away the chill of truths no child should have to learn. Her thin arms came around him.

    "You're going to be something amazing," she whispered, fierce belief in every word. "Something so much bigger than this place. I know it."

    The bathroom mirror slowly fogged over again, obscuring their reflection. But Isaac held onto that moment — the scent of coconut oil and Blue Magic hair grease, the warmth of his sister's arms, the sound of ancient pipes marking time in their tiny sanctuary of steam and shadow.

    It would be the last time they would be this close. Two weeks later, Marcus would go too far and Imaani would end up in the hospital. When she came out, something in her eyes had changed — hardened into a purpose that would eventually lead her to run away.

***

Twenty-two days.

    Isaac marked each one with desperate footsteps through their neighborhood, wearing holes in his sneakers as he searched. The laundromat where Imaani worked evenings. The community college where she took classes in childcare. The small church where she sometimes sat in silence, finding peace in stained glass shadows.

    Their mother's voice grew hoarse from calling hospitals, her cleaning uniform always slightly askew as she rushed between jobs and police stations. The cops were worse than useless — just another missing Black girl in a city that collected such absences like fallen leaves. They suggested the usual: drugs, boyfriends, pregnancy, gangs. Their mother's protests about Imaani's good grades and college plans

CHAPTER 89

fell on deaf ears.

Marcus made a show of concern, calling friends, putting up posters. But Isaac caught him studying Imaani's photo too long, licking his lips. The boy's stomach churned, understanding now why his sister had been so desperate to escape.

On the twenty-third morning, Isaac found her.

She was curled against their apartment door like a broken bird, clothes hanging in dirty tatters. Her carefully maintained braids — the ones she had styled every Sunday while humming their father's favorite hymns — had come undone, creating a wild halo around her too-thin face.

"Ima?" His voice cracked on the childhood nickname.

She flinched at the sound, pressing herself harder against the door. When she finally looked up, her eyes held shadows deeper than the circles beneath them. "I… I can't…" The words seemed to strangle her.

He reached for her hands — the ones that had so often moved gently through his curls — but she scrambled back. "Don't," she whispered. "Please. I'm not… I'm not clean anymore."

Somehow, he got her inside. Marcus was passed out in front of the TV, empty bottles telling their usual story. Their mother was already at her first cleaning job of the day.

Isaac led his sister to their sanctuary — the tiny bathroom where she had taught him about dignity and survival. The pipes groaned their familiar song as he filled the tub with warm water. Steam rose like prayers to a God who had ignored his desperate bargains for her return.

"Let me help," he pleaded, reaching for her torn sleeve.

"You can't." Her voice was hollow, stripped of the warmth that had always been his comfort. Something flickered in her eyes — a darkness that didn't belong there. "The things I did, Isaac… the

FAITH

people I..." She broke down then, sobs wracking her frame.

He held her while she cried, trying to ignore how cold her skin felt, how wrong she smelled. Whatever had happened, they would face it together. They had to.

But in the days that followed, it became clear that the sister who had disappeared wasn't the one who returned. Small changes at first — the way she jumped at sudden movements, how she avoided mirrors, the hours she spent in scalding showers.

Their mother worked longer hours, avoiding the ghost her daughter had become. Marcus watched Imaani with narrowed eyes, a gaze that made Isaac's skin crawl. He took to sleeping in the hallway outside his sister's room, back pressed against her door, a guardian against monsters both human and otherwise.

The changes accelerated.

Isaac would find Imaani talking to herself in corners, whispering names he didn't recognize. Sometimes she'd stare at her hands for hours, tears sliding silently down her cheeks. The worst was when she'd wake screaming, clawing at her own skin as if trying to tear something out.

"He's in my head," she'd whimper, rocking back and forth. "Always in my head. Zachariah." The name emerged like poison.

Isaac tried to piece it together from fragments: her muttered confessions, the news reports of mysterious disappearances, the strange marks on her neck that resembled bite wounds. But his mind refused to complete the picture.

The final week played out like a fever dream:

Monday: Finding her methodically destroying every sharp object in the house, hands bleeding from broken blades. "Can't trust myself," she whispered, eyes fixed on something he couldn't see. "Too many died this way."

Tuesday: The screams that woke him at midnight. She was huddled

CHAPTER 89

in her closet, arms wrapped around her knees. "The children were the worst," she sobbed. "They looked at me with such trust, even as I..."

Wednesday: Catching her reflection in a passing window — for just a moment, her face seemed to shift into something inhuman. She covered every mirror after that, whispering about shadows that moved wrong, about a man's proud smile hovering just behind her shoulder.

Thursday: The silence. No more screams or broken sobs. Just Imaani sitting cross-legged on her bed, writing in her journal with unsettling calm. She looked up when Isaac checked on her and actually smiled. "It's okay, baby bro," she said. "I found a way to make the memories stop."

He should have known then. Should have recognized the peace that comes with final decisions. But he was too relieved to see her smile again, too eager to believe things might get better.

Friday dawned with steam curling under the bathroom door. The pipes sang their familiar song, but something felt wrong. The steam carried a copper scent that made his stomach lurch. Water pooled slowly across the cracked linoleum, tinted pink like the sunrise outside.

His hands shook as he pushed the door open. Steam billowed out, and for a brief moment he could pretend this was just another morning — just Imaani doing her hair, teaching him about life, protecting him from the world's cruelty.

But the mirror had fogged over completely, as if trying to hide the truth it reflected. The steady drip of the ancient faucet counted out seconds that stretched like years. The razor blade caught the morning light, transforming it into something almost beautiful. And Imaani...

The memory fractured, each shard carrying its own specific agony: her skin gone gray and waxy, those painfully empty eyes, the braids she had maintained so carefully floating like seaweed in bloody water. Her final note propped against the shampoo bottle, written in her neat hand:

I'm sorry, baby brother.
  The memories won't stop. Every face, every scream, every drop of blood. They follow me into dreams. He made me his weapon, and I'll carry those deaths forever. What he turned me into... what I became... I can't live with it.
  Be strong, Isaac. Be better than me.
  Remember everything I taught you about dignity and survival. Don't let this world make you hard or cruel. There's too much darkness out there.
  I'll love you always, and I'm sorry I couldn't be stronger. Sorry I couldn't keep my promise to always come home to you. But the person who made that promise died already. What came back was just a shell filled with nightmares.
  Take care of Mama. Keep your head up.
  Be the man your Daddy would be proud of.
  Love always, Your Ima

His legs gave out. He crawled toward the tub, threadbare jeans soaking up pink water. Her skin was so cold when he touched her face, trying to wake her from a sleep he knew would never end.

"Please," he begged, his voice breaking. "Please, Ima. Don't leave me."

But she was already gone. Steam continued to rise from the cooling water, carrying the last traces of coconut oil mixed with copper mixed with despair. And in that small bathroom where his sister had once taught him about life, Isaac learned his final lesson: sometimes love isn't enough to save people from their demons.

The police found nothing in their investigation of Imaani's death.

CHAPTER 89

Just another tragic statistic. But Isaac discovered something they missed while cleaning out her room — the journal hidden between her mattress and box spring, its pages filled with fevered writing about creatures that hunted in darkness. About the man named Zachariah who turned people into weapons. About blood and guilt that wouldn't wash away.

The last entry was dated three days before her death: 'They're real. The monsters. The vampires. But so too are the people who fight them. I see them sometimes, moving through shadows with silver blades. Too late for me, but maybe...'

The words trailed off into darkness, as if she couldn't bear to finish the thought. But she had drawn a symbol in the margin — a sword crossed with a stake. Isaac would later learn this was the Hunter's mark, but right then, it was simply hope. A way forward through grief.

**

He was seventeen when he found the first Hunter. Months of research, following whispered rumors and unreliable leads, led him to an abandoned church on the edge of town. The woman was cleaning blood off her blade when he approached — tall, scarred, with eyes that had seen too much.

"You're too young," she said without looking up.

"My sister..." His voice caught. "She was taken... by Zachariah. Changed. Made to..." He couldn't finish.

The Hunter finally looked at him, really looked. Something in his eyes must have convinced her. "Training starts at dawn," she said. "Be ready to hurt."

He was.

Every morning for two years, she broke him down and rebuilt him.

His body became a weapon forged in pain and purpose. She taught him about blessed silver wire and sword craft, about UV grenades and spiked caltrops, about how to move like shadow among shadows. But the hardest lessons weren't physical.

"You're pulling your strikes," she said one day, after he hesitated on a killing blow. "Still seeing them as people."

"Aren't they?" he asked, remembering Imaani's words about guilt that wouldn't fade. "My sister... even after what they made her do, she was still..."

"That's why they're so dangerous," his mentor cut in. "They keep enough humanity to make you doubt. To make you hesitate. That hesitation gets people killed."

She was right.

He learnt to see past the human faces to the monsters beneath. Learnt to strike without mercy, to end threats before they could spread. Other Hunters whispered about his intensity, how he never seemed to tire.

They didn't understand that mercy had died in a bathtub full of pink water.

Years passed.

He became what his sister's journal had described — a shadow warrior with silver blades. Each vampire he killed was revenge for Imaani. Each innocent he saved was a tribute to her memory. Sometimes, during quiet moments between hunts, he could still smell coconut oil and Blue Magic hair grease.

***

Then came the mission in this new world where Vampire Hunters and the Council of Elders formed a truce. To protect a hybrid child — a girl born of both light and dark bloodlines. Faith, she was called.

CHAPTER 89

He expected to hate her on sight. She was, after all, a vampire. A monster.

But when he saw her struggling to control her darkness, to protect others despite her own nature... something cracked in his carefully maintained walls.

During training, power surged through her like fire, making her movements unnaturally fast and precise. But instead of embracing that strength, she pulled back. Contained it. The effort left her trembling.

"I won't be like him," she gasped. "Won't let the darkness win."

Right then, he saw Imaani in her fierce determination. In her willingness to suffer rather than risk harming others. In the gentle strength that remained despite everything fate had thrown at her.

Training Faith became both a blessing and a torture. Every session reminded him of quiet mornings in a steam-filled bathroom, of gentle hands teaching hard lessons about survival. Faith's dedication to mastering control, her protective instincts toward others — it echoed his sister's spirit in ways that made his heart ache.

He found himself wanting to protect Faith as Imaani had once protected him.

Some nights, he dreamed of his sister. Not as she was at the end, broken by guilt and pain, but as she had been — strong, fierce, loving.

He would wake with tears on his face, the scent of coconut oil fading like mist. And in the training room with Faith, watching her fight against her darker nature while refusing to let it define her, he began to understand what his sister had tried to teach him: the true horror wasn't that monsters existed. It was that they could take someone good and pure and use them to spread their evil. Could fill them with such guilt and pain that death seemed like the only escape.

Faith proved otherwise. Every day, she chose to be more than her bloodline. Chose to protect rather than destroy. Chose love over power. Just as Imaani had tried to do until the guilt became too much.

Perhaps that was his sister's final lesson, delivered through the gentle strength of a young woman who straddled the line between light and shadow: sometimes the greatest act of love is seeing past what someone is. Sometimes mercy isn't weakness — it's the most difficult kind of strength.

For the first time in twenty years, Isaac felt something besides vengeance stirring in his chest. Something that lingered... like coconut oil, Blue Magic hair dress, warm steam and hope.

***

"The blood magic... it isn't about power. Mary isn't trying to become like her brother." Jiangshina's words echoed in the Council headquarters. "She's trying to bring him back."

The world seemed to tilt beneath Isaac's feet.

One word blazed in his mind: Resurrection.

Possible. It was actually possible.

Everything else faded into background noise as his thoughts spiraled around this revelation. Every memory of Imaani — her gentle hands in his hair, her fierce protection, her broken body in that bloody bathtub — suddenly carried new weight. New possibility.

He left Vhik'h-Tal-Eskemon that night. Three days of relentless searching followed. He called in every favor, exhausted every contact in the Hunter network. The trail led through abandoned churches and forgotten cemeteries, each location bearing signs of Mary's recent passage.

He found her in an old cathedral outside Atlanta. She stood before the altar, her minions waiting in the shadows.

"Hunter," she said without turning.

"Is it true?" The words scraped his throat raw. "Can you really

CHAPTER 89

bring back the dead?"

She turned, moonlight through stained glass painting her distinct features in jewel tones. For a moment, she looked almost beautiful. Almost kind.

"My sister." His voice cracked. "Your brother... he took her."

"Ah." Understanding flickered in Mary's eyes. "Zachariah's pets. His Crimson Claws. I remember them — broken things, really. Such a waste of potential."

Isaac's hands clenched into fists. "Can you do it? Can you bring her back?"

"Better." Mary moved closer, but not too close. She was no fool. "I can bring her back whole. Free of the memories of what she became." She smiled, and there was something almost gentle in it. "A second chance, untainted by my brother's cruelty."

Every Hunter instinct screamed that this was a trap. But all Isaac could see was Imaani's face — not as she was at the end, haunted and hollow, but as she had been.

"The price?" he asked, though he already knew the answer.

"The girl." Mary spoke the word like a prayer. "Bring her to me. It's her blood that holds the key — for both of us." She must have seen his hesitation, because she added: "She will not be harmed, Hunter. Rest assured. This isn't about destruction — it's about restoration. About making right what was wronged, in both our cases."

Isaac thought of Faith — her gentle strength, her determination to be more than her blood. The trust she placed in him. His stomach churned.

"How do I know you'll keep your word?"

Mary's smile was understanding. "Because I know what it's like to lose family. To wish for one more chance to make things right."

Isaac knew full well this was insanity. But even the merest possibility of seeing Imaani again — whole, happy, free of the memories that had driven her to that bathtub — overwhelmed every other consideration.

He remembered her final note: *'Sorry I couldn't be stronger. Sorry I couldn't keep my promise to always come home to you.'*

Maybe now she could.

***

The lies came disturbingly easily back at Vhik'h-Tal-Eskemon, each one a betrayal of everything Imaani had taught him about honor and trust.

He played on Faith's deepest fear — her terror of others being hurt because of what she was, her desperate need to protect those she loved. His carefully crafted warnings about failing wards and potential spies preyed on her vulnerabilities. Like a master manipulator, he molded her fears into action.

He wove Zachariah's tomb into their conversation, highlighting its importance to the resurrection while pretending to discourage the very plan he was nurturing. When Faith finally proposed destroying the casket, he made a show of resistance while inwardly marking his manipulation's success.

The guilt nearly choked him during their practices. Every time she looked at him with trust, every time she fought to control her darkness, he saw echoes of Imaani in her determination. Both women struggling against natures they hadn't chosen. Both deserving better than the betrayals life — and he — had handed them.

He hadn't counted on his own heart's betrayal. Somewhere between the fighting lessons and quiet conversations about maintaining control, Faith had become more than just a means to an end. He saw in her the same gentle strength that had made Imaani special — the fierce protectiveness, the capacity for love despite suffering.

CHAPTER 89

"*Dignity isn't what they give you,*" Imaani had said to him. "*It's what they can't take away.*"

But Isaac had given his away freely, traded it for Mary's poisoned promises. Each step closer to their goal felt like another betrayal of his sister's memory. The girl who had endured Marcus's abuse to protect him, who had chosen death over becoming a monster, would be ashamed of what he had become.

Yet even knowing this, he couldn't stop. The possibility of seeing Imaani again outweighed every logical and moral objection.

Watching Faith with Leona had torn something vital inside him — not just because of his own growing feelings, but because it represented everything he was about to destroy. Her chance at happiness. Her future. Her trust.

The memories bled together — Imaani teaching him about dignity in their tiny bathroom, Faith learning to balance her nature in training sessions. His sister's gentle hands in his hair, Faith's determined grip on practice swords. Two women who had breached his carefully constructed walls to find the lost boy beneath.

And he had betrayed them both.

Imaani's final words from her suicide note haunted him: "*Be strong. Be better. Be the man your Daddy would be proud of.*"

His sister had chosen death rather than let darkness use her to hurt others. Yet here he was, willing to sacrifice an innocent woman for his own selfish ends.

Would Imaani even want to return, knowing what he had become? The thought was a knife in his gut as he watched Faith train with Leona, their trust and connection obvious in every movement. He had corrupted everything his sister had tried to teach him about honor and love. Yet he could not stop himself.

Some choices, once made, could never be undone.

"*Be the man your Daddy would be proud of.*"

He wasn't. Not anymore.
And no amount of magic could change that truth.

Chapter 90

The vision released its grip as Faith let go of Isaac's arm.

She found herself back in the atrium on her knees, gasping, tears streaming down her face. The ritual's dark energy pulsed around them, causing the very air to crackle with malevolent purpose. But in that moment all she could see was Isaac's face — both present and past overlapping in her mind's eye. The frightened twelve-year-old boy who had lost everything merged with the broken man lying beneath Leona's enormous figure.

The scent of coconut oil and Blue Magic hair grease lingered in her nostrils, ghostly remnants of a childhood marked by warm steam and sisterly love.

Leona's growl vibrated through the stone floor, carrying the damning finality of primal justice. Her russet fur bristled with barely contained fury as she positioned herself to deliver the kill.

"You betrayed us," Leona snarled, her words thick and guttural as they emerged through elongated teeth. "You betrayed pack!" Her muscles bunched beneath her thick fur, preparing to enact final judgment.

"Wait!" The word tore from Faith's throat, raw and desperate. She lurched forward on unsteady knees, still dizzy from the force of the vision. "Leona, please — you don't understand!"

But the werwulf's eyes blazed with amber fire and ancient purpose as she lowered her large head toward Isaac's exposed throat.

Faith sensed his pulse — not racing with fear of death, but steady with acceptance. He had surrendered to this fate, perhaps had been surrendering since that morning he found his sister cold in bloody bathwater.

"Do it," Isaac whispered, his voice carrying the weight of twenty years of grief. "Do it. Let me go." His eyes found Faith's across the space between them, and she saw that same vulnerable boy who had lost the anchor in his life.

Across the atrium, Mary's hawkish face transformed with anticipation as she watched the ritual's progress from her position by the altar. Farsine's hands moved in increasingly complex patterns, threads of dark energy crackling between her fingers. Both were oblivious to the events taking place outside the energy field.

Faith moved closer to Isaac. Each step felt like wading through deep water.

Amara and the Hunters kept a respectful distance, though they were poised for action.

"You don't understand," Faith said, directing her words to Leona while keeping her eyes fixed on Isaac. "I saw... saw what he lost. What Zachariah stole from him... I felt it."

Leona's head swung toward Faith, though her paws remained planted on either side of Isaac's chest. A low growl built in her throat — a warning that even pack loyalty had its limits. The sound made the fine hairs on Faith's neck rise, triggering instincts that recognized apex predator fury.

"He led us into a trap," Leona snarled. "Used our own bonds against us. Used *your* trust." Her claws flexed against the Hunter's pinned body. "The price for betraying pack is death. It's the way of the wild."

Faith moved closer as the ritual's power pressed against her from all sides. She held out one hand, palm up — a gesture of supplication.

CHAPTER 90

"You weren't there," Faith continued, her voice softening. "In his memories. I was. I felt everything." Her cold fingers shook as she reached out to touch Leona's flank. The fur was hot beneath her palm. "His sister protected him, just like you protect your pack. She taught him about dignity and survival, just like your parents taught you. And when Zachariah took her, broke her... it broke him."

The werwulf's fur rippled as conflicting instincts warred beneath her skin. Faith watched the patterns shift and change, reading the battle between primal nature and human understanding. Faith's voice caught as visceral memories crashed over her again — steam and coconut oil and a sister's desperate love transformed into a nightmare.

"That doesn't excuse treason!" Leona growled, but Faith detected a slight wavering in her tone.

"No," Faith agreed. "It doesn't excuse it. But it does explain it." She moved closer still until she could see herself reflected in Leona's fierce amber eyes. "He thought he could bring her back."

Isaac made a broken sound beneath them — not quite a sob, not quite a scream, but something caught in between. The noise seemed to vibrate through Leona's immense frame.

"If I've ever meant anything to you," Faith whispered, letting her hand slide up to cup Leona's massive jaw. The gesture was intimate, dangerous — one twitch of those powerful muscles could tear her hand off. But she held steady. "If what's between us is something real, if I'm truly pack, then please. Let him go."

A whine built in Leona's chest — high and keening, carrying confusion and anguish in equal measure. Her fur bristled and smoothed in waves as she fought against her nature, as woman warred with wolf.

The wolf won.

Chapter 91

Leona's head shot down, her razor-sharp teeth finding Isaac's neck.

"He wanted to protect his big sister," Faith continued urgently, her voice breaking. "Just like I wanted to protect my parents. We both made choices out of love, Leona. The difference is, I had you to keep me from losing myself. He had no one."

Blood welled from the puncture wounds in Isaac's throat as Leona's teeth sank in, its scent filling the air with copper sweetness. Faith's own fangs protruded involuntarily at the smell, but she forced back the hunger. This moment wasn't about blood or death — it was about choosing something better.

"Please," she whispered one final time. "For me."

The moment stretched like glass about to shatter.

The Hunter squad maintained their defensive positions around the energy barrier's perimeter, weapons ready. Chanting filled the air. Energy cracked and rippled all around.

Amid the chaos of the atrium, Faith's entire world narrowed to the points of contact between Leona's teeth and Isaac's throat. One twitch, one moment of lost control, and primal justice would claim its due.

Then, with agonizing slowness, Leona's jaws released their grip.

She backed away from Isaac's prone form, each movement jerky and uncertain, as if her body fought against the choice her heart had

CHAPTER 91

made. A continuous growl rumbled in her chest, but it carried notes of confusion now rather than just pure rage.

The Hunters around them shifted uneasily, their ingrained training warring with what they were witnessing. Faith caught their subtle movements — hands tightening on weapon hilts, boots scraping against stone as they adjusted their stances. Their heartbeats thundered with discomfort.

Faith moved immediately to Isaac's side, gathering him into her arms. His skin was fever-hot against her constant cold as she cradled his head. Blood trickled from the puncture wounds in his neck, each drop carrying memories of a bathtub, another life slipping away in crimson streams.

"I'm sorry," Isaac choked out, his entire body trembling against her. "I'm sorry. I just… I thought… I'm so sorry." His words dissolved into quiet sobs that shook his frame.

Faith's fingers found his hair, working through the curls just as Imaani had done in that steam-filled sanctuary of their youth. The gesture carried the weight of love and loss.

"I know," she soothed, continuing to stroke his hair. She felt him press into the touch, seeking comfort he hadn't allowed himself since those brief moments in a shabby bathroom.

Behind them, Leona paced in agitated circles, her colossal form radiating confusion and suppressed violence. Amara and Haiden watched on as the wolf demanded blood for broken trust while the woman struggled for understanding.

"I ruined everything," Isaac whispered against Faith's shoulder. "Everything she taught me. Everything you meant to me."

"And I forgive you." Faith's voice was gentle but firm as she bent down to press her forehead against his. The position echoed countless moments between siblings in a cramped bathroom. "I forgive you, Isaac."

A sob tore from his throat — carrying two decades of carefully contained grief.

Faith held him through it, her cold hands offering what comfort they could. She felt Leona go still behind them, the werwulf's amber eyes fixed on this display of mercy she couldn't quite comprehend.

"Go," Faith whispered finally, pressing a kiss to Isaac's forehead. The gesture carried benediction, absolution, release. "Go, now."

She pulled back enough to meet his tear-filled eyes, then cupped his face in her hands: "Be strong, Isaac. Be better. Be the man your daddy would be proud of."

His entire body went rigid as Imaani's words emerged from Faith's lips. A sound escaped him that seemed to carry all the pain of that last morning, all the grief of twenty years without his sister's gentle hands in his hair. His eyes searched Faith's face with desperate intensity, looking for judgment but finding only compassion.

He stumbled to his feet, swaying slightly as blood loss and emotion took their toll. His gaze swept over Faith one last time — a look that carried an ocean of both gratitude and regret. Then he turned and fled, his footsteps echoing through the atrium until they faded entirely.

Faith remained kneeling on the cold stone, her hands still warm from where they had cradled his head.

The choice had been made. Mercy given. Amid the swirling chaos of the atrium, she had honored Imaani's memory by doing what the elder sibling could not — protected the frightened boy who still lived inside a broken man, and kept alive a sister's love that had once made a tiny bathroom feel like the safest place in the world.

Chapter 92

The blood began as a trickle.

Faith watched the first crimson droplet emerge from between the ancient stones of the atrium, tracking its path with her sharp vision. The liquid caught the ritual circle's pulsing light as it wound its way down the wall like a tear. More drops followed, joining together into rivulets that painted the granite with living crimson.

Blood from stone.

The darkness in her veins stirred restlessly, recognizing something primordial in that blood. It wasn't fresh — it carried the musty scent of time, as if the very walls were weeping memories of violence.

"Oh my god," Amara whispered, her voice tight with horror. She fumbled with a device that sparked and died in her hands, its screen flickering with nonsense readings before going dark. "The energy signatures are like nothing I've ever…"

The librarian's words dissolved into a gasp as more blood began to flow. What had started as tears became streams, then torrents. The copper scent filled the air until Faith could taste it on her tongue. Her fangs extended involuntarily, responding to the overwhelming stimulus.

Leona pressed closer to Faith, her bulky shape radiating protective heat. The werwulf's fur stood on end, each hair now charged with the paranormal energy saturating the air. A continuous low growl rumbled in her chest — not aggression, but an instinctive response to protect pack.

The ritual circles began to pulse with angry red light. Faith watched the carved symbols twist and writhe, transforming from precise geometric patterns into something chaotic. The dark energy flowing through them reminded her of blood moving through corrupted veins — hot and thick and tainted with malice.

Faith turned her focus on Farsine.

"This is wrong," the spellcaster whispered, though only Faith's keen hearing caught the words beneath the mounting chaos. "The energies... I can't..."

The spellcaster's obvious fear sent ice through Faith's veins. If even Farsine — who had traded her soul and betrayed her own twin for dark power — was afraid, then whatever was about to happen would be truly catastrophic.

The chanting reached a fever pitch: "RASIE SUFLETUL MORȚILOR ȘI ADUC VIAȚĂ NOUĂ!"

"Hold the line!" Haiden's command cut through the voices. "Whatever comes through, we contain it here!"

But even the veteran Hunter's voice carried an edge of uncertainty. This was beyond their experience, beyond their training. The very air seemed to crack and splinter as reality buckled under the ritual's mounting power.

The chandelier overhead swayed violently, its chains groaning in protest as paranormal winds began to howl through the atrium.

Leona moved even closer to Faith.

"Yes!" Mary's voice rose above the chaos. "Rise! Return to us, brother!"

But Farsine's face had gone chalk-white. Her hands shook as she tried to maintain control of magics that had grown far beyond her ability to contain. Sweat beaded on her brow despite the unnatural

CHAPTER 92

cold filling the chamber.

"No," she gasped. "This isn't... I can't contain..."

The magic surged again, and this time the spellcaster screamed as it tore through her attempted controls. Dark energy flowed through the ritual circles like lightning through metal, transforming the patterns into channels of pure chaos.

Farsine's hands trembled as she wove increasingly erratic patterns in the air. Her movements had become desperate. Faith recognized that instability — she had felt it in Serafin's magic, fractured by the severed twin bond. But this was worse, as if the spellcaster was trying to control a tsunami with a paper cup.

The lid of the stone casket began to rise.

Chapter 93

Faith registered everything with merciless clarity. Dark energy seeped from the widening gap, carrying a stench that made her stomach lurch — grave soil and rotting flesh mixed with something older and more putrid.

Amara's monitoring devices exploded one by one, unable to process the mounting power. Faith caught the scent of burning electronics mixing with the chamber's otherworldly miasma.

"Form up!" Haiden's command cut through the chaos as he repositioned his remaining Hunters around the perimeter.

Farsine stumbled backward from the altar, her face a mask of fear as the magic continued to spiral out of control. The bone wand dropped from her trembling fingers, clattering against stone that pulsed with angry crimson light.

"What have I done?" Farsine's words carried pure terror.

But Mary was beyond reason, beyond fear. She pressed her hands against the casket's surface, her features marked by zealous anticipation. "Brother," she breathed. "Your time has come at last."

The chanting faltered as even Mary's vampires began to sense that something had gone horribly wrong. Their formation broke apart as they backed away from the waves of corrupt energy pouring from the ritual circles. The very air seemed to shudder, reality itself protesting against what was being done to it.

CHAPTER 93

The chandelier's chains screamed in protest. Crystals began to break free, raining down like deadly hail. Faith registered each impact as they shattered against the stone floor, the sound mixing with the increasingly erratic chanting to create a symphony of approaching doom.

"The circles!" Amara's voice carried both fascination and terror as she scrambled to document what was happening in a notebook, her pen flying across the page. "They're not just conducting energy — they're transforming it! The geometric progression suggests…"

Her words were drowned out as the chanting reached a fever pitch. The sound and energy in the atrium became a physical force, driving several Hunters to their knees.

"RASIE SUFLETUL MORȚILOR ȘI ADUC VIAȚĂ NOUĂ!"

"The seals," Farsine gasped, backing further away. "They're not just breaking — they're inverting! We have to stop this—"

But Mary's only response was to press closer to the casket, her hands leaving bloody marks on the stone as she clawed at its surface.

Faith picked up movement within the casket accompanied by wet, organic noises. The darkness in her veins writhed in response, recognizing something in whatever was awakening. Leona trembled beside her, primal instincts recoiling from what was about to emerge.

"Sir?" One of the Hunters called to Haiden, panic bleeding into his voice. "Orders?"

Faith watched the veteran Hunter's jaw clench as he assessed their rapidly deteriorating situation. His hands remained steady on his weapons, but she caught the spike in his heartbeat, the tang of adrenaline in his sweat.

"Hold position," he commanded, though Faith detected the strain beneath his controlled tone. "HOLD POSITION!"

The lid shifted again, rising higher.

Faith's vision pierced the darkness within, and her mind recoiled from what it saw — flesh and tendons writhing and twisting. Something taking shape. A fleshy hand emerged from the casket, skin forming over it in a wave. The fingers were long and elegant, aristocratic even.

The casket lid was thrown violently across the atrium. It crashed against a stone pillar and broke into pieces.

More of the figure rose slowly, wreathed in dark energy that made it difficult to focus clearly.

A man.

Faith's acute vision caught fragments — high cheekbones, a prominent nose that spoke of nobility, thin lips curved in a smile that held no warmth. Black hair fell past his shoulders in thick waves, framing a face that spoke of both privilege and cruelty. But it was his eyes that arrested her completely — dark as night and deep as wells.

He wore the clothes he had died in — rich fabrics now rotted to rags. The air seemed to bend and distort around him, as if his mere presence were an affront to the natural order.

"Brother?" Mary's voice carried the first trace of uncertainty.

The pulsing energy around the stranger smoothed out for a moment, allowing Faith to get a clearer look at his face.

The world seemed to stop.

Faith's blood ran cold.

She had seen that face before.

"No," Faith whispered as the energy field fluctuated. "Oh God, no."

Chapter 94

That same face had been rendered in stark detail in the books she studied at Vhik'h-Tal-Eskemon's library. The images had been accompanied by descriptions that had made her physically ill: eight hundred nobles impaled on stakes, their families forced to watch as they died slowly over days. Turkish envoys who refused to remove their turbans having them nailed directly into their skulls. Children forced to eat their own mothers' flesh while he watched with intellectual curiosity. A room filled with rats, starved for days, then released upon bound prisoners.

The pieces aligned.

Farsine's fractured magic hadn't just failed to resurrect Zachariah — it had reached further back, tapping into something older. She had drawn forth the origin of it all. The first vampire. The Omni-Father himself.

Vlad Tepes stood before them, newly risen from centuries of death, his dark eyes surveying the chamber like a king assessing his domain.

The darkness in Faith's veins recognized its creator, its source. Her own blood betrayed her, yearning toward him like iron filings drawn to a magnet. She grabbed Leona's fur tighter, needing an anchor against the pull.

Everything she was, every supernatural gift and curse, had begun with this man. Her refined senses, her strength, her need for blood —

all of it could be traced back to the monster standing before them.

The world, Faith realized with sickening clarity, *will never be the same.*

Chapter 95

Mary's sharp features transformed as she stared at the man who was decidedly not her brother. Faith watched the change sweep across her face — first confusion, then dawning recognition, and finally pure, unadulterated terror.

The Hunters' weapons began to smoke in their hands as ancient power overwhelmed modern protections.

"No," Mary whispered, stumbling back from the casket. Her usual grace abandoned her as she nearly fell. "No, this isn't… you're not…" Her voice cracked on each word, the sound of absolute conviction shattering like glass. "My brother?" The words emerged as a broken plea, a child's desperate cry for family. "Zachariah?"

But Vlad's cold eyes held no comfort, no kinship. Only that terrible calculating interest as he studied her like an insect under glass.

Faith recognized that tilt of his head, that look of detached fascination. She had seen it in her own reflection during training, in moments when the darkness took hold. The way his eyes cataloged every detail of potential prey, sorting weaknesses and plotting elegant deaths — it was exactly how she sometimes caught herself watching humans. That same intellectual curiosity, that same detached interest in their fragile mortality.

Haiden barked instructions to his squad, but Faith barely heard him over the roaring in her ears. The darkness in her veins surged and recoiled, torn between recognition of its source and horror at what that source truly was. Vlad's legacy went to war with Radu's in her body.

Faith felt her blood become a battlefield. Two opposing forces rippled through her veins — darkness and light, cruelty and compassion, Vlad and Radu locked in eternal combat beneath her skin. Each heartbeat a war drum as ancient powers clashed within her.

Vlad's blood called to her with seductive whispers of power and dominance. It promised strength without weakness, freedom without restraint, a throne built on the backs of lesser beings. But Radu's legacy rose to meet it, carrying wisdom and compassion. Faith felt his strength — not the strength to dominate, but the strength to protect. Mary's mind flashed to a thin Black girl in a rundown bathroom.

Faith looked on with grim fascination as the architect of her species returned to the mortal world.

For the first time in her life, Faith truly understood her mother's fear, her father's desperate protectiveness. This wasn't just about keeping her safe from external threats. It was about keeping others safe from what flowed in her veins — from the capacity for cruelty that she had inherited from this man. This monster. This ancestor.

This was her worst fear made manifest — not that she would be hunted or killed, but that she would become like him. That the darkness in her blood would prove stronger than her grip on her humanity. That in the end, nature would overcome nurture, and Vlad's legacy would claim another soul.

"The energy field!" Haiden's voice cut through Faith's spiraling shock. "It's destabilizing!"

The barrier surrounding Vlad, Mary and Farsine had begun to fluctuate wildly. Cracks appeared in its surface like lightning bolts frozen in glass.

It suddenly shattered with a sound like reality itself breaking.

CHAPTER 95

Shards of pure energy scattered across the atrium, forcing everyone to duck for cover. Where the fragments struck stone, they left smoking craters — holes in the fabric of existence itself.

Faith felt Leona's mammoth body envelop hers, shielding her from the worst of it. Faith could smell burning hair where the energy had singed her.

"Stay behind me," Leona growled, but Faith heard the tremor beneath her fierce tone.

The Hunters scrambled to regroup, their weapons looking like broken toys compared to what they now faced. Blessed silver and UV grenades meant nothing against the originator of the undead. This was the source — patient zero of the vampire plague, a being who had crafted immortality through unimaginable suffering and brutality.

Faith's mind rushed to her parents. Not only was their daughter missing, but she had helped unleash a terror upon the world the likes of which it had never known. She had failed them. Failed everyone. Now the world would pay the price.

Chapter 96

The symbols carved into the atrium floor burst into dark flames. The fire moved like liquid, consuming the patterns before crawling up and then across the walls in defiance of natural law.

Vlad moved through the growing inferno, his tattered noble's clothing creating a surreal image — an embodiment of decay and vitality, death and unlife. The flames parted around him like courtiers before a king, leaving a circle of untouched stone beneath his feet.

Words in ancient Romanian spilled from his lips: *"Ce este această insultă pe care o văd în fața mea? Nu recunoști măreția când o vezi. De ce nu te înclini în fața celui mare?"*

Though she couldn't understand the meaning, Faith felt her blood respond to his words, stirring like a dragon awakening to its master's call. She pressed closer to Leona, grateful for the werwulf's towering presence.

Mary hesitated, taking a step toward the Omni-Father, desperation etched on her face. "My lord, we have been preparing for your arrival," she lied.

Vlad's gesture was almost casual, a flick of his elegant fingers as if brushing away an annoying insect. The impact sent Mary flying across the atrium, crashing against a stone column with bone-crushing force. Faith heard the sickening crack of multiple breaks beneath the roar of the flames.

CHAPTER 96

One of Mary's vampires stepped forward, either brave or foolish. "Great one, I beg you to understand—" he began.

The flames illuminated Vlad's smile, a scientist observing an intriguing specimen. He raised one hand, fingers spread like a conductor leading an orchestra.

The vampire's eyes widened in sudden terror as his flesh began to glow from within. Faith captured the horror in perfect detail — his blood ignited inside his veins, turning them into channels of liquid fire. His agonized scream was cut short as he collapsed into ash that spread across the floor.

The remaining vampires fell to their knees, pressing their foreheads against the stone.

Faith heard the whisper of Farsine's robes as the spellcaster retreated into the shadows behind the staircase. Even Farsine, who had traded her soul for dark power, recognized that what stood before them now was beyond any magic she could hope to control.

"Such weakness." Vlad's first words in English were thick with centuries, each syllable precisely enunciated as if tasting the modern language and finding it wanting. "The blood has grown thin." His eyes swept the chamber with imperial disdain.

Something caught his attention.

His head snapped toward Faith with predatory speed. He inhaled deeply, nostrils flaring as he took in her scent. An unreadable expression crossed his features, sending ice through Faith's veins despite the inferno consuming the atrium.

Mary scrambled to her feet, her bones re-fused, though discomfort was evident in her lopsided gait. She noticed Vlad's eyes locked on Faith.

"My lord," she began, keeping her distance this time. "The hybrid child. I have her. She's mine to—"

Vlad moved faster than thought.

One moment he stood amid the dark flames, the next his hand closed around Mary's throat. Where his fingers touched her skin, it began to blacken and crack like old parchment left too long in the sun. "She belongs to *me*," he snarled, his voice devoid of humanity. "Me alone."

Faith saw something break in Mary — not just her charred flesh but her very purpose. Everything she had sacrificed, every dark path she had walked, every sacred item she had collected, every manipulation and betrayal she had orchestrated had led not to her brother's resurrection but to this — a nightmare reborn.

Vlad tilted his head, inhaling Faith's scent again. When he spoke, the word carried centuries of longing and madness that made her skin crawl: "Justina..."

Chapter 97

The name sparked something in Faith's mind — a memory, a connection she couldn't quite grasp. Her blood stirred in her veins, responding to that single word with a force that terrified her.

The flames crept closer, transforming the atrium into a vision of hell itself. Yet they continued to curve around Vlad as if afraid to touch him, as if even nature bowed to his power.

"Justina," he called again over the inferno's roar, the name emerging as both summons and curse. Faith felt it like hooks in her soul, pulling her toward something she didn't understand but instinctively feared.

Leona pressed against Faith's side, her fur bristling. The werwulf's growl vibrated through Faith's body, carrying notes of pack, family, protection. The sound grounded Faith against the pull of Vlad's presence.

"We need to move. NOW." Haiden's voice cut through the chaos with military precision. "The building's compromised."

As if to emphasize his point, the corruption spreading from the ritual circles began to consume the very stones beneath their feet. Faith witnessed the mansion's death throes — old mortar crumbling to dust, support beams twisting like living things in agony, foundations groaning in protest as dark power devoured centuries of defensive magic, attacking the protective talisman embedded in the walls.

Her nose filled with complex layers of destruction — burning stone, melting metal, the acrid stench of corrupted spellwork, and beneath it all, the copper sweetness of blood seeping from the walls.

Isaac's absence struck her suddenly. She had granted him mercy, choosing compassion over vengeance. But now, engulfed in chaos, she yearned for his steady presence, his quiet strength and unwavering support, even though it had all ended in deceit.

"Faith!" Haiden's command snapped her back to the present. "Move!"

The Hunter leader had already begun directing his remaining squad toward the exit, positioning them to cover their retreat. Amara clutched her notebook to her chest, her eyes wide as she documented everything amidst the crisis. The librarian's scholarly dedication would have been admirable if the situation weren't so dire.

A support beam crashed down near them, spraying burning splinters across the floor. Faith registered the crack of ancient timbers, the groan of stone stressed beyond its limits, the whisper of dark flames consuming everything they touched. The mansion was falling apart, its centuries of history devoured by whatever Vlad's resurrection had unleashed.

More of the ceiling began to collapse, forcing them to move. Faith's supernatural speed allowed her to dodge falling debris, but others weren't so fortunate. She caught the sharp scent of blood as burning wood scored Haiden's arm, hearing the Hunter's carefully controlled grunt of pain.

The corruption had spread to the walls, transforming the white stone into grotesque tableaus of black patterns that writhed with unnatural life. Faith noticed faces forming in the patterns — tortured souls trapped in granite, their silent screams locked within stone. The sight made her freeze mid-stride.

Leona pushed her forward, forcing Faith past the obliterated double

CHAPTER 97

doors and out of the atrium.

The group fought their way through a hallway that had become a tunnel of death. The corruption spread ahead of them like living cancer, transforming everything it touched. It echoed the infection that had gripped Nell's parents.

"Stay close!" Haiden ordered as another section of ceiling collapsed behind them. The Hunter's voice carried forced calm, but Faith caught the spike in his heartbeat and the sharp scent of fear in his sweat.

More support beams collapsed, forcing them to alter their route. The smoke grew thicker, carrying strange colors.

Faith's guilt threatened to overwhelm her as they ran. She had wanted to stop Mary, to prevent Zachariah's return. Instead, she had helped unleash something infinitely worse.

She heard screams from behind her — Mary's remaining vampires discovering that immortality could not be counted on.

They reached a junction where three corridors met. The corruption had transformed the marble floor into something disturbingly flesh-like, complete with pulsing veins carrying darkness instead of blood. Faith's nose filled with the stench of decay.

"Left!" Haiden commanded, but the words had barely left his mouth before that passage collapsed in a shower of burning debris.

"Right!" Amara called out, her knowledge of the mansion's layout proving invaluable. She clutched her notebook with white-knuckled determination, refusing to let go of precious knowledge even as the world crumbled around them.

They turned just as stone and plaster tumbled down where they had been standing.

Faith caught movement in her peripheral vision — shapes forming in the smoke, reaching toward them with fingers made of shadow and flame. Her speed allowed her to dodge their grasp, but one of the

Hunters wasn't so lucky. His scream cut off abruptly as the ghostly fingers pulled him into the wall, leaving nothing behind but bloody handprints on stone.

"Keep moving!" Haiden's voice cracked slightly — the first break in his careful control. "Don't stop! Don't look back! MOVE!"

The front entrance was just ahead, but it had become almost unrecognizable. The corruption had spread — elaborate crown molding twisted into grotesque shapes, marble floors rippled like a bloody sea. A chandelier above the entrance had transformed into something that looked unsettlingly organic, its crystals replaced by structures resembling teeth.

"Almost there," Haiden called out as they ran, but Faith caught the strain in his voice.

The massive front doors stood directly ahead, but the corruption had reached them first. The wood had become something alive, its surface rippling with patterns that seemed to form and dissolve like fever dreams. Faith's nose filled with the putrid scent of supernatural rot.

Chapter 98

Leona charged forward without hesitation, her immense frame slamming into the transformed wood with primal force. The impact sent splinters flying in all directions. The pieces dissolved into ash before hitting the ground, just like vampire flesh.

Cool night air rushed in through the breach, carrying the promise of escape. But Faith's sensitive ears picked up something else — the sound of footsteps approaching from behind. Not the chaotic movement of fleeing vampires, but measured steps.

"He's coming," Faith whispered, the words emerging as a plea. Part of her wanted to turn back, to answer that call of old power. Only Leona's growl — low and fierce with unholy fury — kept her moving forward.

They burst into the night, but the horror wasn't confined to the mansion's interior. The corruption had spread to the grounds — grass withering and transforming into something that looked disturbingly like hair, trees twisting into shapes suggesting tortured bodies frozen in eternal agony.

The night sky above had taken on an unnatural cast, clouds racing too fast across the low, pregnant moon.

"Justina…"

The name floated on the tainted air.

Faith stumbled.

Leona caught her before she could fall, her powerful arms easily cradling Faith's weight. The werwulf's fur bristled, her amber eyes fixed on the mansion's entrance where shadows writhed.

"Don't you dare," Leona growled at Faith, sensing her indecision. "You're pack. You're ours. Not his."

That simple declaration helped Faith fight against the pull of ancient blood. Pack. Family. Love. These weren't just words — they were anchors against the tide of darkness threatening to sweep her away.

The mansion's death throes reached a crescendo as the building's protective talisman failed completely. Support beams snapped like bones, stones grinding against each other as centuries-old walls gave way, the hungry roar of paranormal flames consuming everything they touched.

"The vehicles!" Haiden's command cut through the chaos. "Move!"

They ran, their footsteps eerily muffled by grass that seemed to reach for their ankles with deliberate malice. Faith's speed allowed her to stay beside Leona, one hand buried in fur radiating protective warmth.

They fled from the dying mansion.

Two military-looking jeeps sat just before the tall metal gates of the compound.

One of the remaining Hunters screamed as dark tendrils reached from the house to seize him. Faith caught the wet crack of bones being crushed before the shadows pulled their victim into the depths of the decaying building, leaving only a bloody trail on the grass.

A sound like reality tearing made them turn back toward the mansion. Faith captured every detail of its final moments — how the corruption transformed the gothic architecture into something organic and wrong, how dark flames consumed stone that had become flesh, how the very air twisted around the structure's death

CHAPTER 98

throes.

The building collapsed in on itself. The ground shook as each floor pancaked down, sending shockwaves through the earth. A sound like the world splitting in two echoed across the grounds as centuries of protective magic finally shattered.

Then utter silence, like sound itself had inverted.

As the dust began to settle, Faith caught movement in the ruins. A figure emerged from the wreckage, each step measured despite the chaos. Vlad's eyes found her across the distance, and Faith felt her blood surge.

She stumbled as fragmented images swept through her mind — candlelight on castle walls, a woman's slender hands smoothing emerald silk, petals scattered across stone steps, moonlight casting long shadows through high windows. The visions felt like memories, but not her own.

"Get in!" Haiden's command cut through her confusion. The Hunter leader had already begun loading the survivors into the waiting armored vehicles.

Faith threw herself into the back seats. Leona somehow managed to fold her huge form in beside her before transforming back to human. Amara threw her a spare set of Hunter fatigues stowed in a compartment at the front.

The jeep rammed into the metal gates, which protested for a beat before being torn from their hinges with a shuddering crash. The two vehicles skidded across the narrow dirt road just outside before the wheels found traction and tore away.

Faith's superior hearing caught the sound of sirens in the distance, first responders reacting to an event they couldn't possibly understand. Her keen nose detected traces of corruption on the wind — reality itself bleeding from the wound they had opened in the world.

The vehicles drove on into the night, but mere distance couldn't diminish the weight of what Faith had helped unleash. They had sought to prevent one evil and instead had unleashed something far worse.

The added horror was that part of him had always been inside her, waiting to awaken. And now that darkness had found its source, its creator, its king.

Faith closed her eyes, but she could still hear that name floating on the night wind, carrying promises that felt like threats: "Justina…"

Chapter 99

The adrenaline crash hit Faith as the armored vehicle sped through the night. The darkness within her roiled restlessly, yearning for its source even as they fled.

Smoke clung to their clothes, carrying hints of supernatural corruption that made her sensitive nose burn. Beneath that acrid scent, Faith detected other aromas: Leona's wild musk tinged with exhaustion, Haiden's restrained fear-sweat and the musty sweetness of old paper from Amara's precious notebook.

Leona sat beside Faith in borrowed Hunter fatigues that seemed too stiff for her movements. Her eyes never stopped searching the darkness beyond the reinforced windows, muscles coiled with tension, ready to shift at a moment's notice.

In the front seat, Haiden's hands remained steady on the wheel despite fresh burns crisscrossing his left arm. Amara sat next to him, scanning their surroundings. Behind them, the headlights of the second vehicle illuminated their wake, carrying the remaining members of the Hunter squad.

"What... what exactly did they unleash back there?" Leona's voice emerged hoarsely.

Faith's mind flashed to a line from the prophesy — *"The Eminence of abominations will rise again"*. Mary had assumed that title referred to Faith's birth. Jiangshina had thought it was a reference to Zachariah's return. But the cryptic prophesy had fooled them all again.

Faith closed her eyes, but that only sharpened her memories — Vlad emerging from his casket with aristocratic disdain, reality warping around him, those dark eyes finding hers across centuries with chilling recognition.

"The first vampire," she breathed. "The Omni-Father, as they call him. Vlad Tepes."

The vehicle's suspension groaned as they hit a rough patch of road. Faith's enhanced hearing caught Haiden's quick intake of breath, the slight acceleration of his heart beneath its careful rhythm.

"That's impossible," the Hunter said, though uncertainty seeped through his controlled tone. "How could that happen?"

"The resurrection spell went wrong," Faith replied. Her fingers curled into fists as she recalled the chaos in the atrium — Farsine's fractured magic spiraling out of control, reality bending as something ancient answered the call. "Or maybe... maybe it happened exactly as intended. Just not how anyone on this side of the veil wanted it."

Amara hadn't spoken since they fled; her gaze now fixed on the notebook in her lap.

"You knew," Faith said softly. "The moment you saw him."

Amara's fingers tightened around the paper.

"I've spent years studying vampire history after what happened twenty years ago," the librarian said. "His face... those features... they're in every old text, every arcane manuscript. It was unmistakable." A shudder ran through her frame. "But seeing him in person..."

Faith understood that horror. She had read about Vlad's atrocities in Vhik'h-Tal-Eskemon's library, but reading those descriptions was nothing compared to witnessing that cold intelligence in person, feeling the weight of centuries in his gaze.

Leona's hand found Faith's, squeezing gently. The shifter's touch helped anchor her against memories threatening to pull her under.

CHAPTER 99

But even that comfort couldn't completely banish the shadows gathering at the edges of her mind — fragments of visions she had glimpsed in flames back in Vhik'h-Tal-Eskemon.

"The dragon," she whispered. "I should have known."

"What dragon?" Leona's voice mixed confusion and concern. Her thumb traced circles on Faith's palm, a protective gesture.

"When Serafin was drawing the corruption from my parents…" Faith's voice caught as she remembered that desperate night. "I saw images in the flames. A dragon breathing fire. Longswords arcing through darkness. I couldn't make sense of them then, but…" She swallowed hard. "Vlad was known as Vlad Dracul. Vlad the Dragon."

"The Order of the Dragon," Amara interjected, her academic enthusiasm breaking through her fear. "A Christian military order dedicated to fighting the Ottoman Empire. Vlad's father was a member, which is where the name Dracul — meaning dragon, as you said — originated. His son became known as Dracula, meaning 'son of the dragon' or 'son of Dracul.'"

"Dracula," Faith repeated, hardly believing her own voice.

They drove on for several minutes, the name hanging in the air.

Faith's mind snagged on something else.

"Justina," she whispered.

"He called you that," Leona growled. "Back there, in the mansion. He looked at you and called you Justina."

Faith's throat tightened as another memory surfaced — hours spent in Vhik'h-Tal-Eskemon's library, researching her heritage. A portrait in an old tome that had made her pause. A face that seemed eerily familiar.

"There was a book," she said, her words coming slowly as if dragged from deep water. "An old volume of historical portraits. One of them showed a woman — Justina S, it said. When I saw it, I thought…" She couldn't finish the sentence.

FAITH

Amara had gone very still in the front seat. Faith picked up the librarian's elevated heartbeat, the slight catch in her breathing suggesting she knew something she was afraid to share.

"Amara?" Faith leaned forward, pressing against her seatbelt. "Who was she? Who was Justina?"

The librarian's hands trembled slightly as she clutched her notebook tighter. "Perhaps we should wait until— "

"Please." Faith's voice cracked. "I need to know. He recognized me. Vlad looked at me and saw her. Why?"

Leona shifted closer. Faith sensed subtle changes in the werwulf's scent — how her wild musk intensified as her protective instincts surged. Even Haiden seemed to tense, his grip on the steering wheel tightening.

Amara took a deep breath, gathering courage. "Justina Szilágyi de Horogszeg," she began, her scholarly tone barely masking her tension. "She was a fifteenth-century Hungarian noblewoman of extraordinary beauty and fierce intellect. Cousin to Matthias Corvinus, King of Hungary. She was known for her..."

"Amara, sweetie," Haiden's voice was gentle but firm. "You're stalling."

The librarian's shoulders slumped slightly. "Yes. I suppose I am." She turned to face Faith, her eyes heavy with weight. "I'm stalling because I'm afraid of what this might mean — for you, for all of us."

Through the windshield, moonlight painted the winding mountain road in shades of silver and shadow.

"Just tell me," Faith implored. "Please."

Amara's fingers drummed nervously against her notebook. "Justina Szilágyi was..." She paused, swallowing hard. "She was Vlad's wife."

Chapter 100

The words landed like a punch to the gut. Faith felt her heart seize as the implications crashed through her mind. Beside her, Leona went rigid.

"His wife?" The werwulf's voice emerged as a half-growl. "Are you saying he thinks Faith is..."

"The bride of Dracula." Amara's words carried no mirth. "And not just any bride — Justina was different. Special. Historical records suggest he was obsessed with her in ways that transcended normal devotion."

Faith's keen hearing caught Haiden's carefully controlled exhale. Everyone was out of their depth here.

"The portrait," Faith said, her voice hollow. "When I saw it in that book... I thought the resemblance was eerie, but I didn't..."

A flash of movement caught her eye — her own reflection in the vehicle's window. Her features seemed to shift, overlaying with another face from centuries past. Defined cheekbones, a proud nose, eyes that carried both strength and tragedy. Justina's face. Her face. The similarities were undeniable.

"This can't be happening." The words escaped her like a plea to the universe.

Leona's arm tightened around her. "It doesn't matter who he thinks you are," she said fiercely. "You're pack. You're ours. Not his." But

Faith caught the undertone of fear.

"You don't understand." Amara's voice was tight. "Vlad's obsession with Justina wasn't mere love or devotion. It was darker. More possessive. Historical accounts suggest he saw her as an extension of himself — a vessel for his legacy." She hesitated. "Some texts hint that he conducted blood rituals on her, trying to transform her into something beyond human."

Amara's scholarly tone cracked slightly. "The records become fragmented. But they suggest his experiments with blood magic were driven by his desire to be with Justina for eternity."

Faith was at a loss for words. In the Omni-Father's eyes, at least, she was the rebirth of his greatest obsession. In a twisted way, he got his wish.

A realization struck her. Her parents. Kavisha. Jiangshina. The Magisters. The Council. All those years hiding in Scotland — did they know... or at least suspect this?

"We'll protect you," Leona said fiercely. "You are *not* his. We won't let him get anywhere near you."

Haiden's hands tightened even more around the steering wheel, his knuckles white.

"The global Hunter network needs to be activated immediately," he said. "Every safehouse, every ally we can muster." His military mind took over, pushing back against the preternatural threat with tactical strategy.

"He'll come for me." The words emerged from Faith with terrible certainty. She felt it in her blood.

"Let him try." Leona's reply was instant and fierce. She shifted to face Faith fully, her hazel eyes blazing with fury. "You're not his. You're not some vessel for his twisted obsession. You're Faith, not Justina."

Faith turned to look at Leona — really look at her. She took in

CHAPTER 100

her fierce protectiveness, the way her wild nature strained against borrowed Hunter fatigues, how her hands shook with the urge to transform right now and fight an unseen enemy. Faith's heart ached with everything unspoken between them — possibilities now tainted by an ancient legacy.

Vlad Tepes was back in the mortal world.

The first vampire.

The dragon.

The architect of their species.

Her creator.

Her ancestor.

Her husband.

The horror of that last word echoed through Faith's mind.

The bride of Dracula.

Reborn.

Epilogue

Faith watched her bare foot sink into the wet earth, feeling each individual particle shift beneath her skin. Even this simple sensation reminded her of what she was — human nerves heightened by vampiric senses, allowing her to experience the world in ways that belonged to neither realm completely.

She was a vampire born, rather than turned, unique among mortals and immortals alike.

The Toccoa River whispered behind Vhik'h-Tal-Eskemon as she stood barefoot on the bank, the water glinting in the late afternoon sun like scattered diamonds. The sight momentarily transported Faith to a distant Scottish beach, where a frightened girl had once hidden from her own nature. That memory now felt like a story about someone else.

Faith allowed her senses to expand fully, embracing them instead of resisting. She heard fish darting through the crystal-clear depths, while the scents of pine resin, mountain laurel, damp earth and the wild spice of Leona's skin filled her nostrils as her friend cut through the water with powerful strokes.

Two weeks had passed since Vlad's resurrection — two weeks of discovering that strength manifested in unexpected ways: in the pack bond of werwulfs, in her parents' forgiveness and even in Isaac's painful absence as he wandered in exile. He had taught her how love

EPILOGUE

could drive people to impossible choices and how mercy could be its own kind of power.

Her keen eyes caught sight of Leona emerging from the river, water cascading down olive skin that seemed to glow in the fading light. The sight stirred something in Faith's chest that she no longer tried to deny. It was not just desire but a bone-deep recognition of belonging. Of pack. Of home.

Yet somewhere beyond these sheltering mountains, the Omni-Father's power was growing. She felt it in her blood — the ancient pull, the weight of centuries. He wouldn't stop until he claimed what he believed was his. Until he had her.

Sometimes, she heard that name floating on the wind, carrying centuries of longing: "Justina…"

Let him come. She had found her pack, her family, her truth. She was her mother's fierce love and her father's quiet strength. She was Leona's wild heart and Isaac's complex loyalty. She was Imaani's legacy of sacrifice, Amara's dedication to knowledge and Kavisha's careful wisdom. She was Jiangshina and Serafin's quiet perseverance in the face of unbearable loss.

She contained multitudes — daughter, friend, protector, hybrid. Both shadow and light. Both mortal and immortal. Both fierce and gentle. Uniquely, unequivocally herself.

"Justina…" The whisper reached her again on the cooling evening air.

She lifted her chin, her eyes fixed with resolve. "My name," she declared to the gathering darkness, "is Faith."

***

Dear reader

As I write this note, I'm filled with gratitude that you've journeyed with me through another chapter of the Red Claw saga. Writing these stories late at night at my kitchen table in longhand has been challenging at times, but your engagement and the way you bring them to life in your imaginations makes it all worthwhile.

With each book, I've challenged myself to grow as a storyteller. In this latest installment, I wanted to delve deeper into the sensory world of our characters — to help you feel the chill wind off the Scottish coast, experience the musty expanse of Vhik'h-Tal-Eskemon's cavernous basement library and hear the wolves howling in the lush Blue Ridge Mountains. I also tried to give characters more depth and backstory so you could experience the raw emotions that drive each one forward. My hope was to create a richer experience where you could lose yourself completely, if only for a little while.

As a self-published indie author, writing is both my escape and my passion. Every evening after my day job and when my own little monsters are finally settled, I return to this world of vampires, werwulfs and ancient magic, trying to weave stories worthy of the time you give them. Your support means everything — it's what keeps these stories alive and growing.

If you connected with Faith's journey, felt the fierce love between parent and child, or found yourself caught up in the swirling forces of destiny and choice, I would be deeply grateful if you'd consider leaving a review on Amazon. Even a single sentence about what moved you would mean the world to me and help other readers discover these stories.

Thank you for being part of this adventure. Thank you for giving my characters a home in your imagination. These stories come to life through you.

With heartfelt appreciation,
Anya

Lastly, If you would like to contact me for any reason (such as to point out a mistake!) or simply to say hi, that would be great. My personal email address is:

anyakelner@gmail.com

Printed in Great Britain
by Amazon